Chaos & Flame

CHAOS & FLAME

TESSA GRATTON
JUSTINA IRELAND

RAZORBILL

RAZORBILL

An imprint of Penguin Random House LLC, New York

First published in the United States of America by Razorbill,
an imprint of Penguin Random House LLC, 2023

Copyright © 2023 by Tessa Gratton and Justina Ireland

Penguin supports copyright. Copyright fuels creativity, encourages diverse voices, promotes free speech, and creates a vibrant culture. Thank you for buying an authorized edition of this book and for complying with copyright laws by not reproducing, scanning, or distributing any part of it in any form without permission. You are supporting writers and allowing Penguin to continue to publish books for every reader.

Razorbill & colophon are registered trademarks of Penguin Random House LLC.

The Penguin colophon is a registered trademark of Penguin Books Limited.

Visit us online at penguinrandomhouse.com.

Library of Congress Cataloging-in-Publication Data
Names: Gratton, Tessa, author. | Ireland, Justina, author.
Title: Chaos & flame / Tessa Gratton, Justina Ireland.
Other titles: Chaos and flame
Description: New York : Razorbill, 2023. | Audience: Ages 14 years and up. |
Summary: Two unlikely allies from rival factions, Darling Seabreak and Talon Goldhoard must work together to navigate treacherous House politics and ancient magic to keep their world from falling apart.
Identifiers: LCCN 2022050414 (print) | LCCN 2022050415 (ebook) |
ISBN 9780593353325 (hardcover) | ISBN 9780593353332 (epub)
Subjects: CYAC: Fantasy. | Magic—Fiction. | Interpersonal relations—Fiction. |
LCGFT: Fantasy fiction. | Novels.
Classification: LCC PZ7.G77215 Ch 2023 (print) |
LCC PZ7.G77215 (ebook) | DDC [Fic]—dc23
LC record available at https://lccn.loc.gov/2022050414
LC ebook record available at https://lccn.loc.gov/2022050415

Printed in the United States of America

ISBN 9780593353325 (hardcover)
1 3 5 7 9 10 8 6 4 2

ISBN 9780593619599 (international edition)
1 3 5 7 9 10 8 6 4 2

BVG

Design by Tony Sahara
Text set in Warnock Pro

This book is a work of fiction. Any references to historical events, real people, or real places are used fictitiously. Other names, characters, places, and events are products of the author's imagination, and any resemblance to actual events or places or persons, living or dead, is entirely coincidental.

The publisher does not have any control over and does not assume any responsibility for author or third-party websites or their content.

CHAOS & FLAME

CHAOS

The first time the scion of House Dragon painted the eyeless girl, he was only six years old. She was nothing but a face shaped with finger smears of brown, a darker crooked line that might've been a sad smile, and huge, swirling black holes where her eyes should be.

"I don't know how to save her," he said to his mother when he presented the art to her.

His mother accepted the soft parchment, doing her best to hide the horror she felt at the red-rimmed, furious eyeholes in her son's painting. Casually, she asked, "Why is she in danger?"

"I don't know."

"What happened to her eyes?"

"Nothing yet." The little boy shrugged.

Though the Dragon consort asked a few more delicate questions, he could give her no answers. But he drew the eyeless girl again and again, and told his nurse about her, and his aunt, and his father eventually. That was a mistake, because he was far too old for imaginary friends, his father growled. The consort promised her husband, the Dragon regent, it was only childish play, and their son would grow out of it.

Better an imaginary friend, she thought, than the truth she suspected deep in her heart: her son had been gifted with a boon, but it was a prophetic one, and prophecy always, always drove the wielder mad.

The people of Pyrlanum would never accept a regent with such a wild boon, and to shield her eldest son, the consort extracted a promise from him to stop talking about the girl, and certainly to stop painting her. He must never paint anything from a dream or vision. It was dangerous. The young scion agreed, thrilled to have such an illicit thing binding him with his mother.

And he kept his promise for two entire years, until his mother was murdered.

The day she died, the consort and the scion were pruning in their private garden. She injured herself on a few reckless roses, and when she gasped, the scion saw a flash of vision, in strokes of vivid paint: a fan of dark blue skirts against the harsh black-and-white checkered floor of his mother's solar, golden sunlight smeared in streaks, and a kiss of crimson splattered at her mouth and in her hair. A spilled cup near her hand, leaking sickly green.

It would have been a beautiful painting, had he been allowed to create it.

But the scion had learned his lesson well. His boon was a curse and he did not say or do anything.

Later, when his mother lay dead on the marble floor, the boy realized this was not a game, not a thrilling secret: it was a matter of life and death. Had he been braver, he might have saved his mother from the poison in that cup.

He wailed and clawed at his hair until his aunt, his mother's sister, gathered him up in her arms. "What happened, little dragon, who did this?"

The scion hugged her neck so tightly. "Don't tell anyone," he begged. "I'm sorry, I'm sorry, I couldn't save her, I didn't even try! I'm sorry! Please."

"Hush, hush, it's all right."

"I didn't save her," he whispered, sobbing. "I have to save her."

"It's too late, little dragon," his aunt murmured.

"No," he said again and again. He threw himself away from his aunt and ran to his rooms. Found chalk and old cracked paint pots and ripped paper out of books in a tantrum. The scion drew and drew, scrawling images of that eyeless girl. He refused food, he refused his father and his baby brother, he refused everything but paint, and finally he locked the door, screaming to be left alone unless anybody was going to help.

When his aunt had the door kicked in, the scion's room was a disaster of paintings and spilled color. Wasted effort, childish, ugly pictures. Blurs and shapes that looked like nothing but impressions of landscapes or people, castles and gardens and ships and massive, ancient creatures the Houses called their empyreals. A figure of fire, broad winged and gorgeous. The eyeless girl. His aunt recognized the monsters, if not the girl. Dragon, gryphon, barghest, sphinx, cockatrice, kraken. And the First Phoenix.

But the scion tore the phoenix painting down the middle and threw a heavy book at his aunt. "Bring me a master, to show me how it's done," he cried. "I have to find her. It's soon."

"What is soon?" asked his aunt. She put her arm around him. "Who is she?"

"You'll see," the young scion said, pulling away.

While the young scion lost himself in painting dreams, Pyrlanum descended into violence. House Dragon accused House Sphinx of murdering their beloved consort. The grief-stricken Dragon regent demanded retribution, forcing all the great Houses to choose sides, and reviving the House Wars after more than twenty years of peace.

Bloodshed consumed the land, and the young scion found he could not save the eyeless girl.

"It's too late," he whispered to the disaster of art surrounding him, the night his father—leagues away—massacred the entire family line of House Sphinx.

The new House War raged on for years, and instead of the eyeless girl, the scion painted darkness. Thick black streaks, chunky peaks of gray and angry blue, the underlying red-red-red, heartbeat red, of sunlit memories behind tight-shut eyes. A bruise of purple over green-black, ocean-black, midnight, moonless black.

When his baby brother asked what he painted, the scion only hissed at him, chasing him from the room.

House Dragon took more and more of the country, forcing the other Houses into submission. Finally House Dragon captured Phoenix Crest, the ancient home of the Phoenix, those keepers of peace who had vanished during the first House Wars more than a hundred years ago. The Dragon regent declared himself High Prince Regent over all Pyrlanum.

His family left their northern mountains to occupy the fortress, and there the Dragon scion's aunt was left in charge of the boy and his small brother while their father continued his war. Though House Cockatrice fled Pyrlanum entirely, she managed to hire artists to tutor the scion—Cockatrice had been the house of her birth, after all, and that of her sister. She bought the scion paint and paper, canvas and ink and charcoal. He grew as his skills did, becoming taller and stronger but still very pretty, with a constant flush of fever in his sharp white cheeks, a ghostly gleam in his pale green eyes. He was prone to fits of laughter or staring at nothing, sure signs of madness, the court gossiped. At his aunt's prodding, the Dragon scion learned to be charming, too, and concealed the wildness he felt. He studied language and policy and economics. He flirted and argued and led council meetings during his father's frequent absences. Soon everyone believed his disposition to be merely long-running grief. After all, his mother, the late Dragon consort, had been glorious and special, hadn't she? So her glorious and special son would survive; he would lead them well. Chaos willed it, no matter that his painting boon would be useless in a leader.

But his aunt—she knew the truth of his boon. She whispered to him that she had always had gently prophetic dreams. They ran in their family. Her grandmother had been a brilliant prophet, too. His aunt offered to take the secrets he painted and use them for House Dragon on his behalf. The young scion agreed.

She studied every painting for clues, and when she discovered them, told the High Prince Regent unknowable things: where the last remnants of House Sphinx hid, the location of an ambush, the look of a spy. The High Prince Regent gave her the title of Dragon Seer, and the young scion was glad to have his secret kept so well, as his mother had wished.

Time passed. The scion painted. He dreamed of the eyeless girl but kept her to himself. He had not saved her from the darkness, just like he had not saved his mother. They haunted him, left him wracked with grief some days.

On the morning news reached the fortress that the High Prince Regent had been murdered by House Kraken, the scion woke up laughing. He laughed and laughed, caught in visions of silver swirls of light, hot light, bright light—sunlight!—on the eyeless girl's face. She had survived.

But the scion had not even dreamed of his own father's death.

That very day, ten years after the first time he'd clumsily painted her, the scion sketched the true shape of the girl's cheeks and chin and nose, the wide, eager smile, and bright tilted eyes perfectly shaped, perfectly beautiful, except inside they were churning spirals of darkness. He mixed new colors, thrilled and focused, painting her in long strokes against the entire southeast wall of his bedchamber, directly onto the stone, from crown to chin as tall as the prince was. Her hair curled out into the shadows of the room like a god of storms, and in her pupils dotted tiny explosions of fire.

When his serious little brother ventured into the scion's bedchamber, he frowned at the overwhelming sun on her face, finding the art too intense, too real, and he looked at the scion like he'd never seen him before. "What's wrong with you?" the younger boy asked, knowing nothing of prophecy and its curses.

The scion laughed, determined to keep his brother innocent of his secrets. "I'm only tired, dragonlet," he said. "Leave me to my dreams."

In the wake of their father's death, the scion was made not only the regent of House Dragon, but High Prince Regent, ruler of all Pyrlanum.

Freed by a crown on his head, the High Prince Regent let his generals take over the war, while he took over the tallest tower in Phoenix Crest to paint his eyeless girl again and again. Sometimes he vanished into his tower for days, long enough and sudden enough to foster again those rumors of madness, rumors of a wild spirit or a curse. Each time he emerged, a new painting leaned against the tower walls: the girl in full sunlight, arms crossed defensively, curls flared in a gust of wind and a mask across her eyes. The girl with a sword in hand, strange goggles making her eyes like those of a bumblebee. The girl, older, standing at the top of a cliff, peering over ruins, eyes covered by small masks, one that laughed and one that screamed. The girl in a library beside a hearth as big as a giant's mouth, holding a dagger made of a curving gryphon talon, and her eyes full moons. The girl in the Phoenix Crest ballroom wearing a cream gown, holding the empty air like she was dancing with a ghost, with eyes made of massive black pearls.

The High Prince Regent was eighteen years old when he painted the girl engulfed in flames. The House Wars his father had reignited had raged for an entire decade.

He barely remembered mixing the colors of fire, or throwing his brushes in the corner. With his hands he drew flames like ivy growing up her body, twisting and burning, but feeding her power. He felt it, too, hot and hungry, the promise of melting in such an inferno. The fire licked up the edges of the canvas and up his wrists, twining his forearms with pain.

The High Prince Regent screamed through his teeth, refusing to stop, as smoke burned tears down his cheeks and his hands shook. He closed his eyes, blocking it out, the fear and heat and pain: it hurt so much, the memory of this future pyre.

He woke up alone in his tower room, nostrils filled with the tinge of old smoke, but there was nothing around him except splatters of paint and every image of the eyeless girl, surrounding him, watching him with her pits of eyes, her bumblebee eyes, her full-moon eyes, sea-glass eyes, ghostly fish-bitten dead eyes, and eyes of pearls. Most of all a new painting on a messy unframed canvas: the girl made of flames, her eyes like twin suns.

There had never been a fire eating him whole.

But there would be.

In four years: a high rampart, a bright blue sky, warships on the brilliant horizon, something sticky in his hand, an awful taste on his tongue. And the eyeless girl, standing before him, her lips on his lips. For the first time he could see her eyes not as furious wells of power, but gentle brown with flecks of gold. Then the fire. It would happen. It must.

Alone in his tower room, the High Prince Regent waited for the sun to rise over his land, torn apart by constant war, then he carefully rent the fiery painting into strips and set them alight.

ENEMIES

1
DARLING

I had a dream about the dark.

Not the night, which has stars and the moon to cast shadows, but an all-consuming dark, one that devoured and twisted and changed a girl into something else, something defiant and monstrous. She scrabbled in the abyss with the other women of her house: sisters and mothers and cousins and friends, each of them dwindling away until she was the only one left. When it finally came to pass that she was liberated from that hole, her eyes had learned to live without the light, to love the cool comfort of the shadows. And so she wept in the arms of her liberators, not because she was sad, but because her poor damaged eyes had no idea what to do with sunshine.

I dream of my childhood every night before a battle, which is a lot, considering Pyrlanum has been at this worthless war since before I can remember. Fighting might be a rite of passage, one that feels less triumphant the longer we're in combat, but my dreams are so familiar they've become equal parts comforting and distressing. Lucky me, I learned to make peace with fear long ago.

"Darling, heads up!"

A knife flies past my face, close enough to slice a line across the deep brown skin of my cheek and take a chunk from my ear. A curl that has managed to escape from the twin buns at the nape of my neck falls to the ground. I don't swear at the sudden blossom of pain, just turn to wait for the next blade, ready to deflect it with one of my long knives.

"Really, Adelaide? This close to a battle?" I say, swallowing a sigh.

Adelaide Seabreak, second scion of House Kraken and my adopted sister, grins at me from across the deck of the *Barbed Tentacle*, flagship of the Kraken navy. The wind whips her long brown hair around her face, and even though her skin is tanned, it is nowhere near as dark a brown as mine. They say that all the members of House Sphinx had skin as brown as the leather of their beloved treatises, but there is no one to verify this. I am the only one left.

"How else am I supposed to make sure you don't get bogged down in melancholy?" She stands in a ready position, legs shoulder width apart and feet firmly planted on the deck of the ship. In her cursed left hand she holds another throwing knife, her posture all arrogance and well-earned bravado. She should one day become regent of her house, taking the role of her father, but being left-hand dominant ended that dream before it could even begin. "Chaos touched," the old gossips still whisper when Adelaide is near. The old superstitions of Pyrlanum control the futures of one and all—even within House Kraken.

At least Adelaide has a house to call her own.

"Not now. And don't you have a battle plan to review?" I'm in no mood for her good humor, and I push off from the pile of rope I recline against. I wanted a quick nap, a brief respite in a day too heavy with emotion, not an impromptu knife fight.

"Oh, don't be like that. Really, Darling, it isn't like you'd have to worry anyway. Look! Your boon has already made you beautiful once more."

I touch my cheek subconsciously. The cut is gone, nothing but a line of scab in its place. My ability to heal had made me a legend among the House Kraken Barbs from the moment of discovery and prompted just as much speculation as it had admiration.

After all, how was it the girl with the healing boon had such damaged eyes? Even now I have to wear my smoked-glass goggles, the setting sun still too high in the sky for me to remove them just yet.

My light sensitive eyes are a visible sign that my gifts have limits. I am not invincible.

I stand and walk to the prow of the ship, ignoring Adelaide's platitudes and half apologies. I love my sister, even if we are not of the same blood. I was adopted into House Kraken after Leonetti Seabreak, Kraken regent, saved me from the dark of the Nakumba sewers seven years ago when I was ten. And calling Leonetti my father has been one of the bright spots in my life. But Adelaide likes to push and push until she finds a breaking point. It is just her nature: like water, she flows in and around a person until she finds their weak spot.

The problem is that long before I reveal my weaknesses, I will strike out, and killing Adelaide is not an option even if I wanted to. So, like I have for many years, I find it better to distance myself from her prodding rather than engage her.

"Ignore her, she's feeling the pressure of tonight's mission." Gavin Swiftblade sidles up to me with a grin. The wind tousles his sandy hair, and he absentmindedly pushes it out of his bright blue eyes. The sun has burned freckles into his pale cheeks, giving him a cherubic air. It's a lie, though. I have watched Gavin slide a knife between a man's ribs without the barest flicker of remorse. It's to be expected: the Swiftblades were respected assassins before they turned their backs on House Dragon, defying the High Prince Regent to fight alongside House Kraken.

"Chaos give me strength, are you making excuses for her? We are all feeling the pressure, Gav. That doesn't mean she gets liberty to be an ass," I say.

"I heard that, Darling," Adelaide calls, even though she keeps her distance. She knows better than to provoke me when I'm in a mood, and memory tugs at me a little too hard this evening for me to smile at her gentle mockery.

Even though we have anchored a few miles off the coast of Lastrium, there's not much to be seen of the coastline. It's an unremarkable port city with very little strategic value, but House Kraken spies indicate that somewhere in the governor's mansion Leonetti is being held captive. Sometime last week while my Barbs and I were razing Dragon settlements along the eastern coast, our regent was kidnapped, forcing us to sail around the southern wastes and here to the western coast of the country. It was a hard trip, but the *Barbed Tentacle* is fast, built for smuggling more than fighting, and combined with Adelaide's fair-wind boon we made the trip in days instead of a couple of weeks. Now we have to get to Leonetti before the bastard Dragons move him.

I do not have much hope of seeing my adoptive father alive again. This thrice-cursed war has a way of taking everything one loves and turning it to ash.

For a moment I am trapped again in the garden of my childhood, my mother screaming as one of the Dragon's Teeth, elite soldiers that serve much the same purpose as House Kraken's Barbs, separates my mother's head from the rest of her body. The crimson arc of her blood splattering her everblooms is the last memory I have before someone scooped me up and pushed me through a passageway into the tunnels of Nakumba. There had been over a hundred women and children living in the compound of my childhood.

"So, we gonna skin some Dragons or what?" Alvin Kelpline says, spitting over the side as he leans against the deck railing with Gavin and me.

Alvin is a deckhand and all of thirteen summers old, far too young to be a Barb just yet, but so close to being old enough to draw blood of his own. His mop of dark curls and buck teeth always make me smile. He has the same olive complexion as the rest of House Kraken, pointing to the shared ancestral bloodline that long ago united Kraken and Sphinx.

"You are going nowhere, fry," I say with a grin, ignoring the fear that rises up when I think of innocents like Alvin taking up arms with the rest of us. But the chances are that, like so many other little ones, he will be forced into battle before he is ready. I'll do my best to make sure that doesn't happen. "Show me your stance."

Alvin takes up a ready position, his feet too close together and his shoulders sloped. I adjust his body to fix his form and run him through a couple of drills while Gavin offers the boy helpful tips. It's enough to push away the remaining storm clouds of memory, the movements easy and familiar, and I half wonder if Adelaide sent the boy over. She's always been good at reading my moods.

My smile fades as I imagine Alvin fighting. I was his age when I begged Leonetti to let me pick up my first sword. And two years later I was in my first skirmish when the country estate where we were staying was overrun by House Barghest. Leonetti tossed me a blade and demanded I defend myself.

"Darling Seabreak, if you would be of my House, you will fight like a Kraken," he said with a crooked grin, his weather-beaten skin and tousled salt-and-pepper hair making him seem less like the ruler of a prosperous House and more like a rakish pirate.

On that day I killed my first man, and too many since.

"I miss him, too."

Miranda, Adelaide's older, more earnest sister, stands nearby, her long dark hair braided and her tan skin already darkened with oily soot. Even though the girls share a mother, Miranda has no idea who her biological father is. But Adelaide is the spitting image of Miranda, just without the recklessness. Miranda offers me the inky soot pot, but I shake my head. My skin is naturally dark enough that I do not have to worry about blending into the shadows.

"I think you and Adelaide must have cast some forbidden blood spell to read my moods," I say, changing the subject as I begin to ready myself for the night ahead. I do not want to talk about Leonetti, about how we were not there to keep him from being kidnapped. Instead I wrap a dark scarf around my hair, tucking it tight around the tops of my ears.

"Blood magic? Even with your smoked lenses you have no game face, Darling. Why is it you think you lose all of the time?" Miranda asks with a laugh.

I grin. "Because all of you Seabreaks cheat."

She shrugs. "But your moods are also as easy to read as a Gryphon manuscript. You should work on that."

"It's never a problem in the dark."

Miranda shrugs. "Only you would think spending life in the gloom was the solution to a simple annoyance." She says it without any heat, but the words sting anyway. My instinct has always been to hide in the shadows when things go wrong. Perhaps that is why

I was glad to join the Barbs when Leonetti asked me last year. They get praise for skulking about in the dark, not censure.

But after tonight, no more. I've sworn I'm finished with all of the treachery: the assassinations, the hostage taking that never quite goes as expected, the sabotage. All of it ends tonight, after we've freed my foster father. I have played my role in this endless war. Now I will step aside and let someone else take the stage. Someone like Gavin, whose appetite for violence sometimes seems unquenchable.

"We'll set out as soon as the light dies," Miranda says, cutting through my thoughts. "You and Gavin will be going all the way into the governor's mansion. I'll be remaining on the beach to make sure our exit is flawless."

"Are you certain?" Despite my weariness of killing and treachery, there are few things that bring me more joy than being lead on a mission. I like doing a good job, even if it creates far too many sleepless nights.

"Of course I am. He's got invisibility, and you've got the healing. My poison boon won't do much on a rescue mission, and I've sent the rest to see to the warehouses along the wharf. It's just the three of us. I'll be waiting with the boat so we can make a quick getaway." She lays a cool hand on my bare arm. "I want you to be careful, though. I will *not* lose another family member tonight."

Gavin pops into existence next to us, grinning as we both startle. "Are you kidding? If anyone gets in our way, Darling will slice them to pieces. They'll be dead before they even realize they've lost their heads." He's also foregone the soot, for obvious reasons. He winks at me before disappearing once more, and I roll my eyes at the way he shows off his boon. Maybe if my gift didn't require a measure of pain, I would be more inclined to show off as well.

As Miranda goes over the parameters of the operation one last time, I let my mind wander. The sun hangs low in the sky, fat and round, seeming to quiver with the way the light ripples off the sea. That might just be the smoky goggles that I wear. Either way, the daylight is not long for this world, and I am anxious for us to weigh anchor and be off. In a short while I'll be able to remove my goggles and stride through the dark, where I will be the one with the advantage.

Tonight, I will kill anyone who gets between me and my father.

And then I will lay down my arms once and for all.

2

TALON

I hate city fighting. There's even less I can control than usual: no high ground, too many people, too little maneuverability, dead ends, unbelievable amounts of flammable materials. And usually screaming. My whole life has been this House War, and there are plenty of shades to everything I hate about it, but urban battle is the worst.

I don't hide my dismay from the captains and officials facing me over the long table. Until two days ago this building was a herd-drake stable, and it smells like sour char and musty shed scales. But even war drakes are useless in city fighting, so we commandeered the stables for temporary barracks and sent the plodding beasts to the countryside.

Governor Tillus argued to meet in his mansion, where there is plentiful wine and pasta, and half my field council agrees, but I don't care: this is war, and I won't let them forget that. They already like to talk around me and pretend I'm not the Dragon scion, not my brother's War Prince, because I'm only eighteen, and compared to Caspian I'm forgettable. But I've been leading soldiers and killing the enemies of the High Prince Regent for years. If Tillus came face-to-face with one of these insurgents, he'd probably kneel to beg before he even thought to draw a blade. He's just annoyed the first thing I did when I arrived yesterday was to send his shiny new prisoner away.

We shouldn't even be here. Lastrium is a port town only because they built a decent pier, not because it's strategically useful. Jagged cliffs hem it in, while the city of Sartoria, a day's ride up the coast, has a river and was the old seat of the Kraken regent for centuries, before the fall of the Last Phoenix and the first House War. Sartoria is much more tactically relevant, even though we've had it locked down since my father rekindled the House Wars after Mother died, fourteen years ago. If the Kraken are determined to restart their guerrilla tactics here on the west coast, Lastrium is more suited to a practice run than the real thing. Not worth sending their navy. But Aunt Aurora sent a prophecy that the Kraken navy pulled up anchor and will be here, in Lastrium, in three days.

It has to be a feint. The only thing of use in Lastrium is reserves of fossilized venom we use to make dragonfire. But the Kraken have to expect if they laid any kind of siege to the city and we thought we'd lose it, we'd blow up the warehouse before allowing them to have it.

I wonder if I should just do that now and get back to the Crest. Caspian won't expect me, and maybe I can surprise him in his tower before he forbids me to visit. I've been in Barghest lands leading our combined forces for the last eighteen months, and every time I suggest I come home to meet with my war council in person, I'm commanded to remain away. I have got to get to my brother soon. I'm worried about him, especially given the growing rumors of his madness.

But Aurora's prophecies are never wrong. The Kraken are coming here. So instead of Phoenix Crest, I'm in damned Lastrium.

Captain Firesmith points to the map of the city spread on the worn wooden table. "They can't set fire to the cliffs, so they'll focus on the pier. We should send the remaining ships up to Sartoria."

"All that's left are some cutters fast enough to send messages," one of the city officials, Mara Stormswell, reminds Firesmith.

I say nothing, tracing the defenses of the city with my gaze. They're not good, but they've never had to be. This place is just cliffs, beach, residences, and a few scattered markets and warehouses. Leonetti Seabreak was here for a minute, but they can't have known that. I grind my teeth thinking they might have known that. It doesn't matter now he's gone. But I don't want their spies to be better than mine.

"—their ships can easily keep out of range," Finn Sharpscale says, and I assume he means the limited dragonfire cannons we have. Less than an hour after Caspian appointed me commander of the Dragon's Teeth, I passed the position to Finn instead, because I'd rather be free to fight where I'm needed, not tied down to a certain company. One of the only things I've learned about leadership from my wild older brother is that sometimes it helps if you surprise people with a sudden left turn. If they can't predict you, they pay closer attention. Of course, Caspian takes that to every extreme. I need to be more reliable. Certain. Respected.

Governor Tillus snorts. "Fool Kraken. Naval warfare is useless here." His beard twists as he either smiles or grimaces.

"They aren't fools," I say quietly. They think they can take something from us here, either Leonetti or some kind of retaliation for his capture.

The governor looks like he wants to call us all fools and go home to wrap up in the silks Dragons won for him, under the roof Dragons provide. His family might have sworn to the High Prince Regent, but a mere five years ago they were Kraken. They haven't taken to heart yet what it means to be Dragon.

I stand up. I'm not tall enough to loom like Caspian, but I'm broad and have perfected the way I show my teeth when I smile. It's just like the toothy draconic grin of my helmet when I wear full armor. I want to remind Tillus that no matter who he used to be, no matter what lands these were, it's all a part of the High Prince Regent's hoard now. We must defend it and die for it in a reign of fire, because that is who Dragons are. Not fools.

At my side, Finn stands, too. He is huge, with a scar on the left side of his face that hooks his lips into a permanent sneer. I didn't make him commander of the Teeth only for his skill with an ax, or his loyalty to me.

"We have three days until their navy arrives," I say to Governor Tillus, then skewer each other official and captain with a gaze I know is an unwavering vivid green. The color runs in the family. "I want a complete inventory of everything in the city, Tillus, no matter how small. And I want cannons set up along the cliffs to at least make the Kraken marines' lives harder, if we can't reach the ships. Everybody bring me an idea for additional defenses tomorrow. Be creative. Pretend this city is made of your own precious hoard. We must be ready in two days."

With that, I turn sharply and go.

Finn will give me enough time for my exit to make its point, then follow me to the narrow hostler's office I took for my own.

I move quickly across the cobbles of the inner courtyard from the stable's training arena, where we'd set up the council table and cots for most of the foot soldiers. Everything in a drake stable is made of stone or plaster, because drakes of all varieties tend to have fiery accidents. We have the seven war drakes attached to the Teeth harnessed together with iron gear in the corner farthest from the gates. They're leaning their bodies against each other, twining sinuous scaled necks. Crests of feathers shade their slit-pupiled eyes, but most are looking at me. I stare at them, catching the eye of my primary mount, to remind her who's the boss. She stares back for a long moment, then flicks her row of long spine feathers. I smile and pause to scratch under her scaly chin. She makes a sound almost like a purr.

I glance up at the last streaks of orange sunset. The moon will rise shortly, almost full. Good visibility on the seas tonight, nothing to slow that navy down. I'll eat a quick dinner, wait for Finn, and then go down to the pier myself. We'll check the warehouse. Most of the Dragon's Teeth we have with us are on night patrol, but the few off duty might let me spar with them.

Obviously they'll do whatever I command, but it's better when they want to include me.

Just before I push through the door into the stable building, I feel the distracting pulse at my wrist: Aurora's summons tingling in the bracelet pressed to my skin by my leather bracer. She wants to talk five days before our scheduled meeting, which is unusual. We limit our regular communications by necessity because such distant far-seeing taxes the strength of Aurora's attendant.

I quicken my pace past the stalls where higher-ranking soldiers have doubled up to the hostler's office. Most of the stalls are empty at the moment, as it's near change of watch, but two soldiers lean against their open doors and salute. I put my fist to my chest in response.

Inside the dim office are my own cot, weapons, and armor, plus a field communication kit with the necessary bowl and cleansing glass. I light the oil lamp and pull closed the shutter on the round window that overlooks the courtyard I just passed through. Firelight dances on the three chunks of dragonglass settled in the bottom of the shallow stone bowl. I take one in my hand and drag it softly clockwise in a spiral up to the edge of the bowl and balance it there. The second I drag in a counterclockwise spiral and balance it at an angle from the first. The third I use to draw a six-pointed star across the entirety of the bowl before placing it along the rim. A slight tingle tickles my spine, so I know the cleansing worked—Aunt Aurora says I only feel it because my boon is related to far sight, and if I were a true seer, there would be a thin line of power visible everywhere I'd traced the stones. I trust her word on that and go get some water from the pump just outside the office.

Then I wait.

The water shivers as it settles into the bowl. In an emergency we can connect through rippling water, but this must not be one. I fit my body into a core stance, feet apart and fists together over my stomach so my elbows and arms make a strength triangle. I focus on breathing and settling my blood as the water settles. Aurora can always tell when I'm upset, thanks to the way heat from any emotion makes pink blotches high on my cheeks, and I don't want her to worry about taking care of me tonight. I'm an adult; I can take care of myself. I can control my feelings. *Dragons don't need to hide their emotions*, she soothed me once, when I was nine and angrily stomping around wearing a too-large helmet with full faceplate. *Let your fury and joy and grief show; that's where your power is, dragonlet.* Maybe that was true for a little boy, or maybe it's true for a High Prince Regent. It can't be true for me. I'm not powerful enough for people to respect displays of emotions. Not unless they're calculated displays.

Besides, Caspian's reputation is wild enough without having a scion always too near to exploding.

"Talon," Aurora says, and I glance down at the bowl. Her face shimmers colorlessly against the water, peaceful and lovely . . . except there's a tightness I can see at the corner of her lips. Tension that would be hidden to most, but I know to look for it.

"What did he do?" I demand.

My aunt puts her betraying lips into a thin line and says, "It's been a very bad week."

I clench my jaw and slowly nod. "I can leave now—"

"No, Talon, he wants you there. He said that specifically. But . . . he also said, 'Talon must save her.'"

"Save who?"

Aurora's lashes flutter, and she lowers her gaze in sorrow. "There's only one *her* Caspian has ever concerned himself with since my sister died."

The eyeless girl. His imaginary friend, or whatever she is, a figment of his madness. His muse. The only thing he cares to paint. Even Aurora, whose boon is prophecy, cannot see her. But Caspian has been obsessed with her for my entire life. Aurora believes he must have known the girl as a child; perhaps something happened as his painting boon took root. Either that, or she's a piece of his nightmares, a Chaos-induced hallucination. There are old stories of Chaos speaking to all of us through dreams, but not since the Last Phoenix died a hundred years ago. All our boons are weaker now than they were then, if we have them at all. "What does he want me to save her from?" I ask.

"I don't know," Aurora admits. "He was even more distressed than usual."

"Distressed?" Anger makes my voice low. I hate being far away from them, where I can't do anything at all to help. "That's no excuse for treating you poorly."

"Oh, Talon." She sets her jaw just like I do, and in the water I can't tell if she has tears in her eyes or not. "You need to come home when you finish there, prepared to take over."

"Aunt," I begin, because she's said this before, and I can't. I won't unseat my own brother.

But Aurora cuts me off. "I am holding the council together, Talon, but at *best* they say Caspian is too distracted to rule. At worst, there are the whispers of madness, still, again. We've worked hard to keep his tendencies private, but he doesn't care if people notice he vanishes for days and days, he rarely comes to meetings anymore, and when he shows himself at court, it's impossible to predict if he'll be lucid or wild. The Gryphon physician you arranged for does little to—"

A knock on my office door grabs my attention. I hold up my hand so Aurora stops talking, and I call, "Finn?"

"Scion," he responds through the thin door. "Hungry?"

"Hold a moment." I turn back to Aurora. She's watching calmly, not a hair out of place, elegant and pristine as a portrait—though not like the art of our mad High Prince Regent. I'm told she looks like our mother, but I don't remember. They were both of House Cockatrice, beauties traded by their father to mine in an attempt to allay the spite of House Dragon garnered nearly forty years ago during the previous House Wars. I doubt the bad cross of madness and artistry born in my brother had been the intended outcome of the alliance. "Aunt," I say, "you know my answer. But I will come home after this battle, strong in glory and heart. We will *help* him, somehow, not take his throne. I have to be able to do that. I'm his brother."

For a moment, Aurora's expression stills as if she means to argue, but then she lowers her gaze in acknowledgement. "As you say, scion. But please, be careful. We need you."

"If it were my day to die, you would know it through your own boon, Aurora," I answer warmly, and touch the water to disrupt her seeing. I miss her, but I can't let myself succumb to homesickness.

"Finn," I call, and just as he turns the handle, the nape of my neck tingles. I can't react at all before I hear a massive boom.

Finn throws the door open, ax in hand, but I push past him out into the stable. I run, because I know that sound: an explosion.

Behind me Finn yells orders for everyone to arms. I skid to a stop and look up. The night sky blazes with stars, and the moon is too low—there in the southwest is a ferocious orange glow. Fire.

I run toward the inn across the way from the drake stable. It's four stories, the tallest nearby building. I barge in, ignoring cries of alarm and people pushing to get out. They'll see nothing useful on the street. I need to get high.

Up and up the stairs I run, Finn's bootsteps echoing at my heels, until I reach the top floor and blow through into a private room, to the south window. I shove open the shutters and lean out.

From my dragon's-eye view I can see exactly how far it is to the flicker of red-hot flames. The billowing smoke, spreading lazily across the sky, blots out stars. Half a mile, toward the sea, but still south. I know what that is.

The fossilized-venom stores. Somebody blew up the warehouse.

I stare for a long moment, mind racing. There must be Kraken insurgents already in the city, a forward brigade of their own, before the navy. Barbs. That's what they call their spies and sneaks. They must be preparing for the navy to arrive somehow, but why warn us? Why not wait until the navy is right here instead of setting the city on fire?

Below me the streets are filling with people. Chaos. Disorder. It will be harder to get my soldiers anywhere now. That's plenty good reason to blow the warehouse—when the navy arrives. Not now.

I pull myself back inside and tell Finn, "They blew the venom stores. That fire won't go out for hours, even if we can get people with fire and water boons set up to contain it. I'll send Captains Firesmith and Peak to the warehouses for crowd assistance and to catch any of the insurgents, while Wingry and Fallfar go to the cliffs and pier. Get the Teeth seer looking for anything, but keep your people with me."

We start back to the barracks. Finn says, "What are we going to do?"

"Get our weapons. There's only one good reason for them to do this now, days before their navy is here." I spare a reluctant thought for better spies.

"Distraction," he says, baring his teeth eagerly. With his scar, he looks truly gleeful. "They think Leonetti is still here."

I nod and pause at the front of the stable courtyard, snagging one of the toothlings assigned to me. I send the young girl to relay my orders to the various captains. She's shaking with a heady combination of fear and excitement to see action, bouncing on her toes and fingering the hilt of her smallsword as she repeats my orders before dashing off.

Finn claps his hand on my shoulder. "Let's go drown some squids, Talon."

3

DARLING

The explosion from the fossilized-venom warehouse is visible from the sea. Miranda, Gavin, Alvin, and I all gasp when we see it from where we bob in a small boat less than a nautical mile from the coast. We've been waiting half a turn for the first warehouse to go, for people to crowd the streets and distract the occupying Dragons enough to let us slip into the smugglers' tunnels under Lastrium.

"Oh wow. That's so cool," Alvin breathes, his eyes wide in his soot-blackened face. He's right. It's a beauty of an explosion, all orange and red and smoke, and so bright that my eyes are dazzled for a second. They water profusely, and I dash away the tears as I blink to clear the afterimage of fire and carnage.

"We managed to get everyone out before it went, right?" I ask. The fire is so bright that I debate putting my smoked glasses back on, even going so far as to dig them out of the pocket of my tunic before the flames die down enough and my vision clears so that I can see the cliffs, waves, and my boat companions.

"Darling, always worried about the casualty rate," Gavin says with a sigh.

Miranda shoots him a sharp look. "Yes. Lastrium was one of our cities, and it still is. House Kraken isn't like Dragon. We inspire loyalty. We don't force it."

I nod and pick up my oar. "Great, so let's see how loyal this governor is to the Dragons who hold his leash."

Gavin laughs. "I love it when you talk torture."

Miranda, Gavin, and Alvin each grab an oar, and we make our quiet way to the cave at the base of the cliff. The Dragons may suspect the existence of the smugglers' tunnels that wend their way through the cliffs, but even if so, the way is death for anyone not familiar with the routes. Luckily, we've been using these tunnels to supply Kraken loyalists within the city for nearly a fortnight. With my uncanny sight, Gavin and I will make our way to the governor's mansion quickly by way of the tunnels, returning just as the second warehouse goes, long before they'll manage to put out the first warehouse fire. It's a simple plan, but that's the beauty of it.

The Dragons will never know what hit them.

The boat dips and bobs as we reach the shallows. Even though the coast is rocky, there is a small beach that leads to the entrance to the tunnels, and wordlessly we paddle the boat to it.

We maneuver the small craft toward the shore, and I leap out of the boat and begin to pull it onto the sand. There's enough moon that it seems almost daytime bright to me, and I'm faster than the others. Once we've gotten the boat out of the water, Gavin and I do a quick weapons check, before saying goodbye to Miranda.

"Fair winds and following seas," she says as she hugs me tightly, the common farewell of House Kraken. It is both good luck and a deeper emotional parting, the kind of thing sailors say to their families before they leave for sea duty. It's a reminder that we might not all make it.

I hug her silently before doing the same to Alvin. I didn't want the boy to come along at all, but if Gavin and I don't make it back, Miranda will need a second to help her return to the *Barbed Tentacle*. He practically vibrates at being allowed to accompany us, and I can't bear to look at his happy hopeful expression as Gavin and I leave them behind.

I send a prayer out to Chaos that our mission tonight is successful and the boy never sees true war.

Darkness swallows us quickly once we enter the smugglers' route. Gavin walks with his hand on my shoulder as we make our way through the damp tunnels. There are places in the walls for torches, but I can see just fine even in the belly of the cliffs, where there is little ambient light. One of the House Kraken physicians theorized that my vision was somehow augmented by more than just physical adaptation, and that there was a bit of Chaos at work, since my eyes note far more than they should in the dark. It made a bit of sense, since boons are the result of Chaos in the blood, but I've never thought much more beyond that. Philosophy is for House Gryphon and their talented minds. Maybe I'd have cared if House Sphinx still existed, but I'm a Kraken now; all I care for is action and result.

My boots are wet from jumping into the shallows, and the puddles in the tunnel don't help, but the mesh and leather are designed for just such a landing, and after only a short ways into the tunnel the material begins to dry. I mark time by the upward slope of the floor and Gavin's breathing, close to my ear but as steady and rhythmic as the sea on a calm day. Even if I'd never been in these tunnels before I still wouldn't be lost. The walls point me in the right direction. Marks carved by smugglers of long ago look like nonsense, arrows and stars and crescent moons that would lead anyone unfamiliar with the Kraken House code astray, but which clearly direct me where I want to go: inland and toward the outskirts of Lastrium.

The close press of the walls might make others hesitate, but for me it's strange, almost like coming home. I spent so much of my life hunting and scavenging in the tunnels under Nakumba that the damp walls and stale air are more relaxing than alarming. Of course, these smugglers' tunnels smell a far cry better than the sewers of Nakumba, but still. I'm fairly buzzing with anticipation by the time I've led us through the majority of it, Gavin's hand on my shoulder as I walk the only reminder I have that I'm not alone in the pitch black.

I stop, and Gavin stumbles a bit before he manages to catch himself. "We're at the crossroads that points to the graveyard," I say, unsheathing my long knives and rolling my shoulders to loosen them up. Gavin pulls out his small throwing knives, quickly placing them between his fingers even in the dark. Barbs deal in stealth and speed, and our weapons are the same. No flashy swords for us, thanks.

Gavin places his hand, now full of tiny poisoned knives, back on my shoulder, and I am careful to tilt my head to the right so I don't accidentally get nicked by one of the blades. We've only gone a few steps before his hand falls away as the tunnel lightens considerably, moonlight filtering in from the opening ahead. I take a deep breath and let it out.

We are so close, and my heart beats triple time at being able to soon see my father again.

The tunnel is mostly blocked by thick rumbleberry canes. This early in the season they are all thorns and new leaves, and Gavin and I carefully move them to the side with our blades as we sneak out. The tunnel empties into a graveyard on the edge of town, but the governor's mansion is not far from the cemetery, for good reasons. Smuggling is as much a part of House Kraken as fishing and expedition. It is rumored that the First Kraken had been a pirate, a woman who declared she would not marry the man her family betrothed her to and instead took to the sea. When her family chased her down and demanded she wed, she said she would marry the briny deep. Chaos had granted her wish by twisting her form so that she could forever live in her beloved sea, pulling down ships until she regained her human form and returned to lead her House.

I don't know if it's true, but I love the idea of Chaos granting a wish in such a backhanded manner.

"What are you smiling about?" Gavin whispers as we run to a stand of live oaks on the outskirts of the governor's garden and duck down. There are no guards about, and the curtains to the wide windows of the formal dining room are drawn back so that the household is revealed for all to see. The doors to the garden have been propped open to let in a breeze. It's almost too perfect a scene, like something out of an old House Cockatrice farce. There is a Dragon captain, grizzled and gray in his distinctive forest-green uniform; the governor, a small man with far too much facial hair and a penchant for paisley; and a few others that I don't know. A nearby maid pours more honey wine, even though it's clear the assemblage has already had enough, their voices loud and uncontrolled. The governor bounces a laughing girl much too young for him on his knee while the men make lewd jokes. The girl laughs along with their crass humor. I hope she's being well compensated.

"These fools," Gavin mutters. "Don't they know there is a war happening?"

"Bryanne Seabreak," I say.

Gavin startles. "What?"

"You asked what I was smiling about, and I was smiling about Bryanne Seabreak. Have you heard that story?" I whisper back.

"No, but this might not be the time," Gavin says, pointing to the heavily armed riders storming up the drive. They ride war drakes, large and barely feathered, their scales dull and their forearms thickly taloned. I have never seen such vicious-looking creatures. The drakes in House Kraken tended to be the smaller kind, to fit on ships, their plumage grand and their talons nearly nonexistent. No wonder some of the more grizzled veterans tell horror stories of the House Dragon cavalry. I cannot imagine seeing a unit of those monstrous lizards bearing down upon me on a battlefield.

"Chaos take me," Gavin swears. "Look."

I frown at him and turn back to the company of riders disembarking from the drakes. They wear skirmish armor, leather plating and gauntlets, but no helms. They stride into the mansion like they're going to a fire, which is where they're supposed to be, attending to the warehouse fire near the pier, not here.

"What am I supposed to be seeing?" I ask.

"Did you see who that was?" Gavin asks. At my head shake he sighs. "That is Talon Goldhoard. The War Prince himself, scion to House Dragon. His dad is the one who ordered your House murdered."

"My House is Kraken," I murmur absentmindedly, making the old argument without even realizing what I'm saying. The riders appear in the dining room scene, and there seems to be some yelling, with the governor making the appropriate bows and scrapes and the rest of his guests looking somewhere between chagrined and annoyed at the arrival of their unexpected guests.

"Leonetti has to be here if the War Prince is here," Gavin says. He's right. Why else would a battlefield commander bother himself with a worthless town like Lastrium? The fossilized-venom stores are tactically relevant, but this town is nowhere near as important as a few other locations on the coast.

"Okay, change of plan," I say. I strip off all my armor but keep a bandolier of throwing knives and the sheaths for my long knives before picking up my weapons once more.

I wiggle and rotate my arms, enjoying being much lighter. This is a perfect end to my war. A perfect vengeance. "We're going to kill us a prince, first."

Gavin grins, but it's more like a snarl. "Okay, what are you thinking?"

"I need those lights to go out. While I'm working, you search the residence for Leonetti. Let's show these overgrown lizards what a little Kraken blue steel can do," I say.

Gavin nods, disappearing before sprinting across the garden.

I lean back and wait, watching the newly arrived Dragon soldiers. Unlike the regular troops they don't wear green. Instead, they wear tunics of bloodred under their armor plates, their trousers a snowy white.

Dragon's Teeth.

These are no regular soldiers; these are the High Prince Regent's deadliest, most bloodthirsty troops. Once, their job was to watch over and protect House Dragon's regent, just the same as the Barbs were assigned to Leonetti. But that was before a century of endless wars and Dragons who wanted to add the whole of Pyrlanum to their hoard.

One of the soldiers, a nasty piece of work who looms over the rest, begins yanking the curtains closed. He's just reached the open double doors when the tableau before me dims. There's a shout, and then the boonlamps in the dining room begin to go out one by one. It's a relief to my eyes, and just in time. It's incredibly difficult to sneak in through a closed window.

The moon is plenty bright, its light cool and bathing the world in silver, so I'm careful to skirt around the edges of the garden as I run toward the still-open double doors, blades in hand. I'll only have a few minutes before they figure out how to restart the lines that Gavin cut.

"Someone must have cut the main line to the boonlights." The War Prince stands near the back wall, farthest from the doors. As one of his Teeth heads out to fix the lights, I slip around the doorjamb, trying to seem like just another shadow, but the War Prince tenses.

"Someone just entered," he says calmly, drawing his sword with a soft *schnick*. The rest of his soldiers do the same, but in the dark they cannot see the threat. Despite my caution the scion sensed me, so I give up the pretense of stealth and get to work.

The room might be dark, but I can see everything. I take out the grizzled old war general first, my blade easily parting his throat. He hits the floor with a loud thump, but I've already moved on to the governor, sliding my blade into his heart from behind. He makes a choked gurgle, and as he falls to the floor, his hired company lets out a scream. I push her toward the double doors, and she takes the hint, running out into the garden.

"After her!" one of the soldiers calls, giving chase even as the War Prince snaps at her to hold fast.

The soldier runs right into my blade. It slides into her throat so easily, and then I am spinning to the side so that her body takes the brunt of the ax that comes crashing toward me.

"Show yourself," the brute yells, his face twisted by a scar. I answer him by sliding my knife into his side, letting the poison in the blade do as much of the work as the edge. He grunts, and I dance away before he can bring his ax crashing down upon my skull. Instead, he catches another one of his comrades in the face, felling the man.

I'm beginning to think that it's going to work, that maybe I will get to slide my blade into the heart of the Dragon scion, when the lights come back on, blinding me for a precious heartbeat. I fumble for my glasses, getting them on just as the brute with the ax comes back around, crashing toward me like a drunken man. I dive under the dining room table, somersaulting out the other side and leaping to my feet. There are still four Teeth remaining, including the brute and the War Prince, and I grin at them as I take up a ready position with my knives.

Always fight with a smile, my girl. Leonetti's voice echoes to me across the years, and something hitches painfully in my chest.

Suddenly everything in my soul screams at me to run, to flee. But Gavin is still upstairs somewhere in the house, hopefully with Leonetti. I owe the salty codger my life. So I take a deep breath and decide that this is where my journey will end. It looks like I will die at the hands of Dragons as I was long ago supposed to.

Chaos always has a way of exacting its price.

The brute falls to his knees, the Kraken's Sting on my blades having finally taken effect, and the man and woman who stalk toward me look to the War Prince for guidance. I glance at him, trying to judge whether or not I could get a clear shot with a throwing knife, but he stares at me with a mixture of both wonder and terror. It's a look I've seen before when people see the strangeness of my smoked glasses, and I snarl at him in response.

But then the Teeth are upon me, and I have no other thought than survival.

TALON

The first time I remember seeing her I was eleven and my father had just died.

Caspian painted her against the curving stone wall of his bedchamber. She was made of fire and darkness, coming out of the shadows—out of the constant, violent, streaking darkness that had been the only thing Caspian painted for years before that day. A girl with a grin on her face. Luminous brown skin lit with sunlight—firelight—moonlight—every kind of light he could shine on her with strokes of paint. In one hand she held a curving knife. In the other, a quill. But her eyes were swirling wells of black. As if those dark years stormed inside her, making her as wild and mad as Caspian.

My brother's nightmare stands before me, flesh and blood and poison steel. Just as fiery and beautiful as he draws her, with a smile on her face to tear through anything. And her eyes are huge circles of reflective black, like a pit viper or a butterfly.

She is made of Chaos.

Finn grunts as he falls to one knee, wide hand pressed to his side. Blood trickles between leather plates, not enough to have felled him, but Kraken Barbs put poison on their knives. They think we're the treacherous ones.

Salva and Eovan glance at me, and I manage a tight nod: we're plenty to take her down now that we can see. Her advantage is gone.

She has a long knife against all our swords. But I look back at the eyeless girl, and it's another gut punch just to know she is so completely, vividly alive. *Talon has to save her*, Caspian said to Aurora.

My hesitation costs Eovan his life.

The girl throws two small knives from a bandolier I hadn't even seen, and they hit Eovan: one in the neck, one low on his hip. He keeps toward her at Salva's side, but the girl moves with astonishing speed, ducking under Salva's sword, turning on her knees as Eovan slices where her throat had been, and instead of stabbing Eovan again she grabs the knife in his hip and tears it higher. Eovan cries out, and the girl barely dodges away.

I move around them, giving her no room to back off. She must remain engaged. But they're fighting too close for Salva's sword, and the young Tooth leaps at the girl, grabbing her arm to twist her into a pin. The girl, as if she'd expected it, uses Salva's strength to fling herself around and kick Eovan in the gut so that he stumbles and falls. Blood gushes at his neck from her first knife. She drops again, forcing Salva to release her, and Salva strikes, missing the girl with her blade, but as the girl twists out of range, Salva manages to hit her across the chin with her gauntleted hand.

It doesn't matter. The girl never stops moving; one step flows into the next turn, her footwork swift and dazzling. She flicks her wrists and thrusts her long knife back into Salva; it glances off Salva's armor, but when the girl rolls to her feet again, she holds a long knife in each hand. A grin still splashes across her bloodied mouth, and those strange black goggles glint in the boonlight.

There's two arm-spans between them. I say, "Salva, back off," my gaze on the girl.

She is exactly as she was when Caspian painted her. Fire and shadow. She walked into this room from pitch darkness and destroyed half the Dragon's Teeth, and now it will be just the two of us.

Perhaps it is not madness that touches my brother's mind. Perhaps Chaos claims him more deeply than any of us had known.

"Tell me your name," I command.

The girl spits blood onto the floor, presumably staring right back at me. But I can't see her eyes at all. No matter. Finn breathes hard in the corner of my vision, on his knees, but alive and waiting.

I draw a deep breath and flex my hand around the grip of my falchion. The blade curves slightly and is only a hand longer than her knives, made for swift death and elegance. I like it because I can outmaneuver most swords no matter the skill of the wielder, and I've got my own strength, so I don't need as much weight in the blade. I don't have a buckler or gauche dagger to meet her double blades, but I reach for the claws hooked to my belt in the small of my back and slide my fingers in. It's a modified fingerless gauntlet with short claws in the knuckles that can be used for cutting or blocking, and it will do.

When I face her fully armed, her head tilts and her smile shifts a little so she seems eager and amused. I wonder if it's a mask or if she's really so ready to die.

"I am Talon Goldhoard," I say, "First Scion of House Dragon. Who are you?"

The girl's only answer is to attack.

I meet her blades with mine and push her back. She turns and whips a knife at me; I deflect and turn with her, never pausing. I can move the way she does—with her—because I'm not trying to kill her. I don't want her dead. We need her—for what I don't have the slightest idea. But I believe it in my gut.

On defense, I can react, and we're a little too well matched. She's smaller than me, but so fast, and strong. She knows exactly how to use her speed to keep me chasing, but I know exactly how to angle to drive her slowly in the direction I want. We battle carefully, avoiding the sprawled legs of my dead Teeth and old Captain Ignatius.

The girl surprises me by turning fast and ducking under me. I swing but stumble and barely catch myself before she cuts my throat. Salva cries out. I feel the wind of the blade and set my jaw as I turn my falchion so it lines up along my forearm and drive so close I can see myself in the black glass of her goggles. I lean in, and her long knife almost pricks the underside of my jaw, but my own blade presses across her unarmored stomach just under her breasts. She freezes, hissing in through her teeth, and I slowly press my falchion out, forcing her back as I do. The girl steps away then drops down, twisting, and I almost get stabbed with that poison knife in the same place Finn did.

Salva says, "My blade," and I shake my head once. "Go for reinforcements," I command. Sweat slides in strings down my back. I blink droplets from my eyes. I force my breath slower again, staring at the girl, and she gets to her feet.

"You aren't trying to kill me," she accuses. Her first words to me.

"I don't want you dead."

"Your funeral, War Prince." The girl rolls one shoulder like it's sore, but I think that's a distraction.

"Tell me your name," I try again. "I'd like to know who wants to kill me."

She snorts. "It's a long list."

I let myself smile, too, slow and as dangerous as I can make it. "It's good to have enemies. That's how you know you're living your best life."

"Dragon propaganda." The girl doesn't even finish the word before throwing herself at me. I use the claw and manage finally to catch her left knife between the hooking blades. I twist my wrist harshly, and it turns her long knife so she's forced to release it. I fling it away and drive in before she can draw yet another knife. Her remaining long dagger blocks my falchion, but I step in close again, so we're locked together. The girl puts her free hand to her other, using all her weight to press her knife against my sword. I bend my elbows, letting her in, then with my entire body I throw her against the side of the table.

She grunts as she hits with her hip, winces, but instead of coming at me or folding, she hops and rolls over the table itself, landing on the other side next to the slumped governor, dead in a chair, blood down his brocade coat even messier than his beard was. It's a thought not worthy of my rank, but I'm glad he's dead.

Her shoulders are heaving now, too. I can feel the heat of battle in my face, my heart pumping as hard as dragon wings. I stare at her again, the gleam of sweat on her cheeks giving them shine, her lips, the hand loose at her side curved as if she's about to sprout talons. I can believe it. She's made of Chaos. I have to know her name.

"Leonetti's not here," I say, taunting now. I know that's why she came.

Though the girl's goggles make her eyes empty hellish pits, the skin of her forehead shifts like she's narrowed them, and she stops smiling. "Lies."

I shake my head. "He hasn't been in Lastrium since the day before yesterday." I walk to the table and put my claw against the wood, leaning toward her across broken glasses and spilled wine to emphasize my point. "I sent him away as soon as I got here."

She bares her teeth again. "You gryphon shit son of an eel."

"Are you his child? His lieutenant? A new, too-young wife?"

Her body goes rigid.

"He must not be proud of you." I push where it would hurt me. "Or we'd have heard of a vicious, skilled assassin girl without any eyes."

She refuses my bait. It's irritatingly admirable.

I start around the table so she either has to run through the open doors into the garden or let me drive her deeper into the room.

She doesn't move. Waiting for me. Except she picks up a table knife to replace the one I forced her to drop. No hesitation as she settles it in her hand and the boonlight glints off its relatively dull blade.

Something heady speeds my pulse now. I barely remember she murdered four of my Teeth and another two might still die of their wounds, including Finn if I don't shut this down soon.

I don't glance at him to make sure he's ready. I can sense his hulking shape right where we left him, on one knee, struggling not to fall until he's done his last task.

"Very well, scion," I say, because if she's in Leonetti Seabreak's family, she's the child of a regent, and that makes her one of us. He has a daughter and son at least.

A slight shift of her weight makes me think she doesn't like me calling her that, so she must be one of the Seabreak war orphans. Family, but not a scion by blood.

This time I attack, sudden and fast.

The girl jerks away, lashing out with her leg in the same motion. I expected something like it, so I let her kick my thigh, braced enough it only hurts like a stampeding drake, and wrap my claw around her calf, knocking her back.

We both fall away, and I press my advantage, turning again to drive her toward Finn. It's a dangerous risk, but I slow, as if I'm tired, and the girl gives me no leeway. I wish I could take a hit, but that cursed poison isn't worth it. So I attack again, slicing at her, and she dodges, as graceful as flickering flames and just as difficult to touch.

I hear others behind me: more soldiers, servants maybe. I don't know because I can't spare the focus. If I lose it for just a moment, she'll skewer me. And I'll never know her name.

It almost happens because I'm so caught up, breathless and fierce. I think maybe she's supposed to kill me; that's why Caspian painted her over and over and over again. Perhaps *he* was predicting my death, all this time. Not Aurora.

I falter and she leaps into the gap of my defense, and I desperately drop my falchion to catch her wrist. The long knife is a handspan from my bare neck, her arm trembling with effort. I can feel her breath on my jaw—then I feel pain blossom in my shoulder in the space between my chest armor and the leather pauldron on my shield arm. The table knife.

Of all things, I laugh, low and painful. I shove my wounded shoulder toward her, pulling her wrist around with me, effectively flinging her toward Finn.

The girl remains on her feet, and she never lets go of her long knife. She lifts it, and this time, she'll stab it straight through my throat. She lets herself grin again, in satisfaction, because my sword is on the floor and there's a table knife sticking out of my shoulder, rendering my claw useless.

But her smile falters. I wish I could see her eyes.

She sways, and against all logic I leap forward to catch her as she falls, unconscious, into my arms.

I lower to my knees right away, to the sound of my name called urgently as those soldiers and residents of the governor's household finally come forward, now the danger is past. The girl's head lolls against the handle of the table knife, knocking it and sending pain down my arm and across my chest.

As I carefully lay the eyeless girl down on the bloody floor, Finn growls, "What in the edge of Chaos is she?"

I remove my arm from under her neck, my jaw set against pain, and study her. Finn's quiet, often strategically useless boon is sleep—he can make anybody drop unconscious with only a touch. She discounted him because he was too poisoned to fight. But not to grab her and invoke his boon.

In sleep the girl seems younger, less like a Chaos monster, and a twinge of sympathy cools the fury in my heart. She's probably younger than me, but barely. At war her whole life, who knows what she's lost, who she made herself become.

I let myself skim my fingers against her cheek: her skin is hot.

With those reflective goggles, she could be staring at me still. Eyes like pits, whirlwinds of pain or violence or empty pearls or dead-fish eyes, all the things Caspian has painted.

"Talon," Finn says, drawing my attention to the returned Salva and the cluster of soldiers and civilians staring wide-eyed at me. At her.

"Finn, you get treatment for that poison, then you're in charge here. Once the warehouse fire is out, secure the port against the Kraken navy. Keen," I call to the older soldier propping Salva up. "I want this prisoner secured for travel. We leave as soon as possible. I'm taking her to the fortress at Phoenix Crest."

Home, I think, to set her in the tower surrounded by Caspian's art and finally understand what's haunted my brother all his life.

"Scion," Finn says, and I glance at his blotchy face. "You need treatment, too."

I grimace at the table knife; then I slip my fingers under the strap of the girl's goggles and strip them off her face.

They leave a gentle mark down her temples, almost like tear streaks.

But her eyes are closed, lashes tightly curled, and the lids shifting with dreams. I wonder, as pain makes me light-headed, if I'll ever see what her eyes are truly made of.

5
DARLING

I wake groggy and confused. My head pounds, the room is too bright, and I squint and shield my eyes as I sit up. I'm in an unfamiliar bed, and my body aches and twinges in a way that makes me wonder if Adelaide tried out one of Miranda's poisons on me the way she used to when we were younger. It definitely feels like I accidentally drank one of my sister's treacherous tonics.

"She's awake, my blade."

The voice is unfamiliar. I can't see anything but the barest of outlines, everything haloed in sunlight that burns my eyes. The memory of the failed attack on the governor's mansion begins to come back to me in bits and pieces, and I realize that I must be someone's prisoner. I'm definitely not in a dungeon, which seems strange. The bed I lie upon is too plush for a prisoner of war, so maybe I'm in a House Kraken safe house.

The hand that clamps down on my upper arm quickly disabuses me of that notion.

"You. Get up," another voice says, pulling on my arm. I pull back.

"I can't see anything without my goggles. So you can find them or you can carry me." I might not know what's going on, but the fact that I'm still alive seems to be positive. I should be dead. I remember the War Prince, his blade pressed to my middle, his hesitation. Fool.

My brain quickly spins through everything I know about House Dragon, and it keeps landing on a single, indisputable fact: House Dragon takes no prisoners, and they definitely never show mercy. So why did the most ruthless of them all do both?

Cool glass and leather straps hit my hands as I catch the goggles in midair, squeezing my eyes tightly shut before placing the smoked-glass lenses in place and tying the leather straps. They aren't *my* goggles, but they'll do. The lenses cup my eyes so that none of the too-bright sunshine leaks in, and my eyes water for a moment before adjusting. Within seconds I can see once more.

I sit in a luxurious bed with a mountain of coverlets, in a room meant not for a prisoner but for a scion. The drapes are pulled back, made of a heavy green velvet, and the walls are a deeply polished wood. Household servants stand along the edge of the room, three in all, two women and a nervous-looking man. The House Dragon crest is embroidered on the women's overdresses, a sinuous beast wrapped around a vicious sword. The room also contains a large copper tub and a dress of blue chiffon displayed prettily on a dress stand.

The sight is so unbelievable that I almost laugh.

"Did Adelaide put you up to this? Where did she get House Dragon livery?" I ask. This must be one of my sister's practical jokes. There's no other rational excuse.

But I've forgotten about the hand clamped on my arm, and it isn't until I'm being pulled from the bed that I realize this is no farce. The meaty hand belongs to the brute with the ax from the governor's mansion. The scar marring his face gives him a cruel look, and the murder in his eyes as he looks at me doesn't help.

I land hard on the floor and he releases me, walking away before

I can scramble to my feet. I take up a ready position, and he gives me a disgusted look. "Not much without your poisoned blades, are you, squid?"

"Try me and see just how dangerous I can be, lizard," I snarl. I have no weapons, and I definitely feel a bit woozy now that I'm on my feet, but I know a number of ways to hurt a person, blades or not. "How's your side?"

His face twitches with barely suppressed rage, but he doesn't move. "You will bathe and change into the gown procured for you, and then I will take you to the scion's library. If you are difficult, I will steal your wits from you once more," he says. He grits the words out as though he would like nothing more than to force me to comply, some other command preventing him from throttling me. I file the fact away for later and ignore his threatening glare.

"Steal my wits? You have a madness boon?" I have heard stories of those with the boon to be able to drive others mad, similar to Miranda's penchant for poisons. She can tailor any poison for any situation, her touch deadly if she wishes it. Such dangerous boons are extremely rare, but rumors of them persist from long ago when Chaos granted all in Pyrlanum boons, not just a few.

"No, I have a slumber boon. So if you misbehave, I will put you out once more. Perhaps for another couple of weeks. But the next time you wake up, it might be in a dirt hole." He bites his thumb at me, the sign for a curse upon one's house and not a very nice gesture in the least, before he closes the door behind himself.

"Well," I say with a heavy sigh. "I do not think we are going to be friends."

"My, um, blade," the man against the wall says, drawing my attention. With the immediate threat gone I have a chance to study him and the women a bit more. All have the distinctive pale skin and light eyes of the northern Dragons, hair a fiery red known among the Kraken as the Dragon's flame, and not in a flattering way. There is a rumor that those with such distinctive hair are quick to temper, but this man seems to be more prone to anxiousness, judging by the way he folds and unfolds his hands. The women say nothing; their faces bear the carefully neutral expressions of household staff who have seen entirely too much for anything to be especially scandalous.

"Where am I?" I ask. Outside the windows all I see is sky.

"My blade, as I was saying. I am Niall Softclaw, and I bid you all of the grace and joy of our House to welcome you to Phoenix Crest. Our most esteemed War Prince Talon Goldhoard, First Scion of his House, valiant in battle and dauntless in courage, asks that you join him for afternoon repast in his war room forthwith."

I blink, and blink again dumbly. These Dragons talk in a bit of word salad, and it takes me a moment to parse his meaning. "I'm sorry, did you say Talon Goldhoard?" I'm pretty sure the last time I saw that man he was trying to kill me. Which is fair, because I was trying to do the same to him. I remember how I slid a dinner knife into the War Prince's shoulder, and I laugh out loud. "Pretty brave of him to invite me to share a meal," I say, even though Niall has no idea what I'm referring to.

I'm beginning to wonder if I hit my head, because none of this makes any kind of sense. This seems more like a Chaos-sent dream than real life.

Niall does not comment on my near mania, just bows deeply, and when he straightens, he looks as flustered as I feel. "My blade. My team and I are at your beck and call, but please, let us make haste. There is much to be done." He glances at my attire in dismay, which is fair, since I still wear my clothes from the night Gavin and I attacked the governor's mansion, and I'm half-covered in dirt and dried blood.

"What's the rush?" I ask, because now that I'm considering the copper tub, a nice long soak sounds delightful.

Niall puffs out his cheeks, the first break in decorum I've seen from him. It gives me a small measure of joy, and I think Adelaide would be proud of me. I've managed to unmoor the man in a matter of minutes. That's usually her forte. "The scion greatly dislikes tardiness."

I laugh. "Well," I say, stripping off my clothes and walking toward the tub, heedless of Niall as he scurries from the room. "It looks like today is the day your War Prince learns some patience."

I spend half a turn soaking in the tub, and the next half a turn letting Sarabeth and Janella, the two maids Niall hadn't bothered introducing, pick the snarls out of my hair until it hangs down my back in heavy curls. They want to arrange my locks in some complicated style, probably the horns and plaits the Dragons seem to prefer, but I refuse. I very rarely get to wear my hair down, and I aim to enjoy this respite for however long it lasts.

I put on the chiffon monstrosity, and it turns out to be the ugliest thing I have ever worn. My hair, still damp, tangles in the edges of the ruffles, of which there are at least a thousand. The blue makes my brown skin look jaundiced, and the dress swallows me and makes me look half my age, like a child playing dress-up. Even

Sarabeth cannot help her small moue of despair, and I laugh. "So, it looks like I am to be tortured after all," I say, after securing my goggles over my wet curls. I inspect myself in the full-length mirror the women hold up for me. Even the glasses are ridiculous, the soft leather tooled with flowers and strange birds, the metal filigreed. They offer me a pair of impossibly pointless slippers, but I opt for my boots instead.

I already look like a mess; at least I'll be a fashion disaster that can kick efficiently.

After making the women promise to wash and return my much more useful Barb's uniform, a promise I only half expect them to keep, I follow Niall out of the door. I'm considering overpowering him and trying my hand at an escape, but the brute and a brace of Dragon regulars stand in the hallway.

"Don't you have boots to lick?" I ask the lout sweetly.

"No, I finished that this morning. By the way, how do you like my grandmother's dress?"

I grimace. "I figured this was punishment of some sort."

He bares his teeth at me. "I'm actually surprised it fit you, squid. Either way, you've taken so long that now you don't get to eat. We're going to the Regent's Tower instead."

He gestures for me to follow the three soldiers that lead the way. I hesitate, but the mountain of a man flexes just a bit, and it's enough to get me moving. The man would like any excuse to break my neck, and I won't give it to him.

We pass a number of doorways and take a winding staircase up and then around, so that even though I am trying to mark our passage, I am helplessly confused by the time we approach the ornately carved doorway where the soldiers halt. The engraving depicts a phoenix locked in an embrace with a dragon, their bodies tangled and intertwined so that they could be trying to kill one another or making rapturous love. It's a nauseating piece of art, new from the way the wood glimmers in a much lighter hue than the rest of the doors in the hall, and as the soldiers open the door and push me through, I'm glad of the distraction.

"Climb," the brute says, and before I can respond, the door slams behind me, nearly catching the voluminous edge of my old-lady dress. I pull the material to me just in time, and then I am trapped, alone, in the barely lit stairwell.

For anyone else it would be confusing and dark, but I can see just fine, even with the goggles. This is no siege fortress but a palace. The tower is built from soft white sandstone, and the stairway is lit dimly by a row of flickering boonlamps so grand they probably cost more than a common family makes in a year.

I know Phoenix Crest used to be the seat of power before the fall of the Last Phoenix a century ago, and these boonlamps are relics, so I turn my disgust toward the Dragons instead. How dare they revel in such luxury when half the continent struggles to feed themselves in the shadow of this never-ending war?

I begin to climb the winding staircase, counting steps to help steady my racing thoughts. I have counted seventy-five when a final turn reveals a doorway leaking balmy sunshine. I finish my climb and enter the chamber, ready to fight.

I freeze in my tracks, unbalanced like a storm swell has hit. All around the room, in a hundred or so different paintings, is a girl who looks like me.

No, it *is* me.

I enter the tower in a trance, all of my anger and fear and uncertainty bleeding away as I stare at the paintings, sketches, and even a mural, my life dominating the art. Or, rather, a version of me. Where my goggles should be are only circles of darkness that seem to swirl the longer I look at the pictures. There I am the first time I killed, standing in a patch of purple lovers' quarrel. Here I am laughing beside a bonfire with Miranda, Adelaide, and Gavin, their faces blurred in the picture—but I remember that night. And a life-sized portrait of me walking out of the dark the day Leonetti liberated me from the sewers of Nakumba. The painting is so real it's almost as though I am there once more. The Kraken reached a hand out to me, and I gripped my homemade knife tightly. It had been at least a year since my nursemaid Claudia, one of the last of the women to scavenge the sewers with me, had passed of a wasting sickness.

What is your name, child?

I don't know.

Then, dear fry, what do people call you?

Darling.

"This is why I didn't kill you."

I spin and reach for my knives, my hands finding nothing but damnable ruffles. The War Prince stands in the doorway, his shoulders broad enough they fairly block it.

The night I first saw him I didn't have the leisure to make note of his features, since I was trying to kill him, but now I am annoyed to realize that he's handsome. His jaw is square, hinting at a stubbornness that matches my experience of meeting him in combat. His dark hair is shorn close on the sides, the longish waves at the crown that fall across his tan forehead his only apparent concession to vanity. His eyes are stupidly green, and I think of the waters of the Farglass Sea. His full lips make him look less like a remorseless killer and more like the hero of a romantic poem.

It makes me hate him even more.

"How's the shoulder?" I ask, showing my teeth. I am unbalanced and out of my element, wearing a hideous gown and trapped in a tower full of paintings bearing my face. I've never been one to be overly concerned about manners; now will not be the time I start.

"Better than Finn's side, I should guess, since there was no Sting on the table knife," he says, stalking toward me. For a moment I think I am going to get a rematch, but instead he stops a few feet away, to glance at a painting of me peering out over a cliff, a place I have never been nor recognize. It's maddening, and I dig my fingernails into my palms, the pain balancing me, grounding me in the realness of my body.

I shrug, feigning nonchalance. "Next time I'll make sure to aim for your heart."

He crosses his arms. "There won't be a next time."

"But of course there will, lizard," I say, walking toward the portrait of me leaving the tunnels of Nakumba. The painting does something to me, filling me with a bittersweet ache at realizing Leonetti is still held by these Dragons. Is he being treated as well as I am? Do they somehow have a room full of art bearing his countenance as well?

That seems unlikely.

"What makes you think I'll give you another chance to put a blade in my heart?" the War Prince asks.

I tsk. "I'm still alive, aren't I?"

I turn around to see his expression, but I am disappointed. He's fighting to suppress a smile.

"I wasn't sure when I saw you in that funeral dress," he says. "I'm pretty sure my captain's granny was entombed in something similar."

I scowl. "Trust me when I say I did not pick this dress."

He frowns. "The others I left did not suit?"

I purse my lips and say nothing, figuring that his soldiers must have thought it would be cute to humiliate me. No matter, I did kill a number of their comrades, and I would feel similarly if someone had cut so easily through my Barbs. "Why am I here, exactly? Because of all of this?" I say, gesturing around the tower. "Funny, I did not take a warmonger for an artist."

"That's because my dear brother did not paint them," says a new voice, an edge of humor riding the words. Next to a moth-eaten tapestry, which I suppose hides a different door from the one I entered through, stands another young man, beautiful and lithe. His light green eyes are wide, and his dark hair falls past his shoulders in unruly waves. While the War Prince wears his uniform of red and ivory, this man wears trousers of cerulean and a dressing gown embroidered with a rainbow array of dragons and flames. He's bare chested but pale, as though he spends very little time out of doors. Where the War Prince is all power and intent, this man is all beauty and aesthetic, and looks as though he has never wielded a weapon in his life.

"Cas," Talon breathes, his expression hopeful. The first unguarded expression I've seen him wear. "I— It's been too long."

"Has it?" The man gives the War Prince an enigmatic smile, and

I don't quite understand the exchange. But I still have questions, so I continue with my interrogation, just redirecting my queries.

"You're the artist?" I say, turning away from the man and looking toward the art once more. "Your technique is sloppy," I say, the lie souring on my tongue. The paintings are beautifully rendered.

He laughs, unbothered, the sound too loud in the enclosed space. "You are a terrible liar, little riddler, which is a shame. It was one of the finest skills of your House."

"I am House Kraken," I say.

"You are not," the man says. He says it simply and without heat, like he is correcting a child. "You are House Sphinx. Your true name may be lost to the flames of war, but that does not change your blood or your heart."

"And what, exactly, is your name?" I snap in annoyance.

The man gives me a ridiculously deep bow. "I am none other than the ruler of this thrice-cursed land, or what will be left of it after this war is done. Caspian Goldhoard, High Prince Regent and portrait artist to the tragic."

I grit my teeth as my stomach falls. He said *my brother* about Talon. I should have known right away, but I have not felt this off-balance and out of sorts since the time Adelaide forced me to sail with her through a summer storm. I am not made for conversing with scions and princes; I am made for wielding blades in the dark. I reach once more for my knives, which have not managed to magically materialize in the past few moments, more's the pity. I wonder if there's a boon for that.

Here I have the chance to do what most Barbs dream of doing, killing the treacherous heads of House Dragon, and I am helpless to do much more than admire a few creepy paintings.

"House Sphinx?" the War Prince says. His expression is half-shocked and half-annoyed, as though he has just realized that he is the butt of a joke.

"Yes, dearest Talon, my scion, my heart," Caspian says, hooking an arm across the War Prince's shoulders and pulling him close, even planting an affectionate kiss upon his cheek. The High Prince Regent is a bit taller than his brother, but only by a few inches. It's such a dramatic change from the near dismissal earlier, and it makes me curious about their relationship. "Dragonlet, you have caught yourself none other than Darling Seabreak, war orphan of House Kraken, the best and deadliest daughter of Leonetti Seabreak, who dragged her from the sewers of Nakumba when House Kraken took the ancient city of the Sphinx back from us—though not for long." Caspian laughs. "You didn't know?"

"I surmised only some of it." Talon glares at me like he wishes he'd killed me back in Lastrium. "She can't be the scion of House Sphinx."

I am half wondering if I am already dead, because this, these things Caspian knows, are things not even most scions of House Kraken know. Leonetti swore me to secrecy long ago, and only Adelaide, Miranda, and Gavin know the truth of my origins. Everyone else thinks I am yet another war orphan, low born but talented enough to be of notice, just as Talon clearly had assumed.

And chances are that I am low born of House Sphinx, too, but what I remember of the time before the Dragons ravaged House Sphinx is strange and muddled. I could have just as easily been the daughter of a washerwoman or the scion of the House. Either way, it doesn't matter much to me. I'm a Kraken now, and that's all there is to it.

But how does the High Prince Regent know all of this?

"Why can't she?" Caspian asks, a lazy smile still upon his lips. "She looks regal enough to me. Well, maybe after a quick costume change."

"Tell me how you know, brother," the War Prince says darkly. I don't like how our mutual confusion puts us on the same side of this conversation.

"I remember her, of course. We knew each other as children, and I have worried for so long that she was lost." Caspian releases Talon and shrugs. "You must get yourself some better spies."

I blink, because a spy cannot discover a secret never spoken, and I have only a heartbeat to mark the hurt on Talon's face before Caspian rounds on me. "I daresay the kitten and I have so many things to discuss, seeing as how our father wiped out all of her kin." I try to respond, but all my words and wit die in my throat, leaving me choking on air.

"Talon," Caspian says, turning once more to his brother, "on your way to the council meeting you're late for, please have some food sent up. Oh, and a table and two chairs. Difficult matters are best discussed over food and wine, and I would have both."

"I could kill you," I finally say, because it is the first thing I can get out.

"I will run you through first," Talon says, drawing his falchion, his stupid green eyes flashing a challenge. My threat has shaken him free of whatever spell gripped him when his brother entered the tower. I'm glad of it, for fighting him is better than whatever strangeness is going on with the High Prince.

But Caspian fearlessly touches Talon's sword, wordlessly urging him to sheathe it before he looks over his shoulder at me, and his smile slips just a bit. He's too beautiful, and I wonder if that's his boon, to dazzle with a single glance. It would explain much. "You could, but you won't. There is too much you want from me."

Caspian turns back to Talon, whose jaw remains tight. "Oh, Talon, tell the council that I will be there, but just a tad late. We have to eat and discuss important matters first. And trust me, little brother, when I say we will find time to catch up."

"Soon," Talon insists.

"I promise."

That seems to mollify the War Prince, so that he doesn't resist when Caspian gently nudges him toward the door. Caspian adds, "And if you see Marsden make sure he sends up the honey wine I like, not the vintage he served at dinner the other night. That was disappointing."

Talon shoots me one last look full of hot promise, a warning that nothing is finished between us, even if his duty now compels him to see to another task. I shoot him back a wink, trying to provoke him, but I'm looking forward to seeing him again.

I still need to kill him.

"Next time bring me my goggles that you stole," I call as he leaves. "These are too big."

He thins his lips in annoyance but says nothing else and departs the tower.

Caspian claps his hands, rubbing them together in delight. "Now, where were we? It's hard to focus when you're wearing such a monstrosity," Caspian says as two soldiers enter and post up as guards. Talon is not as certain of my motives as his brother. But as soon as they appear, Caspian shoos them from the room like recalcitrant children. As the soldiers depart, two liveried servants enter, quickly setting up a table and two chairs. I get the feeling that the High Prince entertains here often, the servants' movements efficient and practiced.

"You were telling me how your father murdered my entire House," I say, my voice flat. I have no idea what to do or say, so I opt for bluntness. I think perhaps I would rather be moldering in the dungeon. At least that would be something familiar enough that I would know how to react. This, eating an afternoon meal with the ruler of all Pyrlanum in an ornate tower filled with paintings of me, is like something out of a fever dream.

A pitcher of wine is set before me, and I reach for it and the matching goblet, pouring a healthy measure and downing it quickly. It's sweet and puddles in my empty belly, warming me. I'm not usually a fan of strong drink, but I have lived a lifetime in the past few turns, so I let myself indulge.

"Ah, yes," Caspian says with a grin in response to my plain speech. A separate pitcher is set before him, and he drinks straight from the small carafe, not bothering with a cup. Perhaps the rumors of madness are not rumors after all.

"Let us," he says, reaching for a small roasted bird and tearing it in half, placing part of it on my plate, "first discuss the matter of reparations."

6

TALON

As I leave my brother's tower, I order two Crest soldiers into the room to keep the eyeless girl—*Darling*—from hurting Caspian. Then I storm down the tower stairs, loud enough the servants waiting at the base with food and wine slide out of my way and keep their gazes down. Good.

I curl my hands into fists and stop abruptly. I carefully flatten my hands against the wall. Then I close my eyes and press my forehead hard into the cold stone. Hard enough to hurt. My breath is too shallow, too fast.

I need to calm down. Put a shield of control around myself and hide the mess of feelings churning inside me. I'm furious at Caspian for keeping so much from me—I'm his brother, and his scion; he should trust me. And that girl! Darling. What does Caspian need from the maybe scion of House Sphinx that he can't share with me? I should have insisted I remain. She's dangerous even without a table knife.

I push away from the wall and continue down to the landing. I'm no longer panting with frustration and anger. This is fine. I am fine.

Finn awaits me just past the wretched engraved door Caspian had installed a few years ago. *To remind us dragons and phoenixes both die in fire*, he'd said wistfully. *But only one rises anew.*

"How did it go? Did you leave her body up there?" Finn asks, moving to follow at my right shoulder as I continue striding down the corridor. His voice is low and insistent. He knows even less than I do. Aunt Aurora has worked hard to keep Caspian's madness a secret, to keep his paintings and the obsession with his eyeless girl hidden in that tower room. It won't be a secret for long now. And Caspian won't let me help him scheme out the best way to reveal his plans.

What did I do to earn his mistrust? The thought makes me sick. But in all our lives he's never let me get close to him. Today, when he threw his arm around me, I think it's the first time he's touched me in a decade.

"Talon?" Finn nudges my uninjured shoulder.

"The High Prince Regent is with her," I bite out. "I'm late for the council meeting he should be attending himself."

My captain of the Dragon's Teeth growls a little. He argued hard to put Darling in the dungeon when I refused to slit her throat and hang her head from the Crest gates. Finn hates that she nearly gutted him, and that the Sting from her blade lingers, despite our House Gryphon doctor's constant supervision of the wound. Even now, Finn sweats slightly, his blood running hot from Elias's tonics, which are slowly counteracting the poison. He'll be fine—we've fought this poison successfully before. But the constant reminder makes Finn even less friendly than usual.

I pause and face him. His fist rests on the pommel of his short sword, his battle ax in his room while he's on palace duty, and his jaw is clenched so tightly his skin blanches around the jagged scar. His anger is more vivid than the red of his uniform. "Finn." I put my fist against his chest with a slight thump. "She's Darling Seabreak; I was right about her being one of Leonetti's war orphans. I don't know what Caspian wants with her, but he thinks she's the last scion of House Sphinx."

A wide grin spreads across Finn's mouth. "He'll have her publicly executed, to show House Dragon has finally killed the last of them."

My stomach rolls again. "I don't think so." Before his surprise has a chance to form into questions, I add, "Go take over Crest security from Commander Lightwing. I'll have the Teeth in charge of the palace and reporting only to me."

He clearly wants more, but I turn away and head for the council meeting.

Aunt Aurora catches me before I push open the filigreed double doors of the Phoenix Hall.

"Talon," she coos softly. She slips her hand around my elbow. Her touch is gentle but insistent, and I manage to turn smoothly instead of barking at her like I would anybody else.

"Aunt." I'm barely taller than her, but she's slender and soft, no hint of Dragon malice in the way she carries and presents herself. In my memories of childhood, before Father died and I was sent to be a soldier, Aurora wore pale pink and cream colors, beautiful bright oranges and violet streaks, like the dawn and dusk of exiled House Cockatrice from which she and my mother had been born. It was comforting and let me feel like Mother was still alive. When Caspian took the throne, Aurora abruptly changed her attire to reflect complete loyalty to the familial House of her nephews. Today her gown is a rich earthen brown with an overlay of lace in the green of House Dragon that looks like a pattern of scales. At her shoulder rests the elaborate emerald pin of the Dragon Seer.

The problem is when I see Aunt Aurora so perfectly put together, I instantly remember how ridiculous Darling looked in that puffy confection. Ridiculous and yet still like she'd not hesitate to rip off the hem and strangle me with it.

I should have returned her goggles. They're tucked carefully into a treasure box in my chamber, forgotten until she demanded them back. But she was wearing some. It could only have been Caspian who provided them. Nobody else knew she needed them, and Caspian's intervention explained why they were prettier than the ones I'd taken off her. Delicately made, with tooling in the shape of flowers along the leather. I wonder if she has permanent marks high on her cheeks from the press of straps.

"Talon," my aunt says.

I blink and focus on her smooth white skin and kohl-lined green eyes, instead of unpainted, messy Darling. "Caspian was there, with me and—and her. Darling Seabreak."

"You were correct about her identity, then." Aurora smiles, pleased. Though Caspian denied me an audience with him, Aurora welcomed me home yesterday with enthusiasm. I'd seen unconscious Darling situated in her guest room and made sure—I thought—she'd have her choice of clothing and servants to make her as comfortable as possible, and Aunt Aurora had readied a feast of my favorite foods. She entertained me with gossip and news from the last few months until I was rested and full, ready to tell her everything. One thing we'd shared all these years, more than blood or concern for Caspian's mind, was curiosity about the identity of his eyeless girl. Now we have it. As she watches me, Aurora's smile falls away. Quietly, she says, "You should have killed her when you had the chance. When she was an anonymous nobody."

It's so easy to forget someone as elegant and sweet in appearance can be as bloodthirsty as any Dragon. But Caspian said, *Talon must save her*. I shake my head no. "He said he remembers her from when they were very young. That's why he's painted her."

"How could he have known her, and not your mother or I?"

There's no answer I have to that. "I need the truth, Aunt. I want to know what this all means. His paintings."

Aurora presses her mouth into a small moue of irritation. "It may very well mean nothing. Madness can seem reasonable in trying times, Talon."

I try not to react, though very likely the heat in my cheeks is visible. I hate it when she chides me as she used to when I was a child. We already had this argument last night, and I won't have it again. Though Caspian behaved terribly just now, ignoring me, then acting the doting brother, then dismissing me like I'm nothing, I have to believe he knows something of what he's doing. And if not, that there are answers to why Chaos has such a strange hold upon him. I have to. He's not only my brother, he's my Prince Regent.

"Caspian says she's the last of House Sphinx," I say very quietly, aware of the guards stationed at the council doors and the constant flux of people through the corridors of Phoenix Crest.

Aurora brings a hand with pink-painted nails to her mouth to cover her gasp. "Why, that would explain so many things. Perhaps even how he saw her, but I did not. I never visited House Sphinx before its end."

"You've seen nothing in your prophecies?" I ask, both of us leaning toward each other.

"You know she's eluded my sight, always," Aurora murmurs with another hint of irritation.

"She's got Chaos in her, Aunt," I admit. "Just like Caspian. That might have an effect on your work. Something happened to her, and it changed her, and her eyes..." I'm struck with a deep longing to ask Darling about what she sees. What she saw in the paintings. I could almost guess her feelings as I studied her. She reached to touch one, and her lips parted in something more than surprise—maybe reverence. Maybe grief. Impossible to know with her eyes hidden behind black glass.

Aurora says, "We must discover Caspian's intentions, my blade. This is no way to run a country, much less conquer one."

I want to argue that the war is the problem with the country, always distracting and dividing our attention and resources. But this isn't the place or time. "I need to get into the meeting," I say instead. "And you."

My aunt peers at me, as if deciding whether or not to call me on my diversion. Instead she bows in acknowledgment, delicate fists together, and I reach out to drag open the double doors.

The Phoenix Hall is the most ancient room in the Crest, carved into the mountain itself, its floor set with black marble and its boundaries marked by six massive granite pillars. Each pillar is carved in the shape of an empyreal and decorated with metal and jewels precious to the House it represents: gold and emeralds for Dragon's scales and wings; garnet for the eagle-headed and -winged lion of Gryphon; and for House Sphinx's sister lion with its wise human face, carved ivory. Silver and sapphires glint for Barghest's huge dog, every shade of quartz and amethyst make up the strange clawed and feathered cockatrice, and black pearls trail in the clinging arms of the kraken.

At the head of the hall is a massive statue of a phoenix, the great fire bird that once rose each generation from a different House and led us all with passion and balance. This stone phoenix lifts its wings in arcs to begin the dome of the ceiling. Spun glass and fire opals are set into those wings, glittering like a hundred thousand candles.

Beneath the phoenix's wings is the oval council table, with every seat occupied but for mine, Aurora's, and the tall blackwood throne reserved for the High Prince Regent. They don't expect him in the least: the throne is pushed back against the Dragon pillar. Out of the way.

With Aurora on my arm, I stride toward the table, steps echoing in the sudden silence once all the councilors scrape their chairs away to stand and salute me.

Despite never having spent a decent hour in this hall, I like being here, surrounded by gems and precious metal, beneath the stone of our mountain and under the protection—however imaginary—of the long-dead Phoenix. The last was killed a hundred years ago, and nobody knows why no other has risen since. It shouldn't matter to me. House Dragon rose in the Phoenix's place, and we fight to keep what is ours.

Or what we've stolen. I was raised to protect what is mine, my hoard, and seek more. That's been House Dragon's legacy since its beginning: protection, loyalty, and the strength of wealth. But we're losing wealth because of how hard we've fought to keep it these days. The longer this war lasts, the more we lose. I don't speak about my doubt with anyone, not even Finn late at night around a quiet fire. But this House War is nothing more worthwhile than a habit. A deadly one.

General Bloodscale doesn't sit back down when I gesture for the council to retake their places. He comes around toward me, mouth set sternly. His hair is as shorn as mine on the sides, and the longer top is nearly all silver now, as is the beard he has trimmed into a split horn, and the lines around his unyielding blue eyes have deepened. But in a crisp green uniform jacket with a gleaming gold rondel at his left shoulder and matching gold decorative armored collar, he doesn't look any less strong.

"General," I say, letting Aurora leave me to glide to her seat.

"Scion," Bloodscale answers, glaring up and down at me. I don't even twitch under his domineering study. He was my father's captain when they were young men, and he climbed the ranks with brutal successes even during the relative peace before this new round of House Wars. He led the assault against House Sphinx and the defeat of Barghest, taking me under his wing when Caspian sent me to learn war when I was only eleven. Bloodscale only retired from the front to serve as the minister of war when I took over the field last year. When he deemed me ready. My pulse picks up the longer he stares, but I hold myself still, not quite at attention because I no longer owe him that. He'd see it as a weakness.

Then without so much as the softest change in expression, Bloodscale nods sharply and claps me on the arm. "Welcome back, Talon," he says, ushering me around to the seat reserved for the first scion. It's in front of the Dragon Throne, and Bloodscale pulls it out for me, then takes his own place next to it. "You remember Callis and Freescale, I'm sure," he says, referring to the ministers of prosperity and work respectively, then skips Aunt Aurora to continue to the old House Gryphon representative, Ferl Elysium, and introduces me to the two newest council members, replaced in the eighteen months I've been away from the Crest. The first is Kael Longspine, the minister of the hoard, and House Barghest sent the second cousin of their current regent, a young woman with sapphire earrings as large as teacups named Mia Brynsdottir.

Before Minister Freescale can jump in—I remember he has a tendency to take over this meeting whenever possible—I gently tap my fist on the table and tell them all to give me a very brief update on what they've been doing and are most concerned with in the last year. I need some breathing room as well as grounding in what I've missed.

I regret it almost immediately. The next hour of my life is spent listening to complaints, insistent rhetoric, flattery, and outright bickering about food, money, resources, Caspian himself, and the war. This war that I've lived my whole life straining beneath. I'd rather House Dragon close around our current hoard, which is so much land and money and people, and protect it. Barghest and Gryphon are our allies; we three could easily hold the northern two-thirds of our country. Let the Kraken have the seas and their islands! We have everything else. But I don't have the political capital to say that yet. The Kraken killed our father, the last High Prince Regent. I cannot advocate that House Dragon give up without eradicating them as we eradicated the Sphinx for poisoning our mother.

As we *maybe* eradicated House Sphinx.

I think of Darling again, and Caspian's intensity as he closed around her, dismissing me. I need him; House Dragon needs him! Rational and leading us. He is the one to be listened to. I hope having Darling here fulfills whatever madness or wild boon forced his obsession. Maybe with her at his side, he can step out of it and lead. If I trusted Chaos, I wouldn't just hope—I'd pray.

The two sips of wine I allowed myself go straight to my head, since I didn't get to eat that meal with Darling, and I abstain from the rest. My stomach threatens to audibly growl and my head hurts, so I unlace the collar of my uniform jacket as I remind the minister of the hoard that the people requesting his ministry's assistance are Dragons, and none should be dismissed out of hand.

Someone snorts, I don't catch who, but I think it's the Barghest representative, Mia Brynsdottir.

Freescale, who had to be cut off from his report before it languished in the weeds of compensating farms for what the army takes from their stores, jumps in to say, "There are generational Dragons, and those only recently sworn to our great House, whose motivations may be questionable, scion."

"Because they had little choice in making their vows," I say, trying not to sound sarcastic. House Dragon takes care of our people; we share our wealth with those who join us. With those who do not, we strip them of everything. It's made most of this country ours, but foments a strict us-against-them mentality even among the lowest born. And gives House Kraken plenty of recruitment fodder.

"Like all the soldiers who've deserted in the past months?" Mia Brynsdottir asks with sugar on her tongue.

I meet her gaze, ready to ask her if she'd like to volunteer as a replacement soldier, but General Bloodscale clears his throat. He is the only minister yet to make his report, which I suspect he orchestrated in order to go last and hold the field from the strongest position. I nod at him to go on, and he says, "I want to institute a new penalty for deserters—death. Cowards have no place in our ranks."

I'm glad I haven't eaten anything now. It's hard to argue with the man who taught me most everything I know about my job. I say, "Death hardly encourages our soldiers to return to us."

"Once lost, lost forever," he answers. My father used to say that, too, driving home there is no good loss, and I needed to win every single time.

"I know you've not been in the field in some time," I say with care, but certainty. "But the newest warfare has been unlike previous battles."

"Assassination and guerilla warfare have always been part of House Wars," Bloodscale says.

"But not with such thin resources, general. And not for such sustained lengths of time. We only pay a third of our army well enough that they can support a family—the rest rely on the farming season or building season, and when they have no time to feed their children, they—"

"Betray the High Prince Regent," Bloodscale finishes for me.

I clench my jaw.

"Perhaps the scion can explain to us in more detail why he abandoned his own troops in Lastrium, leaving them to surrender to the Kraken navy?" This from Callis, who I expected to be on my side after her long report on how the war was ruining her ability to keep roads from crumbling even in the Crest itself.

"Are you suggesting," Aunt Aurora begins, breathy with horror, "that our War Prince *deserted* his posting?"

I consider letting Aurora lead the charge and seeing what Callis will say, but this is a waste of time. "I left Lastrium for a number of reasons, minister, including the fact that it's strategically insignificant, the venom stores were already ruined, and I discovered there something very important to the High Prince Regent that required me to personally escort it here."

Everyone stares at me, except Aurora, who lowers her lashes demurely.

"When the time is right, the High Prince will make his plans known," I say, "and we will be ready."

"How true, my dear brother," Caspian says, voice echoing with delight from the far entrance of the Phoenix Hall.

Not one of us noticed the doors shoving open, but here comes Caspian striding confidently toward us, the picture of a leader, except that he's still wearing the long, dragon-painted silk dressing gown over nothing but loose trousers and bare feet. It's tied at his waist, but open over his chest and dragging dramatically behind him in long tails against the black marble floor.

At least he makes an impression, I think sourly. I can't help glancing behind him to see if Darling is there. She's not. The pinch of disappointment is probably just hunger.

"You're late, my blade," General Bloodscale says.

Caspian puts a dramatic hand over his pale chest and stops. "Late?" he says, wide-eyed. "Is it possible for the High Prince Regent to be late for . . . anything?"

Mia Brynsdottir giggles as if he's said the most clever thing in Chaos. I barely control my expression as I realize Barghest sent a new House representative near Caspian's age because they want him to marry her.

Short on the heels of that insight is the absolutely horrible thought that perhaps Caspian intends to marry *Darling*.

Thank the elder serpents I'm sitting down.

Caspian smiles at Bloodscale's grimace and the scatter of ministers agreeing that of course he can't be late, and as he circles around the council table to his throne, he waves at the huge opal-and-glass Phoenix sculpture like it's his best friend. I once again must school my expression.

Aunt Aurora says, "Prince, perhaps you would like to settle our debate once and for all." In her tone is a promise that she knows exactly what he'll say—not because he told her, but because of her prophecies.

"Well." Caspian stands before the Dragon Throne. He holds himself tall, one hand in the pocket of his dressing gown, the other lifted slightly with the palm toward us. He looks regal, cool and calm, every inch the High Prince Regent despite that he's essentially in his pajamas. "I'm sure I don't know what you were debating, Aunt, but I will settle something." His cool face breaks into an impish grin. "The war is over. House Dragon will fight no more against the squids."

I bite back a shocked exclamation.

Bloodscale doesn't even take a moment before he growls, "But your father!"

And while the rest of us sit there, twisted to face Caspian, Caspian lowers himself down, slow and controlled, both hands curling like claws around the blackwood arms of the throne. He looks strong. Regal. He is.

Aurora slips her hand over mine. To reassure, but I can't acknowledge it as I reel. It's as if I conjured this, like a wish boon, or that thoughtless prayer. But . . .

Is it power or madness that Caspian can so easily wave his hand and say, *The war is over*?

"Our father has been more than avenged," Caspian says, "and I get to make that decision, don't I? If not me, only Talon." His ghostly green gaze flicks to me. "Talon, do you disagree with me?"

I have to swallow once to wet my mouth enough to speak. "No, brother. I do not disagree."

Caspian slumps back in the throne, rather triumphantly. Bloodscale is on his feet, while Callis and Freescale are talking at the same time, and Mia Brynsdottir tells Caspian he is wise. The Gryphon representative is silent, studying Caspian too carefully.

"How do you intend us to end this war?" Bloodscale asks after shooting me a disapproving look. I realize I was supposed to ask this. I am the War Prince, after all. The war is my identity.

"That is your job, general," Caspian says, chuckling. A red earring glints from within his tangle of hair. "Feel free to discuss it after I'm gone and send someone to let me know what strategy you've hit upon."

Bloodscale's mouth is such a hard line I almost expect him to start bleeding. He slides his glare to me, and it is like I am a child again, and Bloodscale owns my rewards and punishments. There is such a threat in his vibrant scowl. If I don't do something, he will.

Aurora is right: they'll kill Caspian if he doesn't give them a good reason for this. They'll assassinate him and make me play the role instead.

I get up, a little stilted, and then walk to Caspian's side. I glare at him, too, so he knows I'm furious that he put me in this position by forcing my ignorance of his plans, but I stand next to his throne.

No matter what game this is, I absolutely want the war over, too. I want to stop killing. I want a chance at something else—anything else. We're united in that.

Caspian tilts his head to wink at me. Just like Darling had. Heat rises in my face. How does she fit into his plan? Did they plot this together in an hour? Or is this the end of an *old* plan?

I turn at his side and position myself like a foundation stone. The War Prince supports his High Prince Regent.

Aurora says, "My nephew, will you tell us what has brought this decision after so many years of war?"

"Oh yes." He claps once. "I would have brought her to you, but I'm afraid at the moment she rather clashes with the aesthetic of, well, absolutely everything." He laughs to himself.

"Her?" says Minister Longspine hesitantly.

"Oh!" Aurora stands, touching her temple. "The girl from my prophecy!"

Caspian's mouth curls, and I realize he expected her to do this, to claim Darling as her prophecy. But she didn't see Darling—she told me so herself. This must be her way of making herself a matching foundation stone for him. Good.

For a moment, Caspian looks like he'll disregard her, but he'd better not; she only wants to support him and his rule. To keep him from seeming mad. She loves him as much as I do, though he'd rather not let us.

To my relief, he drawls, "Yes, the girl from your prophecy, Aunt."

In a rush, smiling, Aurora joins us to complete the family trio. She kneels at his other side, happily taking his offered hand. It's performative, but she looks at me, and I nod. We will be stronger like this. Working together.

"What girl?" demands Bloodscale.

"Darling Seabreak, whom I captured in Lastrium," I say, adding my small lie to theirs: "I recognized her from a recent prophecy the Dragon Seer shared with only the High Prince Regent and myself."

Caspian stands up, as if he cannot bear to be still a moment longer. He steps in front of me, the tails of his dressing gown sliding over Aurora's skirts. "That is her name, but it is not who she is. She is the last and first scion of House Sphinx, and as of this moment, her House is reinstated, with all the privileges inherent to the title, and the confiscated homelands returned to her." Caspian spares a look for the minister of the hoard. "And her monies."

Audible gasps and even a groan come from the council table. I try to mark every reaction, the better to ignore my own horror—and delight—but Caspian isn't finished.

"It is done, good councilors. Signed before witnesses this very hour." He starts for the exit, one hand lifted to wave at us. "You have one week to see to the necessary arrangements, and we will have a gala to present the new scion of House Sphinx to everyone here at Phoenix Crest." He spins just to throw us all a grin. "One week from tonight, we're having a party."

With that, he shoves out the double doors and leaves us all in a gaping silence.

Aurora takes my hand again, squeezes it, and I nod once. I'm with her. I push away my surprise, and the hurt that he hadn't prepared me. Hadn't trusted me to help plan this. He'd know I hate the war and hate needless violence if he bothered to talk to me!

But right now, Aurora and I have to salvage what we can from the sprawl of Caspian's wildness.

I draw a deep breath, making my jaw hard, my eyes cold. I will control this.

But I can't stop thinking, over and over, that instead of stabbing Caspian with one of his paintbrushes and escaping through the sewer or something just as dramatic, Darling agreed to be his pawn. She must find the risk worthwhile, because by the end of it, if she plays his game and regains the glory of House Sphinx, she'll be as powerful and rich as House Dragon. His equal.

I can't even imagine what Chaos the two of them might invoke together.

But I can easily imagine what I might have to do to stop them.

7

DARLING

I wake to the too-bright sunshine filtering in through frilly curtains and remember that I am a thrice-cursed, Chaos-touched fool. I would have to be mad to go along with Caspian's scheme, and yet here I lie in a bed meant for a prince.

Or a scion.

I sit upright in bed and fumble for my goggles. The plain smoked-glass-and-leather lenses I demanded, not the ridiculous engraved things Niall keeps leaving out for me. They aren't mine—Talon never returned those—but they're close enough. Familiar in a world that is anything but.

Over the past week I have been fitted and measured, poked and cajoled. Every meal is a spectacle of choices, and every clothing suggestion is a parade of fabrics in a rainbow of hues. To someone used to wearing functional garb and eating sea rations, it's been a bit disconcerting trying to accustom myself to such ridiculous mores. Not to mention the things the Dragons want to do to my hair. Braids and updos and so many flowers. It's made my temper short as I try to establish boundaries. A maid even burst into tears one day because I snarled at her when she tried to attack my curls with a pair of heated tongs.

I still have had no news of my father. I ask, I demand, and the answer is always the same: Leonetti is safe, and I will see him soon enough. Assuming I hold up my end of the bargain. I want to push back, demand to visit with him and refuse to cooperate, but I am as much a prisoner as he is: outmatched and without comrades. And even I hesitate to poke a Dragon.

But as difficult as my transition from assassin to scion has been, it's also been interesting. I have learned that while House Sphinx was theoretically purged from the historical record and left in smoldering ashes, the reality is something far different. Niall found an entire book on the House colors and fashions, and a set of rooms was given to me completely decorated in the style of House Sphinx: succulents and desert flowers, water features that sing, and a walled garden with a sandstone path. It's beautiful and decadent, and when I ask how it came to exist, Niall flushes.

"The House Sphinx spoils have long been enjoyed by one of our most esteemed council members, my quill," Niall says, the proper form of address for a noble member of House Sphinx. That makes me smile, because imagining some salty general getting booted from rooms that once belonged to someone I knew makes me glad, even though it doesn't make them any less dead.

When Caspian asked me to become the scion of House Sphinx, I laughed. I sat in his strange tower room and howled until tears fogged my lenses and I had to wipe my eyes with a table linen. "Are you mad? I'm no prince."

"It is unfortunate nobody seems to remember you but myself," he said, shrugging one shoulder as though we were discussing our favorite jams, not the fate of a shuttered House. "But whoever you are, whoever you are not, I daresay no one shall argue against your claim."

That sobered me immediately, because it would not do to forget who these people are, what they are capable of. The Dragons are strategic and deadly, and it will do me no good to underestimate them.

I climb out of bed and jump up and down a few times to get my blood flowing before escaping to the nearby courtyard for my morning exercises. Niall and the rest of the staff—my staff, I suppose—have learned my routine enough that they know not to bother me until I summon them for breakfast. It's still early, and I use my lone hour of freedom to move through a set of full-body exercises. I would rather train in the yard with the rest of the soldiers—it has been far too long since I sparred with someone—but Talon has refused that request, not even a missive sent by Caspian enough to change his mind. The War Prince might be grudgingly going along with the whims of his Prince Regent, but he still has his limits.

After my muscles are warm and I've begun to sweat, I pick up a couple of heavy, decorative rocks from the rock garden, the additional weight slightly heavier than my knives, but better than nothing. I suppose others might find the comfort of Phoenix Crest a welcome vacation, but all I can think is that somewhere out there my friends are still fighting a war while I am being fitted for ball gowns.

I have just moved through three of the seven forms of attack when a person appears behind me. I whirl, turning the attack toward the new body instinctively, fisting my hand around the apple-sized rock and using it as an additional weight for my swing.

If the person had been a regular soldier, it would've been a good punch, but the blow is blocked, as is the awkward swing of my left hand.

"You're still favoring your right side," Gavin says, grinning as he deflects my blows.

I dance backward, chest heaving from my exertions, breath stolen by my surprise at seeing him in this place. I drop the rocks and launch myself into his arms, and he picks me up and swings me around, laughing.

"How did you get in here?" I ask, lowering my voice with a glance toward my rooms. None of the household staff have entered, but the sun climbs higher in the sky, and it won't be much longer before the day's torture of dress fittings and political briefings begins.

"My boon, of course. The bigger question is, what are you doing here?"

"Why, haven't you heard? I'm the new scion of House Sphinx," I say, hands on my hips. "You should be bowing and scraping and seeking my favor."

Gavin snorts. "The day that happens I will sprout wings and fly off of the nearest parapet. We heard the rumors, Adelaide and I, but I didn't want to believe that you'd turn coat."

"I didn't have much choice," I say, voice low, as there is some movement inside my rooms. I grab Gavin by the arm and drag him behind a particularly large succulent with spiky rosettes. "The High Prince Regent told me his spies know every single Kraken safe house location. He said if I didn't go along with this he would have all of them razed."

Gavin's brows shoot up in surprise. "That's impossible."

"The tailor's shop in Reykia? The old drake stables on the edge of Hiran? He even knew about the tavern in Orso," I say, pulling my hair in remembered frustration. I'd been just as disbelieving as Gavin is now, until Caspian rattled off the locations of our safe houses, one after the other. "I thought it would be better to accept his offer, gather as much information as I can about Leonetti, and regroup than to refuse and sentence every single Barb to death." I swallow dryly, desperate to convince him I'm still loyal to House Kraken. "I'm trying to get to Leonetti, but the High Prince Regent refuses. But he's promised that he's safe, and I believe him."

"So, it's true," Gavin says, relaxing. It's not until this moment that I realize his hand has been hovering near the spot in his vest where he likes to hide his throwing knives. Did he come here to kill me? I'm upset at the thought, but not very. I would do the same if our roles were reversed.

"You said you heard rumors. What have you heard?" I say, looking past him to the door to my rooms to make sure the servants are still minding my space.

"That you had sold out to the Dragons and that you were betrothed to the High Prince Regent himself," Gavin says.

I spit at the words. "I've done no such thing. I want them as dead as you do. Especially the War Prince." At the mention of Talon an image of him surfaces in my mind, and a curious flutter arises in my middle. I cannot hear his name without thinking of our first meeting, the way he matched me blow for blow, surprising in his speed despite his size. He was a worthy opponent, and I still mean to finish what we started. Only, next time with something a bit more deadly than a butter knife.

"I was hoping you'd say that," Gavin says, finally reaching into the pocket opposite the one his hand has been hovering toward this entire time. He withdraws not a throwing knife but a cosmetic pot, blue-green and ornate. "You are in the kind of position we have dreamed about, Darling. You can get close to not only the War Prince, but the High Prince himself. Which is why Miranda prepared this for you."

"What is it?" I say, taking the proffered pot.

"She's calling it the Kiss of Death. A new formulation that she created after we heard the rumors. We were hoping that you had a reason beyond greed for agreeing to reclaim your lost titles, and since you are still faithful to House Kraken, I know it will be no matter for you to kill the heads of House Dragon. This looks to be nothing more than a lip tint, and when handled by anyone else it is just that. But smear it across your lips and it becomes a deadly poison for anyone you kiss."

My brain is slow in parsing his words, and when I finally do, I let loose a short bark of laughter. "You want me to go around kissing Dragons?"

"Not any Dragon. The High Prince Regent. And the War Prince, if you can. They've said the war is over, but we've fallen for Dragon lies in the past and won't be fooled again." Gavin suddenly clutches my hand, folding it around the one that holds the Kiss of Death. "Leonetti is still missing, Darling, and despite your new friend's assurances, we've heard nothing of him. We fear the worst. As long as the Dragons hold sway over this continent, war is inevitable. It's how they are. We have to sever the head and burn the body. And you are a vital part of that."

The sound of a door slamming nearby cuts off whatever else he was about to say. I look around the towering succulent to see one of the newer maids, Beatrice, I think, curtsying at the edge of the yard, her purple overdress embroidered in bright yellow with what I have been told was the seal of House Sphinx, a scroll and quill before a blazing sun.

"My quill," she says. "I am sorry to interrupt your morning routine, but the seamstress is here for your final fitting before the gala tonight. Will you attend to her now, or should I send her away?"

"No, no, I'll see her now," I say. Gavin is gone, once more invisible if not having taken his leave, and I clutch the pot of lip tint in my hand so that Beatrice will not see it. House Kraken has given me a task, and not one worthy of my skills. Better they should have given me poisoned blades to hide within my sleeves, or even a hairpin to slide into a jugular. Instead, they would have me plant my lips upon the High Prince Regent and the War Prince, kissing my way to a win over House Dragon, when neither of the men have shown the slightest interest in me as anything other than a pawn on a chessboard.

And yet, when I think of kissing Talon, there is a heat that rises in my cheeks and a curiosity I cannot quite avoid. Would he be a soft, gentle kisser? His lips were full enough for such a thing. Or would he be a ravenous one, biting and tugging at my lips just as fiercely as he had fought me that first night?

"My quill?"

I clear my throat and focus on the maid who waits for me in the doorway to my sitting room. "Yes, sorry. Have a pot of tea and something hearty brought from the kitchen. I'll break my fast while the seamstress does her work."

The maid disappears back into the room, and I sigh heavily. Kissing Talon Goldhoard is too appealing a prospect, and that just makes me hate him all the more.

8

TALON

It's been a rough week. I've barely slept thanks to constant meetings and interruptions and fires to put out as I work to institute the command of the High Prince Regent and end this fourteen-year war. General Bloodscale is so resistant I'm worried I might have to force him into early retirement, but he's been one of my best supporters, and I'm determined to keep him. The minister of works is the only council member on my side other than Aunt Aurora—and even though she puts on a loyal face to the public, in private moments I can see fear in her eyes. This is so sudden, such a change of policy—not to mention the anointing of a new Sphinx scion—and Caspian so unpredictable, she and I know if we make one wrong move, we'll all be dead. A Dragon's hoard is only as good as what he can protect.

And Caspian won't talk to me. He's avoiding me, just like he's done for years, and I'm avoiding Darling, the instigator and heart of this problem. At least I expect she's chafing under what amounts to house arrest and nearly as many meetings as me, as Aurora and the minister of prosperity pull apart family trees and untangle titles in order to rebraid them around Darling's neck. I made sure half her staff are soldiers dressed up as new maids—pulled from palace guard duty and the eastern battalions so they don't know any of the Teeth Darling killed last month—and I continue denying requests for her to join the regulars or palace guard for workouts. No matter how innocent a request it is on her part, which is doubtful in the first place, the Teeth remember Eovan, and Finn has only barely recovered. Somebody would take offense and try for revenge; then it would be a bloodbath—and I can't lose any more people to her knife.

Caspian sent me a *note* asking I be lenient with our recovered Sphinx scion, and I sent him a response that we could discuss it *in person*.

When I seek him out, he's nowhere to be found or just departed, despite the fact that Caspian doesn't take meetings with anyone but his personal healer, Elias, and the occasional random courtier. I refuse the indignity of yelling at him through his locked door.

I'm forced to use my boon to ensnare him. It's a tracking boon, better suited to hunters and spies than soldiers, but it's also how I knew Darling was in that dark dining room back in Lastrium, and sometimes I can use it to track slightly forward and predict fighting patterns. So I know exactly when Caspian is ensconced in his master suite for his daily appointment with Elias, when they're finished, and when Elias leaves Caspian to be washed and dressed for tonight's gala.

The guards have just flung open the gates of Phoenix Crest to welcome guests through the spangled corridors, the musicians play the opening notes of Swiftwind's "Variations on a Lament for the First Phoenix," wine has been poured, and boonlights twinkle against the mosaic ceiling of the ballroom, and I arrive impatiently at Caspian's suite door, ready. He cannot hide from his own scheming gala.

His first and second valets are within, have been for some time, and as I gather myself to barge in, two maids appear: one holds a delicate ceramic jar with a wax cap and a small liquor cup; the other, a plate of spice cookies. Their eyes widen at the sight of me, and they bow.

"Give those to me," I say, holding out my hands. They quickly obey, and only one girl grimaces. "Now bring sweet coffee for both of us."

The girl who grimaced bites her lip. I wait until she says, "War Prince, there's no more coffee. The fortress ran out months ago and can't get more."

I grit my teeth. Many of our imports have been cut off for years, thanks to the Kraken pirates, and several overseas nations refuse to endanger their people with Pyrlanum trade.

"Fine," I say. "The darkest Pyrlanum tea you can find, then." I nod to the guard stationed beside Caspian's door, and he pulls it open.

These rooms are opulent and barely lived in, a pointless performance for the palace when everyone knows Caspian sleeps in his tower workroom more often than not. I stride over thick rugs and past tall windows overlooking an inner garden—the same one Darling's rooms give her access to. But Caspian is two levels up the climbing Phoenix Crest with no balcony or exterior access. Through the arched doorway I hear Caspian's voice ring out. "The liquor! Wait to do my lips until I can swallow a bit down."

Scowling, I open my mouth to speak, but Caspian glances at me, and shock flits over his expression before he hides it behind a huge grin. "Baby brother!"

Caspian stands up from his stool at a gilded vanity, spreading his arms so that the stiff brocade and silk engulfing him flare like wings. He's in layers of green and gold, and the outer coat has a high collar that gathers behind his head to flare out into spines down his back. "Look," he says, exuding glee. "It unhooks from here and here at my shoulders, and under that collar, so that once I've impressed everyone, these sleeves and outer skirt can drape over the throne and I can dance without tripping over myself."

I have to admit it's as impressive as it is draconic. So I nod and set his liquor and cookies down on the long table stacked with unopened letters and yellowing scrolls. I don't open the wax seal on the liquor jar but say, "We need to talk before we go in there."

The two valets have their heads down, pretending to fade away. The first holds a flat box of hairpins and earrings open on display; the other has a makeup brush in her hand. I nearly tell them to leave, but Caspian is peering at me through narrow eyes. "Is that what you're wearing?"

Clearly he wants the answer to be no. But it's my formal Teeth uniform: bloodred jacket over ivory trousers, real black dragon-scale buttons, and a matching scale pauldron armoring my left shoulder. The dress sheath for my falchion has some of the most intricate black-glass scale mosaic I've seen in my life, and I don't know what Caspian's problem is with how I look. So I just set my jaw and stare at him.

His lips flutter into a fond smile, and he waves me to him. "Come sit down, right here. Ninia, I need that powder back. Faelon, you pour me that liquor, then find something in your box for Talon. Or, no—do we have time to send for the great-grandmother's claws? They might fit."

My brother ushers me to the stool, gently pushing me down, and I look at Faelon, whose eyes go to my left hand, and he shakes his head. "No, Prince Regent, they won't."

"Alas, well, drinks first."

The sound of Caspian's heavy layers sweeps around me, and I look at our reflections in the mirror, telling myself if I have to let him dress me up a bit more for time together, fine. I meet his light green gaze and find myself seeking similarities: maybe the shape of our nose, the square cut of our jaws. My mouth is bigger, and I have a scar high on my right cheek caused by a gauntleted punch from Finn that I should have blocked when we were fourteen. Caspian's long hair softens his entire look, even pulled back in sections and pinned with red jewels. He looks like a bolder but equally beautiful version of Aunt Aurora. Or maybe he looks like our mother. Except his eyes seem more crystalline than usual thanks to dark lines of paint around them, drawn out toward his temples. It reminds me of the black holes of Darling's eyes in some of his paintings. I know he did it on purpose. I wonder what she'll look like tonight, like a prince herself, I hope—and crush the thought.

"My blade?" Faelon asks softly, liquor jar in hand. I shake my head and turn to Caspian.

Caspian takes the cup of liquor and knocks it back. Then he turns me on the stool and touches my chin with two fingers, tilting my face up. He stares at me, through me.

I've worked to be in the same room with him, and now I can't think of all my demands. I just want him to tell me what he's planning. How to help him. How to keep him safe. "Caspian—"

"Faelon, Ninia, you may go," he says, never looking away from me. His hand moves, and then his fingers return, rubbing something cool and soft into my skin along my cheekbones. "It's just to make you glow," he chides softly as I stiffen and try to draw away. "Don't you think I can paint you up without ruining anything?"

I make myself go still, listening for the departure of his valets. When the outer door closes, I say, "I want to know what you're planning tonight."

"Introducing Darling to the world, dragonlet. You know that."

"But what else?"

Caspian snorts and looks directly at my eyes. "Dancing. Drinking. Merriment. Showing off what power we still retain. The war is over, but we are strong. We have our hoard."

"With the lost scion of House Sphinx brought home."

"At our side," Caspian emphasizes. He dabs more of the cream on my face, then purses his lips as he chooses a paint pot and Ninia's discarded brush. "Look up," he tells me, then smiles. "With only your eyes, don't move your head."

I do, rolling my eyes to look at the ceiling. There's a mural of the Drakes of Every Season lusciously painted from wall to wall. Not Caspian's work, but much older. From when the Phoenix ruled here, not House Dragon. The makeup brush touches the inner corner of my eye, cold and teasing, and I blink at the tickle. If I talk, will it mess him up? He's got me trapped for the moment.

And part of me revels in it, in being under my brother's care. I don't wear makeup, but I might if Caspian would do it for me every day. I was so little the sole time I tried to paint with him, a year after Mother died. He let me have a corner of a canvas and whatever color I wished. I covered my hands and smeared in shapes I thought were like his, sad and warm at the same time—until Caspian gasped suddenly and shoved me away, tore our painting into shreds, and screamed until I ran into Aunt Aurora's skirts as she rushed in. After that I was handed to the Teeth permanently, and I had a hundred older siblings in the barracks instead.

Caspian moves to my other eye. When he's finished, he turns to the jewelry and gives a thoughtful hum.

I glance in the mirror: he's used dark lines to enhance my eyes into a true dragon green. Hard to notice if you weren't expecting it, unlike his striking style. And I do look . . . brighter. "Caspian. Give me something. Everything is on the line, and I am working very hard to end this war, to do as you will. But you're avoiding me like a child. It undercuts our solidarity—it undercuts both of us."

"You can handle it," he assures me.

I do not feel complimented. "Why did you suddenly decide this?"

"You want the war to go on?"

"No—but I want to know what changed. Why now? Is it just Darling?"

Caspian says, "This is the beginning. She is the beginning."

"Of what?"

"The end of the war."

"Caspian." I take a deep breath. "What do you know that I do not? Tell me why you trust her. Why are you giving her this? Putting the weight of our future on her shoulders?"

"So dramatic," he murmurs, and I bare my teeth at him, clenching my jaw to bite back this deep anger.

"Tell me."

"Justice?"

"Are you asking me?" I grind out.

Caspian laughs and slips me a mischievous grin. "Justice," he says more firmly.

I don't laugh, and his expression falls. He stops sifting through rings and earrings and chains of gold. Turns fully to me. Nothing shows on his face, a chilling contrast to the makeup and vivid flare of the dragon collar and the garnets glinting in his hair like blood spatter. He's looking through me again.

"She lived in darkness for years," he says.

The breath in my lungs seems to freeze. He doesn't mean metaphorically. There's a lightness in his tone, a dreamy remembering.

"Raw darkness, Talon, and it forged her—it made her eyes, those eyes . . ." Caspian's head tilts as he looks at something that is not there.

If I didn't know Caspian's boon is simply for art, at moments like this I'd think he had one of those ancient, long-lost boons like dreamwalking or mindsight.

"It's our fault," he says. "She was in hiding, desperate and alone and orphaned, because of Father's war."

"They killed our mother," I say, though even as I say it, I know I don't think that justifies slaughtering children.

"Yes." Caspian's voice grows sharper. "We mustn't forget they killed our mother. And we killed theirs in return. And Darling lived in darkness, but it did not hurt her. She did not falter or wither like a flower. In that darkness, Chaos found her and reforged her once already . . ." He pauses as if to drift again, but then his attention snaps entirely back to me, to the moment. "We made her, is my point. Oughtn't we continue making her?"

"I don't like it," I say, meaning this entire conversation.

Caspian lifts his eyebrows. "But you like her."

I glare. "She's dangerous. We can't trust her."

My brother shrugs, shifting silk and brocade. Then he says, "Put these on. Oh, Chaos teeth, your ears are pierced, aren't they?"

The horror makes his voice breathless in a way he was not when he spoke of real horror. I don't understand him. We've been apart for too long. I left and he made himself into this. He never wanted me close.

I accept the little black drops. As I fasten them to my ears, he takes another paint pot and dabs color onto his lips. "Your turn!" He grabs my chin again, and I manage not to grimace. It makes my lips sticky, but he turns my face to the mirror, skin pinched in his strong fingers. To our reflections he says, "We match!"

It's barely a blush of color, and I shake free of him. "We're late already."

"You're the one who wanted a heart-to-heart right now, Talon."

Trying not to huff at that truth, I get to my feet. "Is that what this was?"

Caspian slings his arm through mine and nearly drags me to the door.

"Caspian," I say, planting my feet before stepping out of the chamber.

He glances at me, inquiring.

"No surprises tonight."

"Not of my making, dragonlet," he promises.

We go together, shoulder to shoulder as we should, and it settles something in me.

The gala is being held throughout the second level of the fortress, centered in the Phoenix Hall but spilling out into one of the ancient courtyards and narrow corridors carved into the side of the mountain. A path is made for us by palace guards, and I step back at the wide doors of the hall to let the High Prince Regent enter first. But I keep up at his shoulder, avoiding the sharply scalloped trailing edge of his dragon cape.

It's dazzling inside, boonlights catching jewels and gilded decorations, shining off glasses of champagne and the flash of dancing couples. The music fades with a final trill when Caspian arrives, and he is bowed to in a great wave that tracks from one end of the Phoenix Hall to the other as he makes his way toward the great phoenix statue overhanging the throne. I keep my eyes sharp, note the guards, the Teeth in their own bloodred uniforms, the colors of House Barghest and House Gryphon nearly overwhelmed by the green and gold of Dragon.

Waiting for Caspian at his throne is Aunt Aurora and every member of his council—and a filled flute of champagne, which he takes with a flourish as he faces the assembly with a smile. "Enjoy yourselves at my party, friends," he calls, informal and brash, then drinks most of the wine in a single motion that displays his long neck to anyone's knife.

I catch Aurora's eye, and she lifts her champagne toward me, sips lightly, and then pulls her own performance back on, lovely and flirtatious and just a little bit like the mother of a charming, if foolish, king.

I take a cup of fresh fruit juice—oranges from the dry southern tip of our land where the Sphinx once reigned. The minister of the hoard says something to me, and I respond shortly. I will stand here, I will show my full support to my brother, but that support is martial, is dangerous, and that is not something anybody needs to forget. I drink the juice; my other hand rests on the pommel of my falchion. I watch and I nod; I do not smile as the gala whirls around me. Caspian lounges on the throne, beckons guests to come closer. He knows all their names and ranks, their families and holdings, and charms them, flirts, and expertly tilts everyone away from important subjects, and absolutely away from the declaration we've all come tonight to hear. He promises with a sly grin, a wink, and a toast to peace and prosperity given to us all by the surprising opportunities of Chaos and the benevolent memory of the Last Phoenix.

It is a waste of money. A waste of food and wine, and it's been less than a turn. I need this over with and am nearly ready to storm off and find out what's delaying Darling—though I expect the lateness of her arrival is also Caspian's doing—when Caspian gestures to someone I don't see, and the lights in the entire Phoenix Hall dim.

The sudden shadows cause gasps and startled cries, and the musicians easily transition into a soft march: the "Song of House Sphinx." High against the ceiling the boonlights begin to sparkle and turn like stars against a misty sky.

And there she is.

Framed by the gleaming dark wood of the arched doors, Darling Seabreak stands in a dress of intricate ivory and desert-yellow panels, and a capelet of downy feathers. House Sphinx regalia. White leather bracers lace up her forearms, and there are knives sheathed there. I cannot believe Caspian armed her, but it's such a display of her—their—power. She looks odd, but breathtaking.

And then I realize it: the reason the hall has been made into a dusky starscape, the reason she seems strange to me.

Nothing covers Darling's eyes. They are wide open and glittering dark brown, but filmed over with something—an illusion, a Chaos scar—of eerie, lustrous blue and purple green, a rainbow of shifting hues.

And staring directly at me.

9
DARLING

I hate this.

It's the first thought I have as I enter the gala, the dress moving with me but also weighing me down in an unfamiliar way. I was excited when I saw the gauntlets with their throwing knives, either confidence or foolishness on Caspian's part to allow such a thing, but the rest of the getup left me cold. It's a glorious dress, if unsettlingly just like one that I wear in a painting I glimpsed in Caspian's tower. Did he have the seamstress copy it, or did he somehow paint me in a dress I had not yet worn? The pale colors are striking next to my dark skin, but it is flashy and wholly unsensible. How am I supposed to kick someone while wearing two underskirts, let alone satin slippers? I'll break my toes. Not to mention the boning keeping the bodice of the dress in place. The seamstress had assured me that it is much less restrictive than is fashionable, but I still loathe it. No wonder Gavin and Miranda want me to kiss everyone to death. I wouldn't last five seconds in a proper brawl.

And yet, here I am playing along with whatever Caspian is planning. Because Gavin's bloodthirst won't free Leonetti. Only playing at scion will.

And liberating my father is still my primary goal.

I stand in the entryway of the gala, the dim room making my smoked goggles unnecessary. It's a frivolous example of the power Caspian wields. Even so, I am not the only unhappy clam roped into this event. Talon scowls next to his brother, dressed in the cursed uniform of those bastard Teeth, and I've taken two stalking steps toward him before I realize that the red of his jacket is enough to make me want to plunge one of the tiny blades I wear right into his heart.

Old habits die hard. But more importantly, how am I supposed to kiss a man I so very much want to murder?

Caspian must sense my rising bloodlust, because he intercepts me in the middle of the floor, his long-legged stride eating up the distance. "Friends! We are blessed to finally have the moon in our night sky, the lost scion of House Sphinx, Maribel Calamus!"

A polite round of applause goes up in the room, as well as a few sloppy huzzahs from what I'm supposing are guests who are already well into their cups. Caspian grabs my hand, kissing the back of it before bowing deeply. When he rises, I sink into the damnable curtsy I've been practicing all week just for this moment.

"Calamus? My name is Seabreak," I say through gritted teeth, my smile closer to a grimace. "And Maribel is hideous."

"Ah," he says, pulling me close, surprising me with the movement. "Calamus is a very good Sphinx name, while Seabreak is a Kraken name, and it would be in poor taste to remind our friends that you like to keep such company. And Darling is an endearment, not a name, regardless of your feelings on Maribel. You will learn, I'm afraid, that politics are tedious, and your name is the least of what you will lose the longer you are in this game. But, if it makes you feel better, telling people to call you Darling will make them feel like they've curried favor, so it's all to your benefit in the end."

"I'm not worried about my benefit. I want to see Leonetti," I say.

I've learned it's best to address issues with Caspian whenever possible, before he flits away on some whimsy.

"Soon, soon," he says, his expression distracted. He gestures over my shoulder, and the musicians take up a sprightly tune. Caspian gives me what can only be described as a wicked grin.

"Surely you know the Miller's Jig?" he says.

He doesn't wait for me to answer before he begins maneuvering me around the dance floor in what can only be described as some sort of public humiliation. First we are skipping one way, and then the next, other couples joining the madness as we whirl about.

"What are you doing?" I snap, when he spins me out away from him and then slaps his thighs before holding his hand out to me.

"We are dancing. You're supposed to twirl and pose," he says, confusion twisting his pretty face. I glance around at the other couples and see that in each case one of the partners is laughing and pretending to be a garden statue or some nonsense. One woman has placed her fingers on each side of her head like a bunny, while in another pair one of the men looks as though he is about to fade into a swoon. Is this what the Houses do while their soldiers die in the mud, fighting a nonsensical war? It just makes me scowl.

"I don't dance," I say.

"Then I shall take on the role of the fancy," Caspian says as he poses instead, causing a round of raucous laughter to go up from the onlookers at the edge of the room. Even the other couples stop and begin to applaud the way he's twisted himself into a coy pose, his eyelashes batting at me as though trying to entice me, like a seductive creature of some long-ago fable.

My temper flares. I'm out of my depth. I agreed to play along with this farce in order to keep everyone I love safe and to get my father back, but I did not think it would require me to be the butt of the Prince Regent's jokes.

I spin around to leave, and Talon is there, blocking my exit. I open my mouth to snap at him, but he just bows. "Perhaps you would enjoy a more capable partner," he says, pitching his voice to be heard over the gossip that has erupted. I open my mouth to tell him just what I think of that idea when Talon grabs my hand and pulls me close. "My brother has no idea what the life of a soldier is like. He most likely thinks we have galas after every battle. Let me help you."

Being held by Talon is nothing like Caspian's light touch. Caspian might be taller, but where he is willowy and sylph-like, Talon is hard and muscled. My face heats as I realize that he's doing me a favor, and I give him a quick nod.

"I'm going to talk you through the steps, but it will be easier if you follow my lead," he says, as we set off in another turn around the floor. "First is a bit of a stampeding step clockwise around the room, and the next is the skipping. Do you remember?"

"Yes," I say, trying to focus on the steps. The first two parts go without a hitch, and when I glance over at Talon, he's actually smiling at me.

"Stop laughing at me," I mutter while we negotiate a turn back to where we started on the dance floor.

"I'm not laughing! You're doing great. You should've seen me at my first gala. The next is just a promenade, and then we're back to the sashay and then the pose."

"Those are not real words," I say, but he's already spinning me away so that I can run back across the room and place my hand in his.

"Don't think about it too hard," he says with a laugh as we parade in a line, hands barely touching. I watch his feet, trying to figure out the steps. "It's like fighting: you have to let your body feel the movements. By the time you've thought about the step it's already too late."

"I would rather fight," I say.

"Then let's do that instead."

The next series of steps requires us to circle away from each other, the other couples doing the same. This is the part where I got all twisted up last time, but this time I know better. When it's time to pose, I don't hesitate, instead striking up the ready position like I'm about to fight. Talon grins. Somehow, he's enjoying this.

"Nicely done," he says. "Well, don't hold out on me!"

I move from the ready position into a defensive pose, and I'm half-surprised when he does the same. And before I can think about it too much, I flow toward him, stomping the floor a few inches in front of me. He gives a shout of challenge and does the same.

The music suddenly changes, less strings and more flute, and I recognize "Throw the Bastard Overboard," a well-known Kraken song. I raise my eyebrows at Talon, and he shrugs.

"Do you know the Sea Swell?" I say.

"I'm a quick learner."

Krakens don't do ballroom dances, or if they do I've never seen such a thing. Instead, we stomp and yell and *fight*. Every Kraken dance is really just a way to stay limber for the eventual fight that will come. Seafaring is dangerous business, and every aspect of life revolves around it. Even fun.

Something inside me is aching and sad. I miss Adelaide and Gavin and Miranda and even little Alvin with his too-wide eyes that see far too much. I hate that I am dancing while Leonetti is Chaos knows where, and guilt pierces me. But I am here because I want to keep them safe.

So I will give this room full of fancies a show they will not soon forget. They will remember who I am, even if Caspian would rather have them forget.

I skip lightly around Talon, as though I am looking for an opening. A soldier approaches, and Talon gives him his falchion, just as the other couples leave the floor to give us room. The music rises and dips, and I clap twice, signaling the beginning of the dance.

The Sea Swell is a series of stomps, dragged feet, and kicks. The dancers leap closer and closer to one another, until by the end of the song they come together in a spin. There can be flips and the like, but in this dress that would be disastrous. So I just make do with the more basic steps.

Talon bends backward so that my very slow kick passes over his torso, and he responds by stomping and sweeping a leg toward me that I easily leap over. His smile is gone, and his gaze upon me is intense. It is too late that I remember the Sea Swell is as much a dance of seduction as it is a battle, the moves mimicking the push-pull of attraction as the dancers grow closer and closer together.

At first I think I've wildly miscalculated, even if Talon looks to be enjoying the dance as much as me, but then I get a glance at a sandy-haired youth in the crowd. Gavin? I'm turning and avoiding a strike from Talon so I can't tell, but it's enough to remind me that I have a mission. If I am to kiss the War Prince, I will have to seduce him. Because while I need Caspian's favor to get my father back, I cannot help but think how killing Talon will save so many Kraken lives on the battlefield.

And what better way to seduce an enemy than a dance?

The problem is that Talon *is* a quick learner. For every feint and strike he's there with the appropriate maneuver, which has us stalking closer and closer to one another. After he slides under a switch-leg kick, a move that I can surprisingly do despite the voluminous skirts I wear, I realize that he knows more than he's let on.

The pipes swell, the last refrain of the song, and I spin toward Talon in a way that seems uncontrolled. Faster and faster, before leaping toward him. I half expect him to let me fall on my face, but he doesn't. He catches me in midair just as the music ends. My body slides against his as he lowers me toward the floor, our chests heaving, our faces close enough that his breath warms my cheek.

It's now or never.

I lean in, eyes slightly closed but open enough that I see he is doing the same. So close. A single touch of my lips and his end is writ large.

That is when the room erupts in applause.

I blink and open my eyes. Talon seems just as dazed as I am. I'd forgotten the rest of the attendees, the bystanders watching what they seem to think was a show for their benefit.

"Brother! Scion!" Caspian is clapping hardest of all, his eyes dancing in the low light. He looks like a boy up to mischief, and it's cold water on the moment. He schemes far too much for my liking. "What a magnificent display. No wonder you were so sour at my clumsy attempts," he says with a laugh, the room tittering along with him.

"What? No—" But he cuts me off before I can say anything else.

"No matter! The hour is at hand, and it is time for my announcement. No, don't go anywhere, Talon. This concerns you as well."

Talon has set me a few feet away from him, his expression troubled. Is he remembering the heat and excitement of our dance? I tell myself that my pulse thrums and my skin tingles because I almost killed the War Prince, but I know it for the lie it is.

"Gentle friends," Caspian says, pitching his voice so that it booms throughout the hall. "In the time before this tedious war it was customary for House regents to take a yearly tour across the country, each taking a turn to host the rest. And with the war ended, by my own decree, of course, I announce that I will immediately be sending the delightful Maribel Calamus, scion of House Sphinx, on just such a tour so that she can familiarize herself with the various House regents."

There's a smattering of applause and murmurs of polite surprise, but for the most part the assembled guests are deathly quiet. I'm not surprised. I'm not exactly thrilled to know I will travel through lands that would've killed a Kraken on sight less than a month ago.

"And that is not all!" Caspian continues, waving over a server and handing each of us a fluted glass. "In three weeks' time, at a feast hosted by House Barghest, I will raise the scion to her rightful place as House regent and return her seat on the ruling council to her."

There are audible gasps to that. I suppose everyone thought that I would play at being House Sphinx scion for a while before I was either assassinated or hidden away. Truthfully, it's what I expected as well.

This? This sounds like actual reparations.

"Huzzah!" Caspian yells, and the crowd echoes it back, drinking their fizzy wine half-heartedly. After the announcement Caspian gestures, and the musicians start up another sprightly jig, but I'm in no mood to dance.

Someone grabs my arm, and I turn to see Talon, expression as stormy as a hurricane on the horizon. "You knew about this," he says. It isn't a question.

I yank my arm out of his grasp. "I am no more privy to your brother's machinations than you are. What a ridiculous thing to say." Inside I'm reeling. Traipsing around the countryside will give me a chance to escape. I can win my way back to my friends.

Only to have Caspian declare war once more and murder them all in their beds.

I put the thought aside and realize this is a bad thing. I need Leonetti back before I can see Caspian and Talon dead. How can I save my father if I'm on some stupid cross-country tour?

"Angry faces are unhappy places," Caspian singsongs as he throws friendly arms over Talon's and my shoulders. "Don't worry, dear brother. You're coming along as well. We're going to have a grand adventure."

"We?" I say, recovering before Talon does.

"Why, all three of us! We're going to see all that this fine continent has to offer. Carriages! Sightseeing! Even brand-new wardrobes. Doesn't that sound like fun?"

I force a smile, my grimace echoed on Talon's too-handsome face.

This is going to be a disaster.

10

TALON

I'm too agitated after Caspian's announcement to do more than clench my jaw and glare daggers at anyone who approaches. When one of my Teeth returns to me my falchion, I take the opportunity to shrug Caspian off and stalk over to lean against the throne while he parades Darling around, formally introducing her to the ministers and noblest Dragons. Her fingers twitch every time someone touches her or reaches for her hand; she shifts her shoulders as if to resettle the feather mantle, clearly uncomfortable.

I think about the dance, of how quickly we fell into the rhythm of it together, how good it felt pushing her and knowing she'd follow, and then gasping to keep up when she gave a challenge right back to me. Maybe I should rescind my command against her sparring with my soldiers and pair up with her myself.

Darling clasps her hands behind her waist as the minister of the hoard says something to her, and while her hands are nearly hidden, I clearly see her caress the thin hilt of one of the daggers in the gauntlets. I know what she's thinking, and I feel a smirk pull at one side of my mouth.

The problem is that I like her.

And Caspian is using her, using both of us, all of us, and I'd bet every sliver of wealth in my personal hoard that she's using him, and all of us, right back.

"It's so dim I can barely see anything," Aunt Aurora says at my side.

I hadn't noticed. All I need to see is Darling.

The realization heats up the back of my neck, and I swallow it as I glance at Aurora. Her brow is raised in a quiet reprimand.

Thank Chaos my aunt doesn't know I thought about kissing Darling for that lingering, suspended moment after we danced.

"I'm leaving," I say under my breath, just for Aunt Aurora. It's definitely time for a strategic retreat. Darling is on Caspian's arm; they're surrounded by Teeth and courtiers. Safe enough, and Darling can handle anything thrown at her—even protecting my brother if necessary.

"Hmm, you've certainly been enough of a spectacle this evening."

I wrench my gaze from Darling and stare incredulously at Aurora instead. Compared to whom? Caspian? He's a walking, talking spectacle. For a brief moment before this party I thought we managed a connection, but Caspian promised no surprises only to turn around and announce this grand tour. Not only a broken promise but a flat-out lie. Or a sudden, madness-induced idea. I don't like any of the options.

Aurora's expression softens. She touches her fingers lightly to my forearm. "I'm sorry, Talon. I'm only worried."

I nod. Worried is an understatement for both of us. Stepping back, I bow formally to her. "Excuse me, Aunt, for forgoing a dance with you. There are a number of preparations I should immediately see to, if we are leaving imminently."

Leaning onto her toes, she kisses my cheek. "Be careful," she murmurs, but when she drops back onto her heels there's no hint of seriousness touching her. Aurora glides away, and I head for the exit with enough purpose not to be stopped.

It's a relief to escape the crowd, the noise and perfume, though the return to full boonlight in the corridor has me blinking. The starry sky of the Phoenix Hall was soothing, the pale shadows and flicker of people almost like a dream. Is that how Darling found it? Somehow I doubt *soothed* was how she felt.

I push past laughing Dragons and nod at the guard in Dragon green stationed at the large double doors. I'll find Finn in the Teeth barracks and take him with me to the captain of the palace guard to find out if Caspian put anything in motion for the security of our little jaunt around the country.

But I see Elias Chronicum stepping up from one of the arched stairways leading down into the terraced gardens and turn immediately to intercept them.

Nearly two years ago, before I submitted to the order to replace General Bloodscale at the front, I insisted on a personal physician for my brother or I wouldn't leave. This came at the end of a year when Caspian had had too many episodes in public for me to feel at all safe leaving him. He'd cut off mid-sentence and stare at something nobody else could see, or giggle suddenly, or bar everyone from his tower until he was too exhausted and starving to give commands. His hands were always covered in paint. Aurora and I knew he woke from nightmares often and refused fires in his hearths or even regular candles. As if flames held some special horror for him. The rumors of madness or dreamwalking had begun again, and we didn't know how to counter them.

Except it ended abruptly for no reason apparent to us, and Caspian picked up the reins of leadership more firmly than ever before.

I was relieved until he pulled Bloodscale onto the council and wanted me gone. I spoke with Aurora, and we sent word to House Gryphon, renowned for their libraries and physicians, and Elias came to us. They are the Gryphon regent's first cousin, with not only a specialty in treating boon-related maladies but also a diagnostic boon themself. Elias told me it was not unlike my tracking boon in application. They had such calm confidence that they could help Caspian, I eased into leaving.

But it's been two years, and Caspian isn't any better. Where once I trusted Elias, now I'm angry. They see it in my expression as I bear toward them and blink rapidly before giving me a slight bow. "My blade?" they murmur.

I take their elbow and lead them back down the stairs into the terraced garden. This confrontation has been coming for us both since I returned with Darling and found Caspian just as wild and unpredictable as ever. As we pass a trio of courtiers, I slow down and relax my grip so that it seems a more friendly escort than before, and step us around a row of flowering trees to the end of the stone terrace, where we have a modicum of privacy. I release them.

"My blade," Elias says again, but no more. They wait. Something challenging hides in their gaze, and I'm primed to bristle.

Like many of House Gryphon, Elias eschews most explicit markers of gender in their costume and accoutrement. They're wearing layered robes of exquisite pale material that simply flow around their body and a garnet signet ring indicating membership in the Gryphon regent's immediate family that sits heavy on their light brown forefinger.

"Why aren't you helping him?" I say with slightly more threat than I intended.

Elias keeps their expression as calm as ever. "I do help him."

"He's not better."

"Better than what?" Elias drawls, letting their facade shatter. I see the challenge again, a quiet disdain that I don't know my brother at all and this physician does.

I draw myself up: I'm taller and broader than Elias, so it's easy to loom. "I brought you here to cure him of his illness, of—"

"He's not sick."

Narrowing my eyes, I want to ask if my brother isn't sick, why hasn't Elias gone home? But I want answers more. "He *acts* sick. He's wild, just as prone to mood swings and ridiculous behavior. You saw him in there, didn't you?"

Elias studies me, glass-brown eyes taking in probably more than I'd like. "Did you see him?"

"No riddles, Elias."

The Gryphon gives the impression of rolling their eyes without actually doing it. I feel young, stupid, even though I'm only a handful of years their junior, and the first scion. Elias says, "The Prince Regent knows what he's doing, scion. Did you ever think that? He's doing it all on purpose, playing you and everyone else like a master musician."

I cross my arms over my chest and shake my head. I keep my voice low: we seem alone, but gardens are notorious for eavesdroppers. "Sometimes, but not always. I've watched him fall out of himself; I know I have. I hope you're right, and he is doing everything on purpose, but if he's not, it's not worth the risk."

Elias's body relaxes slightly. "You're worried about him." They have the audacity to sound surprised.

"He's my brother," I grind out.

"You've been away a long time."

"We all have our duties to perform."

The physician runs a hand through their short black curls. For the occasion they're streaked with the rust red of House Gryphon, and Elias grimaces when they remember, pulling their hand down and rubbing the powder between their fingers. *I wonder if Caspian did that to them like he'd insisted on making up my eyes. I wonder how close Elias and my brother are.*

Before I can formulate my question without hostility, Elias says, "I've seen the paintings of her."

I suck in a quick breath. That's an answer to my question, at least. I'm going to have to somehow make Caspian confess just how many people he's told. The extent of his paintings, of his obsession with Darling, was supposed to be a very well-kept secret.

Elias says, "Knowing they depict a real person, a person with whom Cas—the Prince Regent clearly has an unprecedented Chaos connection . . ." There's a shadow in their eyes as they glance away, a shadow that mirrors my own sour feelings about Caspian and Darling having any kind of connection. But Elias continues, "It suggests that his boon takes a form of something heretofore unknown. Artistry, yes, but focused on one thing, one person. A single thread of Chaos. It does affect him strangely, I admit that. But just because we don't understand it"—their voice sharpens—"doesn't mean he's sick. Or mad."

"Are you certain his boon is for painting?"

"Unless he is lying to everyone who cares about him."

"You don't think that's possible?" I snap.

"I trust him," Elias responds, both quiet and steely.

For a long moment I study Elias. They seem sincere. And even if I can't bring myself to be as trusting of Caspian, I am glad he has someone so devoted. "If he is not sick—and I believe you that he is not—why do you think his boon is so difficult for him to process? Is it somehow because of this connection to Darling? Or simply because it is so strong? Chaos has too tight a grip upon him? Even if he does much of this on purpose, I have seen it take control of him. You must have, as well."

The expression on Elias's face is somewhere between annoyance and wonder. Caspian has gotten his claws in them in the best sort of way, despite their better nature. "I have wanted to research in the Gryphon archives, where there are many books about how boons functioned in the time before the death of the Last Phoenix, when they were all stronger than those we are gifted with now. But . . . I also fear leaving him."

Because I understand that entirely, I only smile grimly at Elias and say, "In that case, I have good news: you're coming with us on our ridiculous tour."

Instead of continuing to seek Finn once I leave Elias, I head toward Darling's rooms. She won't be there yet, but I'll wait. When I reach the extravagant suite, I dismiss the palace guard at the door and take her place. I learned to appreciate the isolated peace of night watch my first year in the army, assigned to just as much grunt work as my fellow recruits. Many complained about watch, but I found it soothing, especially high on ramparts or city walls in the middle of the night. I can sink into a boon-driven focus for hours, aware of the details of my surroundings without having to think much about them until something out of place catches my attention. It's meditative. I don't have the opportunity often anymore, and I miss it.

I let my boon awaken and am immediately aware of the empty space around me, the tapestry across the corridor with a tattered hem, a recent stain from spilled wine on the rug to my left, the skitter of something very small in the shadows near the standing candelabra on my right. Inside Darling's suite an attendant waits in a doze. Otherwise I'm alone. I breathe deeply and settle into the quiet awareness. It makes me note the remaining soreness in my shoulder and the uneven strain across my back because of how I've been compensating. The ache in the soles of my feet, the weight of black paint around my eyes, a tickle in my nose. I block it out and keep breathing.

Several servants hurry past, and a couple of courtiers from House Barghest heading for their own guest suite. None of them notice I'm not simply a palace guard, despite the fancy black scales of my shoulder pauldron or my dress uniform. It's not long, maybe an hour, before I sense the approach of three people: two in formation, the one at the fore stomping.

I slide my gaze toward her without moving my head, to see Darling practically kicking her heavy skirts out of her way as she strides—instead of just lifting the skirts in her hands. Something warm kindles in my chest. She's wearing dark-glass goggles again, framed by thin cords of cream-colored leather that wrap into her hair. I wish I could see her Chaos-scarred eyes. And I think of her original goggles, the ones I took from her in Lastrium and put into a lacquered box in my rooms with the rest of my favored pieces of personal hoard. Like a prize, or a special treasure.

When she reaches me, I turn my head, and her lips fall open. I don't quite startle her—but she hadn't realized it was me. "Talon," she says, turning any fluster into something more spitting.

I nod to her and with a flick of my eyes dismiss the two Teeth escorting her. They go, and I say, "We should spar."

She laughs at me. It's mean and pretty. "Right now?"

Clenching my jaw, I shake my head. "You have wanted to work out with the army. I'll allow it, but only if I'm there. Tomorrow. Or any day you're available. I don't know what Caspian's made your schedule into, but we'll be leaving in a few days."

Darling leans on one hip, eyeing me. "Well. I suppose that's as good a deal as I'll get."

"It is."

"Then, War Prince." She bares her bright teeth in a grin. "I look forward to it."

Something about her bearing and expression reminds me of her strange eyes falling to my lips in the Phoenix Hall, and before either of us can do anything ridiculous, I choose another strategic retreat.

11

DARLING

Despite Talon's offer to spar, one I'm looking forward to a bit too much, I have more pressing matters to attend to. Because there are even more dress fittings than before, a revelation that almost sends me into a spiral of despair.

It turns out that none of the dresses I've already been measured for and sewn into are appropriate for Caspian's grand tour, so I am once more put through the paces of the court seamstress and her army of assistants. The morning after the gala, before I have even done my morning exercises or broken my fast, Lady Fringues and her people are at my door, ready to work. She barks orders at them like a general, and when I make the mistake of sighing as I am refitted for yet another dinner gown—honestly, six seems like plenty—one of the assistants snaps at me.

"You should be honored. Lady Fringues is one of the few House Cockatrice tailors left on the continent. Her services are highly valued and respected. She had to cancel several appointments with well-respected scions to fit you in," he says while pinning a dress on me.

I give him a long stare. I still don't believe I'm the scion of House Sphinx, but I doubt any other noble would let him speak in such a way. And appearances are important. Once he wilts a bit, I finally respond. "If she would sew me a pair of pants, I would deeply appreciate that. But these dresses are frankly not to my taste. So I will tolerate this as I see fit," I say. Lady Fringues overhears me. She appears at my elbow, color high in her pale cheeks and anger snapping in her black eyes. Her straight black hair is twisted up in a complicated bun on the back of her head.

"You dislike my designs?" she says, her voice low. The room goes quiet as an ancient tomb, and I can't help but sigh again.

"The designs are lovely. As are the colors. It's just that . . . I'm a soldier. A fighter. I can't kick in this," I say, demonstrating how the skirt gets wrapped around my leg when I lift it. "I can barely move. If I can't fight, no matter how pretty the dress, I'm not going to love it."

A murmur goes up in the room, and the lady raises her hand sharply for silence, which she gets. "This is interesting. Hmmm. Yes, I see the problem now."

She retreats to pull a large drawing tablet from one of the numerous cases, waving over a few of her assistants. She begins to sketch, and as she does, they all murmur in low voices. There are a few glances in my direction, and I realize that she actually listened when she returns and shows me sketches that give me a measure of hope.

"I wish you had raised this issue earlier," she says when I grin at the new designs, "but we can adapt. We'll take the measurements we have and return before you leave with dresses that accommodate your needs."

They depart, and I figure that I am about to have the rest of the day to myself. But there is no time for me over the next couple of days. There are, instead, numerous lessons on decorum, the histories of the various Houses, and fittings for shoes. I even have to pick the drakes that will be pulling my carriage, because apparently

I will have an entire carriage to myself, and it is vitally important that I pick the color scheme.

I hate every single, vapid moment of the exercise. It is only the reminder that I hold the fate of House Kraken in my hands that has me playing along with the farce. Even learning the history of House Sphinx makes me feel a deep sense of unease. I'm a Kraken, but there is something vaguely familiar about the stories of dust storms and seasonal rains. Are they long-buried memories or just a deep longing to understand who my family was?

But as quickly as the emotion wells, I push it away, focusing instead on my goal: Leonetti's freedom. All of this is pointless without that. Despite Caspian's promises I am beginning to worry that I am being played for a fool, and even though Caspian rejects my requests for an audience, I have to believe that he means what he says. What does he have to gain, otherwise?

By the morning of the day before we are supposed to depart I am sick of travel and sick of House politics, and we have not even left Phoenix Crest. I am meeting one last time with Lady Fringues and her team. The changes she's made to the designs are brilliant. There are now cleverly hidden slits in the skirts that allow me to kick, as well as weights in the hem that draw the material away from my legs. Some of the skirts have clever ribbons sewn in that ruffle them up to the bodice. A set of sheer leggings complete the various looks. They're still not my Barb blacks, but they are much better than they were.

I am just being fitted into what I'm told is one of several traveling dresses when the door opens, admitting a flurry of Dragon guards. Before I can object, a woman dressed in shades of green and gold, House Dragon colors, sweeps in.

"Lady Fringues! Oh, what a simply stunning design," she says, walking around me as though I am a dressing dummy and not a person. "I must have something similar designed for me when the Prince Regent is no longer making demands upon your time," she says, taking in the sheer halter neck and fitted bodice.

"Can I help you?" I say, my tone polite. Bland. I can tell a setup when I see one, and this woman is a bear trap waiting for an unwary step. I don't know who she is, but there is something about her face that reminds me ever so slightly of Talon and Caspian.

"Oh, you've met so many people in the past several days," she says, her trill of laughter as false as her lashes. "I'm sure I can't blame you for not recalling."

That reminds me: Caspian did indeed introduce us at the gala. Dismissively. "Oh. You're the aunt."

There's a subtle shift in her expression, no more than a tic, but I can see that the simple comment annoys her somehow. "Yes. I am much more than that, though. I am Lady Aurora, the Dragon Seer."

Ahh. That explains the necklace she wears: a dragon's talon clutching a large, clear diamond. Probably some Chaos-forsaken seal of her office.

When I don't answer, she repeats the phrase slower and a bit more loudly, as though I am simple. "The Dragon Seer?"

It raises my hackles instantly.

I am not stupid. Even though I grew up in the sewers of Nakumba, I know how House politics work. Not because of some long-buried memory of House Sphinx, but because I spent so much time with Adelaide and House Kraken. The House might not have had galas and tailors on call, but there were still minor nobles and their partners scrabbling for favor and concessions. I have seen firsthand how a friendly overture can turn as sharp as a throwing blade, and I am not about to play this woman's game.

But I will have some fun.

"How does it work?" I say, waving the assistant back over so she can finish her adjustments. She gives Aurora a wary look, cementing my suspicions. Never trust someone the servants fear. There is a great deal to be learned about a person by the way they treat those they see as lower than them, and the fear from the tailor at my waist is noticeable.

Aurora gives me a sly smile. "Oh, it's like any other boon. It comes when it wishes, and I am changed after each vision."

"Did you have a vision of me?" I ask, my voice sweet. One of the benefits of my smoked lenses is that they hide my eyes, which makes it all that much easier to lie. There is much the eyes give away, and not having to worry about that tell is its own boon.

Aurora seems surprised. "Why would you think that?" she says.

"Well, the way you burst into my rooms made me think it was something important." I turn back toward the soldiers loitering uncomfortably in the doorway. "Or do your troops make a habit of storming into the rooms of House scions when they are dressing?"

Aurora makes a shooing motion, and the guards leave. "I do apologize. Caspian asked me to keep you company these past few days during your fittings, to ensure that you were well cared for, but I was quite busy."

"Ah. Well, luckily I have been dressing myself for seventeen years."

"How is the fit, my quill?" the tailor says.

"Brilliant," I say, and we retreat behind the screen so that I can be stitched into yet another concoction. Only there are no more, and while I slip into a set of trousers and a loose top, Lady Fringues and her army retreat to make the necessary adjustments.

I do not miss the wide berth she and all her assistants give Aurora.

"Well, it looks as though I have been completely attired," I say with a smile. "Please do not let me distract you from your normal duties."

"Nonsense! You will soon be on the council. We should become acquainted."

And there it is, with a minimum of trawling. I gesture to one of my maids, a woman with brown hair and tan skin who I am rather certain is a soldier Talon assigned to spy on me, and she approaches. I could have sent one of the others, but I quite enjoy sending the spy on errands, a fact I am sure she has noted by the way her lips press into a thin line before she curtsies.

"Please bring us a pot of strong tea and maybe some of those little sandwiches we had yesterday if there are any left." When she's gone, I turn to Aurora.

"I'm not sure what you want from me, but I am in no position to start political maneuvering. You don't have to worry that I'll turn on Caspian, as he truly has a very good grip on my strings," I say, blunt and to the point. "If you're trying to build a cabal or what have you, I am next to worthless."

She laughs as I walk to the sitting room and take the chair I like, the one that puts me in a position to see all the possible entrances and exits. She takes the chair on the other side of the small table with a bit of skirt ruffling and resettling.

"Your performance the other night at the gala was quite impressive. You are quite the talk of Phoenix Crest," she says.

"I could have shown up and disappeared into the wallpaper, and people would be wagging their tongues," I say. "That doesn't explain why you are here."

The maid/spy returns with the tea and little sandwiches cut into the outline of a feather, probably a nod to the House of Sphinx. It's silly. It isn't as if it will make the already delicious food taste any better.

I pour a cup of tea and hand it to Aurora, and there's a moment of surprise before she reaches out to take it, like she didn't expect me to have basic table manners. As though I haven't spent the past couple of weeks being drilled by the protocol tutor Caspian sent over.

"I suppose I was curious," Aurora says, staring at the tea a moment before taking an exploratory sip, the column of her pale throat revealed as she does so. That's when I see it. Anyone else would think it was a mole, perhaps a bit of errant cosmetics. But the tiny droplets in the hollow spot where Aurora's throat and ear meet are definitely blood.

No one ever warned me how messy killing was, but there is a reason Barbs wear black. Killing, even a quick knife across an unwitting victim's throat, is dirty business. The blood gets everywhere, and there have been too many occasions when Leonetti would chide us to take time to clean ourselves up after a mission.

Don't come to dinner bloody! It's coarse. We may be soldiers now, but we will not always be tied to this life, and we cannot forget ourselves, he would say, and anyone fool enough to ignore his warning would get a cuff upon the ear and then a lecture about manners and representing House Kraken.

Sudden tears threaten at the memory, and so I busy myself pouring my own cup of tea.

I say nothing for a long uncomfortable moment, pretending to sip my tea the way Aurora does. I don't drink, though. I am starting to have a bad feeling about this meeting, and while my boon can heal, I don't know if it will keep me safe from poison. Miranda and I were never brave enough to take the chance and try it out.

Despite the jangling of my nerves, I pretend to be nothing more than a bored scion, not rising to the bait she has let dangle. I don't care about politics, but a woman who proclaims herself a seer and then finds her way to getting blood upon her person is dangerous indeed.

"Aren't you curious about me?" Aurora finally says, and for a moment I worry that she's read my mind.

"Only to wonder if you'll be accompanying us on this grand tour," I say, picking up a sandwich and setting it down before biting into it, as though I find it distasteful. How many poisons can be absorbed through the skin? Too many. Is this an assassination attempt, or has my time at court made me paranoid? There's nothing about the woman to make me think she is going to try to kill me, with the exception of the blood, but I touch the hair sticks that are currently holding the mass of my curls in a complicated updo anyway. I have no weapons. The throwing knives were very quickly taken from me after the gala. But I know a dozen ways to disarm an attacker, and a hair stick to the eye would be a painful way to go if it came down to it.

If she has poisoned me, I doubt I will get the chance.

"Oh, I'm afraid I cannot. I have my duties to attend to. Speaking of which"—she sets down the teacup and gives me a bland smile—"I must return to them. Thank you so much for indulging me, and I will see you at the end of your tour when your title is reinstated."

"Thank you for the company," I say, even though we both know that I don't mean it. She leaves, and as soon as she is gone, I put my cup back on the tea tray and explode out of the chair.

The maid, who I am now certain is really a soldier playing at being a servant, hurries into the room. "My quill, is something amiss?"

"What's your name again? Your real name?" I say.

She opens her mouth and then sighs. "Marjorie. Was I that obvious?"

"Most of the servants here walk like they don't want to be noticed. You walk like a soldier." I point to the serving tray. "Have that taken away. And make sure no one touches anything."

She glances at the food. "It's safe. I checked it myself."

Just what kind of orders did Talon give her? The idea that he could've sent someone to keep me safe makes me feel odd, and I dislike the sensation immediately. "That was before the Dragon Seer came to visit." It may seem silly to be so paranoid, but I have a sister who can poison with a touch. Who knows if this Dragon Seer has some treacherous boon of her own?

Luckily Marjorie doesn't make excuses or tell me I am being silly. Instead she puts on leather gloves and removes the tray, stopping in the doorway. "The protocol tutor will be by at the top of the hour. Would you like something before they arrive?"

"No," I say. I'm too anxious to eat. Instead I walk out to my private garden and pace, trying to let the singing fountains and fragrant flowers of a land I barely remember soothe my nerves. I do not like the Dragon Seer, but I cannot figure out why beyond those few splatters of blood. What is it about the woman that is so distasteful, more so than the other minor nobles who bow and scrape and social climb?

And just what kind of game has Caspian roped me into?

12

TALON

I'm not hiding in the drake stable. Cleaning my primary mount's tack and combing her crest feathers is a necessary part of my job. It needs to be my hands oiling her dry spots and my smell pressed into the harness, to firm up our bond. These war drakes are dangerous even when they trust their partner, but if I let others do this work, she might follow the wrong command or decide I don't belong to her at the worst possible moment.

It is convenient, though, that I need to be here for several hours a day before we depart on Caspian's grand tour. Nearly everyone on the council wants a piece of my time this afternoon to exert some kind of control over the proceedings, despite the fact that everything is already arranged. I'm not making last-minute changes to satisfy the rivalry between the ministers of prosperity and the hoard, or adding more time to our stay at House Barghest because Mia Brynsdottir pouts at me over tea for an hour. Fortunately, none of them will follow me into the nest of war drakes. Only General Bloodscale might do so, and he indicated a desire to once again argue that House Dragon declaring the war over did nothing to assure House Kraken would stop fighting—as if I don't know that. We need to follow through by putting down our arms, though, or why should they believe this is real? We've had this argument several times this week, and I won't do it again. At least Bloodscale won't interrupt me here, because he knows better than most that I need to take care of my primary mount like this.

After a couple of hours I've gone over the harnesses and saddle, checking the buckles and new decorative filigree, and put it all on her to make sure it sits tight enough not to chafe and she doesn't hate any of it. Then I take it all off and pack it neatly, and turn my attention to rubbing down her scales and combing the feathers with a fine pick. I file her claws and buff them, especially the large hooking claws on her rear legs. She leans her hips against my shoulder while I'm down there, teasing, and curves her strong neck to bury her muzzle in my hair as if she can groom me in return. The huff of her blood-sour breath down my spine makes the stall seem even hotter, so I remove my uniform jacket and roll up the shirtsleeves. The final part of tending to her is polishing and oiling her scales. I tie on a short apron and get the jar of thick salve. Though she's used this oil all her life, I first dip my fingers in and hold them before her muzzle.

She plants her nose in my palm, snuffling, and dips her head to smear the long line of her jaw through the oil on my fingers. Acceptance.

"Good girl," I murmur. "If I have time once we finish this, I'll dig some of those old flattened copper coins you like so much out of my hoard and tie them under your neck tomorrow. And I have salt fish." Though war drakes don't know language, they can learn a few words here or there, and mine recognizes how I say "good girl" and "salt fish" for sure. She stomps her left rear leg on the stone floor, scraping through the remnants of sawdust.

The scale oil smells earthy and cold, like moss-slick stones after rain up in the mountains of House Dragon's ancient territory. I get to work, rubbing under her jaw and down the muscles of her strong neck. Her scales are warm and smooth, gently pebbled until they get longer near her breast and down her back. I take time with her dry elbows and between her stubby fingers. She chitters at me when I find ticklish spots at the end of her stubby, thick tail—it's more for balance when she really runs than anything else. The feathers there aren't as shimmering as the green and black spinal-crest feathers or the tiny feathers around her emerald eyes. These are fluffier, and their tips curl almost grayish. There's a spot on her right rear, just over the jut of her hip, where some of the scales have rubbed off. She must have done it herself, itching something. I don't let the oil get on the exposed dermis. I'll have to grab a patch before I leave and check it again when I dress her in the parade tack tomorrow morning.

The war drake has been shifting her weight, restless, as I finish, and I make my way back to her head. I put away the salve and wipe my hands on the apron. "Salt fish?"

She dances a little in place and snaps her jaw lightly. It makes a clicking sound almost like laughter.

I step out of the stall and unlatch the metal bucket nailed to the wall between this stall and the next. It's half-filled with little dried fish. I grab a handful and go back to my primary mount. "Good girl," I say, and hold out my cupped hands. She immediately dives in, her thin tongue lapping up the little fish. Though most drakes of other sorts are more omnivorous, the war drakes are true carnivores, and the only food they get is meat—raw in stables, preserved on the road. They don't usually bother with fish, so these little snacks are an excellent treat.

As she finishes, she keeps licking at my palm. I laugh, letting her curl that tongue around my thumb while I use my other hand to gently scratch under her big green eye. Her feathered lashes lower, and she heaves a sigh. "You can rest now, gorgeous," I say. "After tonight you'll be on guard for weeks, so be sure to relax."

"Chaos, I can't—"

My drake and I both startle at the voice. One of the drake's fangs nicks the heel of my thumb as she snaps her jaws closed and shifts her entire body to face the stall opening. She flares her crest feathers and taps her clawed feet aggressively on the stone floor.

"There, it's all right, it's all right," I say firmly. I put my hand at the base of her neck, where it meets her right shoulder, and pat firmly three times. That's one of their training signals for *all's well*.

Darling, standing in the open door of the stall, is silent and still. Which is good.

"Give me a moment," I say to her, turning my focus back onto the drake. I glare into her nearest eye and stand as tall as I can.

"I can go," Darling begins.

"No, don't leave; the drake might want to chase."

"Chaos," Darling says again, quietly.

I rub my hand up my mount's neck, stroking back and forth. "Darling, that bucket next to you has some dried fish in it. Can you grab some and slowly hold it out to me?"

Instead of an answer, I hear the creak of the metal and a shuffle of little fish. Then Darling says, "Here."

Glancing over my shoulder, I see her outstretched hand. I hold mine out, and she tips a few fish into my palm. I bring them to the drake's muzzle again, and her crest feathers finally relax. She licks up the little fish enthusiastically, and I continue patting her.

"Good girl," I murmur. Then I scratch under her eye again. "Get your rest."

As I join Darling at the door, I say, "Let me take your elbow."

Darling juts out her chin but doesn't protest. I cup her elbow and turn her around to leave together. Hopefully my drake will accept this suggestion that Darling is mine, too, so they don't have to be enemies.

We walk down the stone corridor. War drakes peer out from their stalls at us, a few of them being tended by other Teeth or one of the shared handlers. I take a deep breath of the musty smell of scales and char before we reach the sunny exit. Immediately I release Darling. "That was stupid," I snap, regretting it even while I'm saying it. But now that we're outside I can finally react, and, well, I'm having a lot of feelings. Irritation, anger, relief, surprise. A complicated appreciation for how Darling reacted to the war drake's aggression and the ease with which she did what I said. But anger is the most comfortable when it comes to Darling.

"You're the ones pretending monsters can be tamed and kept in pretty little boxes!" She glares at me. "Besides, your apron is stupid."

I raise my eyebrows, incredulous.

Darling raises hers back, mocking. Her goggles are plainer than most that my brother has provided, just spheres of dark glass that reflect the sun behind me like furious white pupils.

We stare in silence for a moment. A few Dragons watch from around the drake yard. We use this arena for training and exercising the war drakes, and the dirt-packed ground is bare of everything and ringed by metal posts. Finally, I reach behind my waist to untie the apron. I ball it up in one hand. "Did you . . . what do you want?"

Darling puffs a big sigh. Her hands are on her hips. She's dressed not dissimilarly from me in trousers and a loose shirt. It suits her.

Chaos teeth, I left my jacket in my mount's stall.

"I need to hit something," Darling says.

"And you thought of me."

"Naturally." She smirks. But then she adds, "You did promise me a spar."

I take a breath. "I did."

"Well?"

It's a much better prospect than returning inside to face meetings and arguments and being waylaid by the council. I have at least a couple of hours before I promised to dine with Aunt Aurora. Besides, I want to test myself against her again, especially since we danced. I nod. "Yes. This way."

I lead Darling away from the war drake yard toward the Dragon's Teeth barracks. It's near the base of the fortress territory, the barracks and offices cut into some caves, and a practice ground that's multilevel and includes several types of sparring fields. We climb down to the lowest, which is unoccupied at the moment. A few Teeth glance at me as we pass, but I wave them off. They'll have to at least pretend not to watch this.

Darling studies everything like she's planning an invasion. Which . . . well. Her suspicion and distaste for Teeth accoutrement certainly are earned. At the edge of the lower sparring field is a shed. I throw the doors open to reveal all manner of practice equipment: weighted wooden swords, blunt daggers, shields, body armor, a few spears, even, though we tend only to use those with the drake cavalry, which is a specialization apart from the Teeth. "Challenger's choice," I say to her.

"Knives," she says immediately. And she winks at me as she shoves past to grab a pair of blunt daggers not even as long as her forearm. She tosses both to me, and I manage to catch them. Darling takes two more, and we head for the center of the field.

The sun passes behind a cloud, and I glance up. The clouds are moving quickly, so we'll have changing light. I settle my feet and wait as Darling scrapes her own boots against the beaten dirt. It's furrowed from battle, and we leave it rough here for optimal practice. Sparring in the rain and mud is one of my Teeth's favored ways to pass time. Afterward there's fire, beer, and close quarters in the cave barracks as we all dry off and retell the best moments to each other.

"What rule?" Darling asks. "I chose the weapons. You lay the bounds."

I smile tightly. "No blood."

She scoffs.

"Caspian would make both our lives miserable if I put marks on your face before this tour."

"Oh, I think your face is the one in danger," she answers with an easy grin.

"It is an awfully pretty one," I agree.

She snorts, but it sounds like suppressed laughter.

Oh, this is fun. Channeling my aggression and frustration into this kind of spar, into banter. Before it can turn too close to flirting, I say, "No blood, and reset after a hit. Four hits is the winner. Or total disarming. Or yield."

"You wish," she says, bouncing on the balls of her feet.

"I won last time, remember."

"You cheated."

"I used all the weapons in my arsenal. Including Finn."

"I bet I can beat you before you get two hits," she says.

"There's nothing I could win from you that I need."

Darling narrows her eyes. "How about answers?"

I stop, shifting my grip on the blunt daggers.

She presses. "Instead of a wager, how about this? I hit you, you give me an answer. You hit me, I give you one."

Slowly, I nod. "Sounds good."

Without even agreeing, Darling flings herself at me. She's fast, I remember that, but her darkness advantage is gone here. I dodge and turn, moving one of my knives into a reverse grip, and slash down.

Darling spins and goes low. I back off, and she follows me, moving almost too fast for me to keep track of both her weapons. I focus on her body language, on defense. I need to keep her from winning too fast. Knives are not my specialty.

There's no sound but the scuff of our boots and our breathing, getting faster and harder. My hair flops in my face, and I wish for my helmet or oil to slick it back. Darling takes advantage, feinting in an identical way twice, and then a third time I think I'm ready for her to change it up in a trick, but she does the exact same thing and just barely gets a hit on my forearm.

I grunt and back off. She does, too. I wait. Darling studies me, I assume; her big round goggles are trained on me. "Where's Leonetti?"

"Prison convoy."

"On the move!" She looks appalled.

It is pretty sneaky, but instead of admitting that out loud, I attack.

I drive her back, and Darling turns quick, lashing out several times in a pattern that I can barely track. If not for my boon, I probably couldn't at all. I see the end point and block her. She's clearly surprised, and I manage to jab the butt of my left dagger against her hip.

We back off.

"Do you remember your real father?"

"Leonetti is—"

"Your birth father," I quickly say.

"Maybe." Darling opens her mouth, then closes it. She tilts her face down. I want to see her eyes again, open and shimmered over with Chaos the way they were at the gala. "I think I do, but there's little way to be sure unless I ever meet someone else who knew him, is there?"

We move at the same time, and I can barely hold my own under the flurry of Darling's attacks. I use my boon to track her motion, and there's the pattern; I can see it like a dance—the way I told her at the gala a dance was like a battle.

Suddenly she gets another hit. With a triumphant crow, she backs away.

I lower my knives to wait.

"What reasons did your father give you for massacring House Sphinx?" She says it almost casually. That's how I know my answer matters.

I wish I had a better one. "He didn't tell me anything."

"You didn't know?"

"I knew, but it was . . ." I tap the blunt tip of the practice dagger to my thigh. "It was presented to me by others. As simple revenge. Sphinx killed my mother, so my father killed Sphinx. A natural consequence."

"Dragons," Darling hisses. She attacks again.

I defend myself. Her attack is faster, vicious. I barely stop one of her daggers from gouging out my eye, and the other ends up dug into my ribs. "Darling," I gasp.

"Who was the first person you killed?" she demands, very softly. She's so near, her dagger against my side.

I stand still, suddenly reminded of my war drake, the beautiful but very dangerous weapon I keep at my side so often. I stare into Darling's goggles. Her shoulders heave. I carefully say, "A deserter when I was fourteen. We found him because it had rained and he slipped and twisted his ankle. We hanged him where we found him."

Darling's jaw muscles tense. She swallows. "Hanged him. That isn't what I meant."

"It's my answer, though. I was in command."

"At that age?"

"What do you think a War Prince is, Darling?"

"And you want this war ended? Really? Caspian doesn't fight, he's completely ridiculous, so I understand why he thinks he wants peace. But you?" Darling drops back with a scoff. "It's all you are."

I think, *But it's not all I want to be.* I swallow it back. I can't say that to anybody, much less Darling Seabreak. Maribel Calamus. Whatever her name is.

Maybe she sees something in my eyes—they're right there for her, after all. Unoccluded. Darling's expression does something that on anyone else I might call softening.

Before it gets worse, I ask, "How old were you the first time you killed?"

Darling turns her head away, looking toward the horizon where the sun is sinking. "Fourteen," she says very quietly. Just like me.

"Do you want it over?"

"That's two questions, War Prince, and no hits!" Darling flings herself back into the fight. She disarms me almost immediately. I narrow my focus to only survival, one knife against her two. My boon can't do much more than it already is, connecting her steps and actions in a trace pattern for me. But Darling is breaking the pattern even as she weaves it. I block her again and again, never following up with an attack. Honestly, I barely could if I wanted to.

"Why aren't you trying harder?" she demands, panting.

My breathing is hard, too, and I shake my head. "I don't want to hurt you," I say lightly, trying to put a gleam in my eye.

Darling laughs once. "Oh, well, go ahead and hurt me—I dare you!" She emphasizes "dare" with an attack.

My whole focus is on her, on the fight, narrowed to this single knife and the Chaos sensation of her trace through my boon. I see her moves a split second before she makes them, which is the reason I know she's going for the throat just as she does it, in time to drop my remaining knife and grab her wrists with my hands.

"Darling!" I snap. Her wrists tense in my hands. I press back.

"Disarmed you," she cries delightedly, even as I've got her pinned. She could squirm or kick me, but her hands are mine.

Sweat cools on my brow as the evening breeze blows, and I'm grateful we didn't end up with an audience. I lower her hands, which are still clutching both practice daggers. This was good. I liked it. Hard, intense, and . . . fun. "You win."

"Damn right." The smile she flashes makes me think she had fun, too. Despite our needling. The too-raw topics we touched upon.

I let her go.

We've got to get back to the fortress proper. I'm sure whatever handlers she slipped—including Marjorie, who better have a good excuse or she'll be running laps all night—are frantic by now. And I need to bathe and get ready for dinner. "Let's do this again."

"Sure," she says, as we put our gear back into the shed. "And you should let me have a real knife. For protection."

"I don't think so." I side-eye her, and she's nearly laughing. I like how quickly she flickers back to humor. It might be how she survived everything she's been through.

Darling shrugs and speeds up, as if the worst way to return to the Crest would be at my side.

I don't mind, thinking that we've fought for real, life-and-death; we've danced; and now we've sparred against each other. I can't help but wonder what it would be like instead to fight at her side.

ALLIES

13
DARLING

The day of our departure dawns cold and drizzly despite the time of year. This high in the mountains I suppose it never gets truly hot, and the gray morning puts me in a terrible mood. I didn't sleep a wink, seeing assassins and plots everywhere and remembering too fondly my sparring session with Talon. I'm not sure which has unsettled me more, the possibility that the Dragon Seer wants me dead or the pleasure I got from the War Prince's company. Both are sand in my underthings: annoying and keeping me preoccupied.

I want my knives and my old smoked goggles and a two-hour head start. Then those blasted Dragons would see what I was made for, not politics and lies, but straightforward combat. I dislike court life, and I am ready to be quit of Phoenix Crest and whatever these Dragons might be plotting.

That is when I see the carriages.

They are ridiculous things, gleaming and frivolous. They look to be new, and if not new then very recently painted. There are jewels set into the wood, the wheels shimmer as if dipped in gold, and the herd drakes that stomp in agitation, ready to be on their way, wear bridles of tooled leather and feathered plumes.

My heart squeezes at the sight of it, along with the numerous trunks being loaded onto each one. There are six carriages, not to mention the handful of wagons that will follow, carrying all of our clothes, cases of wine and ale, and the many provisions needed to feed the soldiers that will accompany us. And there are a lot of soldiers. Despite Caspian's announcement that the war is finished, the country remains unsettled, and travel is not entirely safe. I am not surprised. There are still more reasons to hate the Dragons than embrace them, and I have to constantly remind myself that I am little better than a pampered prisoner, in spite of the luxury I enjoy.

I spot my fake handmaid Marjorie wearing a Dragon soldier's uniform, and we give each other a nod of respect. The next time we meet it might be to kill one another, but now is not that moment.

"Oh, look at this magnificence!" someone says, and I turn to find Caspian towering over me. He frowns down at me. "Have you shrunk since the last time we saw each other?"

"Perhaps I am just weighed down by the excess I have had to endure," I say, my temper getting the better of me. "You do realize that half of Pyrlanum is starving?"

"Only those who wouldn't swear their fealty to the Dragons," he says without missing a beat. "Dragons are very kind to their friends."

"Those are people who had lives until the Dragons came and burned them to the ground," I say. "And being friendly with a Dragon does not protect one from famine or disease. This trip is a waste of resources that should be given to the people," I say. I'm angry. After weeks of dancing to Caspian's tune I've reached my limit. It's been nearly a week since I told Gavin that Caspian knows the locations of all our safe houses, and finding out that they're keeping Leonetti on the move makes me wonder if I've been a fool to trust Caspian in the first place.

Hopefully the Barbs have been able to go to ground since I gave

Gavin the information. Because I can no longer pretend to be a willing participant in this game.

Caspian pauses, as though seeing me for the first time. "You care about the poor, do you?"

"Some of the families with the least are the most generous in this country," I say, the memory of the people I've met and my anger giving me courage. "Which you would know if you'd ever left your tower here. This court exists on the backs of the poor. The soldiers for your armies, the farmers who work the fields, even the poor servants who cart your precious wine around," I say. "Those are the folks who will suffer when winter comes and there are no grain stores."

"And what would you do if you were in my position?" Caspian asks. It's not the question I'm expecting, but I answer it anyway, even though I know I should keep my mouth shut and my opinions to myself. He is, after all, the Prince Regent.

"I would give everyone a voice," I say. "I would let the commoners elect a council to voice their concerns, as it is done in House Kraken." As the House regent, Leonetti had the final word, but his advisors came from every walk of life. He had a council of shipbuilders and one of sailors and even warehouse people he would meet with regularly so that he could address their concerns, and that wasn't even his war council. Leonetti always said it was important to hear everyone's voice as long as they were being honest and genuine. *And even the liars are useful, because you get an idea of what they think to be important,* he would say, laughing.

"A council of commoners," Caspian says. "Fascinating. You simply must ride the first leg of the trip with me and tell me more about this idea of yours."

"I'd rather not," I say, gesturing toward the carriage with the resplendent Sphinx on the front. My beautiful cage for the next few weeks.

"Nonsense," Caspian says. I'm about to argue when I get a glimpse of a blond head dressed in House Sphinx livery bustling around the carriage. It's too bright for me to be able to tell if it is Gavin or some other footman, but a sudden knot of dread sits heavy in my middle. I'm not wearing the Kiss of Death at the moment and for very good reasons. I don't want to accidentally bump my lips against some unsuspecting victim, but the real reason is because poison seems so . . . cowardly. I still want Talon and Caspian dead—Chaos knows I have reasons aplenty—but I would rather do it my way.

After sparring with Talon, I know I at least owe him a proper death, a soldier's death. When I kill him, it will be with a blade, not lip tint.

And I do not have the courage to say that to Gavin just now. I keep remembering how he looked at me like I'd turned traitor, even saying he'd suspected as much, and my blood chills. How will he react to knowing that Leonetti is being kept on the move?

Not well, and that is a chat I will avoid as long as possible.

"Oh. Let us depart before the storm takes hold," Caspian says loud enough that the servants surrounding us snap to attention, but his gaze isn't on them. It's on Talon, who strides toward us through the courtyard. For the first time he wears something besides the bloodred of the Dragon's Teeth, a sedate black jacket with matching trousers and riding boots. The ensemble is probably pricier than it looks.

And he makes the clothing look very, very good.

Caspian links his arm through mine and drags me to his carriage. It seems as though we are both happy to avoid uncomfortable conversations this morning.

The footman, who has to run to get ahead of Caspian and me, throws open the door to Caspian's carriage, startling a brown-skinned man with a riot of curls who appears to be not much older than me.

"Cas . . . ?" he begins, but the Prince Regent makes a shushing motion that halts whatever he was about to say.

"Elias, you'll have to ride elsewhere. I want to be alone with Darling." Caspian doesn't seem to notice the man's crestfallen expression as he goes, instead turning to the nearby footman. "Sparkling wine, please. The good one."

"Who is he?" I say, watching him go.

"*They* are Elias Chronicum, my personal physician. But I have no use of them right now. We are going to discuss politics! In you go."

My face heats at jumping to conclusions, and I start to stammer out an apology when Caspian makes the same shushing motion at me. It's startlingly effective, and I fall silent.

"All of these apologies are tedious. You made an assumption, and you will do better next time. Let us be on our way before Talon tells me once more how this is a terrible idea."

Talon has halted in his progress toward us, and he looks puzzled as I climb into the carriage. I've barely settled into the plush cushions opposite Caspian when a flute of fizzy wine is pressed into my hand.

"Before we can discuss things like the proper way to rule, we must drink," he says. He clinks his glass against mine and drains it, just as the carriage sets off with a jolt.

I watch the long column of his throat work as he drinks, and a feeling somewhere between embarrassment and fear comes over me. He is a beautiful man. But that isn't it. It's more that he wears his power like an old sweater, casually and without thought. Leonetti wore his power like an iron collar, a responsibility that weighed him down. Has Caspian ever paid half as much mind to his people as he does his clothing?

Today he wears a knee-length brocade coat over a matching vest, each embroidered with an explosion of flowers. It's a scion's ransom of clothing, and he wears it with the same carelessness as the dressing robe that draped him at our first meeting. "How much do you spend in a year on clothing?" I ask.

He refills his glass and gives me an arch look. "More than you would like. But! I am happy to satisfy that curiosity, little cat. Here, drink. You'll like it."

I tilt the glass back and swallow it quickly just as he did, and immediately cough as the bubbles go straight to my brain.

"Oh my," I say.

"Strong?" he says, offering to refill my glass.

"Sweet," I say, holding out the flute for more. I've never been much for strong drink, but I may have to reassess that. The Krakens drink a fermented seaweed liquor known as seafire, which is terrible and way more powerful than this. But this fizzy wine is delightful. I enjoy the way the bubbles tickle my nose a bit.

The time in the carriage with Caspian passes too quickly. We finish the bottle and Caspian opens another. My body loosens from the alcohol, and I find myself relaxing for the first time in weeks. I should be putting on the Kiss of Death and looking for an opportunity to kiss Caspian, but I'm honestly enjoying my time with him too much. He's smart and deflects my prying questions with a charm that is infectious, so that our conversation is a delightful sparring match. I feel too comfortable with him, like we are indeed old friends and not uneasy accomplices in whatever game he plays.

It's the most fun I've had in a very, very long time.

Only . . . I am very sure I have had entirely too much fizzy wine.

By the time I have the realization, the carriage is slowing. "Oh, are we here already?" I say, reaching for the curtains and finding that the simple act is a momentous undertaking. "Ahh, Caspian, you have gotten me drunk!"

"Impossible," he says, but his eyes shine a bit too much. "We've only had a single bottle."

"Liar!" I say, pointing to the empty bottle tucked in a corner. "Oh no, this is bad." I rarely let myself lose my composure, and here I am completely zozzled with the Prince Regent. Who I should be trying to kill. "Gavin is going to be so mad."

"Who is Gavin?" Caspian asks, and I clap my hand over my mouth.

"None of your business," I say, but Caspian is now locked on me, his gaze strangely intense.

"Is that your betrothed?" he asks, and I shake my head.

"Of course not."

"Good," he says. All of the mirth has drained from him, and he moves closer to me. "I dislike competition."

"What?" I say, and several things happen at once.

The carriage slides to a stop, and as it does I slither to the floor just as Caspian leans in to kiss me. I'm not sure what he's up to; there's something calculated in his gaze that makes me think he planned this, getting me alone and into my cups so that he could press the advantage. It's deeply unlike him, and my admiration slips a bit.

"What are you doing down there?" he says, looking at where I lie.

"You were trying to kiss me!" I say, not moving.

"Yes, I was. Do you find the thought repulsive?" he says, tone mild. "If you do, I shall cease at once."

"No! But you shouldn't be kissing me. I want you dead."

"Ahh. Well, you would not be the first lover I've had who has felt that way."

There's sadness in his expression, although I'm gazing up at him at such an angle that it could be my imagination. I sigh. "Fine, then." I reach for his fancy vest and pull him on top of me. He's not expecting it, and he yelps as he falls onto me. I plant a kiss on his lips.

"That is not a real kiss," Caspian says, recovering quickly and levering himself up on elbows planted on either side of me. "That is how one kisses their granny."

"I don't have a granny," I say. Too honest. I blame the thrice-cursed fizzy wine.

Caspian's expression melts. "I know, and I'm sorry for that. I'm trying to fix it."

Our faces are only inches from each other, and when he lowers his lips to mine, it is nothing like kissing a relative. It's a nice kiss, but nothing more than that. His lips are soft and full, and his hands tangle in my hair, purposely loosening hairpins.

"Wha—" I begin, but then the door flies open, sunlight slicing across the smoked lenses of my glasses. It's too bright, and I can't quite make out the figure standing there. Behind the glass my eyes adjust slowly as I hear Caspian say, "Give us a moment, would you."

Talon's accusing look is the last thing I see before he slams the carriage door shut.

14

TALON

The beginning of Caspian's grand tour is even worse than I anticipated.

Usually traveling is one of the only good parts of my job because I can be a soldier first. Focused, in charge, with people who share my motives and simple needs. But the third time I brought up security plans for the road to House Gryphon, Caspian threw a fit that deteriorated into a furious argument and ended with his absolutely forbidding me to participate in the tour as his general and commander of the Dragon's Teeth. He insisted I would prioritize the *prince* part of the *adorable title bestowed upon you by the common folk* and threw several items of his clothing at me. *Dress like a first scion, baby brother.*

I own exactly two jackets that aren't uniforms: a vivid emerald-green velvet and a very plain black jacquard. I hope my brother likes me in black.

It's too late to change my mind by the time I mount my war drake for departure and realize her luminous scales are a green so dark they glint black even in the rain and I've ended up making a statement Caspian probably approves of.

The first day only gets worse as it drags on: drizzle and heavy skies slow the carriages, and the herd drakes smoke when they cough; pennants hang limp and sad instead of snapping prettily; servants cram into the carriages to avoid mud; even my soldiers are grumpy. If Finn had come, he'd be shooting me dark looks but teasing the soldiers around him with old stories and promises, at least keeping morale high in the army. I can't do that. I can only lead by example, chin up and no complaints. But my lack of uniform holds me apart, and I ride at the front of the parade instead of ranging among the ranks as I prefer.

Then when we stop for midday break I find Caspian and Darling apparently debauching each other.

Shock—at Darling—and fury—at Caspian—lock my mouth shut, and I stare a moment too long. I'm somehow disappointed in myself. As if I had anything to do with it! I tear away to snap commands and make sure Elias is looking after Caspian and Darling before eating my meal with the Teeth. I sleep with the Teeth, too, in a tent barely suited to a captain, much less a first scion.

The next two days only improve weather-wise. The sun and a cheerful breeze turn the harsh landscape prettier, wildflowers blossoming in pastel rainbows along the road as we parade through the low foothills leading northwest from Phoenix Crest and its lonely mountain. I don't have any trouble avoiding my brother or Darling—they seem to agree it's for the best that we give each other a wide berth. Elias remains at Caspian's side—the two of them often spend all day in the High Prince Regent's carriage. Darling refuses to ride in her opulent carriage for more than a couple of hours, but she doesn't know the first thing about riding drakes. If I were feeling charitable, I might offer to teach her, or let her ride with me. But I am not. The sergeant I assigned to Darling weeks ago—Marjorie—offers, and Darling declines, choosing instead to climb on top of her carriage.

I nearly laugh, but I manage to turn it into a huff and glare. She looks right at me; the cut glass decorating her goggle straps glitters in the sun, but the lenses are night black. Her head tips up in challenge. In that moment she looks more like a painting than a real girl.

I turn away, telling myself if she falls to her death—good.

Of course, Caspian makes a production of it when he realizes what Darling has done, turning the entire episode into a grand joke to the point of climbing onto his own carriage and dragging a disgruntled Elias with him.

I continue to ignore them all.

Deep on the third night, someone slips into my tent, and I instantly have them on the ground by the throat, blade to their jugular.

My eyes adjust quickly to the dim red light from low fires outside. The neck under my hand shifts—I smell charcoal and a sweet flower.

"Talon," rasps my brother.

I lean back into a crouch. There's barely room in here for Caspian's sprawled form, my clothes and weapons, and my sleeping pallet. The canvas roof angles down sharply toward the door flap. I'm silent as I lean over to light the charge on the small boonlamp, then slip my knife back to its place next to the head of my pallet. "What do you want, Caspian?" I whisper.

He sits, rubbing his neck, and crowds over to plop next to me. The blue glow of the boonlight catches his messy long curls, the line of his collarbone where his robe has slipped, a sheen of sweat on his forehead, and the depth of his dilated pupils.

There's a smear of darkness under his left eye.

Caspian stares through me as I study him. Impatiently I rub at the mark on his cheek. It smears like soot. "Have you been painting?"

"Sketching," he murmurs, face twisting in disgust. "Painting is better."

I settle myself, try to relax into a less threatening posture. He's drunk or high or in the grip of his boon madness. Why else would he seek me out? But gently I ask, "Why?"

"Oh," he giggles, listing forward. I catch his shoulder and he looks at it, startled, but then pats my hand. "Did you know you can paint over paint? A whole picture, just let it dry and paint over it—with the right kind of paint, of course, and sometimes you have to sand it down or the—the texture will be apparent. But if you do it right you can just paint it over. Hide the original. It's still there, a ghost!" Caspian gasps a laugh. "Maybe somebody could carefully excavate it, but otherwise only the person who painted over it will remember, and as time goes on, even that person forgets everything but what was new-painted. Maybe even forgets there was an original painting in the first place. Is it even still there if nobody remembers it? If nobody knows it could be excavated? Isn't that a neat trick?"

"Yeah," I say, gripping his shoulder.

"Do you remember when Mother died?"

My mouth goes dry. I'm quiet long enough, Caspian leans in, nudging at my hand with his shoulder.

"Ah, no," I whisper. "I remember the time, but not . . . the day. Not what happened." Shame closes my throat. I should remember. She was my mother.

"It's all right; I'm—I'm glad you don't," Caspian says. He pats my hand again. "It was awful. And Father hated—well. Father was furious."

"He went to war."

"Against the Sphinx for supposedly poisoning her right there in her own garden!" He says it like it's funny. Lighthearted punchline to a very cheerful joke.

"Supposedly?" I demand.

"Oh, you know, evidence was found—it was all very aboveboard. They were angry, you see, for Father marrying a lady from House Cockatrice. Not their Sphinx daughter, whom he'd *supposedly* been courting before Mother."

"Not a good reason for war."

"Oh, Talon." Caspian laughs loud enough someone outside will hear. "Is there ever a good reason for war?"

I grind my teeth and say nothing.

"Anyway. Do you have wine?"

"Caspian, no, I don't, and if I did, I wouldn't give you any. I'm going to take you back to your carriage."

"No, let me stay here."

"Sleep here?" I say incredulously.

"Just . . ." He leans back, half on the pallet. "Just for a moment." His eyes close.

I stare. His eyes dart beneath his lids, and his lips twitch as if he'll speak again. He folds his long fingers together on his stomach.

"Caspian," I ask, suddenly urgent. "What were you sketching?"

He smiles. "Darling."

Of course. That's all he paints. It hurts, though. For a variety of reasons I'm ignoring. "Are you going to marry her?"

"What!" Caspian sits up straight.

"You were just reminding me this war began again fourteen years ago because our father did *not* marry a scion of House Sphinx. Now you—you have one. And you were kissing her."

Caspian carefully puts both hands on my cheeks. His skin is cold. "Talon, dragonlet, you need to get better at hiding your emotions and thoughts while we visit all these Houses."

I allow him to hold my face. "I don't want to be better at that, Caspian. Why shouldn't people know what I think and feel? It doesn't change how good I am with a blade, or my strength. If people know me, they won't try to take what's mine thinking it would be easy."

My brother strokes his thumbs under my eyes, then lets his hands fall away. "Such a good Dragon," he whispers, almost lamenting. "I don't know if it's impossibly naive or gloriously just." Caspian falls back onto my pallet. "Either way, it could get you killed. I'd prefer you remain alive."

As familial affection goes, it's weak, but more than I've had in a long time, and my heart burns with it.

Caspian hums to himself as he curls on my pallet, drawing the thin wool blanket against his chest. I sigh, leave him with the boonlight on, and take my weapons outside. At the nearest fire I sit, falchion across my lap. As the dawn slowly approaches, I think about the First Dragon, a woman who made herself a coat of rough iron and drake scales in order to protect her family from greedy men intent on taking everything that was theirs, including their lives. She begged Chaos to help her be strong enough and was transformed into a massive dragon with iron scales. Our first empyreal.

If Caspian thinks I'm a good Dragon, I won't let that be a weakness.

We arrive at Furial, the seat of House Gryphon, after five full days of travel. Thick granite walls surround the large and lively city, and as we march up the main street, people line the way, some waving, others merely observing, intent as if they're memorizing everything to write down or tell to their grandchildren someday. At the head of the parade, I remain solemn, nodding to those who wave, but keep my eyes moving, looking for danger. Numerous soldiers behind me in the caravan will be doing the same. It's crowded but nothing more. Here there are few signs of the war that has chewed up the southern half of our island.

A roar of laughter and awe rises behind me, and I assume Caspian did something extravagant, but I do not turn. My drake dances slightly beneath me, her claws clicking the cobbled street. Her feathered crest flares, too, and I pat her neck. Her scales are sleek and warm from the afternoon sun.

The street winds slightly upward toward the northern quadrant of the city where the manor complex of the Gryphon regent rises in ancient, mismatched stories stacked like a tumble of old books and scrolls. Some stories are granite like the city wall, others dark wood, a few whitewashed and painted with lines of beautiful red calligraphy. The roofs are all flat, and the facade hosts numerous wide balconies, as if to welcome great flying creatures. I wonder if they've always been symbolic, or if the First Gryphon and his children visited hundreds of years ago. Before the front entrance a garden of evergreen and pale rock spreads in rows like the rays of a star. We ride up the central ray, toward an arc of people resplendent in red waiting to greet us.

I direct my drake to the left, and soldiers spread out in a rest formation, allowing the carriages to pull up. Their drivers place Caspian's in the middle, with Darling's to the right, and attendants dash to open doors and hand them out.

Caspian flicks his long embroidered green coat behind him and offers his hand to Darling, who wears a suit of wide layered pants and fitted bodice, with lace over her arms and trailing down her back, all in the ivory color of House Sphinx. She is beautiful in that color, in contrast with her dark skin and beribboned black curls. Only her goggles distract, these an elaborate mask of creamy-looking white leather that flares around her eyes and temples like wings. It's part of her hair styling, too.

She must hate it.

But she takes Caspian's hand and allows him to escort her toward the waiting House Gryphon. I dismount and follow just behind, knowing I mar the display of their riches and power.

Gryphon regent Vivian Chronicum smiles as we reach her. She looks exactly the same as she did the last time I met with her: a small, whip-thin woman in her twenties, with brown skin even darker than Darling's and curls cut close to her skull. A scarlet gown falls gracefully from her narrow shoulders, with an off-center belt at her hips holding keys and a small dagger.

"Welcome, Prince," she says, expression open and warm. Almost as if she likes Caspian.

Maybe she does. Two years ago she was less effusive with me.

Caspian says, "A pleasure as always, O wise and beautiful Gryphon. Let me introduce to you the equally wise and beautiful scion of your sibling House Sphinx." He draws Darling ahead of him, and Vivian reaches out both hands.

"My welcome, and the welcome of all our House, Maribel Calamus," Vivian says.

"Please, call me Darling," she murmurs, a muscle working in her jaw.

Beside me, Elias steps up, apparently unable to wait longer. "Regent," they say.

Vivian's smile broadens into a grin. "Elias! I am so thrilled to see you home."

Elias hugs their cousin, wrapping her slight frame with their larger.

While they embrace, Darling mutters, "Sibling House?"

Caspian answers her, leaning in. "Haven't you heard the origin story of the First Gryphon and Sphinx?"

"Oh, of course," Darling says harshly. She's definitely lying—or at least doesn't know the same story we do.

Before anyone can continue, Vivian pats her cousin on the cheek and turns to us. "You must be looking forward to rest. I'll have you shown to your quarters, and perhaps in two hours we can meet for dinner?"

I step up. "I will check the accommodations before the Prince Regent or Sphinx scion may settle in."

Vivian frowns. "Surely you trust our preparations, War Prince. We are more than allies with the Dragons."

I bow formally. "Trust is not the question, my sage. It is my duty, and having maintained rituals of politeness would not help me sleep should anything happen to the head of House Dragon or Sphinx." Without waiting for any answer, I turn to Arran Lightscale, who's in direct command of the squad of Teeth with us. "The library wing?" I ask Vivian Chronicum, and she nods, a little amused and a little offended. I bow once more to all the gathered regents and sweep around them into the manor house with Arran and the Teeth at my heel.

The inside of Gryphon Manor is as eclectic as the outside, with dark corridors that open into oddly shaped rooms and the occasional dead end, and staircases you must first go up a half flight before you can get down to a lower level. Thanks to practice and my boon, I'm in no danger of becoming lost and lead the Teeth toward the library—it is the grand heart of the manor, multi-floored with ladders and balconies and a warren of stacks and tucked-away reading carrels. Both times I've visited House Gryphon, my party has been put into the hall of guest rooms that curls around the south side of the library.

We split up and I remind the Teeth to do their jobs, but be respectful. I begin in the larger guest suites, clearing the one I assume will be Caspian's first. I move from the narrow balcony to the shared balcony of the neighboring suite, checking everything. I'm only just starting in the second suite when the door flies open and Darling strides in, Marjorie and an attendant assigned by Caspian's people wearing Sphinx livery behind her.

Darling halts immediately when she notices me.

"I'm not finished," I say.

"I don't care. I'm tired, and this is ridiculous."

"Is it?" I position myself right in front of her. An obstacle.

She grimaces. She's a warrior, too. But instead of letting herself agree with me, she says, "I can check my own damn room, Talon."

"Be my guest."

When Darling moves, I go with her. I follow her into the bedroom, into the corners. Not only looking for danger, but marking what Darling herself does. I can't trust her. At first she huffs softly, then glances over her shoulder at me with the distinct body language of a glare. Finally Darling whirls around and hits me in the chest. "Cut it out."

"No."

"Talon!"

My jaw clenches. "I won't let you take advantage of my brother."

"*What?*"

I don't reply, staring right at those smoky glass goggles.

"I'm not the one taking advantage in this scenario," she hisses.

"You kissed him."

"Are you jealous?" Darling demands, a little breathless and incredulous, but driving even closer to me.

It's difficult not to grab her and shove her away. I keep a stranglehold on myself. Hard and calm I say, "No. I'm warning you, Darling. I won't let my guard down, even if he does."

"You're acting like a child." Darling steps back, turns away.

I watch her stomp to the windows and throw open a drape. Light pours in around her. She doesn't flinch. We stand there, her back to me, both of us quiet, for a long moment. In the sitting room, Marjorie and the Sphinx attendant are moving around, settling things. I should just go. Leave her to finish the sweep of her suite or not. Whatever she wants.

Darling's shoulders move in a sigh. "The stories Kraken told of the First Sphinx and Gryphon empyreals didn't mention a relationship between them."

I say, "The First Gryphon and the First Sphinx were twins. They were traveling together, seeking the answer to an ancient question or looking for a long-lost book of boons, and a horrible storm separated them. When the storm ended, they were each alone. Terrified, they begged Chaos to bring them back together, and Chaos made them mirrors of each other: one a sphinx, lion and human; the other a gryphon, lion and eagle."

"Did they find each other?" Darling doesn't turn around.

"I think Houses Gryphon and Sphinx had different endings of the story. You should ask Vivian."

Now Darling does look back at me. "No Sphinxes to ask."

It's on my tongue to tell her to make up her own ending, as the first scion of her House, but it's too fanciful for me. Instead I bow and leave.

15

DARLING

There is something about House Gryphon that makes me incredibly melancholic. It isn't the rain of the past few days, or the way the house looms. It isn't even Vivian, who looks vaguely familiar, like someone I once met but never properly knew. At first I think it's a kind of sadness over seeing a prosperous House when both the House of my birth and the House that adopted me lie in ruins, or even a bit of cabin fever from long hours trapped in that blasted carriage. Then I realize it's because of Talon and the way he accused me of trying to seduce his brother, like I'm some scheming noble attempting to secure my place and not a hostage myself.

Could he really think so little of me?

I chide myself for the thought. Why do I care what the haughty War Prince thinks of me when he makes a spectacle of himself parading around on that near-feral beast of his? If I'd planned properly, that kiss would've spelled Caspian's doom. My only concerns at this point should be figuring out the current location of Leonetti's convoy and seeing Talon and Caspian dead. I still have the Kiss of Death tucked away in a box of cosmetics, and even though I keep expecting to see Gavin appear at every turn—I was confident he would be waiting here for me in my rooms—he isn't anywhere to be found.

I worry that he and Adelaide have given up on me. It has been over a month since I was taken in Lastrium, and the war is theoretically over. What are they doing right now? Still fighting? Or in hiding, waiting for the inevitable next strike?

"My quill."

Marjorie stands in the doorway, her Dragon uniform traded once more for House Sphinx livery. The smile I turn on her is bitter.

"Are you finished playing soldier, or is Talon just looking to make sure he can track my movements?" I ask. She inclines her head respectfully, not taking the bait.

"Andra and I are here to help you out of your clothes so that you can rest," she says. Her words are demure, but there is a flash in her eyes that makes me think she returned to my side on Talon's orders.

"Fine," I say. I'm still in a bit of a mood, travel and this whole planning-a-double-murder nonsense conspiring against my better nature, but I want out of the ridiculous clothing I wear more than I want to fight.

Marjorie and Andra help me undress, carefully stowing each ivory-feathered piece, and once I am in my underthings, I shoo them away. "I'm tired. Give me a couple turns to rest and then I'll dress for dinner."

"We will draw you a bath while you rest," Marjorie says with a deep bow, before she and Andra withdraw.

Once I am alone, I close all the drapes, so that the room is in deep shadow. I rip off my smoked lenses and rub my eyes, the shadows soothing. The door to my chamber opens and shuts behind me, but I don't turn toward the sound. I've been waiting for him.

"I thought they'd never leave," Gavin drawls, appearing next to me. I'm not surprised by his presence. I've been around him and his boon enough to sense him, even when my eyes cannot see him.

"Where have you been?" I ask, turning toward him. I want to hug him in relief at seeing a friendly face, but his expression is anything but welcoming. This version of Gavin is all business, and I'm made awkward by realizing he isn't quite as glad to see me as I am him.

"Here. There. Around. I don't suppose you heard the one about the House Sphinx regent defiling the High Prince Regent?"

"'Defiling'? You sound like a farmer's wife gossiping in the marketplace. It was just a simple kiss."

"And yet, he is still alive," Gavin says, sighing. "You aren't even wearing the Kiss of Death."

"Poison is cowardly, Gav," I say, but there's no heat to my words. Even to my own ears I just sound scared. Then it hits me: I don't want to kill Caspian. I actually sort of like him, and the way he plays on people's expectations of him. "Get me a blade of some sort, and I'll end them both. But don't ask me to become something I'm not." At least with a blade I can pretend it's a fair fight. And it's as good a way to stall as any.

"Adelaide said you wouldn't do it," Gavin says as I walk over to the bed and collapse into its soft form. Even though the curtains are closed and there are no candles lit, I can see Gavin's disappointment clearly.

"Killing the Dragons would only make them martyrs," I say. "Caspian isn't popular even within his own House, and Talon is as paranoid as they come. If Caspian were to drop dead after so much as looking at me, Talon would figure I was to blame. I'd be put to death and the war would continue. Can House Kraken really handle an assault on the safe houses from the Dragons?"

Gavin sits next to me on the bed. "No. And most of the families we have tucked away have nowhere else to go."

"So what do you want me to do, Gavin? I'm worthless here. Help me escape and we can plan our next attack." I want to tell him about Leonetti, about the prison convoy. But I don't. I'm not sure why, and I know I'll regret it later. But there's something about the set of Gavin's jaw that makes me think this is about more than a political assassination. This is personal for him, and I don't want to know what he'll do if I refuse to dance to his tune.

"No. You're more useful here," Gavin says. "Even if you won't assassinate the princes."

The disappointment in his voice is so strong that guilt unwinds in my middle. "Just get me a blade, Gavin."

"No. You're right. If you're suspected of killing them, you'd be executed immediately. I think . . . I think you playing at Sphinx regent is much more useful."

I narrow my eyes at him. "How so?"

"Wars are expensive, dearest Darling. And with your newly filled coffers and newfound friends, you can help us more than you know." Gavin kisses me on the cheek while plucking out the bejeweled comb that holds the mass of my curls. My hair falls around my shoulders, and he stands to go. "Plus, you may not realize it, but your pretty face can be a weapon. No, you should remain here. Dazzle the princes."

"'Dazzle' them? How am I supposed to do that? Weave love charms of kelp and hill daisies?"

Gavin laughs. "That's silly. You can't find kelp this far inland. No, you're just going to have to use those lips for something besides murder." He tugs a curl. "And leave your hair down. You're prettier when your curls run wild." At my incredulous look he tips my chin up toward him. His eyes meet mine, and there's an expression there I don't quite understand. Regret? Or something else? "You can make them want you, Darling."

I pull away, putting a bit of space between us. I have nothing to say to his sweet words. I hate that he's talking about me like I'm one more weapon in the House Kraken arsenal, but isn't that what I've been the last few years? I've killed for House Kraken, participated in attacks that would've been called merciless and foul by Dragon regulars, and I never once had a single shred of remorse. But now here I am, pampered and coddled, and I'm balking like an ill-tempered drake.

Gavin strides toward the door, the spell broken. "I'll be back as soon as I make contact with Adelaide and we can come up with a new plan. But if you don't mind losing a few of your trinkets, these should help buy grain for the war effort," he says, examining the hair comb a bit more closely.

I wave dismissively. "Take what you want. Just . . . take me with you. Please," I say. There is a sudden dread weighing heavy in my middle, that staying here will somehow turn me into someone I don't want to be. I can't explain the feeling, but I do have the sense of losing myself ever so slowly.

"Darling. Even if you won't murder those Dragon bastards, you're still far more useful here than with the Barbs. You know that."

He disappears from sight, the door opening and then shutting again the only sign of his departure. I wonder how many other jewels he'll take on his way out. Gavin told me once that when the Dragons executed his father, he stole from nobles to keep his younger brothers and sisters fed while his mother fell into a deep depression. I'm sure he knows which baubles in my stash will fetch the best price.

I just wish he cared as much about me, and the toll of playing along with these Dragons.

But even though the sadness overwhelms and chokes me, I feel a deep sense of shame at letting House Kraken down, of keeping any shred of information about Leonetti secret. Gavin's disappointment seeps into me even in his absence, as cloying as any perfume and as toxic as one of Miranda's poisons.

And then, before I can second guess myself, I dig the Kiss of Death out of my cosmetics bag and place it next to the smoked lenses on my dressing table, the small pot a promise and a threat.

By the time I head to the evening meal my mood has improved a bit, but not much. After a bath and a costume change—I swear there is a different gown for each hour of the day—I descend the stairs to dinner. The House Gryphon guard who leads the way is careful to keep the boonlight away from my eyes even though I wear my smoked lenses. And when I arrive to the grand dining room, the space large enough to hold a harvest festival, I find that the boonlights are strategically placed to light the space but also keep it dim so that I can remove my lenses.

"I hope you don't mind my audacity, cousin," Vivian says, coming forward to clasp my hands in hers. She wears a simple, fitted sheath dress in a brilliant emerald, and her blue-black skin glimmers in the low light.

"Actually, it's quite welcome. I know my smoked lenses make some nervous, so I am happy to be able to stow them for our first meal together." I remove my goggles, the motion made easier by my loose hair. I took Gavin's advice and left my hair down, still an oddity for me. Even so, Andra had been distraught to find that a number of my hair combs were missing, and I had to soothe her anxiousness by saying they probably fell off the wagon during our travels. Besides, I am still far from looking like a beggar. I wear a buttery-yellow dress with magenta panels hidden within the split skirt, the hem weighted so that when I walk there is a flash of color and bare leg. I was not sure that the dress worked, but I quite like the way it moves around me.

I am the first one to dinner, so while the servants pour bubbly water—I politely decline the wine, my lesson learned—Vivian and I strike up a friendly conversation. I mean to ask her about the First Gryphon, but we end up talking about Caspian instead.

"You two seem quite friendly," I say, after she relates a story about him and an ill-fated game in the House Gryphon maze when they were younger.

"Oh, he is like the unruly cousin I never wanted," she says with a laugh. "My mother was quite close with the Dragon consort, and when she passed, we were equally devastated."

"Ah," I say, suddenly feeling like I've stumbled into quicksand. "I'm deeply sorry. I know that some believe House Sphinx responsible for her death." It's a vague enough statement that my etiquette coach would be proud.

"Yes, well, I'm afraid House Gryphon has never held that belief.

House Dragon's evidence was hardly convincing," Vivian says, her words bland like she is not committing several kinds of treason with such a simple statement. "We even had a few of our members with truthseeking boons question the household. Besides, House Sphinx had no previous history with blood magic, so it's unlikely they could have engineered the consort's death."

A chill runs across my bare arms, even though the room is warm. "Blood magic?"

"Yes," Vivian says. "Blood magic is the only way to undermine a truthseeking boon, and it was clear someone in House Dragon knew something, but we could never figure out who."

"But, and please forgive my ignorance, what exactly is blood magic?" I say, a note of exasperation entering my voice. "I honestly just thought it was a nursery tale." I feel like there is so much I still have to learn, and everyone keeps assuming I know more than I do.

"Ah," Vivian says with a short nod. "My apologies, I forget not everyone spends their days steeped in the old lore as we do here in House Gryphon. Blood magic was an actual thing, a series of barbaric and archaic rites from before Chaos touched our land. In these days of fading boons some are turning to the old ways to try to gain a measure of power. Blood magic is destructive, and not just because it requires a sacrifice of some sort to work. The old histories tell us that it also takes a toll on the user."

"Do not forget to mention how blood magic is most often used for things like prophecy and skinstealing," Caspian says, sweeping into the room with Elias by his side. "Both destructive boons that are rumored to drive their users mad."

"Skinstealing?" I ask.

"Taking on another person's form," Vivian explains, with a polite smile. "Caspian. I see you still enter a room like a summer storm."

"Everyone enjoys an unexpected shower. It keeps life interesting," Caspian says, gesturing for a servant to bring him wine. Elias looks on with exasperation but says nothing.

"Darling. Do you have a boon?" Caspian suddenly asks.

I blink. "Pardon me?"

"Caspian," Vivian says, censure in her tone. "You know that question is rude."

"Only because strong boons are rare these days," he says. "A hundred years ago children who were born without boons were seen as an oddity. They were shipped off to be tested and analyzed, in the hopes that there was some cure for such a malady. Now wondering if someone's talent is Chaos-sent is somehow a gross faux pas."

"Must we discuss this again," Elias mutters. I say nothing, because I get the sense that this is an ongoing argument that I want no part of.

"Yes," Caspian says. "We must attack this matter head-on. Identify the cause of the fading boons and mitigate the damages. Those gifts from Chaos made this country what it was. We've been at war for so long many have forgotten that we have numerous enemies outside of our borders. Such as Avrendia. What will we do when they finally sail to our shores and try to claim our lands for their own?"

"House Gryphon has been hard pressed to conduct research when we are constantly being dragged off to fix your broken toys, my blade," Vivian says, her eyes sparking in the low light. "Which is why I was quite pleased at your declaration of peace. Once things have resumed the normal rhythms of life, we will take up our research once more."

Caspian laughs and sips at his wine. "Viv, you are such a brat."

"I learned it from the best," she says, and they both start laughing in a way that makes me wonder if perhaps once upon a time they were a bit more than just friends.

Judging from Elias's stormy expression, they are wondering the exact same thing.

"What about that theory you sent me?" Caspian says, mirth fading away so that his gaze is focused on Vivian. "The one about the loss of the empyreals being the catalyst for the decreasing boons?"

"Empyreals?" I ask, because that is yet another term I thought was mere myth. "You're saying they're real?"

"The tales about the First Beasts aren't only stories, you know. Once, the House regents were more than just petty humans," Caspian says, gesturing dramatically with his glass of wine. "They were the leaders of their people, able to shift into dangerous beasts to protect their own. The regent of House Sphinx could be a sphinx in truth, the House Dragon regent could become a dragon, and so on and so forth."

"Yes, and I have a theory about that," Vivian says.

"Is it somehow contained in that droll 'Death of the Phoenix' essay?" Caspian says, swirling his half-empty glass in a pretend display of boredom. Once I would've believed his ennui was real, but now I see the tension in his shoulders that gives truth to the lie.

Caspian is very, very interested in Vivian's answer.

The regent of House Gryphon gives Caspian an enigmatic smile. "It is! I'm glad you asked. I was afraid perhaps you hadn't received my letter."

"Ah, my apologies for not sending a response. I was quite occupied with a new endeavor," he says, this time gesturing in my direction.

"Where did the empyreals go?" I ask. "I mean, if they ever truly existed." I am still not convinced. But then again, I've never had much use for things that were not right in front of me. It's hard to philosophize when you're scrabbling for survival in a sewer or trying to navigate a battlefield.

"They did," Elias says. "I've read the texts."

"Yes. As have I," Caspian says. "Which is why your theory intrigued me, Viv."

Vivian stands. "Well, since the War Prince seems to be taking his time, why don't we adjourn to the library? I can show you the scroll I found while we wait. It should explain everything."

We stand, and I fumble to place my goggles back onto my face. Caspian takes Vivian's arm, leaving Elias and me to follow behind.

"So," I say, giving them what I hope is a friendly smile. "You're related to Vivian?"

"She's my aunt. I lived here in Gryphon's Seat until I was summoned to attend to Caspian."

"Have you been Caspian's physician for long?" I ask.

Elias gives me a cold look. "Long enough to know that he tires quickly of new toys."

I grimace and say nothing else. I have the feeling Elias and I will not be allies.

We make our way up a staircase, down another, and through a twisting hall until we arrive at a brightly lit multistory room full of rows and rows of books. Real books, bound in leather and edged in gilt lettering. There are thousands of them, and I gasp at the hoard. It's a fortune in paper and ink, and the artifacts displayed throughout the room are nothing compared to the tomes that line the shelves.

"Darling," Caspian says in a wry tone. "Have you never seen a library before?"

I shake my head. "I don't . . . think so?" House Kraken doesn't have a library, at least not anymore. Books tend not to do so well at sea, plus ships are cramped, and there isn't much space for such things. If there had been a Sphinx library, it was most likely burned to the ground. "Not a lot of use for books in the Nakumba sewers," I say, trying for humor to defuse the situation.

It has the opposite effect. Vivian's expression goes from amused to horrified, while Elias looks away, ashamed. Only Caspian is unmoved, a short nod as though he understands completely.

Vivian recovers and clears her throat before she moves to a scroll that has been laid out, decorative crystals weighing down the ends. "I had it pulled from the archives specifically for your visit," she says. She gestures, and the boonlights are moved so that I can take my goggles off once more and lean over the scroll with Elias and Caspian, the colors brighter and the artwork more vibrant without my smoked lenses.

"It's called the *Fall of the Empyreals*. It dates to more than a hundred years ago, when the Last Phoenix disappeared. From the texts I've studied, that was the last time anyone saw a true Regent, a human able to shift into something more."

"It's thought that House Dragon killed the Phoenix in a fit of rage," Caspian says, tone dry. "And knowing the temperament of my ancestors, it's probably true."

"Only a hundred years ago? How is it that no one knows the truth?" I ask.

"When the empyreals fell, we lost a number of records," Vivian says. "There was a virulent plague in the immediate aftermath which devastated the land. Not to mention the other challenges we've had finding historical records. The library here burned to the ground, as though the Last Gryphon wanted to take the knowledge with him. All that you see here has been retrieved from other places. My House has worked tirelessly to gather every scrap of knowledge from across the continent."

"This is where you should wonder just how many of these volumes were taken in the fall of House Sphinx," Caspian says, his whisper loud enough to carry.

"Quite a few," Vivian says. "And House Gryphon will be happy to make copies and return the originals."

I'm only half paying attention to Vivian and Caspian's banter. Instead my attention is locked on the artwork before me. In it men and women wail as though in pain, while each of the House regents—Cockatrice, Gryphon, Sphinx, Dragon, Barghest, and Kraken—fall from the sky, twisted in the throes of death. Over it all is the outline of a fiery bird, the shadow of a phoenix.

"It's said in a number of accounts that Houses resolved their differences in battles using their true forms," Vivian says, her voice low as we all take in the painting. "It's why we refer to the heads of our Houses as regents. The true leaders of the Houses, the true princes, were the empyreals who protected those who swore loyalty to the House."

Talon chooses that moment to throw open the main doors of

the library and stride in. He bows, and as he rises, his apologetic gaze falls on me. His lips part in shock, and I grow hot at the way he stares at only me, as if I'm the most important thing he's ever seen in his life.

It's a terrible thing to realize that I actually missed his presence. As though I don't have enough to think about.

16

TALON

I'm on my way to dinner when I sense it.

A trace that shouldn't be there.

It's difficult to be certain so far outside my territory, away from places I've mapped and the foot traffic I know through memory and boon. But someone, something, who did not quite belong, moved through the corridor outside the guest suites.

I am alone in the quiet hall. A woven runner softens the hardwood floor beneath my boots; the boonlamps hum. I stop and close my eyes, reaching with my boon. Just a moment ago two people moved side by side, with purpose. Unknown to me, likely Gryphon attendants. Before that, a fading trace from a handful of Teeth, striding on duty. Someone rushed the opposite direction. Just at the edges of what I can track with the weird Chaos of my boon shimmers Darling's darkly luminous trace, leaving her suite along with her attendant and Marjorie.

And weaving throughout it all, someone who moved wrong. Slow. Pausing, restarting. Then walking along with purpose. Pausing again. The small swirl of the trace where the person hesitated before moving on again like nothing was wrong.

Maybe nothing *is* wrong. But my gut says otherwise.

Opening my eyes, I follow the trace in its stronger direction. I'd like to know where it came from, if it stopped at Caspian's suite behind us, but it's too faded already.

I let the rest of the traces fade from my awareness, too, and focus only on this odd one. The owner of the trace is a stranger to me: that's the most I can tell.

When I pass the Dragon guarding the entrance to the library wing, the soldier nods to me without signaling there's been any incident. So the person I'm tracking either fits in enough that one of my soldiers didn't mark them, or the Dragon couldn't see him at all. I've never heard of an invisibility boon, and I don't think people are born with chameleon boons anymore, but it never hurts to be cautious.

As I follow the trace around an abrupt left and up into a narrow stone staircase, I slow. This is bad quarters for a fight. I should notify someone, but the trace fades more and more with every delay.

My falchion, though a slender, short blade, is too long for the staircase. My claw is sheathed at the small of my back, and I reach under the green velvet jacket to fetch it. Fitting it over my knuckles, I hold it close to my body and slip up the stairs after the trace.

On a landing, the trace seems to hold, brightening slightly. I glance out the small window. It overlooks the side garden and part of the busy town beyond. Roofs bleed with the red light of the sunset. The trace exits at the next landing, out onto one of the wooden balconies that line the third level of the rear wing. I keep following. The trace lessens with every step, so I speed up, ready, as it leads me through a tall, narrow window into some kind of study, out into a corridor dim with only one boonlamp, and down a half flight and into a row of narrow empty servants' quarters. Then down again, a wooden stairway this time, exiting through a door half-hidden by a curtain. I startle a Gryphon attendant when I slip out. They gasp and bow, then move on with a little frown over their shoulder at me. I'm on a grand staircase, at the edge of a marble landing decorated with ancient helmets in the style of Houses Gryphon, Dragon, and Barghest. Our official allies. I follow the trace down the broad stairs into the very front foyer of the manor house, where I first entered this afternoon.

There I pause, though the trace didn't. It goes right, toward the Gryphon family wing. I don't follow it. The course is nonsense.

I resheathe the claw under my jacket and plop my fist onto the hilt of my falchion. The trace didn't seem to have a goal. It was slow, then faster, blending almost perfectly and then hesitating as if confused.

Like it was learning the house.

I sigh, blowing at some of the longer curls that have fallen over my forehead.

Maybe danger. Maybe a new Gryphon attendant. Someone like Elias reacquainting themselves with the admittedly confusing architecture of House Gryphon.

I head quickly through the house toward the western yard, where the carriages are docked and the war drakes stabled. The soldiers have set their command there, though they've all been quartered alongside the Gryphon House guard. Arran Lightscale is there, and I get his attention as I stride toward the drakes. He meets me halfway, and I tell him I want the watch rotations tightened up. "Not friendly territory?" he murmurs, and I press my lips in a line. After a moment I say, "Better to be sure. Tell everyone to be alert, trade out sooner if they need to. Anything strange I want reported."

Arran acknowledges, just as the yard's nighttime boonlamps flare to life. The sun is down, and I'm extremely late for dinner.

I turn on my heel and hurry back toward the dining hall. I'm nearly there when a maid in Gryphon red stops abruptly. "Oh, my blade, there you are!" She curtsies, a little flush on her cheek.

"Apologies," I say. "Please lead the way."

She does so, but we're stopped at the dining room because the party has made its way to the library. Back near where I started before I even noticed an awry trace.

At the entrance to the grand library, I shove the doors open and enter, bowing deeply as I prepare further apologies.

But when I glance up, my eyes catch on Darling, standing beside the dark hearth with its low dancing flames, framed by gilded books.

It's exactly one of Caspian's paintings.

Exactly, from the vivid yellow-and-pink dress, to the extravagant curls free around her face and shoulders, the little fire, the tall red book right over her shoulder. Except in the painting the girl's eyes are a maelstrom of black and Chaos purple, pitted and awful. Darling's eyes are wide, bare under the dim boonlight, round and human and glinting like oil-slick rainbows.

I swallow back all my words and tear my eyes from her to find my brother.

Caspian gazes back at me, for the slightest moment looking devastated. Then he breaks out of it, like snapping open a silk fan to hide behind. "Brother, you're late!"

I bow again: I'm the one hiding now. "I am sorry for it," I say much more softly than I intended. I feel strange. Unmoored. First the odd trace, and now the painting.

Footsteps coming toward me. Caspian says, "We were just

discussing how the loss of the Last Phoenix may have caused the weakening of the country's boons."

It's difficult restraining myself from immediately challenging him about his boon, which seems plenty strong, whatever it is. But Caspian clearly waits for my response, staring pointedly at me.

Belatedly, I remember the Gryphon regent and her cousin alongside us. Not Darling: I could never forget her presence. It would be easiest to agree with Caspian's theory, but I've read the histories of our House, too, and what supposedly happened, and instead I say, "It matters less that the Last Phoenix died than you think."

"Oh?" says Vivian, with interest.

Darling says, "Surprise, surprise, War Prince."

Caspian waits expectantly.

I continue, "Before the Last Phoenix died, the Phoenixes died regularly. And a new one was born every generation. So what I want to know is why have no new Phoenixes been born in a hundred years?"

My brother claps, delighted. "Not just a grunt after all, dragonlet."

"It's a good question," Vivian agrees. She smiles indulgently. "I'm uncertain there's any way to discover the answer, however. Not without more details regarding exactly how the Last Phoenix died."

I glance at Caspian, who makes a moue rather like a shrug, and I say, "You must know we believe our great-grandmother killed him."

Vivian nodded. "But not why, or how."

"Do Dragons need a reason?" Darling asks, sweetly.

I say, "You'd know if we did not."

Caspian laughs. "Children," he chides, but he's already turning, attention diverted by the display of an old calligraphy set in a nook between two shelves. He waves lazily at Elias to join him, and Elias pushes up from the armchair in which they'd ensconced themself to wait out the discussion.

Vivian moves to Darling's side and says, "I'd love to show you those books recovered from House Sphinx."

Darling bites her bottom lip and nods.

I glance at Caspian, who is directing Elias to move one of the ladders along with them as they round the far edge of the main library. I follow Darling and the Gryphon regent in the opposite direction.

"This place is incredible, even in recovery," Darling says to Vivian, who smiles again and touches Darling's elbow lightly, showing her around one of the corners and into an alcove that opens like a chapel, shelves arcing on three sides and a display table like an altar in the center.

"We value knowledge above all else," Vivian says as if it explains the entire world. "Here, Darling. This we believe belonged to the last Sphinx regent."

She's indicating a leather-bound book propped on the table, set with delicately carved ivory lettering: *The Tenets*.

Darling leans in, one hand hovering as if unsure she should touch. But she pulls back, then looks at me before saying bluntly to Vivian, "This shouldn't be mine. Even if now I am the First Scion of House Sphinx, with whatever privileges that brings, this is an heirloom. I do not even know if I mattered at all, before. I might've been the daughter of a launderer. Or cook."

"It's yours," I say. I don't understand this hesitation at all. If I were the last Dragon alive, if I even thought I might be, I would want everything that had been of House Dragon. What we have, what we build, what our family and ancestors have built makes us what we are. That's what we have to protect.

"Because Caspian says so," Darling says bitterly.

"You earned it," I answer.

Darling finally looks at me, disbelief large in her expression.

"You fight," I continue. "Take it." I can't help the hard frown I make.

She glances down again.

Vivian studies Darling's ducked face for a moment, then reaches for her chin. Darling doesn't stop her, and Vivian tilts Darling's chin up so their eyes meet. "You survived, Darling. That's what you did to earn it. And sometimes survival means being who you have to be."

Darling's jaw tightens, and Vivian releases her, glancing at me. Darling does not. Her attention returns to the book, and she reaches out again, more confidently. Just before she touches the final letter of the title, Caspian's voice calls out:

"Ah! Here it is!"

Darling actually startles, and Caspian keeps calling. "Come here, everyone! Vivian, Darling, dears, I need you."

I bow to let the summoned women pass and follow them again, this time toward the end of the library where Caspian is halfway up the ladder, posing with a fist on his hip. Elias steadies the ladder from the marble floor.

"There you are!" Caspian says with a bright grin. "Look at this, Darling." He gestures extravagantly at the glass globe set upon the shelf between rows of thin volumes of what seem to be ledgers. The globe rests on a golden stand, and inside, just visible through the glint of boonlamps, is a curving dagger as long as my hand.

I peer up. The blade isn't metal. It's darker than steel, a rich gray brown almost like a drake's claw, but dull along the curled bottom. Only the tip is sharp. The handle is dark, too, and set with vivid red gems along the pommel.

"Tell us what this is, Vivian." Caspian caresses the tips of his fingers along the glass.

"It's the Knife of Scholarship," Vivian says lightly. "The oldest heirloom of House Gryphon, made from the First Gryphon's own fore-talon, at least six hundred years ago."

"Amazing," Caspian says rather dreamily. He stares at it for a moment, and none of us break the silence.

I don't like this at all. Caspian gazing at the dagger so strangely, and with the afterimage of the painting Darling versus reality Darling in my thoughts. "It looks beautifully made," I say, to say something. "And smooth. We have some ancient weapons made from dragon claws—spears and halberds, because of the size of the claws. And they have ridges on them, growth patterns. Those made from older dragons have thicker—"

"Yes, Talon." Caspian shushes me. "What is important, friends, is that weeks ago Darling and I spoke of reparations to House Sphinx, and Vivian—" Caspian stares at the older woman. He suddenly seems commanding, especially towering over the rest of us. "Gryphon regent, for your House's trespasses against House Sphinx, you will pass the Knife of Scholarship to Darling Calamus, the First Scion of House Sphinx. Honor her rise to your equal regency."

Stunned, we all stare at him.

Vivian draws a breath but holds it, her lips parted slightly.

As I stare at him, I know for all his madness, his playing, there is something he's doing with this elaborate game.

Elias says from Caspian's knee, "Prince Regent, perhaps House Gryphon should be accorded the honor of negotiating this reparation." Their voice is carefully coaxing—I've never heard them speak to Caspian this way. Like they barely know him, too.

"We do wish to honor our cousin House," Vivian says with equal care, but not coaxing; she is firm.

"Caspian," Darling says, exasperated. "I don't want their ridiculous knife."

Caspian turns his gaze onto Darling, and it's cold. I automatically step closer to her. My brother says, staring only at Darling, "Is it not true, Vivian, that House Gryphon gave over stolen maps of House Sphinx and their city that allowed House Dragon to infiltrate their stronghold swiftly and murder the entire family?"

Darling's hand presses against her stomach, and I want to touch her back in support. It would be easy to hate my brother sometimes.

Vivian says, "It is true."

Elias gasps, and their hand tightens on the ladder rung.

Caspian finally looks at the Gryphon regent, his mouth pressing into a grim smile.

But Vivian adds, "I did not realize anyone knew of our involvement."

Caspian shrugs.

The Gryphon regent turns to Darling. "It was my eldest brother, who was regent fourteen years ago. I would not have, I can promise you. I do not know what I would have done when House Dragon came with their demands, but not that."

Darling nods. She's shaking very slightly, and the hand on her stomach becomes a fist.

I'm the only one to notice Caspian reach for the glass globe, and I move too slowly to stop him as he lazily shoves it off the high shelf.

Everything stops as the globe falls, glinting in the boonlight.

I shift to put myself in front of Darling, gripping her arms just as the globe shatters on the marble floor.

She jumps at the crash and for the briefest moment returns my grip. Her hair tickles my cheek and—

Then Vivian is crying out Caspian's name, and Darling tears away from me.

The Knife of Scholarship lies in a nest of glittering glass, chunks and shards scattered in every direction.

"You might have broken it," Vivian is snapping. Attendants and a handful of soldiers have poured into the library, gasping and shocked. I turn and motion my men away.

"Take it, Darling," Caspian orders.

Darling takes a careful step, but I hold my hand out to stay her because Vivian has backed away in her slippers. I crunch over the shards in my boots and pluck it up. The handle is warm, strangely so, and the knife well balanced but much too light for its size.

"Talon," my brother warns.

I don't look at him, only at Darling, who taps the toe of her own boot pointedly for me. I meet her gaze. "You don't want it," I say. It's a question.

"I want a weapon well enough." The hint of a smile graces the corner of her mouth. Then it falls away. "I don't think I have a choice."

"That's right," says Caspian, stomping heavily down the ladder. Elias jerks away before offering their hand again.

"You're a menace," Vivian says in what would be a snarl from a less refined woman. She waves a few attendants nearer to deal with the glass. "I no longer wish to dine with the Prince Regent."

Caspian sets a foot on the floor, gently crunching a shard of glass. "This Prince Regent is no longer hungry." He releases Elias and airily wanders away.

"I'm still hungry," Darling mutters.

"Ah, good. Let me feed you, Sphinx scion." Vivian gestures for her cousin and spares me a scathing glance. I am no more welcome than my brother.

I hold out the dagger to Darling, turning it in my hand so that she can grip the handle. The talon is smooth against my palm. Darling grasps it, and for a moment we're both holding it.

The moment ends, and she takes the dagger as she turns.

I bow to their three backs.

"Come," Caspian says when I rise. He's at my shoulder like a wraith. "You need a drink."

17

DARLING

Dinner is an awkward affair, to say the least. Once we reach the dining room, I try to return the blade to Vivian, but she refuses. "Caspian may be an old friend, but he is still Prince Regent. His word is law. And when he gets like this, there is nothing to be done for it," she says while tearing into a small roasted bird. "Keep it. But perhaps when next we meet, House Sphinx would see fit to return it as a gesture of goodwill."

The meaning is clear, and I incline my head in gratitude at her speaking so very plainly that I don't have to wonder at the layers of meaning in her speech. Not all of these royals are so blunt.

After we eat, I flee to my room. The Knife of Scholarship is warm in my hand, like a living thing, and there is something about the blade that makes me yearn to soar through the sky. It's a silly feeling, and when I place it in the case Marjorie brings me, I am sad to part with it.

"Could you find me a sheath that will fit the blade?" I ask, stroking the handle one last time. I understand why Vivian was so angry. It really is a beautiful blade. But it's also a chance to show that House Sphinx will not be shamed, that we will demand retribution for the wrongs done to us. The rage I felt at knowing that House Gryphon played a part in the murder of my family, of everyone I knew, took me by surprise. But it was also justified.

Plus, I may not know much, but I know how to deal with bullies.

After Leonetti saved me from the sewers of Nakumba, I was moved in with the rest of his war orphans: children adopted into House Kraken either because they had no parents left or because their families had fled the violence and no longer had the means to care for them. It had been a strange transition from my previous life, and my damaged eyes had been cause for much teasing. At least until I made it clear that anyone who tried to pick a fight with me would end up the worse for it.

I'm starting to think that politics is very much the same way.

Once the dagger is tucked away, Andra returns to help me dress for bed. I've just stepped out of the gown when Marjorie enters with a frown, a slip of paper in her hand.

"Someone just slipped this under the door," she says, handing it to me. I don't recognize the wax seal on the letter, but I rip it open anyway.

> *Meet me in the center of the maze.*
> *We have much to discuss. R, L, R, R, L, R.*

I don't recognize the handwriting, and I frown at Marjorie. "Did you see who left it?"

"No, my quill," she says. "Should I get the guard?"

"No," I say. It could be from Gavin. I don't like the way we left our last conversation, and maybe he and Adelaide have realized that I can be more useful away from these Dragons and back with my Barbs. It's a feeble hope, but after the scene earlier tonight I am anxious to get some distance from Caspian and his mercurial moods. "But this requires different clothing."

I dress quickly in something more suited for skulking about in the night: black trousers and a fitted black top that is meant to go under a traveling dress made of a sheer material. My boots go back on, and I find a dark-colored scarf to tie back my curls.

I have no weapons, the Knife of Scholarship has been put away and I don't think I'll need it, but I put on a swipe of the Kiss of Death at the last moment. I'm not sure why. Maybe because Gavin's opinion means too much to me.

Andra and Marjorie watch me go with identical expressions of disapproval, but I ignore them. I am far more comfortable in the shadows than at a fine dining table, and I am pleased to find that the boonlamps have been lowered in the hallways out of respect for the late hour. I tuck my goggles into a pocket on the side of my trousers and enjoy the freedom from smoked lenses and leather straps. Despite my earlier ire Vivian has been nothing but kind, and I truly believe that had she been regent at the time, House Sphinx would still stand.

Not that it matters much in the scheme of things.

I pass a few guards, both Dragon and Gryphon, but they just give me a nod and go back to their duties. It's strange, and I wonder if this is what it means to be a noble: even though I should clearly be sleeping, the guards would rather look the other way than accidentally invoke my wrath.

It saddens me to know I now have a bit more in common with the nobles than I do with regular soldiers. Especially since it's very likely that one day soon we will face each other once more on a battlefield.

I have been at war too long to believe in Caspian's tenuous peace. Even if I want to.

I find the gardens easily enough, despite the twisting corridors, and the night air is cool on my face as I step into the grass. The fragrance of everblooms, heady and cloying, scents the air, and moonlight silvers the landscape, carving out everbloom bushes and climbing drake's breath in shadows and bright. Something in me loosens, and I relax into the beauty of the night. This is my domain, gloom and moonlight, not galas and fine dinners.

The maze is easy to navigate, especially since I have the directions in the missive Gavin sent. It makes me wonder just how long he's been prowling the grounds here. Somehow I had the impression that he was stowing away with us in the caravan among the luggage and liveried servants of our retinues, but now I doubt that. Surely Adelaide has Gavin up to more than just keeping tabs on me. If it were me, I would have had Gavin kill Caspian and Talon. It makes me wonder why Adelaide hasn't just used Gavin in such a way. He has as much reason to want the Dragons dead as any of us. After all, they killed his father.

So why hasn't Adelaide let Gavin have his revenge? It's a question I should've wondered about earlier, but I've been so unbalanced over being thrust into this new life that I haven't let myself wonder overly long at the strangeness of it all. He could just as easily slip into Caspian's chambers as he did mine. Is it because she wants plausible deniability if a Dragon is murdered, or is it because she fears the Dragons would kill Leonetti in retaliation? Which makes it even more strange that Gavin and Miranda would ask me to poison the Dragon princes.

I stop suddenly, in a courtyard with a series of spilling fountains, only halfway to my destination. The tumbling water provides a nice counterpoint to the chaos of my thoughts. Or could it be that Gavin is using me for his own devices? That feels right, more so than Adelaide being in on some poison plot. I hadn't thought too hard about being asked to kill the Dragon princes. We Barbs have spent many an evening around the fire talking about what we would do if we had the chance to take out one of them, ending the war once and for all. But never have we discussed poisoning.

So who exactly is asking me to kill the Dragon princes? Adelaide Seabreak, scion and future regent of House Kraken, or Gavin Swiftblade, disgraced Dragon and current House Kraken assassin?

When I see the boy, I plan to find out.

Annoyance, at my too-trusting self, at being trapped playing a role I don't want, at my lack of choice, hurries my steps, so that I make the rest of the trip in a fraction of the time, arriving at the center of the maze in a huff. This courtyard is larger than the others I passed through, the pavers wide and made of a pale stone that seems to reflect the moonlight. Everbloom bushes line the outside, and a deep pond takes up the center, luminescent fish darting in the shallows beneath lily pads and other water plants. It's a gorgeous space, and it reminds me of the courtyard where I spent the last moment of my childhood.

A pond with golden fish, the sound of a stringed instrument, and the soft laughter of men and women enjoying a late evening meal. And the shouts of soldiers as they interrupted it all.

"Am I dreaming?"

I turn, the man behind me making my breath catch. It's not Gavin, but Talon, looking rumpled and entirely too appealing. His hair is askew and his tunic is unbuttoned. He wears no shoes, and he is decidedly unsteady on his feet.

The War Prince is very clearly drunk.

All of my annoyance and questions for Gavin flee, leaving me standing there a bit dumbfounded. Talon's expression is completely unguarded, and the lopsided grin he gives me steals my breath. "Darling," he says as he steps toward me out of the shadows. "Chaos is mocking me."

"Chaos makes fools of us all, but I think in this case it is Caspian who bears the responsibility for your state," I say. The two of them disappeared after the incident in the library, so the guess is not a wild one.

"Ah, I believe you are correct, my quill," he says, sketching an elegant bow. "My brother has gotten me drunk and lost in the Gryphon maze."

"Well, then, I suppose it's a good thing I have the directions out," I say.

He raises a brow in my direction. "Are you sure you would not rather duel? To the death?"

I laugh. He is surprisingly steady on his feet, but his eyes are wine bright and he has no weapon. He keeps smiling at me, and I like this version of Talon.

The thought is a splash of cold water on my good mood. I cannot afford to like Talon. I have sworn to kill him and his brother. And while I am not certain about House Sphinx, House Kraken stands by its word. "Perhaps some other time. Let's get you to bed, War Prince."

Talon holds out his hand and bows to me deeply. "Then we must dance instead."

I blink. "What?"

"Caspian told me that we were coming to the maze to dance.

And I want to dance." He leans in, his breath warm on my ear. "There is no dancing at war, but there is quite a bit of dancing at court. The only good thing about being at court, honestly."

I'm surprised to find that Talon enjoys dancing, but I'm also not surprised. He is naturally good at it, so I bow to him as well. "Fine, then. A dance and then we take ourselves to bed."

As soon as the words are out of my mouth I realize they could be easily misconstrued, and Talon's slow grin means he is thinking the more debauched meaning. "To sleep," I clarify.

"If you say so" is his tepid response, but the heated look he gives me liquifies my insides.

I take Talon's outstretched hand, and he begins to twirl me around the garden in a simple harvest dance, a step-turn-step-turn that is completely unlike the court dances I've learned or the dances we shared back at the gala. This is simply our bodies pressed tight against each other as we twirl and step around the pond. No extravagant leaps or turns, just two people enjoying the night.

It feels so much more salacious than it is, and something begins to flutter in my middle. Whether panic or excitement, I'm not quite certain. But I do know that I have no desire to go to sleep.

Talon begins to sing as we move, his voice low and steady, an old ballad about a woman gone off to war and the husband and children she has left behind. I stare at him.

"You know the 'Ballad of Jessamyn,'" I say, emotion flattening my voice.

"Of course," he says, murmuring next to my ear, the sensation maddening in the best sort of way. "I am surprised you know it as well."

I know the melody because Leonetti used to sing it to me when

I first came to his household, a feral child too used to fighting and not used to kindness. The song is about a woman who leaves her home to fight in a war—which war is never stated—and the ballad doesn't disclose the tragedy until the last stanza, when it's revealed that the children and husband Jessamyn misses are in their graves, not their beds.

"'Tucked away, tucked away, holding her heart,'" Talon sings, his voice deepening and slowing as he approaches the final stanza. "You are so beautiful," Talon finally says. "Fierce and proud despite everything we have done to you."

I stop and pull away. "Talon—" I begin.

He sweeps me back into his arms, holding me too close. "It's such a short time since we met, but I've been looking at you my whole life, in those paintings. I've known you as long as I can remember. Except you never had eyes, and I didn't know what it meant. And now that you're real, here"—he tightens his hold, his bright green gaze drilling into me as he murmurs—"your eyes are still so mysterious. I look in them, and it feels like Chaos is looking back. I can't pull away, Darling. Tell me that's your boon, to enchant with those dark eyes of yours."

"It's not," I say, my breath hitching in my chest. "And you are drunk."

"Through wine lies the truth," he says, his face searching mine. "I don't know what to do with you, and what Caspian wants from you. From us. But I want to know; I want to know you. It isn't Caspian with a connection to you. I'm the one who's been looking for you my entire life."

I swallow hard. Because I know what he means. Too well. I've come to appreciate and even enjoy his company, sharp words and all. There is something heady about fighting with Talon. About being held in his arms. He sees me. Me.

Talon leans toward me. He is going to kiss me, and I very much want that. I'm not playing at seduction, and yet I've somehow ended up in a moonlit garden with a beautiful boy after all.

That is when I remember the Kiss of Death that I swiped across my lips.

I move quickly, stepping backward. Only we are at the edge of the pond, our dance bringing us closer to the stones that line the edge than I was expecting, so that my heel catches. Our arms are entwined, and Talon's eyes widen in shock as we fall into the water.

I surface, sputtering. Talon stands as well, climbing out of the pond. There is a lily pad on his head, and he plucks it off, dropping it into the water. He offers me a hand, but I ignore it and clamber out on my own, shaking a bit from the shock of the chilly water and the almost kiss.

"I suppose that is Chaos reminding us we have an early morning tomorrow." He's stiffly polite, the cold water apparently chasing away his wine haze, and I give a short nod.

"You know the way out of the maze?" he says.

"I do."

He gestures for me to precede him. I grit my teeth and reverse the instructions in that mystery letter. It's quick—but silent and awkward—work making our way free of the hedges.

Talon bows politely. "I will bid you good night. Sleep well, scion," he says, and does not give me a chance to reply before departing, his long strides quicker than necessary. I watch him go, wondering what in Chaos's name is wrong with me. I'm wishing I'd never worn the stupid Kiss of Death. Yet, I could have kissed Talon and been done with it. So why didn't I?

As I head back to my warm, dry bed, my thoughts aren't on having failed to kill Talon. They're wondering what it would be like to kiss him for real.

The thought is entirely too appealing, and I curse myself for a fool. I cannot have romantic feelings for the War Prince. It is more than madness.

It would be a death sentence.

18

TALON

I understand now why Caspian drinks so much. His world is always tilting because of his connection to Chaos, and alcohol makes it seem like everyone else tilts, too. He said to me last night, "Each sip brings you a little bit closer to me, little brother," and so I didn't stop when I normally would. Later, Caspian dragged me into the garden and stole my shoes.

I remember everything with a perfect clarity—the feel of grass between my toes, the dizzy spiral of stars, the relaxed slump of my shoulders, the dream that Darling was there, how easy it was to be with her in those shadows on bare feet, the dance, the song, my confessions, and especially I remember how wrong I was that she would welcome a kiss from me. I was a fool.

This morning we're packed up and ready to depart by midmorning, and I've been ignoring the High Prince Regent as he makes his elaborate farewells, flirting with the Gryphon regent as if he hadn't pissed her off so thoroughly last night. I mount my war drake and jog her up and down the line. The cool northern air feels good.

I ride at the fore of the parade all morning, trying not to brood but instead enjoy the journey. It will be two days to what remains of House Cockatrice, the ruins of an ancient manor built against a cliffside. Most of House Cockatrice fled to Avrendia when they were exiled in the previous round of House Wars, and after my mother died and Father began his revenge, the rest followed. Only a few lesser members remained, and the ruins are tended by a collection of older folk rather like a priesthood—devoted to the memory of their House and praying, I've heard, to the memory of the Last Phoenix. It will be awful, I'm sure. But for most of the journey we'll be crossing the bottom spur of Dragon territory. That's the part I'm excited about. I've rarely gotten to explore my family's lands since we took over Phoenix Crest and have only visited the ancient fortress of House Dragon twice since my father died. Caspian won't explain why this stupid tour isn't including House Dragon, but he muttered something about Phoenix Crest being the true seat of our family now. I hate that.

By lunch the terrain is rocky, and what remains of river valley trees has given way to the dark needles of spiny evergreen and junipers with misty-blue berries. We pause at a thin waterfall, and I eat quickly before leading my Teeth with our war drakes up a steep incline. We dismount to stretch our legs and let the drakes loose for a few minutes. They'll sniff around and dig at the rough earth with their huge rear claws and let us know if wild drakes are nearby.

From up here the view is spectacular: a silver ribbon of the Phoenix Blood River winds out of the distant blue mountains, surrounded by swaths of dark forest as far as the eye can see. We'll follow the road southeast into the foothills of the Hundred Claw Mountains, where the forest is thick and cold, camp at the far edge of the forest, and break south tomorrow late morning. I can't help staring north at the pale blue sky, looking for the flicker of dragon wings. My only good memories of my father are of him telling me stories of a whole claw of dragons turning against the wind, sun glaring on scales. It's just legend these days. But we all look.

Back at the convoy, Caspian waves me over to where he's sharing lunch with Elias and Darling. I ignore him again, but catch Darling watching me through her smoky goggles before she clenches her jaw and looks down.

I'm not sorry about ignoring Caspian, but she doesn't deserve any petty revenge from me. When everyone loads back up, I nudge my war drake toward Darling's carriage and knock high near the roof where I can reach. She pushes the gilded door open and tilts her head up expectantly.

"I'm sorry," I say. The rest catches in my throat.

"What for?" Darling demands.

I grip the thick leather reins tighter. This can't be harder than leading a charge into battle. "Last night. My behavior was inappropriate. I'm sorry for making unwelcome advances." With that I bow from my high seat and shift my weight to indicate to the drake she should move.

"Talon!" Darling doesn't quite yell, but she's insistent.

I glance back at her.

"It . . . wasn't."

It's my turn not to understand. "Wasn't?"

"Un—um." Sometimes the goggles make it difficult to read her more subtle expressions, but right now Darling scowls. "Inappropriate." She juts out her chin as if daring me to say any more.

It wasn't unwelcome, that's what she started to say. I force the hand on my thigh to relax, and I take a breath. We can fix this. Find our way to something resembling ease or at least alliance. "Ride with me?"

Her brow rises incredulously. "On that absolute monster?"

I shift my foot to urge the war drake to dance a little in place. The drake tilts her head and ruffles her brow feathers as she sidesteps on her massive rear feet. Her forelegs are shorter, with hand-like claws, and she flexes them so the claws gleam sharply under the sun. I grin and look back at Darling. "I think you can handle her."

Darling presses her lips into an amused line. "I've seen what she can do. And no thank you."

I can't blame her. War drakes don't eat human flesh, but they've no problem tearing it to ribbons and breaking bones. Some of them like to scream battle cries, and they can sound hideously human. But before I can be too disappointed, Darling grins back at me. "I have a better idea." With that, she swings out of the carriage door, grips some of the ostentatious gilding, and climbs onto the roof. She bunches her skirts awkwardly as she settles, then gestures around her. "Best view from up here."

I laugh once, and my war drake curves her neck to stare at up at Darling with a single bright green eye. It's like a faceted emerald, lashed by short, downy feathers. War drakes are the deadliest of their species, and the prettiest—especially compared to the more plodding herd drakes like the ones pulling the wagons and carriages. Those walk on four sturdier legs instead of two, with armor on their short necks and bellies, but their spine scales can come in a rainbow of colors.

"Chaos, you *are* gorgeous," Darling says softly to my drake. "But I won't be so charmed by just a pretty face."

It seems a warning for me, too, and I let myself appreciate the compliment.

Ahead, Arran Lightscale signals to me, and then the convoy is moving again. Darling's driver pokes at the herd drakes with his steering prod, and they lumber into motion. I hold my war drake back from the long strides she prefers in order to keep her beside the carriage.

For nearly an hour we ride in silence. Darling takes everything in from her height, especially when we pass an outcropping that lets her see down into the river valley. Then we're under the spiny evergreens with their reddish, scaly bark and towering height. The shade is cool and silent. When you ride war drakes, the birds tend to huddle in their nests. There's just the jangle of tack and crunch of wheels on fallen needles. And the war drakes' claws in the road, their occasional barks or sighs.

"Does she have a name?" Darling asks me suddenly.

"Not that I've given her."

Darling scoffs.

"Feel free."

"Hmm. Vicious. Shadowstrike."

I shake my head and rub my knuckles against the knobby ridge over the drake's shoulder.

"Kitty?" Darling teases.

The war drake flares her neck spines and makes a little bark. I slide a glance up at Darling. Riding like this, my head is level with her ribs. "Kitty it is."

Nothing in the land around us changes, but I know the moment we cross into Dragon territory. Home. It's mine. My family's blood has watered these roots and the peaks for generations. It's rough and bold, beauty only found in majestic chunks of stone, ice-cold lakes rippling with winter light, or sprays of miniature purple thistles. It's hard to live here. But it's mine. Ours. Part of the great hoard—no, the foundations of it. And here it's the shadows of spiny evergreens and soft decaying deadfall. I breathe it in.

"What is it?" Darling asks, leaning over the edge of the carriage to look down at me.

I have no idea how she knew something changed in me. I study the way the light catches the edges of her curls and glints on the smoky lenses of her goggles—strange and beautiful. Then I look out at the forest. Darling is not going to share my sentiments. "We're in Dragon territory. Just the southern tip."

"Isn't it all Dragon territory now?" Her voice is tense.

"Not like this," I say quietly.

We ride again, and I hear Caspian's bright laughter barely muffled by the walls of his carriage. Darling clearly hears it, too. She sighs in frustration and says, "I don't understand your brother."

I bite back a terrible laugh. Then I gesture with my chin toward her driver, who might be able to hear us over the clatter of the carriage and the herd drakes' clomping feet.

Darling grimaces but continues anyway. "It's just . . . he sent me into the maze last night, too. What does he want from . . . us? Why do that? I've been turning it over and over and . . ." She shrugs. "I don't see the strategy."

"He has one," I say, shocked at the revelation of Caspian manipulating us together.

"Or he thinks he does."

I incline my head.

"He should at least tell you," Darling snaps. "Why does he push away people who care about him? And he treats people who try to be his friends so rudely."

There's nothing I can say to that. It almost sounds as if Darling cares about my brother. My feelings about that are disastrously messy: It's good. I want Caspian to have allies. Friends. Or more, if that's . . . what they want. But I want Darling to want me.

"Do you know what his real boon is, Talon?"

My name instead of my title startles me into looking at her again.

"It's not just a boon for painting," she adds. "The way Chaos is . . . all around him somehow, it can't be explained by a talent boon."

I nudge Kitty nearer the carriage, and the drake prances carefully. I reach out to hold on to one of the handles disguised as a golden serpent. "It *is* painting," I insist quietly. "Somehow Chaos bleeds into him, into his paintings, or through his paintings. I've seen him paint in the grip of Chaos."

Darling scowls adorably. The skin at her temple pinches where the goggles press. "Could he have two?"

"Two boons? I've never heard of that." Suddenly I remember I told Elias to find more information about bleeding Chaos or changing boons in their family's library. I wonder if they managed it, or if there was too much distraction. I can't believe I forgot—I let Caspian divert me. First with his antics and then with his wine. And Darling.

"It might just be you," I say, though it feels like the words are dredged out of me with a cold fork.

"Me!"

"You've seen the paintings. The ones he cares about are all of you. You must admit that Chaos helped him create them. How else could he have known you? I don't believe it's because you met when you were young. That he remembers you as the Sphinx scion. If that was the case, they'd all be paintings of you as a child. No. He painted you because of his boon. He knew you because of Chaos."

"Me." She draws her legs up and props her arms on them as she contemplates my words. "You think his boon isn't painting, but . . . something that lets him paint true things?"

"Or something that connects you. Your boon and his, somehow a bridge between each other."

Darling rolls her eyes. "I certainly don't dream about *him*."

"Maybe it isn't two way," I insist. "Caspian's could simply be stronger, and so all the Chaos bleeds his way."

Darling frowns deeply. "The paintings, the way they are true, it's almost like a prophecy boon, except I've never heard of one of those being so focused. On a person. They're supposed to be messy, aren't they? Though I haven't heard much about anything like this magic and history," she adds bitterly.

"Aurora doesn't believe Caspian is a prophet, and she should know."

"I think she's dangerous." There's a stubborn angle to Darling's chin.

"She is my aunt. The only person who has looked out for Caspian—for me—since our mother died. She would not hurt us."

"I didn't say she'd hurt you." Darling frowns. "But that's all Dragons care about, isn't it. Yours. What's yours."

My war drake—Kitty—dances a little to the side, wary of the change in my bearing. "Darling—"

But Kitty throws her head up, teeth bared to taste the air. Her sinuous body is taut under my thighs, and I cut myself off, just as alert.

"What?" Darling breathes.

I lift my hand to signal the soldiers behind me, but it's too late.

Dozens of deadly minor drakes swarm out of the forest. The size of big dogs, they're vicious and mostly claws, teeth, and spines and travel in packs.

First they go for the herd drakes tending the wagons at the rear of the convoy.

"Teeth!" I yell and grab the reins in both hands, wheeling Kitty around. She screams her battle cry. It's echoed back by the rest of the war drakes. We have four with us, including mine.

The wagons stop, attendants and drivers panicked and climbing to the roofs, while Darling clambers *down*. One driver slashes the ropes, and two herd drakes bolt—lumbering but fast, drawing a handful of the minor drakes after them. The Teeth have headed for Caspian's carriage, and the foot soldiers and regular cavalry are defending however they can.

"I need a damn sword," Darling demands, clinging halfway down the carriage.

I unsheathe the claw at the small of my back and offer it. "This is too close contact."

"I'll manage," she says, and hops the rest of the way to the road.

I lean over and grab her arm. "Darling—"

"Talon," she says, and even with the goggles I know she's staring right into me.

I release her. She rips away her skirt and dives into the fray.

With my falchion in hand and my war drake's claws out, I follow.

There are so many minor drakes. Fearless, they charge everything, never alone, so attacks come from multiple sides, and often below. My drake cuts them down with her powerful rear claws, but it's difficult with me in the saddle—I can't reach the littler drakes. But my war drake knows her training, and when I fling myself down to the road, she stays with me.

The Teeth have Caspian's carriage surrounded, and so I just start killing. The minor drakes snap at my legs, and I slash with my falchion, kicking, too. One bites at my free forearm, tearing through velvet and into skin, but I fling it away and spin, cutting the next one through the neck so its head goes flying. I hear war drakes scream, but also the cries of humans, and I step over the body of one of my soldiers. Only the Teeth are in full leathers. We expected human attackers, if anything. And not in Dragon lands.

The minor drakes swarm, but their numbers dwindle. The worst remain, the smartest, slick and fast, and at least two of our war drakes are down. I push Kitty out of the way with my shoulder, then turn to face the minor drakes that had her cornered against two huge trees, but another minor drake leaps onto my back. Its claws find purchase on my sword shoulder, and I brace for pain, turning as I do to try to slam it into a tree trunk. Its fangs find my neck.

Then I'm tackled, and the minor drake screeches, flying off—Darling is there and stabs a sword into its guts. I roll to my feet and cut off its head.

Darling grins at me. Bright drake blood streaks her face and she's got a sword in each hand. "At least nine left—we're down two Dragons, two herd drakes, and none of the Teeth; nothing got into the carriages."

"Good." My shoulder hurts, and there's a sting in my neck. That was too close. But Darling saved my life. Here comes another minor drake, charging us from behind Darling. I pull her closer and turn, blocking the attack.

Then we're fighting back-to-back. It's like a dance, hot and heady, only the music is screeching drakes and the clash of steel on scale. My falchion is covered in gore, and Darling's borrowed swords, too. We make our way toward Caspian's carriage, but a minor drake leaps over the carcass of a dead herd drake, aiming for Darling.

I yell and stab at it, saving her, and now we're even again.

It's over.

We're breathing hard. Our shoulders press together, rising in tandem with each other. My pulse races. It's like I can feel the fire of battle passing between Darling and me, hot and perfect. A brilliance scorches up from my stomach and becomes a grin like the bearing of teeth.

I turn to Darling, and she's grinning right back at me, face a mask of bright blood and black-hole eyes. I want her, so badly. At my side. With me. It's overwhelming how much I want. My hands ache with it, nearly reaching for her, just to feel her arms in my grip, her hands. To laugh with her and share this.

You saved my life, I think as I stare at her. Her lips part, and she nods as if she can hear me, and agrees: *You saved mine, too.*

We tried to kill each other so recently, and here we are. Flooded with battle fury, relieved, comrades. I know what it's like to fight at her side now.

I remember Caspian's message: *Save her. He must save her.*

I put my free hand on her shoulder. It's grounding. My heaving breath slows, and awareness of the pain in my arm and shoulder returns, but that's the worst of my injuries. Darling seems uninjured, all the blood on her that bright fire orange of drakes'. I scan quickly around the battleground, see attendants climbing off the carriage roofs, Arran Lightscale organizing the remaining soldiers, a few injured sitting down in place, and only the two dead. Elias climbs out of Caspian's carriage, their expression urgent as they move to the nearest injury. The living herd drakes will need to be rounded up, the dead tended to, and we need to keep going and find high ground for the night. But for the moment it's calm.

I squeeze Darling's shoulder, then take out the cloth folded in the flat pouch on my sword belt. It's for cleaning the blade, but I step nearer to Darling. "Close your eyes," I say, lifting the cloth and reaching for the button holding those elaborate goggles to her head.

Darling catches my wrist. Her lips part as she studies me. I wait. Finally she releases my wrist, but unfastens the goggles herself. The strap barely tangles in her battle-wild hair. When the goggles fall away, her eyes are shut; two perfectly clean patches of skin surround them. I carefully accept the goggles and wipe the lenses with my cloth, then hold them back up to her eyes. Gently. Darling fastens them again and abruptly punches my wounded shoulder.

I grunt at the pain, and she says, "Your turn."

We make our way toward Elias's makeshift workspace. They've an open bag of supplies beside them and three soldiers waiting to be patched up. "Talon is hurt," Darling says, batting at Marjorie, who darted over in obvious distress at Darling's bloody face.

"It can wait for my turn," I say. "The bleeding isn't bad; it's not deep."

When Darling scowls, I lift my arm. It hurts, but I have full movement.

Elias nods. "Good. Darling, if you're healthy, go help Jerem stanch his bleeding."

Darling goes, and I turn to look for Arran Lightscale, but my brother is standing there.

Caspian is pale—even his normally bright pink lips. But there's no other sign of distress, not even a drop of blood or hair out of place. He stares at me with wide eyes.

"Are you all right?" I ask gruffly.

My brother throws his arms around me. I catch him, shifting my weight at his jarring hug. Caspian squeezes, pressing his cheek to mine. "It's so hard sometimes," he whispers.

"Caspian," I begin.

"So hard, Talon, what I do. To let things be."

Frowning, I push at him. What he does! He hid in his carriage. But Caspian tucks something into my jacket. It crinkles.

The High Prince Regent steps back, a lopsided smile on his mouth now. He's as changeable as a toddler. "Glad you're well, brother. I'll just go see about those drat herd drakes, why don't I?" Then he laughs and steps lightly around a smear of mud on the road.

I gesture for Arran to go with Caspian. Then I pull the paper out of my jacket. It's a sketch in charcoal, the kind Caspian had smeared on his hands when he snuck into my tent last week. In it, Darling and I fight under the shade of spiny evergreens, back-to-back. Surrounded by wild drakes. Both of us smiling. It's elaborate. Complete. Shaded and detailed. Definitely drawn before we were attacked.

A chill slides down my spine. My mouth goes dry. This isn't like a painting of Darling standing before a hearth that turns out to be true. This was an ambush.

He knew.

He didn't stop it.

Two of my soldiers—his Dragons—are dead.

We were all wrong about him. I don't know if this counts as prophecy, but it's enough to condemn him that Caspian *knew*.

I shove the sketch back into my jacket and furiously join in the cleanup.

19

DARLING

After the wild drake attack the rest of our journey to House Cockatrice passes in relative calm. The days drag on as we make our way through the mountains, and I spend most of my time back on top of my carriage watching Talon ride up and down the line. He doesn't stop to chat with me again, but I think it has less to do with me and more to do with whatever new tension has erupted between him and Caspian.

The High Prince Regent is more reserved after the drake attack. I'm not sure if losing two of the soldiers, their ashes tucked away in one of the supply wagons to be returned to their kin, has reminded him what a silly idea this trip was or if it's just another one of his moods, but he spends less time with Elias and me, deciding to remain alone in his tent more often than not. It's enough of a change in behavior that Elias asks me if I know what is amiss with him, and when I assure them I do not, they make excuses and go off to check on the soldiers injured in the wild drake attack. I end up spending the evenings by myself, practicing with the short swords. After the drake attack no one wanted to take them from me, and even Talon no longer seems to be alarmed by the idea of me with a weapon. I suppose everyone has figured I'm not going to kill the Dragon princes the first chance I get.

I keep telling myself that there are reasons that I haven't attacked

Talon and Caspian outright. The odds are against me, for one. A direct attack would quickly result in any number of Teeth and Dragon regulars cutting me down where I stand. But that doesn't keep me from waking in the dead of night and carving open either of their throats. During the interminable hours of travel I try to come up with a dozen different ways I can kill the princes now that I have two very nice swords and a throwing dagger tucked into one of the hidden pockets in my traveling cloak. But the truth is I don't want to kill either of them.

I've spoken with Talon and Caspian enough to know that they are no more enamored of this war than I am. And after the past few weeks there's something about them that makes me think they're telling me the truth, that the war really is over and we have to move toward the future.

Which is how I decide that I am going to ask Caspian to release Leonetti.

After the scene at House Gryphon it seems like a good idea. It's the only logical plan, to be truly honest. I've grown to like the Dragon princes, and I realize that there are far worse Dragons who could be in charge. Such as that brute, Finn, with his snarls and grandma dresses. Or that awful aunt of theirs, with her strange blood flecks and lying eyes. After realizing what the alternatives could be I can't imagine hurting Caspian. Or Talon.

Most especially Talon.

I should be upset by the way I feel when I see him, by how I find myself looking for his long-legged stride whenever we make camp at the end of an endless day of travel or how I feel bright inside whenever I see him looking at me. I should be scandalized by the way he seeks me out as well, whether to spar or just to show me some silly trick his war drake can do. I know the soldiers watch us with dark looks, marking our conversations. We would spend even more time together if it wasn't for his duties, but it's a good thing we're not too often together. The gossip would be unbearable.

I know what Gavin would say, that I am too easily swayed by a pretty face and that the war will never truly be over. He wears his anger like armor, fitted and snug. But I'd already promised myself that I would stop fighting long before I even met the Dragon princes, and I'm so tired of battle, of the blood and death and agony. Maybe these last few weeks as a scion have dulled my edge, but the idea of killing Talon just seems so impossible. I've even developed a soft spot for Caspian, with his maddening habit of speaking in riddles.

A true peace, with everyone learning to work together toward a future that benefits all of Pyrlanum, is a heady thought, and I find that I want that much more than some kind of revenge. Especially since I don't know what House Sphinx did or didn't do. What if they did kill the Dragon consort long ago? How can I hold the Dragon princes responsible when even I don't know the truth? At some point we have to move forward, and how will that ever happen if we never even try?

It's a lot to mull over, but by the time we arrive at the ancestral home of House Cockatrice, I've made up my mind. I'm going to ask Caspian to release Leonetti as part of my reparations, since he seems so enamored of making amends. I'm mentally preparing a speech about leniency and moving forward, because I have learned that where Caspian is involved it's best to be well rehearsed, when the door to my carriage opens and closes. I blink in surprise as Gavin materializes, this time wearing the livery of some other House.

"Is that a flaming chicken on your chest?" I ask, taken aback by both his sudden appearance and his attire.

"It's a cockatrice. Look, I don't have much time. I wanted to give you a heads-up that you need to be careful. This place isn't what it seems."

"What do you mean?" I say, a chill running across my skin.

"It's basically a museum," Gavin says. "I don't even know why they've decided to bring you here. There's not a scion to be found. They've all fled to Avrendia."

My dread dissipates and I shrug. "I already knew that. Caspian told me ages ago that some of these stops were more about appearances than anything else. That doesn't mean it's a trap, Gavin. If the Dragons wanted me dead, I never would've left Phoenix Crest."

Gavin stares at me, wide-eyed. "'Caspian'? You're that familiar with our sworn enemies? In only a few weeks?"

"Gav. It's over," I say, leaning back against the plush carriage seat. "The war is over. It's time to put it aside and rebuild. Unless the battle rages on?"

Gavin shakes his head. "It's just as the High Prince Regent, *Caspian*," he says in a tone like the word is something foul in his mouth, "said. They've surrendered. A flying messenger drake was sent to Adelaide with the terms, which even she said were far more favorable than expected."

I sit up, and I can't quite keep the smile off my face. "And Leonetti? Is he returned?"

"Not yet," Gavin says, dashing my hopes. "They want a meeting at House Barghest with all of the House scions and Prince Regents in attendance. Which is clearly a trap."

"Is it, though?" I say. "If they sent a messenger to Adelaide, they could have just as easily killed her. She should send a representative. I'm going to be there. I could speak on her behalf."

Gavin scoffs. "Oh, how quickly you forget where you've come from. And your vows."

"What vows?" I say, crossing my arms. "My promise to always do what's best for House Kraken? Did Adelaide really want me to kill the Dragon princes? Or was this just you all along, Gav?"

There's a knock on my carriage door, and Marjorie pulls it open just as Gavin's boon renders him invisible. "Is everything all right, my quill?" she asks, her expression troubled.

I clear my throat. "Yes, everything is fine. I was just practicing a soliloquy I was preparing for the High Prince Regent's amusement. It's from the famous House Cockatrice play *A Scion Refused*. Do you know of it?"

"No, my quill. It should only be a few moments longer, and then we will be granted entrance to Mount Klevon. It seems we made better time than they were expecting."

"Thank you, Marjorie," I say, and she gives me a worried smile.

"Are you sure everything is okay?" There is real concern in her voice, and I nod.

"Perfectly. Everything is just as it should be."

Marjorie closes the door and Gavin reappears, his scowl now morphed into something sinister. "You're getting really good at lying. Nobility suits you."

"Gavin, just think this through—"

"I have. And I can't believe you picked them over me," he says, voice low.

"I'm not picking anyone. I'm choosing peace, and you should consider that maybe there's more to life than fighting and killing. Look, I'm going to talk to Caspian, ask him to pardon Leonetti as one of my reparations—"

"Your what?" he says, lips twisted into a sneer. "Look at you. Reparations? How quickly you've forgotten your place. Politics are for the nobles who don't like getting their hands dirty, Darling. You're a Barb. You chose a different path."

"Lower your voice," I say, pointing to the carriage door. "And I chose the only path that was open to me at the time. Am I supposed to keep killing because it's easy?" I take a deep breath and let it out. "No more, Gavin. No more killing, no more fighting. The war is over, and there are other ways to win the day. I'm going to speak with Caspian, make sure that this meeting is legitimate. There's plenty of time on the journey to House Barghest to discover whether or not this is a trap, and act prudently rather than flinging blades at every shadow."

Gavin shakes his head, his expression bitter. "No. You've made your choice. And now I will make mine."

Before I can say anything, he's gone, turned invisible once more. He slams out of the carriage, flinging the door so hard that the sound of the wood cracking can surely be heard up and down the line.

Marjorie appears, expression troubled. "My quill?" she begins, and I force a too-bright laugh.

"Oh, I do not think it was latched all the way. The wind must have caught it."

She nods and closes the door once again, accepting the lie even though the air is still.

Power, it seems, truly does have its privileges.

The town surrounding Mount Klevon is much smaller than that of House Gryphon, most of the shops shuttered and boarded up. After Gavin leaves, I decide that I've had enough of waiting in my carriage, so I climb out to explore the empty cobblestone streets. Our caravan seems to be the only people in town. Once upon a time this was a place where artists created and sold their wares, the remote location apparently provoking creative bursts that led artists from all over the world to journey here. House Cockatrice was well known for smaller artists' colonies throughout Pyrlanum, but Mount Klevon had been the crown jewel.

During the last century of occasional House Wars, House Cockatrice attempted to abstain from violence. From what I've read, it seems that they believed themselves to be above war, as art was a higher calling. They'd been mostly chased out decades ago, but when the Dragon consort died, those remaining should have taken a stand, since she'd been a daughter of their House. The Dragons pressed them to choose, and the last of House Cockatrice here had fled. So the Dragons had claimed Mount Klevon for their own.

By the time the main gates open to admit our caravan into the House Cockatrice ancestral home, Marjorie fetching me from my perusal of an intricately carved door frame to take me back to my carriage, my mind is not on greeting the caretakers of Mount Klevon or even on the heated looks Talon gives me when he thinks no one sees. It's on Gavin, and the fight we had in the carriage. Have I really forgotten where I've come from? What would Leonetti have me do? Kill the Dragon princes or find a better solution to a difficult problem?

I cannot believe my adopted father would want me to poison my enemies in cold blood. He was never even a fan of the Sting we put on our blades, shaking his head whenever he would see us coating our Kraken steel.

The Sting was always meant to be for pirates and outsiders, not our own cousins. Ahh, this war has made monsters of us all.

The memory gives me confidence in my decision, and as we ride through the ornate gates to the courtyard proper, I decide I will find Caspian and ask him to release Leonetti right away. I disembark from the carriage, ready to make my case to Caspian. But I am unfortunately waylaid by a pale-skinned man with unnerving eyes as he bows before me.

"Welcome to Mount Klevon, my quill. I am Josiah Aesthetos, the head caretaker here at Mount Klevon. I welcome you to our remote home."

"Thank you, I am delighted to be here." I glance past him to see if I can spot Caspian, but he and Elias are already walking into the manor house, far ahead of me.

"I invite you to explore the manor on your own," Josiah continues, mistaking my distraction for fascination in the statuary that crowds the courtyard. The woman engulfed in flames that has a place of honor in the midst of the space, a reflecting pool at her feet, is eye-catching, but not where my interest lies.

"Oh, thank you," I say, and Josiah bows deeply.

"Your rooms are ready, and I can have a member of my staff take you directly there if you wish, but Mount Klevon is a place that begs to be explored, and I hope you will do us the honor of enjoying our collection of sculpture and art."

"Okay," I say, because I've never been one for art. I enjoy paintings as much as the next person, but I've never had cause to linger over such a thing. But Caspian is gone for now, and I realize I'm excited to do a little exploring, so I thank Josiah and head into the manor house.

The place is nothing like House Gryphon. That was all dark wood and twisting corridors, the dusty scent of books and scrolls permeating the house. Mount Klevon is all glass and arches, the light flooding the space in a way that makes the room feel larger than it is. The floor bears an intricate mosaic depicting a woman falling off a high cliff. She is engulfed in flames just like the fountain in the courtyard, and I wave over a brown-skinned woman wearing House Cockatrice livery, her long straight hair braided to the middle of her back.

"Yes, my quill?" she says, her expression kind.

"I had a question about the floor. The woman in flames. Is that some sort of House Cockatrice sigil?"

"House Cockatrice gave birth to the First Phoenix," Caspian says, sweeping into the room from an alcove. Elias is behind him, the healer looking upset. It's easy to see why. Caspian is pale and his eyes are wild. The shadows under his eyes are deep enough to look like bruises, and his attire is disheveled like he woke from a nap. Elias whispers to him in a low voice, urging him to get some rest before dinner.

"Stop nagging at me," Caspian snaps, less like the ruler of a country and more like a petulant child. "The hour grows late and my work is not yet complete."

"Caspian," I begin, but he cuts me off with an upheld hand.

"Darling, not now. I believe we were about to hear the story of the woman on fire."

The caretaker shifts her weight from foot to foot. "Ah yes, my blade. You are correct that the woman is the First Phoenix. But that is a story better told by my husband, Josiah."

"Oda is correct," Josiah says, entering the room, Talon and a host of Teeth following behind him. "I had planned a tour of the chapel and the rest of the grounds after the evening meal. Which should be ready momentarily."

"We should take that tour now," Caspian says, and Talon clears his throat.

"Not until my Teeth secure the rooms," Talon says, tone stiff.

"You and your tiresome security," Caspian scoffs.

"I'd also like to enjoy at least one well-prepared meal on this journey," Talon snaps back, "as opposed to wearing out our welcome before the first course has even been served."

I clear my throat as everyone looks anywhere but at the Dragon princes. "I'm absolutely famished," I say. "So if I get a vote, I'd like to eat before the tour, because I definitely do want to see the chapel."

"It is best enjoyed at sunset," Josiah says, giving me what seems to be a grateful smile. "But I am happy to accommodate whatever the High Prince Regent desires."

"Ugh," Caspian says, sighing. "I suppose some things cannot be rushed. Fine, let us eat your ice river fish and be done with it."

Josiah bows, and his wife, Oda, gestures for us to follow her. As

I walk to the dining room, I make an attempt to speak to Caspian, but Elias is there before I can make my move, so I have to settle for walking behind them.

"Thank you," Talon says, falling into step beside me.

"Oh, it was nothing. But is Caspian okay? He seems more erratic than usual."

A muscle in Talon's cheek flexes as his jaw tenses. "My brother keeps his own counsel, so I couldn't say."

"He looks like he may be having trouble sleeping," I say.

"He's always been that way. Ever since our mother died. I remember waking up in the middle of the night, his screams echoing throughout the Dragon manor," Talon says. "Night terrors, the healers called them. The awakening of a powerful boon."

This seems like dangerous ground to tread, so I change the topic slightly. "Your mother was of House Cockatrice. Did she have an affinity for art?"

"Yes, but she preferred to beautify her world with flowers. Growing them, arranging them, preserving them. I remember she always smelled of everbloom and sun drops, her two favorite flowers." Talon laughs and shakes his head.

"What's so funny?" I ask.

"You. It's far too easy to talk to you. You make me want . . ." He drifts off, not finishing the thought. And before I can prod, we are in the dining room, a grand open room with a balcony that overlooks the ravine that abuts Mount Klevon.

But as I settle into my seat, Caspian sullen and Talon trying his best to engage our hosts in the kind of small talk necessary for such awkward meals, I realize that Talon didn't need to finish his thought.

Because I know exactly what he means.

20

TALON

Dinner is remarkably pleasant.

We eat delicious, delicate food unlike anything I'm used to at Phoenix Crest and certainly nothing like army food. Darling's appreciative noises show she concurs, and we share a small smile. Caspian's Chaos-mad behavior falls away; he's loose and flirtatious with everyone, drawing us into conversation as if we're family long comfortable with each other—even Sir Josiah and his wife, Oda. The mood of our High Prince Regent relaxes Elias, too, who engages Oda about medicinal herbs growing only here in Cockatrice lands, and conversation takes a turn toward repartee when Josiah recites a poem intended to teach a healer's apprentice which plants are helpful and which poisonous. Caspian answers with a poem of his own, and soon the two of them flash back and forth with quotes and lyrics.

It sidelines Darling and me, but I don't mind, glad to see Caspian behaving like a prince for once. Then Darling leans toward me, and, just soft enough for me alone to hear, murmurs a line from the "Ballad of Jessamyn" that suits their game. That's the song I drunkenly sang to her in the Gryphon maze. I don't know how to reply, so I only stare at her a beat too long. Darling's mouth quirks up in a crooked smile. I wish I were more of a poet for the first time in my life.

The only dark note to the meal is when Caspian drags us back around to the story of the First Phoenix.

It's tragic and I've always hated it. Every version involves love forbidden across class or House, secret kisses, furious parents, vows, and a gorgeous girl throwing herself off a cliff only to burst into flames and soar high. There is always a promise that justice cannot be killed and will rise again and again, reborn in the flames of the Phoenix's heart. Literally. Supposedly, all the Phoenixes ran hot, with a constant fever of righteousness.

It's ridiculous. And anyway, there hasn't been a Phoenix in over a hundred years, so whatever was in the last one's heart wasn't everlasting. Or wasn't stronger than her enemies. I don't listen as Sir Josiah and his wife Oda trade off telling. I eat. Caspian wheedles his way into the storytelling, then laughs outrageously at the Phoenix's death. There is fish soup on his collar.

Darling says, "I'm sorry I asked."

That jolts Caspian out of his chair. He flings up his hands. "Enough food! Take us on our tour—the sun must be near setting by now!"

As Josiah and his wife hurry to comply, Caspian darts around the table and takes Darling's hand. He tucks it into his elbow and grins before parading her out onto the great balcony after Josiah.

I sigh and quickly take the last two bites of my whipped turnips before following. We were supposed to have dessert, and I feel very petulant about missing it.

Elias and I walk together, not needing to speak. Yesterday I managed to find them alone and ask if they'd found anything about boons in their family's library to help understand Caspian.

They hadn't. Boons had been so different before the fall of the Last Phoenix, and in the intervening years their House had shouldered as much disruption as the rest, unable to engage in true research on exactly why. Elias reluctantly admitted that there were essentially no records of boons causing madness until the last hundred years. "It is possible that it isn't Caspian's boon itself giving him trouble, but its strength. Any powerful enough boon might be stressing the cracks for anyone these days."

I accepted it and thanked them for doing their best with Caspian. Of course, Elias was offended by the suggestion they might do otherwise.

Sir Josiah leads us to the marble balustrade. The balcony overlooks terraced gardens gone rather wild because of the lack of staff here, though they maintain an obvious organizing principle, and that principle is color. This time of year is lush with blooms, including small trees blossoming bright pink and fuchsia. The low sun casts fire over everything, including the valley beyond the gardens and the mostly deserted city. Its elegant lines and pale, steepled roofs seem ghostly, an imprint or a dream. I think of my mother, who grew up here. Maybe right here. Standing where I stand.

Sir Josiah is pointing out the names of the terraces and the small gate to the private forest. The road we drove up through town. Then we turn to the marble arch right against the cliff that leads to narrow, worn stairs and the rest of the magnificent House Cockatrice.

We climb up the face of the cliff—which is also the face of the manor itself—pausing at several balconies. Some are guest rooms, and I have already been here, but most Josiah shows us are various studios used in the past by scions of House Cockatrice for their art. Their insides are light, airy spaces lit with the remains of whole arrays of lanterns.

I hold my attention more on Darling—who seems to appreciate the openness of this place, or perhaps just Josiah's paternal sensibilities—and my brother, who remains on his best behavior.

I haven't asked Caspian about the sketch. I don't want to listen to him lie to me. Again. I want him to come to me voluntarily and invite me in. Trust me. Maybe that's what the sketch is meant to do. But what does he expect me to think about only this little shred of information?

Maybe he doesn't even remember hugging me and giving me the drawing.

Nor have I shown it to Darling, though I considered it. What point would it serve? It would upset her, make her mistrust us again. Caspian, at least. I'm not sure she trusts me—except, she must. We fought side by side, saved each other's lives. That is a knot that can't be untied. And in the aftermath of the battle with the wild drakes, it's almost been like we're friends. I didn't even try to take the swords back from her, and despite my injury approached her two mornings to spar. It was good, and *fun*. A better way to be close to her under the careful observation of my soldiers than hanging around her carriage as I'd done that day. There are too many Dragons and Teeth who remember what it means that she was a Barb. We need to move slower, let mistrustful others see how we're building up a connection. A friendship.

Real peace is too complicated for me to imagine, but I'm starting to hope we can end this war. Not because Caspian says so, but because if Darling and I can find a way to bridge the distance between Barb and Teeth, maybe the whole country can.

I'm so caught up in my thoughts I barely notice when we enter the chapel.

It's dark and small. Ancient. A cave cut beneath an overhang at the pinnacle of these cliffs, the chapel is mostly in shadow. Old, hard-to-see carvings of each of the six empyreals decorate the stone roof, and the balustrade here is nothing but misshapen rocks held together by crumbling mortar. Caspian directs us to the carvings. "Look." He points at the Dragon. Its chest is set with a fist-sized piece of topaz. "We have a shield called the Heart-Plate of House Dragon, said to be made of that front piece of the First Dragon's chest armor."

My father showed it to me once. It was dull yellow, shaped something between a triangle and heart. Set in the back with leather straps to hold. Father said, "Strike me with your knife," and because even as a child I knew better than to hesitate when he commanded me, I did. The blade shrieked against the shield but did not harm it in the slightest.

Sir Josiah gestures to the Cockatrice on the ceiling. It is a ferocious-looking long-necked bird with flared wings, and its one visible eye is an amethyst the size of my fist. Each empyreal has jewels set into their carving: the Gryphon's claws are red garnet; crescent pearls gleam in the tips of the Kraken's first tentacle; sky-blue sapphires are the Barghest's fangs; and ivory shards make the mane of the Sphinx.

"This place is ancient," Caspian says. "Our mother made a garden when we were small, shaped like a six-point star. Each ray held flowers in these colors. And in the center were violets. Just plain violets. Do you remember?"

He's talking to me, though staring only up at the empyreals on the stone ceiling.

Through a thick throat I say, "She constantly tended the violets. They were—weeds."

Caspian laughs once. "Beautiful weeds. They'd take over if she let them. Eat up the space of the more delicate pinkshade and bloodwort and . . . the white ones."

"Sun drops," I say.

My brother nods absently.

Elias steps beside him. "Is there something for the Phoenix?"

It works to snap Caspian out of his sliding mood. "Ah!" With a grin he turns to Sir Josiah, and the older man moves aside from his place at the edge of the chapel balcony. He gestures at the cliff wall, right where it meets the balustrade. There's a shadow there. We all move closer.

Against the gray stone is what looks like a smeared black handprint. Left by fire.

Darling drifts nearer, reaching out as if to put her hand against it. I understand the impulse. The print—if that's what it is—is much smaller than my hand. But might be exactly Darling's.

"It is said the First Phoenix left this mark after she fell," Josiah says, not in a hushed storytelling voice, but plainly. As if it is too important to exaggerate. "After she burst into flame, she flew up here and grasped there to drag herself back onto the balcony."

"I want to see the top," Caspian declares. He walks away, into the darkest part of the chapel.

"The—" Josiah hurries after Caspian, to arrive first where a small wooden door leads into the cliff itself. "Here, Prince Regent, allow me."

The door opens with a creak, and Caspian slips past. The rest join him, except Darling, who remains beside the fiery handprint.

I wait for her.

But when she finally moves, it is not to go after Caspian: she leaps up onto the balustrade, nearly taking my breath away.

Darling clings to the edge of the cliff as she stands carefully, balanced in her boots on the old rock wall. Wind tugs at her layered skirts and the stray curls loose from her braid.

My heart pounds in my throat. I take a slow step. I can't startle her, or she'll fall hundreds of feet into the valley. The sun has set and she is a dark silhouette against the feathery blue sky.

"Darling," I say carefully. Like she's a feral wolf.

Her only answer is to lift her hand to her head. In one violent motion she rips off her goggles and drops her hand. The goggles dangle against her thigh. I want to add them to the other pair I have, that I took from her the night we met. One is just one, but two is the start of a hoard. I have a very Dragon-like urge to hoard everything I can of Darling Seabreak.

There is so much light beyond Darling: silver and gilded clouds pulling away from the low western mountains. But below the world is twilit, soft with shadows. Darling's shoulders lift in a sigh.

"What are you doing?" I ask, taking another step closer. I'm going to choke on my own pulse if she doesn't come down. Two more steps and I'll be near enough to grab her if the very old, absolutely untrustworthy wall crumbles under her feet.

"Wondering what it would be like to burn on the way down."

"How about we not find out what the way down feels like." One more step.

Darling shifts her weight to drawl at me over her shoulder, "Why, Talon, you sound nervous."

"And you sound like Caspian," I say through my teeth, and take the final step.

With the light behind her she already looks surrounded by pale blue fire, and her wide eyes do that sharp Chaos sheen. Darling wrinkles her nose at my comment.

I lift my hand and offer it to her.

First she tucks her goggles into a pocket hidden in the fold in her skirt. Then she studies me as if contemplating something. It turns out I can't read her expression very much better without her goggles. Her eyes are too vivid, too big. Her lips part, but she says nothing. Then slides her hand into mine. I don't move. Let her take all the action. It's safest that way.

Darling steps down, giving me her weight through nothing but our clasped hands. When both of her feet are on the solid chapel floor again, I expect her to pull away. She doesn't.

She looks up at me instead. My pulse quickens again for entirely different reasons.

My fingers, my palm, they feel like they're on fire.

The thought falls out of my mouth: "It's like your hand really is a flame."

Darling gasps, and her fingers twitch tighter around mine.

"Darling."

She nods once, twice. Slowly.

I kiss her.

Our linked hands press between us, and my mouth is suddenly against hers, too hard, but Darling wraps her other hand around my waist, under my jacket. Clinging to my shirt, pulling us closer.

I touch her jaw, angling her head, and will myself softer. My lips, my closed eyes, my tense shoulders. Darling presses our lips together again and again. Small dry kisses. I breathe her in. Her skin is so warm; she smells of hair oil and the dinner wine and something light and smoky.

Darling leans her whole body into mine, and I hum eagerly, deepening the kiss for a moment before drawing back to look at her.

Her lashes flutter as she opens her eyes. They are all I can see, so close they blur. I swallow and stroke my thumb on her cheek.

The distinct sound of clapping, slow and sarcastic, interrupts us.

My entire body jolts, but I don't leap away. Neither does Darling. Together we turn to Caspian, who waves his hands at us. "The others are just behind me," he singsongs.

That erases my reluctance to let go, but I look at Darling first.

She seems resistant as she lowers her eyes and untangles her fingers from mine. Then goes back to the balustrade. I reach out and grab her wrist. "Not so close," I say in a low voice.

I can feel her roll her eyes. But she doesn't climb back up.

Caspian says in one of his higher performance voices, "Now now, little brother, no pushing pretty girls off balconies. We don't have Phoenixes anymore, do we?"

"Thanks to whom?" Darling reminds him.

He laughs and does a skip hop like a dance.

I frown. He was fine a few minutes ago, but the mood is off now. Caspian is slipping again. His grin is not a good one. His gaze unfocused. Seeing me staring, he wrinkles his nose in imitation of how Darling does it. Instead of cute, it's awful. Caspian laughs at my expression. High pitched and wild.

Elias comes up behind him, slipping a hand under Caspian's elbow. But Caspian jerks out. "No room for more lovebirds in this dim chapel," he says with unnecessary cruelty. Elias's lips press into a line.

Behind them Sir Josiah tries to melt into the wall.

Caspian leans toward me and whispers very loudly, "It's not time for this yet, little dragon."

"Time for what?"

He shoots me a disbelieving side-eye and dances toward Darling instead. "Did you know I painted you here once? Here, no—" Caspian grips her shoulder and turns her, then takes her face in one hand. His fingers are like a pale spider stretching its legs across her brown cheek, his palm on her mouth. I reach out to drag him back, but Darling takes care of herself, slapping his wrist away to reveal bared teeth.

"Don't you want to see?" Caspian pouts dramatically. "Talon, you come position her; she clearly doesn't mind your touch. I'm sure you recall the painting."

"No," I say firmly. I do remember the painting, now that he points it out. It was sunset, right here, and Darling's eyes glowed in an eerie blue that mirrored the sky. Like you could see straight through her skull to the sky behind. All those paintings had disturbed me, but this one had been among the most unsettling.

I meet Darling's angry gaze and nod once, promising to take care of this. "Let's go, Caspian."

He puts a hand to his forehead and wilts a little. I slip near enough to catch him if he gives us a full swoon.

Elias says, "I can escort him. He might need one of the tinctures that I—"

"I'm not sick," Caspian snaps at his doctor.

Elias's nostrils flare, and they look ready to snap back. At their High Prince Regent.

Offended, I put myself between Caspian and Elias. "Let's go, Prince Regent. Thank you, Sir Josiah," I say to the older man desperate to vanish. He bows stiltedly.

Darling says, "War Prince."

Startled, I look right at her, a little too openly. She's frowning, but there's worry in it.

I try to smile with reassurance, wishing I could squeeze her hand. Or kiss her again right now. Remind her I'm Talon to her now. Still.

She sighs, relaxes a little, and says, "Caspian, try to get some sleep. I need to talk to you in the morning."

Caspian just giggles like she's said something adorable.

I put my arm around his back and hold his waist so I can firmly guide him away.

He goes without protest but starts to sing softly, a nonsense lullaby about a pair of proud chickens that our mother used to sing.

We get halfway down the long maze of balconies and stairs before his song drifts away and he says, "Why aren't we still in the chapel?"

My grip tightens. "You were being mean."

"What!" He laughs. "I'm not mean to any of those people we were with. I like Elias very much, you know."

"You don't show it." I remember what Darling said the other day about Caspian being cruel even to those who obviously care about him. My stomach hurts. I wish I hadn't eaten any of that wonderful food.

"Oh, I'm very nice to Elias," Caspian murmurs. "And they're *very* nice to me."

There's an edge to his voice that makes me worry Caspian is taking advantage of Elias's feelings. I grit my teeth. We go back inside the manor through the dining room, clear of dishes now, the candles doused. Two boonlanterns glow near either door. In the corridor we pass several Dragon guards and Dragon attendants. Only two of the Cockatrice stewards. I wonder if the House truly will return here if Caspian successfully ends the war. Will he invite the other side of our family home?

I find his room while Caspian leans against me, languid as he walks. His head lolls slightly, and he stares up at the airy ceiling, higher and more arched than anything in Phoenix Crest.

At Caspian's door, I tell one of the Dragons to send for tea and water, but inside I dismiss his attendants, telling them I will care for him but call them if necessary.

His room is wide and bright, pale marble and dressed in diaphanous yellows with splashes of dark gray. Elegant and stately.

Caspian goes to the vanity and collapses bonelessly in the ornate chair. He stares into the copper mirror. The reflection makes him seem bright as a sun. But Caspian leans forward, putting his elbows onto the polished wood and shoving aside a few powders and hair accoutrements. He says to himself, "I'll always look like this."

"Tired?" I stride to his trunk and the wardrobe where his things have been unpacked even though we leave immediately in the morning. I jerk the door open.

"Young. Beautiful. Haunted."

I snort, sorting through the clothes for something he can sleep in. "You'll get wrinkles, I assure you, and white hairs—you're already giving them to me."

"No, I'll never be old."

"You aren't immortal."

"Oh, living forever isn't the only way to only ever be young."

A chill clutches my spine. I spin. *"Caspian."*

But he only touches one long finger to his forehead in the mirror. "I could die right now. Tonight."

I feel like he isn't talking to me.

"Do you think Aurora wishes to return here, lead Cockatrice for me?" Caspian asks, voice normal, as if he wasn't just drifting along suggesting he was about to die. He leans into the chair and rocks his head back, the knot in his throat working as he swallows.

I ignore him. My hands itch to unsheathe my falchion. Instead, I open myself to my boon.

Someone is standing right behind Caspian, invisible.

They appear just as I throw myself at them—a knife in their hand, driving at Caspian's very exposed neck.

I hit them in the arm, dragging and spinning around to throw them away from Caspian.

It's a young man my age, in Cockatrice livery: he grunts as he hits the floor, glares at me, and then right there vanishes.

I take out my falchion. Caspian says, "Talon, where did he go?"

"Stay right there," I command my brother, reaching for the trace of the assassin.

It's easy to find, knowing he's there.

I know it: this is the same trace I tracked throughout House Gryphon. It's been with us the whole time.

"You can't hide from me," I say, staring at the spot where his head probably is. "I know exactly where you are."

The trace moves, and I move to block Caspian, falchion out.

"Let me—" Caspian says, picking up the ornate chair like he'll throw it.

"Don't distract me," I say. I keep myself between the assassin and Caspian.

Then he darts in, and I barely follow him—I turn to use my shoulder to hit him, take the blade if I must—I'd rather not, because any assassin is probably from Leonetti and they use poison.

I slice with my blade, and the assassin darts away again: I feel a rush of wind and dodge, kicking where his legs must be. I don't hit anything.

My breath is already hard—it takes too much effort to track someone invisible and actively in motion with nothing but my boon. It's not a strong boon!

I yell for the guards.

The assassin hisses and sprints away.

"Stop him!" I yell when the door opens, but the guards don't see anybody but me and Caspian behind me.

I let myself have a second to glare at my brother and order him, "Stay here." Then I'm off. "Secure the prince," I say over my shoulder to the Dragon guards.

I feel for the trace and run. It's heading out, toward the main exit. No misleading me, just trying to escape. If he makes it into the gardens, into town, I'll never find him.

But I'm getting closer: the trace is stronger. I focus with everything I can. Down the corridor, past doors—there's a servant picking themselves up like they were pushed over by nothing. I take the corner fast and leap down a shallow flight of stairs, landing in the entryway. I hit hard, bending into a crouch and stab out.

My falchion hits a body. Blood appears in an arc as my blade pulls free. It splatters the floor. I keep going, reaching.

The assassin appears, clutching his side. Blood seeps through his fingers. His other hand has a blade. He grins at me, vicious and eager.

I think I know him.

I attack, shoving the familiarity away.

His blade is short, but maybe—probably—poisoned. I can't let it nick me, and that makes us fairly evenly matched. We clash, I dance away, and then he feints left and vanishes again.

It must be his best trick, and he tries to use it to confuse me, moving right and then left around me. I don't move. I know exactly where he is, but pretend I'm more exhausted than I am.

He springs—I spin. I catch him in the gut. He reappears, stuck on my falchion. Eyes wide, mouth open. Then he grimaces at me, blood in his teeth, and instead of pulling free he shoves closer and raises his dagger.

I let go of my falchion and grip his wrist with both hands to keep the point away from me.

My boot slips; we fall back.

It hurts, jarring through my bones. I bite my tongue and blood gushes. But I don't let go. He's on top of me, straining all his weight to stab down with the dagger. I hold on, push back, trembling with the effort and trying not to choke on my own blood.

"What is—" yells a very welcome voice. I can't answer, though, teeth gritted.

The assassin leans into me, his blood spilling down my blade that's trapped between us now. His lips move over bloody teeth, as if he's saying something. "At least, you," I think he says.

His knife is a breath away from my cheek; that's the only reason the Dragons and Teeth surrounding us aren't knocking him away. That, and I'm their War Prince. If I can't survive this, I don't deserve to.

"Gavin," I manage.

It startles him. His body jerks, and his eyes fly to mine. The pressure in his arms gives just enough; instead of pushing him away I can squeeze his wrist with all my might.

He gasps and drops the knife. I turn my face away and roll us. He cries out in pain, and I pick up his poisoned knife, straddling him, and grimly shove it into his neck.

Gavin Swiftblade dies.

I'm breathing harshly. My whole body aches. I'm covered in blood. Mostly his.

He was a Dragon once. I blink. I knew him when we were kids. His family . . . My father turned on them. Their father betrayed us first. I don't know. I don't care right now.

"Chaos," growls Finn, kneeling beside me. "Are you all right, my blade?"

I nod. Still staring down at Gavin. My vision is spotty. "Secure this whole place," I say quietly.

"Are there more?"

"No, I don't think so."

"Seabreak."

I suck in a breath. Hold it. My tongue is tangy and sharp with blood. "No."

"But—"

"No. Finn." I finally look up at him. His scowl is mostly concerned. His Teeth are just behind him, worn from traveling hard. They were supposed to meet us here after settling Leonetti in House Barghest.

My head hurts, and I still can't focus well. I see little spots of purple silver, rainbows wavering over my vision. It's pretty. I like it. That's a bad reaction to have, I know; I just can't help it.

"Talon, are you sure, because I've come from Barghest, and we are certain Kraken is planning an offensive there. They're amassing their navy far off the coast. And the Barghest regent is dead."

I sway.

Finn catches me in a strong arm. "Talon," he says, tight like he's trying not to panic. "Are you poisoned?"

"No, I—my boon. I used it too much. Just lock this place down." I raise my voice at the end, to make sure the Teeth around us are moving.

"Darling Seabreak—"

"I'll take care of her," I insist. "Just do as I say."

"First I'm getting you some water, and food." Finn glares at me.

I let him help me to my feet.

We stare down at Gavin Swiftblade, and that's when Finn sighs. He nudges Gavin's leg with his boot. "We should get rid of the body. We don't want anyone to know that a former Dragon did this. Tried this."

As I look at Gavin's bloody face, his limp, lifeless body, I feel nothing but distant, hollow sadness.

21
DARLING

After the kiss, that delightful and poorly timed kiss, my nerves are aflame, jangling at the remembered roughness of Talon's lips pressing against mine. So when the War Prince takes Caspian back to his room, a good call since the last thing we want is a repeat of the incident at House Gryphon, I take myself to one of the indoor gardens we passed on our tour of Mount Klevon. I can't quite trust myself to return to my rooms. I'm sure Marjorie would glean that something has happened before I could even concoct a believable lie. So I find a patch of night-blooming flowers, not everblooms but something equally fragrant and cloying, and collapse on the grass beside them. When I first arrived in Leonetti's island house, I was enthralled by the gardens, acres of fresh, living things that bathed in the sunshine. There was nothing of the sort in the sewers of Nakumba, and I have forever thought there was something Chaos-blessed about a garden. No matter where it might be.

Besides, I'm sort of hoping that perhaps I can get another dance in the moonlight with Talon. This time while he is sober.

There are a million tiny voices in my head, yelling that kissing Talon was a bad idea, but I ignore them all. Those few stolen moments are the best thing to happen to me in a very long time, and I'm not quite of a mind just yet to listen to my better sense.

But thinking about the kiss has me thinking about the First Phoenix, and that burning handprint on the balcony of the chapel high above the ravine. Before I quite know what I am doing, I am standing and twisting and turning through the corridors, heading back to the chapel of the First Phoenix, returning once more to see the place for myself.

I cannot quite explain the spell that overtook me when I saw the chapel. It seemed familiar, yet exciting and new. I didn't say anything to Talon, feeling too silly to indulge in flights of fancy with his scowling seriousness. My sudden decision to walk along the crumbling balustrade had been mostly to torment him. I love getting under his skin, and just because we are no longer at odds does not mean that causing his stoic expression to dissolve is any less enjoyable.

But I mostly climbed atop the railing because there was something within me that wanted to fly. I had half a notion that if I leapt to my death, I would burst into flames and soar, screaming in joy and fear all the way down. I, of course, have no intention of jumping. I have no desire to test the limits of my healing boon, and death is far from one of my many desires. But still . . .

What would it be like to burn all the way down?

When I arrive in the chapel, the various empyreals glinting in the low light of the boonlanterns, I am not alone. Instead, Caspian is in the room as well, muttering and swearing against the wall.

"I cannot see a blasted thing, but another boonlantern will draw attention, and we do not want that. No, we do not."

"High Prince," I say, my voice low to keep from startling him. "I thought you returned to your rooms."

"Ah yes, I did, but there was an assassin, and I realize the timeline is compressing, ever shorter, faster and faster. Chaos help me, but I have been set to a thankless task," he mutters. I blink, and he turns on me. "Are you real? Or a vision?"

"Caspian," I say, as one would to a skittish drake pup. I'm reeling a bit from the word "assassin." Could he—could Gavin . . . I clench my jaw and make myself calmly continue. "It's Darling. And I'm real. There's no assassin here. Perhaps we should get you back to your rooms?"

"Nonsense. Of course there's an assassin."

He's so dismissive and strange, but he's also right: If he isn't imagining the assassin, it doesn't mean it's Gavin. I'm sure there are plenty of people who want Caspian dead.

"Come help me, Darling."

He gestures me forward, and I hesitantly step toward him. His eyes are wild, and now I know what they mean when they talk about a person being Chaos touched, the energy of creation flowing through them so strongly that they lose contact with reality. But when I get closer, he seems perfectly lucid and just points to a ledge an arm's length over his head. It's part of the stone of the dome and extends out all along the chapel. "If I give you a boost up to the ledge, do you think you could pull yourself up?"

I blink. "I . . . yes. Caspian, what is this?"

"The beginning of what was supposed to be, and the end of everything." At my look he gives me a heart-melting grin, turning on the charm. "Don't worry. You might fall, but you definitely will not die."

That sounds ominous and too like my earlier line of thought. But I'm at a loss for what to do. "Perhaps you should just return to your rooms. Didn't you just say there was an assassin in Mount Klevon?"

He waves my words away. "That's being dealt with. And do not give me some nonsense about returning to my rooms. I will remain here until either you or I get up onto that ledge. And you've met my brother. He has nothing on me when it comes to stubbornness."

I look up at the ledge, which is all of a foot wide. It's going to be impossible to climb up there, and the wall below is smoothly carved cave wall. I sigh. I'm not sure why I am indulging Caspian. Perhaps because it has already been a strange night. "Have you ever done a Kraken's Throw before?"

He brightens, like a child handed a sweet. "Ah! Yes, I forget how you sailors love your tosses and acrobatics. I have read of such a thing, and I believe I can manage."

Sometimes on a ship, especially in a sudden storm like the sort that comes up in the southern seas, it takes too long to climb to the top of the mast to cut the sails. In that case, we have a way to throw smaller members of the crew up toward the mast's nets, a move called a Kraken's Throw. It's little more than cupped hands and an upward thrust, but the thrower needs to know how it works as much as the person being thrown.

But before I let Caspian begin tossing me around the chamber, I have to ask him about Leonetti. I finally have him alone, and when am I going to have that luxury again?

"Before I go risking life and limb for . . . whatever this is, I want to ask you something—"

"Yes, yes, I will pardon Leonetti and reinstate him," Caspian says with an irritated wave. "Honestly, it's going to be a nonissue in a very short time."

I relax and laugh a little. "You knew I was going to ask."

"I already put the pieces in motion before we departed. Now, Darling, I do not want to be a bore, but"—he links his fingers together before raising and lowering his hands in a mimicry of a Kraken's Throw—"hup hup!"

I sigh and lift my foot, placing it in his palm. "On the count of three. One, two, three!" On "three" Caspian boosts me high into the air, but he's misstepped and we're both off balance. I reach out for the ledge anyway, my fingers brushing the stone. For the briefest of heartbeats I think that I am going to catch it, but then my fingers slip, and I crash hard onto the stones below.

"Oh. Well, that didn't work," Caspian says as I gasp in pain. I am pretty sure nothing is broken, and even if it were, in a few moments it would be fine. But Caspian doesn't know that, and his careless affectation irks me.

"Just why do I need to be on that ledge in the first place?" I ask when Caspian gestures for me to get up. My pain has faded away into embarrassment. Once I would've been able to make that ledge easily, but these past few weeks of soft living have made me weak.

"Let's get you up there first and then I will tell you. Come now. Hup hup!"

I grit my teeth. "You need to plant your feet and be a foundation that does not move."

Caspian laughs, as if I've told a great joke, but he spreads his stance into something stronger, leaning his back against the wall. I nod and place my foot into the basket of his linked fingers once more. I hope he's strong enough for this.

On the count of three again, he hefts me straight up. I manage to grab the ledge immediately, pain exploding along my fingertips as I split a couple of fingernails. But I put the agony to the side and focus on pulling myself up onto the ledge. It's more difficult than I thought it would be. The ledge is too narrow, and by the time I've gotten myself lying along it, I am breathing hard, my muscles taxed.

"There," I pant. I lie on the ledge on my belly and look down at Caspian. "I have arrived."

"Excellent. Now I just need you to pluck out the eye of the cockatrice right there. But do hurry—I have a feeling we'll have company at any moment."

I very carefully stand before turning to where Caspian points. Up above my head a little ways away is the flaming rooster empyreal. The cockatrice.

"Caspian. You want me to steal the jewel."

"I know, I know, stealing is wrong. But look at it this way: I am the High Prince Regent, and everything in this land is part of my hoard. So, not stealing at all! Now take that knife you have hidden in your boot and—" He makes a stabbing motion.

I gape at him a moment before inching along the ledge to the spot with the Cockatrice. I don't understand why Caspian is so erratic, but even when under one of his spells, he makes a curious sort of sense. I wonder if perhaps he is more moved by Chaos than anyone has considered.

I think once more of the stories of his boon and what it could be. I've never believed the lie that he painted me because he knew of my plight, or because we had met once as children. It was the stuff of fables, not real life.

But a boon of prophecy is also something that belongs to the old stories, so I am unsure. What I do know is that when I look down at Caspian in the low light, his face tilted up toward me, he doesn't look afflicted by madness. He looks desperate and worried.

And that makes me hurry to accomplish the task he's set me to.

After pulling the knife from my boot, which I surmise Caspian must have felt when he tossed me into the air, I go to work on the eye of the Cockatrice. It's an amethyst roughly the size of my fist, and the stone of the cave crumbles easily under the tip of my blade. I make short work of it, and then I am holding Caspian's amethyst.

I toss it down to him, but as he catches it, I lose my balance, slipping off the ledge. There is a moment of weightlessness, and then I am falling, the contact with the floor vicious. I land on my right side, and I can't help but cry out as I do. There's a sickening crunch and a moment of surprise before the pain slams into me.

I am lost in a haze of agony. Caspian is talking to me, saying something about fetching Talon and the Teeth, and I raise my uninjured left hand to wave him off. I don't even think he tried to catch me.

"No, wait," I say. I cough. There's blood in my mouth after I cough, which is no good. That means internal damage. When I roll onto my uninjured left side, I feel around the rib. Definitely broken. Internal damage takes longer to heal, but as long as I can convince Caspian to wait, I'll be able to at least hobble back to my room and sleep through the healing process of my boon.

"Darling," Caspian says, crouching over me. "You need a healer. I'll fetch Elias."

"No. I don't want—" There's a sudden crunching sound as my arm resets itself, and I groan at the pain. Just because my boon heals doesn't mean it feels nice. Pain is part and parcel of the process. "My boon. Just give me a minute and I'll be able to walk it off."

Caspian sits back on his heels. "Ah. Now I understand."

Once my arm has finished setting itself, my rib does the same, and after a few deep breaths I'm able to sit up. I still feel bruised and out of sorts, but I can make it back to my room. "Understand what?"

"How you survived Nakumba. I thought Chaos guided you and your blighted eyes, but I see now Chaos remade you into what you needed to be." He smiles at me. "My mother always assured me that Chaos provides. *The path may not be quick or direct, but in the end, Chaos will win out.* I never quite understood what she meant, but the longer I live the wiser her words seem."

"Yeah, great," I say, finally climbing to my feet. I'm dizzy, and I'll need to eat after such a big healing, but at least I can get back to my rooms. "So now you know my secret."

"And you know mine. Luckily we are both adults who know how to keep matters to ourselves. Come, I will escort you back to your rooms."

We leave the chapel, Caspian secreting the amethyst away quickly. But we've only gone a short way before we encounter the brute from Phoenix Crest, the tall, pale-skinned blond man that Talon called Finn.

"My blade," he says, bowing deeply to Caspian. "It is not safe for you to be out and about. You should return to your rooms and remain there until we have secured Mount Klevon once more. The assassin is dead, but might have compatriots." Finn glares right at me.

"Dead?" I say, my stomach dropping at his words. Surely Gavin hadn't been so stupid to try to attack Caspian within the stronghold of Mount Klevon? Adelaide couldn't have ordered something so risky—so is this what Gavin meant by making his own choice? My heart pounds, which is not helpful, since I am quite sure I am still injured.

"We took care of him," Finn says, his words half snarl. The way he looks at me, I know he wants me to know Gavin's dead.

I stumble, and Caspian catches me. "Goodness, this is upsetting," Caspian says. "It is far too late for this much excitement. We will return to our rooms with haste, as you have suggested."

Finn watches me with narrowed eyes as we go. He and the rest of the Teeth will suspect that I was somehow behind this. And just when I've secured a promise of Leonetti's release.

My sorrow over Gavin explodes into rage. Why couldn't he have listened to me? Why did he have to be so hardheaded? Now he is dead.

And it is all my fault.

"Caspian," I say as we draw near to the corridor that leads to my rooms. "You must believe that I had nothing to do with this. And neither did House Kraken. Adelaide would never."

"Let us not discuss this right now," Caspian says, his tone brusque. "You clearly need to rest. We will deal with politics on the morrow. Good night, Darling." He releases me, and when I sway but remain on my feet, he sketches a bow in my direction before leaving to return to his rooms.

My heart sinks. I did everything right. I tried to get away from the killing and bloodshed, and here it is finding me anyway. Gavin is dead, and Leonetti is still held hostage, and I am a fool who cannot escape the same tortuous patterns of my miserable life.

I return to my rooms, waving off Marjorie and Andra when they wake to help me change into nightclothes. I use my boot knife to cut the dress away, pulling my goggles from the pocket and throwing them against the wall. They hit the plaster hard enough to leave a dent, but it does nothing for the ache in my chest.

And then I throw myself onto my bed and give in to the pain and sorrow clawing at my heart, crying myself piteously to sleep.

FLAME

22

TALON

My head aches. Most of my body is sore from the fight with Gavin Swiftblade, and I've barely slept since. That's no good for traveling hard, but there's nothing I can do about it. Caspian insists on pushing late tonight in order to arrive tomorrow midday at House Barghest. Their regent is dead, and the wake for him will be tomorrow night.

According to Finn the regent died in an accident. Not even a suspicious one, though Finn was extremely suspicious. That's one of his best qualities. He told me about the man's death in the early hours of this morning as we washed up in the tubs behind the Teeth's temporary barracks. We both were covered in blood and smoke from the fast pyre we'd made for Gavin Swiftblade. Finn nearly had to prop me up by the end of it and pushed me into one of the back cots for a nap. I woke after a bare hour of shimmering Chaos nightmares to shovel some food into my mouth and find my brother. Caspian was focused on getting the entire party on the road. I didn't have a chance to do more than confirm he was well enough before I was swept up into his urgency, too.

We've been descending toward the coast for hours now, and I'm ranging toward the front of the convoy with Finn at my side. The first time he heard me refer to my war drake as Kitty, he laughed loud and delighted. I did not tell him Darling gave her this name. I want to tell him. I want her riding at my side. I need to talk to her about the kiss. About Gavin Swiftblade. About anything.

Finn jokes that his war drake needs a name, too. His drake is an even larger beast than Kitty, vivid green and missing a chunk of his shoulder ridge, with fangs so large and old they've cut through the drake's bottom lip and scarred over in a perfect sheath. He's extremely ugly, but Kitty likes him, preening a little to show off. "Bluebird," I suggest, trying for incongruous. Something even less dangerous than Kitty. Finn approves and starts whistling at his drake, wondering if he can teach it to respond to such birdsong commands.

At our very brief lunch break I asked Elias for something to make my head better, and they gave me a shot of a truly heinous tincture. It hasn't drained away my headache yet.

Darling frowned at me when I drank the medicine, but did not say anything from across the temporary camp. She looked tired, too, moving slowly, her hair unbound. She was wearing one of the simplest of her dresses: a sheer overdress of linen and lace that whispered over the tight bodice and trousers beneath. The under layer—the bodice and trousers—was what she'd been wearing that night in the House Gryphon garden. Now she has a sword belt rigged across her back to hold the two swords. It ruins the lines of the dress, according to Caspian's distracted wail when he saw her this morning.

When my mind drifts back to last night, or darts back with the urgency of the chase, it isn't the smell of blood or Gavin Swiftblade's final words that overwhelm me. It's the kiss. Nothing could possibly eclipse such a memory. I wish I could ride with Darling, or find an excuse to walk at her side. I want to touch her wrist. Tell her what I did. Ask if she knew him. If she knew he was here. I won't ask if she was part of his plot. I don't need to: she was not. I trust that. Darling did not know Gavin would try to kill Caspian. No matter how suspicious Finn is, how many narrow looks he shoots at her, I don't care.

I could only offer Darling a tense smile as she climbed back into her carriage.

Finn is regaling me and the nearest Teeth with a story I've heard before, escapades from our early years in the army. This one involves a lightning-scarred tree, old socks, and a goat. We were thirteen. It was a good summer. Maybe my only good summer.

Before I can put in a line about stuffing a sock in Finn's mouth so he wouldn't get us caught with his talking, a huge crack splits the air.

My falchion is out, and Finn moves with the Teeth to flank me as we wheel around.

There's no attack. But our party is startled. Human exclamations mingle with the sharp barks of war drakes and the low annoyed moans of herd drakes. "Keep alert," I say, unnecessarily, and push Kitty to jog toward the carriages. Caspian's is only now stopping, and Caspian sticks his head out the door. But my focus is on Darling's carriage, which jerked to a stop and lists awkwardly to the right. The driver hops off, tossing reins to the nearest soldier, and he and Marjorie bend to inspect something under the carriage.

"Darling," I call when I'm in range. "Are you all right?"

"She's fine," Caspian snaps from his carriage.

Her door swings open. She grimaces as she looks at me but nods. Relief is sharp. I glance back at Marjorie. "Is it broken?"

"Absolutely not," Caspian cries. "We don't have time for this."

The driver stands with a grimace. "Axle."

Marjorie nods.

"Of course," comes Caspian's scoff. "Darling!"

She scowls at him.

"Come ride with me. We'll push on." Caspian waves at Darling's driver. "Move the most necessary luggage onto the wagon, then stay with however many soldiers you need and fix it, before making your way after us to House Barghest."

I choose five soldiers quickly and tell them to help.

"Darling," Caspian snaps again. "Let's go."

Darling's entire physicality shifts into hostility at his tone. "I don't think so, Prince Regent."

My brother narrows his eyes dangerously. "You can get in my carriage or run alongside like one of the beasts of burden if you'd rather."

"With that sweet talk how could I refuse?" she says, coated in sarcasm.

I nudge Kitty in between them and offer my hand down to Darling.

Her mouth falls open, then she snaps it shut and her jaw clenches. But she shoots another look toward Caspian then nods once at me. Determined.

Caspian calls for everyone but those remaining to get going. His carriage door shuts with a sharp clap.

I wait, eyes all for Darling.

Slowly she takes my hand. I move Kitty two more steps until she's flush against the carriage. "Put your left foot there on mine, and then step up and over."

"In front?"

"Yes."

Nodding, Darling mounts without even a second's hesitation. Her sheer skirts bunch awkwardly, but she adjusts them as best she can to perch against the soft curving pommel of the saddle. I lean away from the swords strapped to her back and guide her right foot over against mine. It doesn't quite reach; she's too short, and the saddle's not made for two. "All right?" Darling asks, and I say, "You should settle back a little."

Throwing a look at me over her shoulder, she does so, and then her perfumed curls are in my face and nearly all her weight is in my lap. I'm very glad for the swords as a hard barrier between us. Regardless, my whole body tenses. I push it out with a shaky laugh. We were closer last night.

Darling laughs, too. "It's so high."

My war drake curves her neck to stare at Darling with a single bright green eye. She blinks, and the curling feather-lashes waver.

"Hello, Kitty," Darling murmurs.

Her tone is so gentle it nearly guts me. She said she didn't want to ride a brute like a war drake, but she's not afraid. She's easy on Kitty's back. However, if I take too big a breath, Darling will feel it. I shake my head in chagrin at myself. The reins are still in one hand along with the drake spur in case Kitty gets too stubborn, my arm pressed to Darling's ribs. With my other hand I gently push her hair to one side. It's a loose cloud of curls with only a few small braids holding it off her temples. The rest falls around her neck and brushes my chin and cheek. It smells like everbloom. That's the scent in the oil. "Ready to move?" I manage to sound only slightly hoarse.

She nods, and I look up to signal the front of the line to start. Darling waves at her driver, and I squeeze the war drake with my legs. The drake takes a few slow, long steps.

"You can hold on to the saddle here," I show Darling. "Or this bony ridge over her shoulder. But don't hold her feathers."

Darling touches the drake's ridge with both hands, then slides one up her neck along the sun-warm scales. "They're so smooth."

"If you scratch along her spines, she'll love you forever."

She does so, and Kitty arches her neck in real pleasure.

When I push Kitty into a jog, Darling sucks in a breath, and one of her hands finds my knee. Her fingers dig in. But she holds her seat well, leaning with natural balance.

We jog past everyone, and neither of us glances at Caspian's carriage. Though Darling probably is just concentrating. At the front, I sit back, and the drake slows again.

"Isn't this cozy," Finn says.

I raise my eyebrows at him. Whatever else, I'm still his War Prince.

He drops his gaze contritely. But his lips remain pressed in a flat line. It makes his scar blanch.

Darling, staring at Finn, leaves her hand on my knee. It's fine. Good.

Then she says, "Have you thought that these war drakes are rather more like cockatrices than dragons?"

"How dare you," Finn starts with a snarling edge.

But Darling shrugs. "They walk on their rear legs like a chicken; they've all these feathers. And that eye . . . it's like an emerald. A jewel like—"

"From the chapel," I finish.

"My blade," Finn says, disapproving of my taking her side.

I remain silent. I can see her point but know she's also needling him.

Finn finally smiles. "I suppose you had ample opportunity to study it so late in the dark with the High Prince Regent."

Surprise makes my body go rigid in a way Darling must feel. She tips up her chin, ignoring Finn.

My second-in-command's smile turns into a wide, mean grin. He bows in his seat and pulls his war drake aside. "I'll check the rear, shall I?" He goes.

After a tense moment Darling shakes her head, brushing her curls along my jaw. It's almost soothing. "That drake of his is really horrid-looking," she says.

I hear the rest of the sentence clearly: *just like him*.

But I ignore it, frowning at his accusation. "You went back to the chapel? And Caspian was there?" My inquiry sounds like a demand.

"So?"

So, indeed. I pause. She's here in my arms, trapped unless she wants to do what Caspian said and run alongside the convoy. But I'm not angry with her. "I told Caspian to stay in his rooms. Under guard."

"Because of—of the assassin."

I see Gavin's slack face, sprawled dead limbs. Blood. I taste it in the back of my throat. It isn't like I haven't killed before. Younger than Gavin and for less of a reason. "Yes," I say softly.

Silence smothers us as we ride. Sunlight pierces through the trees. The road here is furrowed dirt, hard and caked. It makes for uneven steps, but Kitty has a smooth gait. I have no idea how to say what I want to say. I'd rather tighten my arms around Darling and try to press my thoughts and feelings from my body into hers without words. Press my lips to her temple. My nose in her hair. I want to but don't.

She seems to sense I'm trying, and her hand on my knee moves: she pats me, then her fingers glance over the back of my hand where it rests on her hip. She settles both hands onto the pommel of the saddle. Our only contact is her thighs and backside barely in my lap, and the tickling sensation of her hair on my jaw.

"Talon," she says very softly.

I wait.

"I didn't know."

"I didn't think that you did," I say immediately.

She nods.

"I am the one who should have been more prepared. He was following us for a long time."

"How do you know that?" Darling flicks a glance back at me.

I take a quiet breath. This shouldn't be difficult. It isn't a secret. "My boon. It's a tracking boon."

"You're a hunter."

Inadvertently my arms tighten around her. I force them to relax.

"You didn't need the lights," she says, sounding strangely relieved. She leans back, truly settling against me.

After a moment I realize she means all those weeks ago when we met. When we fought in Lastrium and the Barbs cut the lights. She stabbed me with the table knife. I stole her goggles.

We ride for a few moments. There are more questions I should ask. But I don't want to. I don't want this ruined or tense. I just want to be with her. And I want to kiss her. Kiss her until that's all I can think of, no blood, no assassins, no plotting or war. No wild Chaos-touched brother with impossible plans. I move her hair aside again—it will immediately drift back into my face. But I say quietly, at her ear, "I would like to kiss you again."

Darling shivers. "In front of everyone," she chides. "I don't think your ugly boyfriend would like that."

I huff softly and pull away. Of course, I can't go far. "He'll get used to it."

"Presumptive of you to think I'll let you," she says, flirtation foremost in her tone.

The war drake dances a little to the side, wary of the change in our bearing. Darling clutches at me, then releases me like I'm on fire. She laughs and holds on to Kitty.

We ride in a more comfortable silence. The questions between us can hold for a while, I think. What we aren't saying. This is enough.

Except there is one thing that hardly has to do with Darling and me. I ask, "Do you know why Caspian went back to the chapel?"

She sighs. "He stole the amethyst from the ceiling."

"What? Why?"

"I have no idea, but he was desperate for it."

"I'll ask him."

"Think he'll tell you?" Darling needles.

I don't. My face feels heavy with the weight of my frown.

Darling nudges my ribs gently with her elbow. "He does have a plan. The amethyst eye, the gryphon dagger. He's after something."

I think of the drawing Caspian gave me, the one of the two of us battling the wild drakes. I should show her. It's in my jacket. I keep it on me because I don't want it seen without my permission. It's mine now. The madness of it, the promise in it. Darling and me together. That prophecy is mine. Like I want Darling to be mine. "I think so," I whisper.

Darling nods. Her curls tickle my lips. "I just don't know what it could possibly be. And if it's something good or terrible."

Before I can think of how to respond, she twists around to really look at me. I have to avoid the arc of her sword pommel. She says, "If you figure it out, tell me."

I look into her goggles. In this light I can almost see the shape of her eyes through the smoky lenses. "If you figure it out," I repeat more gently, "tell me."

Darling promises. I do the same.

If this were a different world, I'd kiss her right now, soft and slow. That would mark the promises we made, bind them in front of my soldiers, my brother, the long road, and the open sky. But it is this world, and I don't.

23
DARLING

The kiss has changed everything. And it is all I can think about. As I ride with Talon, the warmth of his body seeping through where his hand rests on my hip, leaving what feels like a brand, I'm not thinking about Gavin. I don't think about his last moments or why he had to rush into a situation he hadn't properly assessed. I should be. I should be mourning! But instead I am trying to figure out a way to make it all work: freeing Leonetti, convincing House Kraken to work with the Dragons toward peace, and Talon.

I want it all, and I want Talon by my side until I get my fill of him.

He is not the first boy or girl I've felt like this about, but usually the fascination burns hot and fierce and fizzles out in a few days or weeks. And I want to let what is between us run its course. I know my mind will be occupied with nothing else until it does, and there is so much I have to do. At some point I will be regent of House Sphinx, and I will have to rebuild and figure out just what it means to have my own House.

But before I do, I want Talon. A few days, a week at most and we can go our separate ways. After all, what more can there be between us but a little physical exertion? His Teeth have been giving me death glares all morning, and he is a Dragon. The War Prince. It would never last.

This is how I convince myself that the things I feel for Talon aren't a disrespect to Gavin's memory. Gavin understood bodies and their urges. He was always the one to encourage me to go after someone I wanted, and I did the same for him. It hurts to know we will never pass a tin cup back and forth and share our stories of our romantic conquests again, and every time I think of him, I am so angry. It's easier to focus on something else instead.

Talon pressed against my back, his war drake stepping lightly along the road, is an excellent distraction. I hope Gavin's ghost, Chaos protect him, will understand.

When we arrive at House Barghest, a long hard ride that leaves everyone in a dark mood, there is no celebration to greet us. Instead, mourning banners in deepest violet drift off the turrets and ramparts, the misty, gray day making the purple material hang morosely. Servants and stable hands come out to wrangle the drakes, and their conversations are marked in low tones. There are no aristocrats to bow and scrape for the High Prince Regent's arrival. The wake is scheduled for tonight, and as is the custom, the House scions will remain cloistered until it is time to celebrate the life of their regent.

Instead, as Talon hands me carefully to the ground, a liveried House Barghest servant offers to show me to my rooms, while Marjorie oversees the unloading of the single trunk I was able to bring along. Before I depart, I shoot one last heated glance at Talon, and the look in his eyes smolders.

"I'll find you later," he says before turning Kitty around to see to matters of his own. I watch him go, a moment too long, and when I turn back to the servant, Talon finally trusting me enough to let me check my own room, Finn sneers at me before following his prince. I ignore him, my head held high, and follow the servant into the fortress.

While the other House seats were pretty things with defense as an afterthought, House Barghest is nothing but an imposing defensive structure. The walls are made of thick stone blocks, and the massive structure backs up to a sheer sea cliff. I've sailed past on the seaward side, and I know there are cannons that line the ramparts for any who dare to get too close. The entrance features a portcullis and murder holes, and the only decor that alleviates the grim facade is a stained-glass window in shades of darkest gray. The thing depicted there is a huge, hulking dark beast with four legs and a face with a short muzzle and snarling fangs. A barghest.

The servant escorting me has not once met my eyes. I am beginning to think they do things a bit differently at House Barghest, because every servant I have seen looks like the joy has been ripped from them. The whole place gives me a feeling I dislike, like I have walked into a shadow on a chilly day and cannot find my way back to the sunshine.

I make it to my rooms with a minimum of fuss, although the moment with the servant leaves me unsettled. I refuse his offer of tea or a spirited beverage and pace until Marjorie arrives, two somber-faced youths carrying the trunk between them. When they leave, I round on Marjorie.

"What is this place?" I ask. "I know the regent just died, but the servants . . . they seem like someone has stolen everything they love. Surely their regent wasn't that beloved?" Everyone in House Kraken seemed to love Leonetti, but I still can't see the House being this distraught over his passing.

Her nose wrinkles in distaste. "Did no one tell you?"

"Tell me what?"

"House Barghest is served by indentures, people who owe the

House money. They work in exchange for their debts, signing contracts that can be as long as ten years."

"What? How can that be?" I say. "Why would Caspian allow such a thing?"

Marjorie gives me a strange look, as though she cannot understand my dismay. "The High Prince Regent doesn't concern himself with the affairs of other Houses, my quill. Would you like me to have a bath ordered for you before the wake this evening?"

I nod, and when Marjorie moves off to see to having the water brought up, I begin to pace. If the High Prince Regent doesn't concern himself with House affairs, why would he take the artifacts from House Gryphon and House Cockatrice? Why would he twist himself into knots over "reparations" and reinstating House Sphinx? There's something about the whole thing that isn't sitting well with me, so I go to see the only person who can answer my questions.

Caspian's rooms are in the same corridor as mine, and the soldier guarding the door isn't Finn, but another of the Dragon's Teeth. When he sees me, he gives a slight bow and opens the door to let me in without knocking.

"Ah! There you are," Caspian says when I enter. He's in a state of disarray, as usual, his trousers unbuttoned and a dressing robe thrown over his naked chest. A brass tub sits in the middle of the room, and children who look too small to carry buckets fill it slowly. Caspian doesn't seem to notice them at all.

"How did you know I was coming to see you?" I ask, my suspicions about him having a prophecy boon flaring anew, and Caspian shrugs.

"I figured you'd want to see Leonetti as soon as possible, and I don't think you'll get much help from the House scions."

I freeze as Caspian's words land, my brain slow in parsing their meaning. "Leonetti is here?"

"Yes. Of course. Did I not tell you that? I thought you knew... huh. Always shifting, I have to be more cautious... If you aren't here about Leonetti, why are you here?"

"To ask you why you would allow this House to enslave their own people."

"Indenture is not slavery."

"It's close enough," I say. "You have to do something about it. But first I want to see Leonetti."

"Absolutely not. On both accounts. I have no desire to interfere in House business. And Leonetti is off limits for now. You cannot see him until after you are installed as the regent of House Sphinx. Then you can make a claim of reparations against House Barghest, who technically holds him now, and demand Leonetti's release."

"This is ridiculous," I say, my voice rising. "I have gone along with your utter insanity, playing a game where only Chaos knows the rules, and you won't even let me see Leonetti." My anger is hot and sudden. I haven't been this angry in a very long time.

"After you're named," Caspian says, his tone mild. As though he is discussing the chance of rain, not the fate of my adoptive father. I have never wanted to hit the High Prince Regent more.

For a moment I wonder if Gavin was right. What if this was all a trap? A ruse to get those who hate the Dragons into one place.

My hands fist, and Caspian's eyes flick to my shoulder, where the hilts of the blades I wear are visible. "You also may want to consider disarming while in House Barghest. They do not take kindly to such indignities."

"I don't particularly like watching families sold into labor," I say, pointing to a hollow-eyed little girl with wild curls dumping a bucket of water into Caspian's bath. "But we must all make do."

Caspian sighs heavily. "I will talk to the new regent after he is named. He is but a child and will be easily swayed. There is a way these things are done . . ." Caspian trails off, watching another child dump a bucket and leave. "I dislike the practice greatly as well. I will urge the new regent to do away with it altogether."

"And Leonetti?" I ask, hating the hope that enters my voice.

"Later," Caspian says. "I promise your father will soon be free of all of this."

The tub is now full, and Caspian begins to unrobe with the help of his valet. I take it as a dismissal and sketch a quick bow as is expected before leaving.

"Darling."

I turn around, and Caspian stares at me with a frown. "Be wary of jeweled serpents."

I blink. "What?" I say, but Caspian is already turning back to his bath as though he hadn't even spoken. I take my leave.

Out in the corridor I'm too agitated to return to my rooms, so I ask a passing servant how to get to the gardens. But when I get to the entrance, I am informed the gardens are off limits due to the preparations for the wake, and the soldier guarding the door suggests I walk the ramparts instead.

"It's a good place to work off some energy," he says, a hopeful glint in his eye. "I could accompany you, my quill, if you would like."

I wish for half a moment he were Talon before thanking him for his generous offer and assuring him I can find the way by myself.

There are several staircases to get to the ramparts, and the last reminds me strangely enough of Caspian's winding staircase to his tower. Only, when I get to the top, the door does not open out onto a room full of paintings of my life, but rather a stunning view of the ocean. The water is choppy and froths, as though the seas share my agitation.

"It seems I am not the only one who needed a bit of air."

Aurora, Talon and Caspian's aunt, walks with a retinue of ladies. I don't recognize any of them, but they titter when they see me. I didn't realize she'd be here, but of course. Instead of Dragon regalia, Aurora wears a deep purple dress. She does not wear the gaudy medallion from our last meeting, but a decorative collar that appears to be an emerald dragon wrapped around her neck.

"Oh, do you like it?" she asks, when she sees me studying it. "It was a gift of the previous House regent before his passing."

"It's definitely striking," I say, Caspian's words still fresh in my mind. Prophecy it is. I have to tell Talon.

"Join us, will you?" Aurora says, the other women watching me silently. I'm reminded of the wild drakes that attacked our caravan, the pack of them snarling and biting.

"I am afraid I am not very pleasant company after the day's travels," I say apologetically.

"Ah, of course," Aurora says with a smile. She whispers something to the woman closest to her, and everyone but Aurora turns and walks back the other way, a couple of the women throwing glances over their shoulders.

"There, now it is just us," Aurora says, her voice too bright. "Will you walk with me? Surely after all the time you've spent with my nephews we're practically family."

There's a threat in her voice, and her insinuation is clear. "I'm afraid I've spent more time with my maids, but I thank you for your concern." I don't move from where I stand, refusing to let her intimidate me.

"How sad that you've already forgotten the teachings of your etiquette tutor," Aurora says with a laugh, and I cross my arms.

"So true. But then again, I was a soldier long before I was a scion. So let us speak in the manner of soldiers, plainly and directly. I don't trust you, and I have no idea what you want with me, but I have no desire to be roped into your political maneuvering."

Aurora laughs, the sound high and clear. "My, you are refreshing. Now I understand why my nephew is so fascinated with you." She steps closer. It's perhaps meant to intimidate, but I stand my ground. Her lipstick is too red for her pale skin, and I remember the blood behind her ear at our last meeting. There is something unsettling about the woman, and I have to wonder just how she became the Dragon Seer. Did she twist Caspian's gifts to her own purposes, or does a prophecy boon run in the family?

"I have seen you," she says, her voice flat, her friendly affect evaporating. "I will not let you destroy my House or my nephews."

"Your House is Cockatrice, correct?" I say, and she startles a bit. "I can assure you that the House is still there, though it seems it suffers from a distinct lack of courage. Very beautiful art, though." Before she can respond, I turn to watch the waves, the dismissal clear. "Next time you threaten me, bring some steel along with it, because I can guarantee you that next time it happens, I will not hesitate to draw my sword."

I don't see her reaction, but I sense her pulling back. The nice thing about my goggles is they hide my eyes, and I know she's trying to parse whether or not I would cut her down. That is the benefit in being a former Barb. My reputation precedes me.

"You are not long for this world. Chaos will take you back to the sewers where you belong," she says, venom in her voice, before she departs in a swish of skirts. I stand and watch the sea for another long moment, just breathing in the salty air, so familiar and yet so different on this coast.

I want peace, and to rebuild House Sphinx. Once I am regent, I will be able to use my resources to help Leonetti rebuild House Kraken, and without a war the country can finally move forward to something that works for everyone beyond the elites. It's a good goal.

But how am I supposed to survive the aggravation of politics?

24

TALON

Publicly I have to pretend that House Kraken is the worst of the great Houses, because they are our enemy, but it's definitely Barghest. It isn't just the indentured servitude, which is awful enough—cheating, somehow—but their coastal fortress is dull and ugly, and seems like it was built by someone with a lot of money to spend on what they've heard is a good defense. Not anyone who has actually ever defended a city. The walls are thick, the murder holes plentiful, but most of the corridors are too narrow, and they twist and turn instead of connecting this tower to that rampart directly. There's no way to get anywhere efficiently, especially not with a complement of soldiers or holding a weapon larger than a dagger. I suppose once the walls are breached, this architecture would confuse the enemy long enough to buy more time to evacuate. But it takes too much time for my soldiers and me to clear the guest suites.

The inner buildings are just as ugly, but fitted with velvet and gilded molding, and decorated in styles from every other House. There is Dragon green and gold predominantly, so that none mistake their allegiance, but I also see stained-glass windows Sphinx was known for, though done in muted colors, Gryphon feather patterns in the curtains and even the uniforms of the servants, delicate Cockatrice mosaics, and dogs everywhere.

Not just dog motifs, but actual dogs in the courtyards and gardens, and we displaced an entire kennel to house our war drakes.

After settling them, I quickly bathe and re-dress in a formal uniform, since there is a wake tonight. I take reports from Finn and Arran Lightscale on our way to the inner council hall for a meeting. Arran fills me in on the state of security in the fortress and the additional Dragon soldiers who joined us here. All security is being tightened thanks to the assassin at House Cockatrice, though we've kept that as quiet as possible. Finn passes on reports from his lieutenants on the recent movements of the Kraken off the coast, the safe houses cleared out here in Barghest territory, Leonetti's accommodations, and the sorry troops House Barghest keeps. They're mostly indentured and untrained. Cannon fodder, Finn says with disgust.

I remember arguing about the Dragon army at the last council meeting I attended, because we needed to release a third of the soldiers to return to their homes for the harvest season. That decision was put off by Caspian's declaration concerning Darling. General Bloodscale hasn't released them at all, citing the need for organized dispersal given the so-called end of the war. I intend to make certain any farmers who desert aren't punished in the meantime. Once this tour is wrapped up and we're back at Phoenix Crest.

A sudden worry about where Darling will be when that happens distracts me from Finn's next words. I want her to be with me. At my side. In my arms. But she'll certainly have to be south at the House Sphinx estates.

It's strange that Caspian didn't include Sphinx in this tour. Perhaps because that will be Darling's eventual destination. Or—I recall Darling saying Caspian seemed to be collecting items—Caspian didn't need anything from House Sphinx that he didn't already have in his clutches.

Darling should be attending this council. I stop in my tracks. Finn's shoulder knocks into me—the corridors are so damn narrow.

"My blade?" he says.

I turn, patting his arm reassuringly. To Arran I say, "Go find the Sphinx scion. Bring her to the meeting if she's able."

Arran doesn't flinch, just trots off.

Finn, however, gives me a dark side-eye.

I hold his gaze, brows raised expectantly.

But my friend says nothing. Merely scowls and resumes his thoughts on placement of guards during the wake.

The Barghest council hall is an overly warm room with a massive hearth at either end, blazing with fire, a long wooden table set with a runner of what seems to be beaten silver and jewel-encrusted goblets. Tapestries hang on the walls, depicting fox hunts and the daughters and sons of various Houses bathing in skimpy robes meant to represent their Houses. I go immediately to the head of the table and turn over the goblet there, knowing Caspian won't show and wishing to refuse anyone else the chance to take his seat.

Finn smirks at me—he's always been good at reading my moods and intentions. I wish he could release his anger at Darling, or at least stop letting it feel personal. I think, though they'd both deny it, that they'd get along if their families hadn't been at each other's throats their whole lives. Neither one of them coats their words with sugar or lets me get away with the same. They both believe in justice with their whole beings. It's just they think justice means different things.

Mia Brynsdottir, the niece of the recently departed House Barghest regent, bows lightly to me and gestures for one of the servants at the hearth to pour wine for Finn and me. Mia takes a seat across from me at the table, which is her right, seeing as this is her House. Despite her already pale skin being drawn with tension, and the deep purple mourning veil over her hair, she isn't cloistered with the other scions before the wake tonight. I don't care why—we'd have had to drag at least one of them to this meeting. Mia at least is familiar with Caspian's lack of decorum, and I know her name. I do wonder, though, if she's still got her sights on marriage to my brother.

Just before I speak, the doors push open again, and Aunt Aurora enters.

Relieved, I stand and go to her. "Aunt," I say as I take her hands.

"War Prince," she replies, squeezing. Her bright blue eyes flick over my face, taking me in. I lean down and kiss her cheek. She isn't wearing her Seer seal, but rather a dragon collar encrusted with emeralds that belonged to my mother. I don't know if Mother liked it. I wonder, not for the first time, but definitely sharper than ever before, why Aurora's prophecy boon did not warn her of my mother's murder.

Pushing morbid thoughts aside, I tuck Aurora's hand into my elbow and escort her to a seat next to mine.

"How are you?" she asks softly. "I know about the incident at Cockatrice. How embarrassing to have happened at my old home."

"I'm well, Aunt," I say. It's what she expects me to say, publicly like this. "I have no regrets about the assassin."

"Sent by Kraken, I assume?"

I nod. "We had some intelligence that the last of the Swiftblade family had defected to Leonetti."

"I have just spoken with the young Sphinx scion." Aurora nods her thanks at the servant who pours her wine. "She was taking air on the ramparts. Perhaps I ought to have invited her along."

I let my expression relax, glad Aurora is on my side in this, despite Darling's own suspicions about my aunt. Aurora supports me. And Caspian. I say, "I've sent for her. We need to incorporate her into these things."

Finn says, "Better to keep an eye on her."

"Especially with those squid ships stalking our horizon," Mia Brynsdottir says with a delicate shudder.

"She is the scion of House Sphinx and has as much right to be here as you," I say.

Mia lowers her lashes, but her hand on her goblet tightens.

"I fear she prefers to be more than that," Aurora says.

"How so?" I demand. Anger heats up my spine.

Aurora touches my wrist with gentle fingers. "I apologize, my blade. It is just . . . a vision given to me by Chaos."

Mia Brynsdottir gasps softly.

I force my aggression down. On the other side of Aurora, Finn has his war face on. Hard and hiding every thought and emotion. "Tell us, Seer," I say.

Aurora's eyes flutter closed, and she leans back in her hair. "It was Darling. Her eyes were hidden behind strange goggles made with clear green glass, and she sat in . . ."

My aunt opens her eyes to look at me, widening them. Fear pinches her mouth, but she adds, "She sat in the Dragon Throne, my blade."

I see it, too. Staring at Aurora's wide eyes I can see Darling enthroned. A Dragon. The possessive side of my heart thrills at the idea.

"Oh no," Mia cries, hands pressing to her chest. "Caspian cannot possibly consider marrying that—that orphan."

"She couldn't take it by force," Finn reminds her.

"What else?" I ask Aurora through my teeth. "Did you see anything else?"

"A scar," Aurora whispers. "Like from fire. It licked up her temples and marred the line of her hair."

My pulse is racing. I breathe deeply and ignore Mia Brynsdottir's talking to look at Finn instead.

Finn stares at me hotly. Knowingly.

Aurora says, "Caspian will have to fight his entire council if he wants to make her his consort. And the people! Not to mention Kraken would refuse to accept it."

"The High Prince Regent is in no position to do such a thing," Mia insists. She presses her hand flat to the table, rings gleaming. "For so many reasons, not the least of which are his own proclamations! The only and last remaining scion of House Sphinx, if that is what she is, cannot marry into Dragon! Her heirs will need to be Sphinx scions, and His Majesty cannot provide her with such."

My mouth goes dry. Because Caspian might not be able to do such a thing, but I could. I swallow to wet my tongue and say, through ringing ears, "Aurora, when did you have this vision?"

"What does that matter?" demands Mia.

"Often my prophecies are triggered by a change in destiny that Chaos wishes might be revealed," Aurora explains. She reaches for my hand. "It was the evening two nights ago. I had begun my journey here already."

I nod. And again. We were at House Cockatrice. That is when I kissed Darling. And killed Gavin Swiftblade. I take a deep breath again. "Fine. I will discuss this with the High Prince Regent." Mia tries to speak, but I cut her off. "My brother will not marry Maribel Calamus, I promise you that. Now, let us finish this meeting quickly, so that we may all prepare for your regent's wake."

I meet Mia Brynsdottir's eyes, then Aurora's and Finn's, making my certainty known.

It is not long before we've completed the little discussion on other immediate topics we can manage without Caspian, who, of course, never does arrive. Nor does Darling. If she was on the ramparts, perhaps Arran couldn't find her. I dismiss everyone. We all have jobs to do before the wake, to ready the fortress for the night and whatever comes of the Naming ceremony tomorrow—and the Kraken fleet offshore.

Once we stand, Aurora touches my cheek. "Be careful, Talon," she says, brushing her thumb against my skin.

I nod my promise. Thoughts of marrying Darling are too thick and hot in my throat. It's such a good idea. This kind of alliance could not be overlooked, would not interfere with House Dragon, but would signal even stronger backing of House Sphinx, reparations, the end of the war, forgiveness. I can't believe it hadn't occurred to me before. Caspian has distracted me too well. Made me jealous. I wonder what he knows.

I leave, heading directly for Caspian, and Finn follows me.

He nearly growls my name when we're alone.

I allow him to catch up, but he's forced to walk just behind me unless he wants his broad shoulders to brush the wall.

"Talon," he says again, urgently.

"It's fine, Finn." I smile. "Better than."

Finn grasps my elbow and drags me to a stop. He doesn't even look for anyone watching. I do, pointedly. But there's nobody. Finn says, "Talon, I know what you're thinking, and you can't marry her, either."

"Yes, I can." The smile doesn't fade. "You've got to see that I can."

His jaw clenches. "Caspian wants something from her, or he wants her for himself. For something." Finn leans closer. The skin around his scar is pinker than usual. "They've spent so much time alone together. I'm not the only one who's noticed they've become close very quickly."

"It's not like that." I put my hand flat on his chest. Finn has half a head on me, and this close, crushed in this stupid narrow corridor, I have to tilt my chin up. "Darling and my brother are not . . ." My lips betray me as I think about kissing Darling myself. They twitch back into a smile. A lovesick smile.

Finn notices. His mouth opens. He just stares at me.

Quietly, I say, "I could be happy married to her, Finn."

"I've never seen you like this," Finn hisses. I can't tell if he's frustrated or shocked. "You've never been this way with anybody—in fact, you've seemed totally oblivious to seduction attempts or even flirting."

I frown. "I haven't—"

Finn laughs once, loud as a bark. But it's not an amused laugh. "You have. You really, really have. We thought, some of us, that you just weren't interested."

"I've had more important things to think about than sex," I chide, pulling my hand back.

"You still do!" Finn explodes. "Even more! What is it about Darling Seabreak that's making you like this? Made my rigid, never-had-a-dirty-thought-in-his-life War Prince act like this girl, this enemy, is your soulmate. Like you'll catch on fire if you don't touch her!"

"Are you worried about Darling's virtue?"

"I'm worried about *yours*!"

I blink at him, stunned.

Finn blinks back. His expression slowly bends into a grimace. He's blushing.

So I wait. I have nothing I could possibly say.

Finn looks away first. Over my shoulder at the wall. He sighs through his teeth. "I don't trust her," he says quietly. "You shouldn't, either."

"But I do. Finn." I wait for him to drag his gaze back to mine. "You should trust *me*."

He immediately looks chagrined.

"Trust me. Believe Darling doesn't have to be our enemy. Keep your guard up, but believe we might end this war for good."

"Yes, my blade," Finn says.

"I'm going to talk to my brother. You have orders to pass on. I'll see you at the wake. Maybe convince you to share a drink with Darling and me—as allies."

His teeth clearly grind together, but he says again, "Yes, my blade."

I'm reeling just slightly from what Finn has revealed—not the least of which is that my soldiers talk among themselves about my lack of experience. Of course they do, but I shouldn't have to think about it. I open up awareness of my boon—just in case—and hurry up an unnecessary flight of stairs in order to cross a hallway and go back down to be on the right level for Caspian's suite.

I knock, and hearing voices inside, I push the door open. I barely catch the alarm in the face of the Dragon guarding the door before I stride in, but it was Elias's trace alongside Caspian's, and no strangers. From the bedroom I hear a flurry of movement and cursing.

"Caspian?" I call, moving through the sitting room for the bedroom.

My brother kneels on the floor, hands folded demurely in his lap. His hair is mussed, his face flushed, and he's half-dressed. He smiles prettily at me. "Little brother?"

At the window stands Elias, back to me, hands pressed to the sill as they lean into the breeze. They should turn to acknowledge me but don't.

Frowning, I take my hand off my falchion hilt and stare at Caspian. "What are you . . . doing . . . on . . . the floor?" Even as I ask the question, the answer sinks in. By the last word I regret being born.

Caspian smiles at me, almost pityingly. "Do you really want me to answer that?"

"I do not. I—" Quickly I fall into anger. "I can't believe you, Caspian. You ran us ragged getting us here, and now you're dallying in your chambers instead of joining our war council?"

"I was feeling unwell, Talon, and sent for my physician." His voice is exquisitely innocent.

Elias spins at that and bows. "As you are much improved, I will take my leave, my blade."

I do them the courtesy of not looking in their direction. My neck is hot enough; I don't need a blush crawling up my cheeks, too. I remain glaring at Caspian as he turns a sweet smile onto his paramour.

"Thank you, Elias," Caspian purrs. I have no idea if he's needling me or Elias. "I'll see you later."

Elias has not stood from their bow, only deepens it, then flees.

"Now, Talon, what can I do for you?" Caspian remains on the floor but shifts to recline with his back against the bed and one knee drawn up. As if the rug is a throne.

"Why did you drive us here so fast, if it wasn't to get something done?"

"I *was* getting something done, brother."

My mouth snaps shut so hard my teeth click. I glower. Caspian returns my gaze with a lazy grin.

I step closer to loom over him. I want to demand to know what his art boon truly is: simple prophecy, or does he paint things into existence somehow? Command Chaos? I ought to demand he explain what other drawings or paintings have yet to come true. But he always shuts down direct questions. So I say, "Aurora had a vision."

"Did she?" he drawls.

"Darling, as the Dragon consort."

Caspian's brows fly up. "Truly!" He laughs. "Well, not mine, obviously."

All my previous excitement feels like chunks of blemished gold in my stomach. "Caspian."

"Talon?"

"Have you painted that?"

His eyes narrow. "Have I painted what?"

"Similar visions?"

"Ah, ha ha, just what do you think my boon is, dearest brother?"

I cross my arms over my chest and wait.

Caspian mirrors my pose from the floor, tucking his arms awkwardly together like he isn't sure how a human should do it. "Aurora's visions aren't enough for you, these days? You don't . . . trust them?"

I clench my jaw and still refuse to reply.

"I see." Caspian suddenly jumps to his feet. He drifts into my space and touches his hand to my neck so a thumb flicks my jaw. "You shouldn't trust them."

"Caspian," I breathe, shocked. "You have visions, too."

He blinks slowly. "None of them are real. Visions. They're inherently untrustworthy, even when they're true."

He's confessing to me, from personal experience.

"Sometimes," he says dreamily, "you have to be somewhere very soon, very fast, and then . . . nothing. Or at least nothing you recognize." Now Caspian's mouth twists bitterly. "Other times you recognize everything and it still doesn't matter."

"Caspian." I put my hand against his, holding it against my neck. "Aurora's vision, of Darling, I want—"

Caspian shakes his head. "Hush, hush, it's not time. Not your time, still mine, for a little while."

I swallow my first response, that I can marry her, that she can be *a* Dragon consort. But something about his words send a chill down my spine. "What do you mean? Your time?"

He shakes his head. "Talon, tonight is the last night before the Naming, and then the tour will be over. Who knows what else will be over. Go, enjoy yourself. Even if it's not time for all these visions, you should be with her."

Still I hesitate, and my brother rolls his eyes. He pats my cheek. "Go. This wake will be rowdy and bright, something we all need. I promise I'll still be here in the morning."

"You . . . approve, then?" I think we're having the same conversation for once but can't ever be certain.

Caspian grins with all his teeth. "Oh yes, little dragon. Go let yourself be conquered."

The unexpected benediction feels so good, so final. I throw my arms around my brother.

"Oh," he says, surprised. "Didn't see that coming," he teases as he returns my embrace.

I laugh a little, too, holding tighter. There's a flicker of excitement in my chest, a promise, like there is a future for us, especially if Caspian can see it. I can't wait to find out if Darling feels it, too.

25

DARLING

I am more than fashionably late to the wake for the last House Barghest regent.

The regent, Eagen Brynson, is laid out in the main hall, his body draped with riches, flowers, and an abundance of fresh fruit as is the custom. Right before the Naming tomorrow the body will be burned, the family each given a measure of ashes to spread, and Eagen Brynson will be naught but a memory. Soldiers guard the body, seemingly to keep the hollow-eyed indentured servants from pilfering it more than anything else. I pay my respects quickly. I won't have it be said that I breached some kind of etiquette by skipping it altogether. Once I've made my curtsies to the dead man and his guards, I follow the sounds of celebration out into the gardens.

There's been no effort to dim the boonlanterns in House Barghest so I wear my goggles as I walk out into the daytime-bright gardens. A fortune in lanterns has been strewn about the trees, and it seems that the entire crush of humanity sits at one of the many tables erected for the wake. Servants walk around with flagons of wine, and quite a few of those within House Barghest got a head start, judging from the flushed faces and raised voices. I see Aurora and her ladies at one table and pretend not to notice the Dragon Seer when she waves me over, most likely for her to try once again to get her hooks into me. Our conversation on the ramparts was enough to last me a lifetime, and I keep walking. Caspian holds court at another table full of pretty youths, a musician playing a rousing drinking song that they're all shouting along to. Caspian sings, but there is a haunted look to his face. I wonder what he's seen, and if he would tell me if I asked. I avoid that table as well.

It turns out that I'm not really in the mood for company.

The wake has spilled out across manicured lawns and behind trees, the gardens larger than they should be judging from the size of the fortress. I look for Talon, hoping to find him clustered with a group of Teeth, but I see neither him nor the elite Dragon soldiers. I swallow my disappointment. I wanted to apologize for not attending his war council, but as I look out across the gathering, it seems like I may not have the chance. Perhaps he found something better to do.

I stand in the midst of the revelry and think of Gavin.

It's hard not to, and my anger has faded enough that a hollow ache blooms in my chest. He should've been here by my side. Tomorrow Leonetti will be released, and I'll be named regent of House Sphinx. The war is over and we will begin to rebuild, and instead of enjoying his life, Gavin is gone, anonymous and forgotten. It's a poor end to someone I called a friend, and I wish I could go back and change things. Change Gavin's mind. Could I, if given half a chance?

The scent of everblooms tickles my nose and pulls me from my dark thoughts, so I leave the party and walk through the gardens searching for the flowers. There's a path that leads past a series of ponds that spill into one another, meticulously manicured hedges and shorter moonflowers lining the stone on either side, but no everblooms. I follow the path over a footbridge to an iron gate, the scent getting stronger as I walk. The gate is partially open, and with a push it swings soundlessly, opening out onto a field. It's darker here, the boonlanterns fewer, and I take my smoked lenses off as I walk through the gate, enjoying the cool night air on my face.

Here is a place that time seems to have forgotten. The garden is overgrown, an abundance of climbing everbloom running wild over crumbling foundations, and I realize it must be an older part of the fortress that has been abandoned. The walls here have fallen down, and the entire place has a neglected air. A low stone wall leads to a sheer cliff edge, fire ivy running along the stones and over the side, and that's when I hear a shout of joy followed by a chorus of laughter.

I follow the sound and find a small fire, and surrounding the fire are Talon's Teeth. I don't see the War Prince, but the rest of the soldiers seem to be singing a song and playing some game that involves leaping over the low-burning flames. I stay back, away from the circle, not just because I see Finn laughing and drinking deeply from an opened wine bottle, but because even at a distance the fire dazzles my eyes.

"Do you want to join us?" a voice says, and I spin around to find Talon smiling at me. I cannot help but return his grin.

"Ah," I say with a laugh. "I'm afraid I would be terrible company." I have no desire to spar with Talon's friend. Not right now. I get the sense they are close, and wine has a way of making even the meek bold. I don't want to see what it brings out in Finn.

"Oh." Talon says. He starts to take a step back, but I reach out and grab the front of his jacket to hold him in place. He's wearing his uniform, dressed in the bloodred of the Dragon's Teeth. The sight should alarm me, make me put him aside, but I don't.

"Will you walk with me? I think I could manage a bit of conversation."

His expression brightens, and he offers me a bow. It reminds me of the night of the gala, weeks ago, when he saved me from humiliation in the arms of his brother. He stands, and the look of delight on his face makes my breath catch. "I would be honored."

We turn away from the soldiers and walk back the way I came. "What is this place? I came through an iron gate, but this looks like it's supposed to be part of the gardens."

"This was once the castle gardens, back when House Barghest were farmers. They used to grow enough food in these fields to feed their entire House," Talon says, gesturing to take in the space that extends all the way to where the land drops off. "That was before they decided it was far more profitable to be landowners and lease the land at an exorbitant rate to other farmers. Also, I hope you can see, because I am nearly blind."

"I can see just fine," I say, looping my arm through his. "You're just going to have to follow my lead."

"As long as you don't lead me right over that cliff back there, that sounds lovely."

I laugh, and something in me loosens. "I'm sorry I didn't come to your war council."

"Tell me you were doing something vitally important and much more fun. Like having your hair braided."

I smile. "I was helping my maid carry buckets of hot water so I could bathe. Scandalized her and half of the kitchen."

"Ah. You saw the children."

"Talon," I say, stopping in a puddle of moonlight near an overgrown grape bower. "They sell their people into indentures! Children who are barely old enough to walk work in their kitchens fetching knives and maintaining cook fires."

Talon grimaces. "I know. I wrote to Caspian about it, last year. He didn't respond. Aurora says he's been hesitant to provoke House Barghest since they fund so much of the war."

"Of course they do! What better way to acquire more land than buying it from a farmer who can no longer feed his family because an army has taken his stores? Or even worse, burned his fields?"

"We don't burn—" Talon begins, before I place my fingers to his lips.

"I'm not blaming you," I say. "Chaos knows House Kraken has done things in the name of strategy I'm not proud of. I'm just saying . . . it's a good thing this war is over. It's a chance to right some wrongs. I've been thinking what it will mean to have my own House, and I think it's a chance to do some good for Pyrlanum."

Talon takes my hands in his so that I'm facing him. "I agree, which is why I have something to ask you." The moonlight picks out the details of Talon's face, so that he looks to be painted in shadows and silver. Is this one of Caspian's paintings? If not, I wish it were, so that I could see this version of Talon again and again. Not as the War Prince of House Dragon, but as a boy staring down at me with excitement and hope and determination.

"After tomorrow, when you're House Sphinx, what would you say to a partnership?"

I blink. "Like a business relationship?"

He frowns. "No, I meant like . . . an alliance. Between you and me. For as long as you want or need it."

I tilt my head and stare at him. Surely he isn't suggesting what I think he is? "Are you asking to be my consort?"

He swallows, more nervous than I've ever seen him. He says

softly, "And maybe your husband, eventually, if the arrangement works out."

I smile widely, an effervescent happiness bubbling up in my middle. So much for getting him out of my system. "Talon!"

His lashes flutter a little, and he looks bashfully away. It's very endearing. "I am a fool."

"Ah well," I say, stepping closer to him so that mere inches separate us. "Do you think you could tolerate being my fool?"

He answers by taking my face in his hands and touching his lips to mine. It's gentler than our last kiss, exploring, asking a question that I answered back at House Cockatrice. I want this Dragon, and now that he's mine, I will not let him forget it.

I deepen the kiss, biting Talon's lip before slanting my mouth across his again. His fingers dig into my hair, and he presses his body fully against mine. I wrap my arms around his waist, and his lips wander from my mouth, tracing up my jaw to my cheek, and finally he kisses my temple.

"There are little impressions here," he says, breath hot against my skin. "From your goggles." Talon kisses me there again, and I tilt my head for him. I close my eyes, and he kisses lightly over my eyelids, little feathering kisses that are almost like laughter. I feel my smile returning, and Talon kisses my mouth again.

That's enough of being slow. I find his sword belt and unfasten it. It falls to his feet with a clatter, but we're far enough away from the rest of the revels that no one hears it.

He leans back a little, panting. "Darling. Before we go any further. Are you sure?"

"Talon, I have never wanted anything more. I am sure." I smile widely and pull him into the deeper shadow of the grape bower, the nearby everblooms scenting the air. I urge Talon to his knees and he leans back in the thick grass, and then I straddle his waist, the skirts I wear pooling around us.

The heat of him presses against me, and I slowly unfasten the buttons of his jacket so that the delicate white of his shirt is revealed. It gleams in the moonlight. My palms press to his chest, and I drag them slowly down under the red jacket. He stares at me through the darkness with a heated gaze, waiting, patient enough to let me take the lead. "I've never . . ." he whispers.

I lean down so that we are nose to nose, his face taking up the entirety of my vision. "Let me."

"Please," he says, tilting his chin to kiss me from below.

And then there is nothing but our bodies together and the headiness of a stolen moment.

26

TALON

I escort Aunt Aurora to the Naming ceremony the next morning, both of us in Dragon finery, bold green and gold. Aurora wears her glinting Seer brooch and smiles softly at me when she takes my arm and squeezes it. "My Talon," she says. "I'm proud of you, you know. Your mother would be."

"I hope so," I manage, because my memories of my mother are faded and overwhelmed by what came after her death: war and anger, struggling under the pressures from my father, fear of Caspian and for him.

"I know so." Aurora reaches up to smooth hair off my forehead. "You look so handsome. This is going to be a big day for us."

"For all of Pyrlanum," I say. New regents for Houses Barghest and Sphinx, the release of Leonetti Seabreak, and hopefully a formal treaty ending the war, signed by all of us. At least, I'm trying to be hopeful that the Kraken navy outside will lay down arms when Caspian recognizes Leonetti and Darling. Even the House Gryphon regent was invited here for the ceremony. Soon someone from Cockatrice will be invited home as well. And Darling and I are *engaged*. She likes me enough, respects me enough, to make me her consort. Maybe even loves me. It certainly seemed so when she touched me last night.

I can't quite stop the joy at the thought from showing just a little bit on my face.

"Is that a smile?" Aurora teases me.

I glance at her, then away, only slightly embarrassed.

"You've rarely smiled like that since you were a boy."

"I smile," I protest.

"Tell me, nephew." She leans into my arm.

Darling and I decided not to say anything publicly, not yet. There are too many people to speak with first. But Aurora is one of those people, and my family. I pause and lean closer. "Your vision, Aunt, of Darling as a Dragon consort, it was close."

She begins to frown, and I hurry on, letting my smile widen. "You don't have to worry about Caspian trying to make her his consort. I'm going to do it." I laugh a little at the end, remembering how Darling had said *my fool*.

My aunt's lips fall open in shock. "Talon!" she breathes.

I step back, holding on to her wrist, and bow over her hand. "It will be a strong alliance, and I—I want it."

"Caspian—"

Still not looking at her, still bowed, I say, "Approves. Please give me your blessing, too. I know you and Darling haven't gotten along, but—"

Aurora turns her hand over, taking mine in both of hers. "Of course," she whispers. Her fingers whiten as she squeezes, her nails glinting bright gold.

I look up quickly, eager for her blessing, but surprised at her reaction.

My aunt's expression is tight and unhappy. "Talon, the things I've seen... I want you to be happy, but I worry. Caspian is...."

"I know his boon is strange, Aunt. You must know it includes some kind of prophecy, like you, visions that come to his art. But Caspian told me himself that the visions aren't always completely accurate. Aren't always the entire story. We have to act with what we know, what we can count on. I can count on Darling."

"Oh, nephew." Aurora visibly rallies herself into giving me a brave smile. "If this is what you want. We will... find a way. Today is going to change many things."

She says it as if the changes might not be good ones, and I nod sharply. "Necessary changes."

For a long moment Aurora studies me. Her round green eyes are very like mine, bright and solid—nothing like Caspian's dreamy, Chaos-touched eyes. Or Darling's, which I long to study for hours. Finally, Aurora nods back at me and says, "Necessary changes, indeed."

Together we enter the House Barghest ballroom. It is a long room of dark wood and small windows. Sunlight shines through in narrow lines, and boonlanterns fill the rest with bright light. At the far end is a hearth carved from black stone in the shape of a massive hound's head, mouth wide and fanged, fire flickering as if from its gullet. The room is filled with Dragons and Barghests, lined up to witness the ceremony. Beside the hearth Caspian already sits in a chair draped green. Aurora and I make our way toward him. There are four other chairs, each draped in the colors of their House: red for Gryphon, pale blue and silver for Barghest, cream for Sphinx, and black and sea blue for Kraken.

Leonetti Seabreak stands before his chair. The old man has been washed and dressed in finery well suited to his stature and status, expensive black velvet and a mantle sewn to look like fish scales. The long sleeves fall over his wrists, hiding the manacles I know to be there. Four Dragons guard him, positioned just behind his chair, hands on hilts.

My gaze slides from him across to Darling at her own chair, waiting with Marjorie in the uniform of House Sphinx. Darling is gorgeous. I feel my face soften as I look at her, the creamy lace on those shoulders I kissed last night, the drops of pale topaz at her earlobes, where I buried my nose to breathe her in. My breathing picks up, and I can't help it: I grin at her. I don't care who sees.

Darling smiles back, sharply. Her goggles are very delicately made, the gilded floral ones of tooled white leather she wore to that first gala where we danced. She tilts her head meaningfully toward Leonetti.

I try to break from Aurora to veer in Darling's direction, but my aunt keeps a hold of me. "Talon, we need to begin," she says, barely moving her smiling lips.

"Yes," I acknowledge, instead bowing formally to Darling, eyes never falling from hers. She licks her bottom lip and tucks her hands behind her back. Like she must or she'd reach for me.

I let Aurora drag me to my brother. I'm slightly distracted when I realize the Gryphon regent is not at the red-draped chair, though Elias stands beside it in their own ruby regalia.

"She won't be making it," Caspian says to me as we reach him. He shrugs and sips his wine. It's still morning, but I don't have to say anything: Aurora takes the cup from him and hands it off as if nothing is wrong.

"Prince Regent," she says, curtsying for him.

Caspian waves her up. He's fully, formally dressed for once, including some touches of polished armor covering his left arm. A gilded tabard fits over it all, embroidered with a bright green dragon and fire-orange phoenix twined together in flight. The design from his tower doorway at Phoenix Crest. I raise my eyebrows at it, and he grins lazily. He looks like a High Prince Regent.

Once I take my place at his right and Aurora to his left, the party of scions from House Barghest enter. They slam the doors open to the blare of a trumpet and stride down the length of the ballroom in a swirl of pale blue and silver. Mia Brynsdottir and her uncle Silas, the brother of the recently dead regent, along with three others in the immediate family, and at the rear is the young boy. First Scion of House Barghest. Darvey Brynson. He's only eleven, I think, much too young for this, and his father has just died.

The boy wears a long blue robe and a small white fur—they all have fur—and around their necks are collars of silver and what appear to be silver-tipped wolf teeth.

Caspian stands. "Let us begin!"

The boonlanterns are dimmed. Several people in long purple tabards enter, holding trays of small clay cups. The servers wear half masks in the shapes of the various empyreals, and when they offer everyone a cup they say, "The shared blood of Pyrlanum," softly.

We're meant to take a cup and answer, "Chaos bless the scion."

I attended the Naming of Vivian Chronicum, the Gryphon regent, several years ago and participated in the toast despite my young age. It's an herbal liquor brewed from honey and mixed with spring water to lower the alcohol—just as the blood of empyreals was thinned with our human blood, supposedly. I take my cup, which is barely a thimbleful, and say nothing.

The servers spread the cups, leaving a single larger cup, rather more of a beautiful spiral bowl, for the first scion, who will drink it and become the regent.

"I thought it would be here," Caspian murmurs.

He frowns deeply, almost glaring at the group of Barghest scions. Over his head, Aurora catches my eye.

"What?" I ask quietly, leaning down.

Caspian brushes his hand in the air dismissively but continues to peer around. He's blinking in a way I don't like. As if to blink away a vision.

I look to Darling, who is watching Leonetti awkwardly hold his cup with his hands chained. Her jaw is clenched, and I won't be surprised if she charges over there to make a scene freeing him before the ceremony. I won't stop her, either. He should have been unchained before this.

A noise from my brother draws my attention back to the Barghest scions. They've moved into a crescent facing Silas Brynson, not the young Darvey. The older man holds the regent's bowl. Not what I expected, but easy to understand, given House Dragon would balk at a child his age for regent, too.

Nobody seems bothered; only a few people share surprised glances. Except Caspian. He leaps to his feet. "No, no, no," he says, waving his little cup enough that a few drops fly out. Probably most of it. "This isn't right. Darvey Brynson is the first scion."

Mia bows to Caspian with her hands clasped around her cup. "High Prince Regent, my blade, my nephew is so young, so inexperienced. We have chosen Uncle Silas for very good reason. He, too, is a scion of Barghest."

"No!"

"My blade!" says Aunt Aurora, hurrying to Caspian's side. She smooths a hand down his arm. "Please, this is unexpected but not without precedent."

Caspian whirls to Darling. "Well?" he demands.

Darling opens her mouth, then snaps it shut to glare at him. "Well, *what*?"

"Surely some of my fellow regents protest the ousting of a first scion? Certainly I would never stand for anyone"—here Caspian sweeps his glare throughout the ballroom—"attempting to undercut *my* heir."

"This is Barghest House business, Dragon," says Leonetti Seabreak in a gravelly, unused voice, but firm enough to be a command. "If it were Dragon business, your opinion might matter."

Caspian gapes at him. The silence in the room is only amplified by subtly shifting material and a few distant whispers. I'm rather stunned to silence myself. But as I stare at Leonetti, I realized where Darling learned her brand of politics.

Then a peal of laughter shatters the quiet: it's Caspian himself. He laughs so hard he bends over, dropping his cup. It tinks against the stone floor and rolls in a thin splatter of honey liquor.

Leonetti's mouth twists up in confused disgust. Of course, he's never witnessed Caspian at his worst. Most of these people have not. They've only heard the rumors.

I grasp my brother's elbow and keep him standing. He leans toward me, as if his mirth has collapsed his knees.

Everyone is watching.

"Caspian," I hiss, fingers tightening. "Gather yourself."

"Oh, I'm gathered, my brother, my little dragon, darling." And he sets off again, laughing.

"Continue!" Aunt Aurora says loudly, spreading her hands to indicate the entire Naming ritual.

I nod and maneuver Caspian back to his chair. My own cup of liquor is dripping onto my fingers.

Beyond me, I hear the ceremony continue. Someone calls out the name of the last Barghest regent in full and his mother, who ruled before him. Then they call Silas's name, the second scion become the first, and I sit Caspian down, kneeling beside the chair. I look up at his face. Sweat gleams at his temples. His perfectly slicked-back hair is falling into pieces as he slumps.

"It's fine, Talon," he murmurs. "It will be. This part doesn't matter. They'll see the first scion is the first scion. When . . . after . . ." His eyes shut, and he leans his head back.

I have no idea what to do. I clasp his hand. "It will work out. And when we drink to Silas Brynson, we can then drink to Maribel Calamus, the regent of House Sphinx."

Caspian looks at me. His eyes are faded, hazy. Maybe he's just tired.

"We want that more, don't we?" I murmur.

"It's not . . ." Caspian says. He trails off, staring at me, and suddenly he looks so sad.

I want to ask what he's seen, but Caspian whispers, "I won't be able to marry his niece. Silas wants my throne; you'll have to watch for that."

"We'll do it together," I whisper back as Aunt Aurora steps

forward and takes our place leading House Dragon in raising the cups to drink all at once. The room shouts, "Chaos bless his fang!"

And it is finished.

Caspian's mouth twists into a self-deprecating smirk.

The cheers rise, and everyone is calling congratulations to Silas Brynson of House Barghest.

I stand, keeping a hand on Caspian's shoulder. He lifts his face to watch the proceedings imperiously. As if he's above it all—a little late. It worries me, not only for him, but for our standing as the dominant House.

Darling has her arms crossed, alone. I wish to go to her, or ask her to our side. But it's her turn. I wait for her to look at me, to meet my gaze, but there's no time. The servers return with more trays of small liquor bottles, and this time they refill cups using the same phrase, "The shared blood of Pyrlanum."

The spiral bowl is brought to Darling. She takes it in both hands, reverently. I want to kiss her cheek, stand behind her, touch the small of her back, anything to show I am here, we will do the rest of this together.

"Accept it well," Leonetti says to her.

Darling's eyes widen, and she looks at him, seeming haunted.

Just then a distant *boom* hollows the air.

I blink: I know that sound. It's cannon fire.

Just as I think it, the floor beneath my boots trembles.

Then the boom comes again.

A Dragon's Teeth lieutenant yells from the entrance, "The Kraken navy is on the attack!"

My training overwhelms my surprise, and I call, "Dragons, to your posts!" We sent out new orders for this last night before the wake, and everyone should know where to go. I need to get Caspian to safety, then join Finn and the Teeth at the command we chose, on the third level of the inner fortress.

"Wait!" Caspian stands. "Release Leonetti Seabreak! He will have his people stand down."

The High Prince Regent looks at Leonetti as he says it, and the Kraken regent hesitates.

"Stop, Caspian," I say. "We need him as a hostage if he isn't on our side in ending this."

"Talon!" Darling strides toward us.

Finn appears at Leonetti's side, he and the four Dragon guards caging the Kraken regent in.

Before any of us can argue further, Aunt Aurora screams.

It is ear-piercing, awful. She falls to her knees, clutching at her own face, gilded nails dug into her forehead hard enough to draw blood. My heart stops beating for a moment.

The entire room stares at Aurora. Another cannon blast rumbles against the outer wall.

"No," Aurora says, her voice raw. "It is . . ." She falls forward and catches herself on her hands. Then she turns to stare at Caspian. "You have betrayed us." Blood wells in the crescent marks her nails left on her forehead.

I step in front of my brother.

But he only laughs once.

Aurora points. "Regents! Scions! Listen to me! Caspian Goldhoard has betrayed us. I have seen it. I have seen his plot to destroy the Houses! He is going to undo Pyrlanum itself. We must—we must . . ." She sways, clutching her chest. "Talon . . ."

I can't help it—I go to her. Falling to one knee, I take her elbows to hold her upright. "Aunt."

"You are the Dragon, you . . ." Her eyes are unfocused. "You are your father's heir. Drink the liquor! The blood of empyreals. Yours." She sways.

Silas Barghest yells, "I have long suspected Caspian Goldhoard of treachery! House Barghest will not stand behind him any longer."

"Take the cup, Dragon scion!" another voice yells.

Someone tries to push a cup of the honey liquor into my hand. I shove them off. "Stop this. I am not—"

"Oh, this is ridiculous!" Caspian himself cries. "I don't have time for this!" He flings up his arms and storms away.

"Caspian," Darling calls, but she can't get to him through the crush of people.

"See how he doesn't care!"

"He's mad!"

"Always has been!"

I thrust to my feet, but Aurora holds my sleeve. "My blade," she says urgently. "You must take over. You must—Caspian is mad, wild; you've seen it." She raises her voice to say, "Talon Goldhoard! Dragon regent!"

I look at Finn. "Take the prisoner, and then meet me in the command."

Darling grabs me. "What are you doing? Let him go." Boonlanterns reflect in the lenses of her goggles; she doesn't seem human.

I turn my hand to take her wrist. "I can't, not until his navy stands down."

"They're attacking to free him! So do it—earn their surrender!"

"Will they stop?" I tighten my grip. "Darling, will they stop, or will they keep coming, under his command?"

"Give us a chance!"

Aurora presses close to my shoulder. "Us? I thought you were engaged to my nephew, not still clinging to your past like a squid."

Darling sucks in a breath and jerks away from me. She takes two steps backward, then turns and shoves through the crowd.

I can't breathe for a moment. Cries and overwhelming noise press against me.

Aurora touches my cheek and I startle. She says, "I'll speak with Leonetti Seabreak, Talon. Try to convince him to make the same deal with you that he had with Caspian. You do your job, my blade. My *regent*."

Still staring past the tangled crowd after Darling, I can only make my mouth move, but no sound comes out as I say yes.

27

DARLING

I chase after Caspian, unshed tears burning my eyes behind the smoked lenses of my goggles. How could everything go so wrong so quickly? One moment I was excited for a future with Talon at my side and Leonetti as an ally, and now I am right back where I was months ago, longing to free Leonetti and cursing Dragons and their treachery.

My breath hitches when I think of Talon's expression of surprise, the way he immediately deferred to Aurora when things looked bad. Anyone with a lick of sense can see she is after the throne, or at least after a useful puppet she can control. The look she and the new regent of House Barghest exchanged makes me think they've been planning this for a while, and I cannot help but wonder what her next move might be. Marry that Mia Brynsdottir to Talon so that the two of them can better control the realm? Most likely. And that beautiful fool will walk right into the trap, because he's too good to do otherwise.

I grit my teeth when I think of Talon. All of his soft words from last night are meaningless in the harsh light of day, and I am a besotted idiot for thinking that someone nicknamed the War Prince could lay down his arms and learn to be a kind and just ruler. Did he even mean anything he said last night? Or was it just more Dragon politicking?

For a moment I think of Gavin. What if he was right? What if this is all my fault because I didn't kill the princes when I had the chance?

Chaos take them all!

I push aside my hurt and anger to focus on the immediate goal: Caspian. Perhaps this can be salvaged. If I find Caspian and make him return, make him give me my title and care of Leonetti, maybe I can send word to Adelaide and the fleet that this is a foolish endeavor, that her father is free.

But I have to find Caspian first.

I push through the crush of people and servants, and someone yells after me, grabbing the edge of my dress to stop me. I shove them off, roughly, and my blood thrums, and I run after Caspian. There's no sight of him in the hallway outside the great hall, and it's only by chance that I see a flash of scarlet turning a corner.

Elias.

I run after the doctor, catching them before they can disappear behind a door. I drag them backward by their robe. They spin around in surprise when they see me.

"My quill—" Elias begins.

"Save it. Where is he? Caspian? Where did he go?"

"The ramparts. He was rambling on about a tooth of some kind—" Elias breaks off, their expression one of worry. "I'm going to get my kit. I think maybe he's had some kind of break."

"What did he see, Elias?" I ask, too bold in my desperation. Elias opens their mouth, whether to object or to equivocate I'm not sure, so I save them the effort. "I know he has a prophet's boon."

Elias's shoulders sag, like they're relieved to have someone to share the secret with. "I don't know, but it's bad. The last time he was this worked up was . . . well, it was right before the War Prince brought you to Phoenix Crest."

I don't know what to do with that information, so I turn and run toward the ramparts.

My trip through the fortress is a quick one. The narrow halls are surprisingly empty, but I suppose that makes a strange kind of sense. There isn't a lot of reason for the servants to stick around. If I were here against my will I would flee at the first sign of trouble as well.

I run up the narrow stairwell to the ramparts, thighs burning from the exertion. It's been too long since I was in a proper fight and my fitness has suffered while on tour, and as I explode out onto the ramparts, I'm surprised to find them empty, the cannons unmanned.

"They're just decorations, the greedy fools," Caspian says.

"So now you're a mind reader as well?" I say.

"Ha! Not a chance. That boon doesn't actually exist. I only know about the cannons because I examined them our first day here."

"You knew this was going to happen."

"I had an inkling that this was a possible path, that Barghest would provoke Kraken to ensure the war continued. Enough of that, it soon won't matter. Come help me find this blasted tooth."

I ignore him and look out to the sea. There are only a handful of Kraken ships, and even fewer Barghest ships. But there is a line of ships flying a strange flag far on the horizon, a bright yellow thing I do not recognize. Not only that, but the formation of the Kraken ships isn't one of attack, but of defense. Nothing adds up.

"They're mercenaries, if you're wondering," Caspian calls. "House Barghest at least is single-minded in their devotion to a goal, even if their sense of aesthetics is something that belongs in a nightmare."

Caspian is on the far corner edge of the ramparts, crawling around the massive statues of slavering hounds. Barghests, I suppose. His clothes are grubby and ripped, even though he can't have been looking for more than a few minutes. For some reason the tabard he wears gives me a strange sense of familiarity, although I cannot place where I've seen the design before.

Caspian exclaims in surprise and pulls free a large crystal with a pointed end. "Smaller than I was expecting," he says. He turns to me. "Where is your dagger?"

I frown and pull out one of the throwing knives I've managed to tuck into my waistband. Caspian huffs out angrily. "No, the Gryphon blade. Where is it?"

"In my rooms," I begin, and Caspian leaps down from the ledge. He's on me immediately, turning me around and pushing me toward the stairs.

"Go. Get. It," he says, emphasizing each syllable as though he is speaking to a child. "And hurry. Otherwise, all is lost."

I should argue or balk. I should bring up Leonetti once more, but I find that I am caught up in the same urgency that drives Caspian. I don't know what he's seen or what he's doing, but I believe that he's working toward some purpose greater than what the rest of us can imagine.

Or perhaps I'm just angry enough that I want to see what kind of havoc a half-mad prince can wreak.

I sprint down the stairs, catching my skirt on something sharp and just letting the material tear. I rip off the epaulets and take out the earrings. A fleeing servant rushes toward me. She drags a little boy along by the hand, and I stop her long enough to push the earrings and feathered epaulets into her hands.

"Take these," I say before she can object. "You'll need the funds."

"Thank you, my fang," she calls as I move past her and back to my rooms. I hope all of the House Barghest indentures have used the nearby battle to flee.

And I hope those thrice-cursed House Barghest bastards never find them.

The door to my rooms stands open, and I am relatively unsurprised to see them ransacked. Things are unraveling quickly, and I only hope that the Gryphon dagger is still where I hid it.

I move toward the bureau, pulling out a drawer and feeling underneath for the blade. I'm not sure what made me hide it. Some Chaos-borne instinct, perhaps? Elias's words come back to me, how the last time they marked this kind of behavior in Caspian was before I arrived to Phoenix Crest. Why has Chaos tied me and Caspian together in such a way? What terrible thing did Caspian see that somehow concerns me? It has to be more than the fall of House Sphinx, doesn't it?

I've just freed the dagger from its hiding place when there's a soft scrape behind me. I grab the blade and roll to my left just as a sword slams into the stone floor, mere inches away from where I knelt.

"I always knew you were exactly what you seemed." Talon's friend Finn stands nearby, a short sword clutched in a white-knuckle grip.

"An assassination attempt already?" I say. "I haven't even been named regent yet, lizard."

"And you never will be, squid." Finn holds up a small pot of gloss.

"I knew you were using Talon. It's too bad you won't get the chance to use this."

I laugh, the sound forced even to my own ears. "It's just lip tint! Yes, that is definitely my grand plan. To kiss Talon until he is delirious and leave a scarlet mark upon him so everyone knows he is mine." The jest is closer to the truth than I like, and my heart skips a beat in my chest at Finn's cruel smile.

"You think me stupid, but I've spent the past few weeks hunting down the last of your Barbs with my sister and extracting the truth from them. You call this the Kiss of Death, correct? It doesn't affect the wearer, but one kiss and the victim dies an excruciating death."

I swallow thickly. I don't have time for this.

"You're wrong," I say, marking my possible paths to the exit. I'm thankful for my goggles, as their smoked lenses allow me to search my escape routes without Finn being any the wiser.

"We'll see what Talon thinks," Finn says, lunging for me. He isn't leading with his sword but with his free hand, and I remember at the last possible second that he has a sleep boon and a single touch will render me unconscious. I spin out of the way, rolling over the bed before pulling out one of my throwing knives and launching it at Finn. The blade buries itself deep in his right shoulder, and he grunts in pain but doesn't drop his weapon.

For a moment I want to finish him. I could. There are two more throwing knives buried in the layers of my finery, and I could launch one at his throat, revenge for killing Gavin. But Caspian is waiting on me, so I turn and run out of the room and back to the ramparts, my steps far outpacing Finn's.

Boots thunder behind me as Finn gives chase, but the narrow twisting and turning corridors work to my advantage. Once I am certain I am out of his line of sight, I duck into a long disused garderobe and wait until Finn runs past. Then I count ten heartbeats before dashing out and running down the hallway back the way I came, to the stairwell that leads to the ramparts. I have no doubt that in a few moments Finn will rally reinforcements, and the fortress will be crawling with Teeth intent on my demise. I have most likely just signed my own death warrant.

All I can do is hope that Caspian's prophecy is worth it.

28
TALON

I take steps two at a time to get to the room we chose for commanding our troops here at House Barghest. I hear the echo of cannon fire, but it isn't hitting the fortress anymore, presumably because the ships in the harbor have turned to fight each other.

A handful of Teeth and regulars hurries behind me, ready to disperse where I need them.

The room is a guest suite we seized on the third level, with access to a stretch of ramparts from which we can see the entire bay and most of the ocean-facing part of the fortress. Last night, before the wake, we pushed aside furniture and stacked chairs, propped the bed upright against the wall, then brought in two long tables. That's where Captain Jersey of House Barghest stands when I burst in, pointing to a map of the coastline as he gives orders.

In the whole room there are only Barghest soldiers. Not the low-ranking indentured, either, but the third daughters and sons of the richest Barghest families, with bought ranks and little battle experience.

"Catch me up," I say, joining Jersey.

Arran Lightscale is at my elbow and gestures for the Dragon next to him to head out onto the ramparts for lookout.

Captain Jersey hesitates. His mouth twists momentarily. He's got a solid decade on me and is only distantly related to Silas Brynson, but seems to have the same watery blue eyes.

I scowl. "Catch. Me. Up."

"Ah . . . War Prince." Jersey stalls with my title and the pause.

Every Barghest soldier in the room has their hand on their sword.

Just then the lieutenant Arran sent outside darts back in, voice panicked: "Sir! There's ships flying the Vir'asvan merc flag! They're coming up from the northeast and attacking the Kraken ships. And the . . ." Lieutenant Kennar stops, taking in the strangely tense atmosphere.

"Yes, lieutenant?" I say, eyes all for Captain Jersey.

"The ships protecting the bay are all flying Barghest flags, not Phoenix Crest."

"Is that so?" I ask Captain Jersey. House Barghest has been vocally against peace for weeks. Just how far were they willing to go against Dragon to sabotage Caspian's plans?

Jersey nods, but it isn't for me. His soldiers draw their blades and attack.

It isn't a long fight, barely even a skirmish. My Dragons and I take them all out in moments. I personally stab Jersey through the neck, jerking my falchion out with an arc of blood that splashes onto the next Barghest's cheek. She widens her eyes as Jersey's body collapses half on the table, and immediately drops her blade, falling to her knees. Three remaining Barghest soldiers do the same. There are six of them dead. One of my Dragons has a gaping wound on her upper arm, but we're otherwise unscathed.

Fury clenches my jaw, and I have a hard time getting out any commands. "You," I say to the soldier who surrendered to me. She looks up from her knees.

"War Prince."

"What do you know?"

"The—we—House Barghest hired the mercenaries from Vir'asva, and..."

"Spit it out."

"My cousin is on one of the ships, and he warned me to be ready, that they weren't to let Kraken start the fight, or end it."

I nod. My fury is melting into something darker, heavier. "Arran."

"Sir." Blood covers his sword. He doesn't bother to wipe it off now.

"Take control here. We are taking House Barghest in the name of the High Prince Regent."

Arran's expression twitches, but he doesn't ask his question. I glare until he says, "Regent... Talon?"

My face is so hot. "What matters is that the High Prince Regent is of House Dragon."

"Yes, War Prince."

"I'm going to find Finn, and the Kraken and Sphinx regents. I will bring them here, and the High Prince Regent. We will take Barghest and defend the coast but end the attack on Kraken. Hold command here. If anyone surrenders, let them; if they resist, no quarter."

"Yes, sir," Arran says, echoed by the rest of the Dragons.

"Defend what is yours," I say almost gently. It is the beginning of the Dragon's Teeth motto.

The Dragons in the command room yell back, "With strength and fury!"

I leave.

As I jog down the narrow stairs, I think about how my entire life has really been spent defending what is *not* mine. Stolen land, stolen lives, pieces of a hoard taken by force and might and certainly not for anyone's good. I did it for my family. Because my father told me to, because my mother was murdered. Then I did it to hold Caspian up with the only tools I had. Just yesterday I believed it was working. We were stumbling toward peace, toward bringing Pyrlanum back together. I was engaged, imagining myself happy as consort allied to a different House. Had it been a dream? Last night with Darling? Smiling, kissing, all those soft sounds she made?

I have to rub violently at my eyes as I reach the main floor. Indentured servants scatter before me, hands full of silk and stolen pearls. Good. I ignore them. I push through and snag the first Dragon I can. "Where did the Dragon Seer take Leonetti Seabreak?" The soldier doesn't know. I ask about Finn, whom they saw crashing down a hallway toward the guest rooms.

Reaching out with my boon, I search for Aurora's trace. There is so much anarchy, people have crossed over their own traces, moved in hurried packs, the traces are an awful tangle . . . I give up. Asking will be faster right now.

The next Dragon I find is one of the guards from Phoenix Crest. They're on their way to join their fellows on the ramparts with crossbows. They escorted Aurora and the Kraken regent to Aurora's guest room.

I bid them strength and fire and head for Aurora's rooms.

If I can get Leonetti to believe me, to understand that I want peace between Kraken and Dragon, and that the Barghest betrayed us both, maybe we can salvage something. My Dragons will absolutely follow me, and if we turn them to Barghest as an enemy, that will make it easier. I don't mind that my House works best with a designated enemy. I feel the same.

There are no soldiers guarding Aurora's guest rooms, and I push the door open.

My aunt's name dies dry on my tongue at the sight before me.

Aurora stands in the center of the room, her grand green-and-gold gown sparkling in firelight, not boonlights. Her hair is wild and down around her shoulders. She has her arms open. Leonetti Seabreak is tied to a chair, his jacket open and shirt torn to display his bare chest and streaks of blood there, painted into a rune of some kind.

Before I can move, the knife in Aurora's hand flashes, and she drives it into Leonetti's stomach.

He grunts, punched out and horrible, and Aurora's fist disappears into him.

She rears back, flinging the knife aside, and then dives forward again to dig both hands into Leonetti's body.

I can't move. I am trapped by horror. She's up to her wrists, reaching under his ribs. Nausea boils up my throat as she clenches her teeth and braces her whole body to shove in, and then she rips backward.

She lands on her bottom on the floor—it's then I notice the array sketched onto the wood. The rug is rolled aside, and there's a diagram in blood, drying brown, elaborate.

In Aurora's hands is a fleshy chunk of meat. Muscle.

I know what it is: a piece of Leonetti Seabreak's heart.

"Aurora!" I finally yell, drawing my falchion.

She ignores me but speaks a word I don't understand: the bleeding meat cupped in her palms catches fire.

The array beneath her glows bright red, then turns vivid purple silver, rainbow purple, the flashing colors of Chaos I have seen reflected in my brother's eyes. In Darling's.

Aurora sucks in a huge breath, taking in the eerie white smoke from the charred flesh in her hands.

I start toward her but stop at the edge of the array. I don't want to break it, touch it, smear it. It's so wrong. It seems to waver in my vision, sticking to my nostrils, the back of my throat like a living thing. This isn't just burning flesh; it's *wrong*. Beyond Aurora, the Kraken regent slumps in the chair, his chest a blossom of blood, a gaping wound. His head lolls back, awful, his expression lax in death.

Darling's adoptive father. I gave him into Aurora's custody. He's dead. Not just dead but brutally murdered for this awful magic.

Aurora's back arches; she flings her arms out. The chunk of Leonetti's heart plops to the floor, landing with a small *splat*.

Chaos sparkles around Aurora: it becomes like bubbles of light. They each grow and then pop.

We're left suddenly in nothing but torchlight. Flickering fire.

Aurora turns to look at me, and her eyes are pure violet rainbows, filled with swirling Chaos. Her lips part. She says in a ghostly voice, "I see them, flying! I see them—they kiss—they die." She shudders through her entire body. "Darling! She'll kill your brother with a kiss!"

My aunt collapses.

I stare at her sprawling body.

She's always been faking her prophecy boon. This is blood magic.

It's been years since I was in danger of vomiting at violence, but I stumble back, a hand clasped over my mouth. My aunt, my *family*, she—she murdered this man for nothing but a vision. For power. For a fake boon.

The room spins.

I duck out, lean against the wall, and breathe carefully.

"War Prince?"

I nod, uncaring who it is, when I see the uniform in my blurry vision. "Take Aurora Falleau into custody. In chains, do you understand? And I want—I want Silas Brynson found and arrested, too."

"Yes, my blade."

Someone else echoes it.

There's blood on my hands, and I don't know how it got there. I need . . .

I take another deep breath. The corridor is strangely quiet. Everyone must have fled these rooms already. I need Darling. I need to find her, be the one to tell her about Leonetti. And Caspian. He promised Darling her father would be all right. Did he not see this? Did he not care? What does he care about?

I push off the wall. I have to keep moving, keep acting. When things are settled, we can all have a real talk.

A Dragon soldier stalks out of the guest room with Aurora dragging behind him, barely on her feet. She's dazed, her eyes still sparking Chaos. It can't be true, what she saw, but isn't the point of this sacrifice to force a true vision?

Before she's hauled away, she suddenly turns to me, reaching with hands like claws. "Talon, Talon!"

Her gaze is unfocused. Her hands covered in gore. My heart hurts, but I let her have one of my hands. Her nails dig into my wrist as she clutches.

"It was a true vision, Talon," she hisses. "Trust it. If nothing else. That magic is true. I saw it. She kisses him and he dies."

I shake my head; I can't believe it, but Aurora is so insistent. She digs her nails deeper, and the pain focuses me.

"I believe you," I say quietly. "Go with this Dragon. We'll keep you safe, Aunt."

"Oh, Talon, nephew, little dragon," she murmurs, listing to one side. The soldier catches her, eyes wild as he looks at me.

"Go," I say.

The Dragons take Aunt Aurora away.

"Talon," grunts Finn.

He grabs my shoulder, turning me around.

I begin to ask for his report but frown in confusion at the blood on his shoulder, soaking his uniform.

Finn sees the direction of my gaze and scoffs. "Your lover did that. I'm sorry, Talon, but she's a traitor."

"Darling?" I frown.

My friend holds out his large hand. Cupped in the palm is a small jar of paste. It looks like someone's paint pot. Makeup. I shake my head and look questioningly at Finn.

"The Barbs use poison, Talon." Finn tucks his chin and stares into my eyes with all his earnest certainty. "I had intelligence they gave some to Darling. This was in her room. I just confiscated it."

"What?"

"It's lip balm. Poison lip balm. If she wore it, and kissed you, you'd *die*."

I step back.

"She didn't deny it," Finn continues, almost respectful. "I'm glad. We finally know where we stand."

"This . . ." I reach out but don't quite touch it. There is blood streaked on my hand where Aurora clutched it. "This is poison. For kissing. And you found it in Darling's room."

It doesn't matter what Finn was doing in her rooms, searching them. Not anymore. My breath is shallow. Nausea won't stop churning, churning in my stomach.

"Yes," Finn says.

Just like that everything stops. Like the moment water becomes ice. I am just as cold.

I see them—they kiss—they die!

Aurora saw it.

I snap my gaze to Finn's. "We have to find Darling and Caspian. Now."

29

DARLING

I have no sooner burst onto the ramparts than I am assaulted by Caspian. There's no other word for it. One moment he is standing near the edge and watching the navies battle in the harbor, the next he is roughly pulling me along by the arm, muttering about time and circumstance.

"Here, here, you must stand here," he says, placing me on a flagstone. A look down and I see I am standing on some kind of strange symbol, sketched out in a rust-brown color. A glance at Caspian reveals his bleeding hand, and I grab it.

"What happened? What are you doing?" I ask. I'm still winded from my run through the fortress, and Caspian gives me a rueful grin as he pulls his hand back.

"I am saving you. And Pyrlanum. But mostly you."

I try to take a step backward. There's something in Caspian's tone I dislike, a fatalism that causes goose bumps to rise up on my arms. "Caspian—" I begin, but he holds out his hand.

"Where's the Gryphon dagger?"

I reluctantly give it to him, and he's no sooner taken the blade than he grabs my hand and makes a deep slash across my palm. I gasp and yank my hand back, but I find that I haven't actually moved.

"It's quick, isn't it?" he says, voice soft. "The poison? There was a philosopher over three hundred years ago who tried to make it a sort of medicine. A lot of people died before the Phoenix stopped him."

I try to speak, but my mouth is filled with cotton. I cannot move at all, yet I somehow remain on my feet. In the distance the boom of cannons echoes to us, doubling in its frequency, and I hope that means Adelaide has realized that she must fight back.

"I have to admit," Caspian says as he produces a cup and gathers the blood that flows freely from my hand, "that this was much harder than I imagined it would be. That, of course, is no fault of yours. But when Talon brought you to Phoenix Crest, I realized that I had to bring everything together immediately. It was time to give in."

I try to say something in response, but nothing comes out. Not even a squeak.

He marks another sigil on the ground, directly in front of mine. My eyes are the only thing I can move, and as I blink, I wonder if that is because my boon is already fighting back against the poison.

"This was always about you, my dear Darling. But this must be so terrifying for you," Caspian says, standing as he finishes and putting the bowl of blood aside. He stands right in front of me, so that he is once again where he stood when he cut me, right in my line of vision. "So let me tell you a story.

"Once upon a time there was a prince who saw too much and knew too much. He saw the way his aunt looked at his father, and the way his mother was unsettled by the things the boy painted. She told him to stop, and so he did not show her the picture of her death. The picture of his aunt pouring the tea Mother enjoyed every afternoon in her garden."

I try to move my hands, but there is no sensation there. Just a curious emptiness. But Caspian's words drag me away from the panic of my body not working and into the tale he spins, which is less fantasy and more history.

"After the boy's mother died, he found himself angry, angrier than he had ever been before. But his anger just made him *more*. He started to see things he shouldn't, and sometimes he would ask questions that others found too hard to answer. So he lost himself in his painting.

"His father was also enraged, and the boy's aunt realized she had made a terrible miscalculation. She thought she would easily step into her sister's place after a few months of mourning, but it turned out the man had loved his wife truly and was devastated by the loss. Perhaps madness ran in the family, yes? And so she began to drip poison into the Dragon's ear. Lies the boy could see through. Lies that fueled his anger and made him yearn to be able to show the world the truth."

I swallow, and the movement is such a surprise that I try to move my pinky, or a toe. But that is still more than I can manage. And yet somehow, Caspian notices.

"Your boon is truly a marvel, Darling. Already you're healing from the Gryphon poison. Time! Ah, never enough time."

He moves away to a small chest, one I hadn't noticed until now, and begins to drag it over to where we stand, all while continuing his story.

"Unfortunately for the boy, truth isn't something Chaos was interested in. Chaos wanted nothing but its own channels returned to it. Its power. Its dreams." Caspian sits back on his haunches and sighs. "I apologize, because I have always been a better liar than a storyteller. Aurora taught me at a very young age the art of the lie.

In case you don't know, it's one part truth, two parts what others want to believe. She convinced me that I should let her pretend my boon was her own, to protect me. She said my mother would have wanted it so. I agreed; I was too young to stand up to her. But, Darling, I have always seen you. From the very beginning of my boon—you are the thing I sketched and painted. You should see the oldest of those childish drawings. They are truly frightening. Only streaks of color and swirling dark holes where there ought to be eyes." Caspian shivers performatively.

The sound of firing grows in intensity, and I look toward the harbor. I can't quite see what is happening, but whatever it is draws Caspian's attention for a moment.

"Ahh. You will be glad to know that Adelaide has begun a counterattack, and quite a successful one from the looks of it. Good for her. But back to you.

"I have always painted you but never understood why. I truly am just as baffled by my boon as anyone. It is prophetic but not broadly so. There is only one future for me, and you are somehow the key. When I was younger, I thought perhaps I was to reinstate you to your rightful position, but Chaos has never made anything so simple. When I was eighteen, I had a truly horrifying waking dream—a prophecy. And I painted you engulfed in flames. That's when I understood. This ritual will undo everything that has been stolen from you. From all of us, Darling!"

Caspian begins to lift things out of the chest, showing them to me one by one.

"The Eye of the Cockatrice, that one you know, since you helped me acquire it. Talon of the Gryphon, you know that one as well, although I regret that I had to be so utterly vile to Vivian over it.

Barb of the Kraken, taken when my father ransacked the island house of Leonetti a decade ago. Feather of the Sphinx, acquired in the same manner, I'm afraid. Tooth of the Barghest, which you saw me find just now, and of course, Scale of the Dragon, my own House treasure."

Caspian lays the artifacts around us, so that they form a circle. I realize I am able to move my head, track his movements just slightly. He smiles, the expression somehow sad.

"Your boon has nearly conquered the poison, but it won't matter. You see, my story is almost at an end.

"Chaos showed me how everything rested on a singular artifact, a shame hidden by my family for generations. This." Caspian holds up a jar. He pries the cork with his teeth, then reaches in to drag out a large red fruit, dripping and fresh. Only it isn't a fruit, it's a heart, somehow still beating a slow rhythm. "It seems that the old Dragon killed the Phoenix and preserved her heart. I found this in the lowest levels of my family's hoard, wrapped in seaweed and protected by fire. A little melodramatic, I suppose, but Chaos does seem to love the absurd."

Caspian holds the heart up so that I can see it, and as he does so, an errant cannonball slams into the ramparts behind him. Far enough away that we aren't hurt, but close enough that debris from the fortress spatters us.

"Ah yes, I shall hurry it along," he says. Not to me, but to Chaos, I suppose, since they seem to be good friends. "Either way, Darling, I want you to know that I am sorry it turned out this way. Talon does care for you, you know. It's just that the timing really is all wrong. Time has a way of doing that. I could have been in love with Elias, if I didn't have this mess to fix. I hope they will forgive me as well."

Caspian holds up the heart, still pulsing in his hand, and takes a bite of it so that blood squirts, trickling over his fingers and painting his face with gore. I am desperate to escape, but the poison still has too much of a hold over me.

"I am sorry that you had to be part of this," he says, chewing and swallowing. And then he pulls me toward him and kisses me, his still-bloody lips touching mine.

I try to pull back, and there's a sound, a shout of alarm. I think it might be Talon, but Caspian's lips are fused to mine, and they are *hot*.

I try to pull away, my hands coming up to push at his chest as I gain control of my body. But I cannot do any more than that. Tears flow and fall down my cheeks from behind my goggles, but I am helpless, trapped in Caspian's madness and by his kiss. His lips leave mine, and heat bursts around me, too bright; it hurts; my goggles shatter from the flames.

And the world is naught but fire.

30
TALON

I don't even hesitate to reach with my boon for Darling's trace. I have it before it occurs to me I should have sought Caspian first.

Darling's trace flares in my awareness, almost hot and crackling. So easy to find, to connect with. I let that recognition stoke my anger. I know her so well I could track her if she'd been gone for days and her trace nothing but a faint echo. But right now her trace roils, because when she ran out of that guest room and, there, left down the narrow corridor, she was more than upset.

Taking Finn's wrist, I drag him along after me. My eyes are half-lidded; I'm sunk into the staticky energy, the rope of lightning that is Darling's trace. It flashes silver and Chaos rainbows, and I follow. Up and over, stumbling in my hurry.

As I cut right into a stairwell, I nearly smack into Elias Chronicum.

"Elias!" Finn says, reaching around me to steady the physician.

Elias focuses on me, mouth set, eyes wide but intense. "Are you looking for Caspian?" They clutch their bag to their chest. "He was heading for the ramparts, and I keep checking, but there are soldiers everywhere. Injured."

There's blood on Elias's vest. Not theirs.

"I'm going after Darling. Come with us." I push around them.

"I need to find Caspian."

"They'll be together," Finn says, pulling free of my grip to take Elias's elbow instead. "We might need your skills if she gets to him."

"What? No." Elias keeps up as they argue.

Finn says, "Do you have poison antidotes?"

The edge of fear is cutting up at my anger as I continue after Darling's trace.

"It depends on the poison, of course," Elias snaps.

"Barb poison?"

"They have at least—eighteen I'm aware of, to varying degrees of—" Elias struggles to speak. I'm taking the stairs two at a time, nearly running around and around. It's a spiral stair and will let out onto one of the highest ramparts just beside the lookout tower.

Finn growls something back at Elias.

At the top of the stairs is a narrow half-circle landing and an arched doorway. I shoot through it, following the thread of Darling's trace, and wince away from the sunlight. Out under the bright sky I smell smoke, and cannon fire booms. There's yelling below me, but I ignore the battle to scan the dark stone ramparts for Darling. Nothing, but her trace keeps going, a jagged path to the tower entrance.

A sharp laugh draws my attention up.

Two figures stand on the open tower. The sun gilds Caspian's wild hair, and he's holding something dark in his hand, stalking close to Darling. She doesn't move at all.

"Caspian!" I yell, sprinting for the tower. Harsh salt wind and smoke steal his name away.

The whistle of a cannonball barely warns me before it slams into the tower. Shards of stone slash at my temple. I stumble forward, coughing. I wipe my forehead with my arm and dive into the shadows of the tower stairs, grabbing the lintel to swing myself in. The stairway is so narrow my shoulders brush the stone wall as I charge up. "Caspian!" I yell again.

Just as I leap out onto the top level of the tower, Caspian puts his hand on Darling and kisses her lips.

My stomach drops. I'm too late! But before I can shove them apart, Caspian pulls back and looks right at me. He raises a bloody hand and waves fingers at me just as Darling ignites.

I'm punched in the chest by a blast of raw power.

Heat throws me back against the parapet. I nearly tip over but manage to twist and fall to my knees against the stone, arms up to protect my head.

Fire roars, and the waves of heat are too much. I lift my face, but the air is scorched. When I look, my eyes water, aching.

Where Darling and Caspian stood is a tall, blue-hot pillar of fire.

No—behind the pillar of fire my brother hunches over, clutching at his stomach. His expression is twisted, and he opens his mouth in a scream. He stumbles back and suddenly arches upright, arms flinging out, and the skin from his chin down his neck and chest flays open to reveal emerald scales.

I see massive fangs, green-black spines, and the monster that was my brother grows in fast fits, scaled flesh blossoming out, and his arms curl into huge fore-claws. Wings burst from him, sharp and jagged.

The dragon in front of me screams.

I clasp my hands over my ears as the cry tears through me.

It leaps into the bright sky, fanning its wings out, blocking the sun. Those wings pump, and it lifts up and up, screaming again. It is so huge. He—my brother—gleams beautifully in the sun.

Then the pillar of fire dims. The conflagration pulls in, narrowing, shrinking. It's moving. It sways.

And the fire becomes wings.

Feathers like sparks fly toward me, scattering. They burn where they touch me, smoldering against my uniform and smearing ashes on the stone of the tower.

She takes off, too, a great fire-winged bird of red-orange-gold, trailing embers.

The dragon screams for her, and the phoenix opens its beak to return the call. Her cry is just as piercing and raw, but it pulses through me like a clarion note.

I think my heart stops beating, and so does the whole world: every heart stops at the shriek of the Phoenix Reborn.

Then my pulse is racing again, and the phoenix joins the dragon, flying higher and higher. She is smaller than the dragon, who can turn and twist around her with his sinuous body three times over. They reach for each other, spinning in a dance of scales and feathers, just as painful to stare at as the sun itself.

I pull myself to my feet, never looking away even as it hurts, even as I can barely breathe.

The empyreals fly up and into the brilliant sky until they are nothing. Gone.

My ears ring; I'm panting. Pain flickers to life where feathers burned me, where stone shrapnel sliced at my hairline. There are no more explosions, no cannon fire, but distant screaming that is both far away and right beside me.

"Talon," Finn says.

He puts a hand on my shoulder. I blink, turn my face to him, slowly like my neck is an ancient set of gears.

"Talon." Finn's grip is bruising.

I mouth his name. Did he see it? Did anyone? How long did it take? Am I as mad as Caspian?

Caspian.

I sway.

Darling.

"Come over here," calls an urgent Elias.

Finn and I manage it. Elias stands at the parapet, staring out at the sea.

"Sweet holy Chaos," Finn breathes.

The sun shines prettily down on the bay, where several ships are floundering, broken into pieces and sinking, dragged around in the clutches of massive red-black tentacles. As I stare, one tentacle lifts a Barghest ship half out of the water and throws it into another. The beast rises out of the roiling sea. It is a kraken, of course.

Whatever Caspian did, it has changed our entire world.

ACKNOWLEDGMENTS

Like Talon and Darling's engagement, we'll keep this brief:

We'd like to thank our agent, Laura Rennert, and her team at ABLA. Laura has a great game face when we say, "Look what we did!"

Thank you to everyone at Razorbill, for your early enthusiasm and support. Especially to our editor, Rūta Rimas, who is a champion, not just because she asked for more Kitty chapters, and to designer Jessica Jenkins, who worked with artist Marisa Ware to give our book a package just as cool as what's inside.

Thanks to our families, because they put up with us.

And Tessa would like to thank Justina for making her have fun even when she didn't want to.